DOLL'S
EYES

Also by Bari Wood

The Killing Gift

Twins (*Dead Ringers*)
with Jack Geasland

The Tribe

Lightsource

Amy Girl

DOLL'S EYES

Bari Wood

WILLIAM MORROW AND COMPANY INC.

NEW YORK

ISBN 0-688-12440-2

Printed in the United States of America

To Jonathan and Pamela,
Alexis and Zachary

I tell the future. Nothing easier. Everybody's future is in their face. . . . But who can tell the past—eh? You lie awake nights trying to know your past. What did it mean? What was it trying to say to you? Think! Think!
Split your heads.
—From *The Skin of Our Teeth*, THORNTON WILDER

DOLL'S
EYES

PROLOGUE

"HIGHER! HIGHER!"

He was out on the swing again, demanding to be pushed, and her meek, mild, stupidly accommodating son was pushing him. Up and down the little one went; she could see excitement on his face even from there.

"Higher," he screamed, "higher, Mikey . . ."

She backed away from the window, and the voice faded. The house was quiet and finally clean. The floor shone, the rug nap stood up, the air smelled of pine oil out here and of butter cookies in the kitchen.

She went back to the kitchen and looked up at the ceiling again.

She still couldn't believe it was there. They'd been in this house almost a week and she'd seen it every day, but it was one of those things you keep having to reassure yourself about because it's too good to be true.

A pulley.

She went to the brown paper bag on the counter and pulled out the roll of clothesline she'd bought in town this morning. It might be too thick for the slot in the wheel, but she wouldn't know until she tried.

She got the ladder out of the broom closet and leaned it against the wall, then moved the table out of the way, taking time to lift each end so she wouldn't scuff the floor. She positioned the ladder under the pulley, then unwrapped the clothesline. It was coated and sprang loose like a snake uncoiling.

She climbed three rungs of the ladder, looped the line around the wheel, then pulled, and it dropped smoothly into the notch. The wheel was sticky; she worked it until it ran smoothly, then climbed down and went over what she needed: hobby knife, paring knife, enema bag, and so on. She laid a fresh towel out on the counter and arranged the implements in a gleaming row on the white cloth.

Only the enema bag would be hard to explain if anyone saw it. But she'd say she wanted to wash it out since it hadn't been used in a while and everything . . . everything . . . gathered dust.

She went back to the front-room window.

Her boy would be going to meet his friends soon. They'd been there less than a week and he'd already made friends.

"Higher," the little one yelled.

The sun on the lake cast ragged patches on his face as he zoomed up on the swing, arching back. "Higher . . ."

The little one was pretty, but so were the whores who hid in doorways on Meade Row back home. She missed home, couldn't understand what had possessed her husband to rent a summer place in the mountains. It was pretty too, with the lake, mountains, endless miles of trees, but prettiness was a snare that lulled you into thinking it was a good world, and it was not.

Mike stopped pushing; the swing lost momentum. The little one tried to get him to go on, but Mike shook his head. The little one tried to push himself, but couldn't get much height, he slid off the swing. Mike walked to the path cut through the trees and the little one stood alone in the clearing, watching him going away.

His shoulders heaved. He was crying, and she thought, *I'll give you something to cry about,* just like her mother used to say.

Mike disappeared and the little one was alone. It was time. The clothesline would go around his knees, the pulley would do the work. She could see how it would look in a couple of minutes and felt a thrill that was closer to pleasure than anything she'd ever felt before.

She opened the front door and called him.

● ●

HE HEARD THEM TALKING IN THE KITCHEN. SHE MUST BE TELLING them he had to be sent to bed without dinner.

He climbed up on the top bunk and tried to fall asleep, but it hurt too much. Tickled too, where blood still oozed a little.

He wanted to wash again, but they'd see him sneaking to the bathroom, and climbing down would probably make the bleeding worse.

It got dark. Mike came into the room and he closed his eyes and listened to his brother getting undressed.

"Hey, faker," Mikey called up softly.

He didn't answer.

"You hungry?"

He kept quiet.

"God, she's got you bulldozed, don't she? Well, I got some cookies down here if you want them."

"I'm okay," he said.

"Sure. You can take it, kiddo. I'll put the cookies next to you in case you do get hungry."

He didn't say anything.

"She's a big old shit windbag, kiddo."

The bed frame shifted as Mikey climbed into the lower bunk.

" 'Night, kiddo," Mikey whispered.

" 'Night," he whispered back.

The moon came through the window and made odd-shaped patches that moved across him as wind off the lake blew the trees. The light looked cool, but he imagined it was warm enough to dry up the blood. The pain wasn't really bad anymore, and he *was* hungry. He felt along the edge of the bunk and found a paper package. Mikey had wrapped three cookies in a napkin and he sat up carefully so he wouldn't pull on the cuts, then unwrapped the cookies and ate them, looking out the top half of the window at the moon on the lake. He brushed the crumbs carefully into the napkin then crumpled it and wedged it on the top of the open window where *she* wouldn't see it and lay down again.

He couldn't tell anyone what happened today; no one *to* tell except Mikey. But she'd said if he told Mike she'd make it worse. He couldn't imagine what that would be like and didn't want to find out.

The patches of moonlight kept moving and made him feel dopey, forgetful. He'd forgotten what he'd done to deserve what she'd done today; it must have been pretty terrible, about the worst thing you could do short of killing somebody.

If he'd done anything.

He stared hard at the moonlight until he got *that* idea out of his head. Of course he'd done something, he just didn't remember what, and if he could forget what he'd done, he could forget what *she'd* done. "Way to go," Mikey would say.

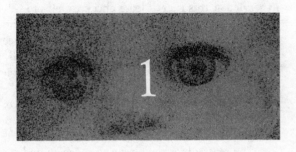

1

Eve closed the sitting room door, went to the phone, and dialed the only number she had for Sam. When he'd left, they'd agreed she'd only call for emergencies. But she'd called once a week for seven weeks and they'd have a fast, morose conversation that consisted of his trying to get off the phone and her trying to keep him on. She'd give up after a few minutes and say, "I just wanted to hear your voice, Sam. I love you."

He'd mumble back that he loved her too, then he'd hang up, and she'd wait with the phone to her ear until the dial tone kicked in. Today probably wouldn't be any different, only she'd gotten sick again this morning, as she had every morning this week, and she thought she was pregnant. She didn't feel pregnant, exactly, but didn't know what it would feel like.

She wouldn't tell him until she was sure. She'd put off going to a doctor because she didn't want to hear that she *wasn't* pregnant and was afraid to hear that she was.

She was a mess, she thought, smiling a little to herself as she picked up the phone and dialed. She got a truncated ring, then a click, then a machinelike voice intoned the NYNEX coda for oblivion:

"I'm sorry, the number you have reached, 518-555-8797, is not in service at this time. Please check to be sure—"

Eve slammed the phone down before it finished. She must have dialed wrong; he was her husband, had always been responsible, he wouldn't just vanish. Maybe he hadn't paid his bill, but then they say "temporarily disconnected," which translates *You have reached the number of a deadbeat.*

If he'd moved, his mother would know where. But Eve had the jitters as she did every time she called him and had probably just dialed wrong.

She reached for the phone to try again and it rang. She grabbed it, hoping it was Sam, knowing it was not.

"Eve, it's Meg."

"I recognized your voice," Eve said drily. They'd talked to each other on the phone almost every day for over twenty years.

"I need help," Meg said.

Meg used to call just to talk or make a shopping date. Then Eve's mother died eight months ago and Meg had changed along with everything else. Now they were user and usee, with Meg as user.

"What kind of help?" Eve asked warily.

"You know."

"I can't do it."

"Won't, you mean," Meg cried.

"Listen to me, Meg." The French doors from the terrace opened and Eve's Aunt Frances glided in.

Eve said, "It's over, gone and done. Go to a storefront reader and adviser, find a gypsy caravan." Frances stood in front of the doors, listening.

Meg cried, "Oh, God, I need you! I'd do it for you if I could."

Which was probably true.

"This'll be the last time. I swear it," Meg said.

"That's what you said last time."

Meg knew enough to keep quiet.

"Okay, Margaret, I'll meet you at Burt's in forty minutes. But it's not going to do any good. It really is over."

She hung up, faced her aunt, and said, "It *is* over. I'll try and fail."

"How do you know?"

"Same way you know you've lost a tooth. You feel it missing."

"You haven't lost a tooth since you were eight," Frances Tilden reminded her gently.

"Shit . . . okay. But it *is* over."

"I hope so, dear," her aunt said, and glided across the room as if she were wearing a chiffon gown. In fact, she had on flannel slacks and red cotton socks; she'd probably left her walking shoes on the terrace so she wouldn't trek mud through the house.

Eve waited until she left the room, then went upstairs to change. The house was silent; no one was expected for dinner. Mrs. Knapp, the cook, had gone to see her daughter in Hartford, and Larry must be out back doing something with one of the cars.

Eve stripped and washed at the shell-shaped granite sink in what had been her mother's bathroom. She'd moved into this room after Sam left to prove something to herself or her aunt. She wasn't sure what.

She raised her head and looked in the mirror with water running down her face. There were circles under her eyes, her cheekbones stuck out, and she'd lost weight, not gained it, but she'd read that weight loss was common in the early weeks of pregnancy.

● ●

MEG WAVED AT HER FROM THE DIM BACK SECTION OF THE OLD roadhouse. Eve crossed the barroom behind the few afternoon regulars, who stared into their drinks or at the monster TV hung on the wall next to the shelves of glasses, and slid into the booth across from Meg.

"Thank you," Meg said humbly.

"Let's get this over with."

"Don't be like that. It means a lot to me," Meg said, and Eve realized her old friend had come to rely on the *thing*.

Eve should find a better word for it; *gift* didn't fit. Gifts were good, and this had probably cost her her husband and turned her best friend into a dependent fool.

Her aunt called it a talent—a polite word, but Frances could find a polite word for rape. Talent didn't fit; *power* didn't either because it implied control.

"I brought this." Meg drew a long, knitted scarf out of her leather bag and laid it on the table. Mary Owen, who'd gone to grammar school with Meg and Eve, but not to Rosemary Hall or Wellesley, came to take their orders.

She had on slacks with a good crease in them and a clean starched shirt, and Eve thought she looked better turned out than they did.

"Nice scarf," Mary said, touching it. "Feels like cashmere."

"*Mixed* with cashmere," Meg said. "I knitted it for Tim—he wore it all winter."

Tears filled her eyes and Mary blushed and asked quickly, "What can I get you?"

"Gin and tonic," Meg sniffled. Eve ordered 7-Up, which her aunt swore by to settle gastric distress.

"Now what?" Eve asked gently when Mary left.

Meg wiped her eyes and Eve saw pain in them. The questions were always about pain . . . the answers caused more pain.

"Tim's found another woman," Meg said.

"That's absurd!"

"No, it's not. He used to be home by six every night, all weather. Now two, three nights a week, it'll be after eight. His clothes are wrinkled, his shirt looks like he's taken it off and put it back on; ditto his tie."

Mary brought their drinks. Eve sipped the 7-Up, the liquid hit her stomach like falling ice cubes, the nausea locked her in for a moment. She grabbed the table edge, shut her eyes, and thought, *Leave me alone . . . why can't you all just leave me alone . . . it's over . . . I can't help you. I never could help you because knowing doesn't help . . . knowing makes it worse . . . just leave me alone.*

"Eve?"

The nausea ebbed. Eve opened her eyes.

"Touch the scarf," Meg said softly in a voice that was almost seductive.

"I don't have to touch anything to tell you that Tim loves you, and if he doesn't—if there's someone else—what good will knowing do?"

"He could clean out the accounts and take off with her."

"Horseshit. He can't touch your trusts, and you know it. How much do you have in trust, Meg?"

"I don't know."

"If I know you, you know to the penny. How much?"

Meg clasped her hands on the table, twisted them, and said, "Seventy million, seven hundred twenty-two thousand."

"And in those famous accounts you're so worried about? Twenty, maybe thirty thousand?"

Meg nodded miserably.

"So it's not the money."

"Of course it's not the money," Meg snapped, "it's that I keep imagining him with *her*, can't stand to touch him or have him touch me. I want to gag when he kisses me. It's ruining us, Eve—I've got to know. You remember you told me Tim Junior didn't have Lyme disease, and that Grandmamma's emeralds were in that old safe deposit box in Millbridge we'd forgotten about. And that Old Man Whitney *was* going to make Tim a partner and *not* to serve the old man poached salmon when he came to dinner because he hates fish."

It was such a short list of small favors, little things that had made her friend's life easier. Not grand, dark, or painful, not the work of a mortal woman usurping God's power. Then why did it feel so black and demonic, why did she hate it so much?

Because it had probably cost her Sam, had driven her father away from her mother and killed her grandmother.

But *it* was over.

"I can't do it, Meg."

"You could try, couldn't you? Maybe there's a little left."

Eve looked at the scarf, and her heart started pounding because she was suddenly afraid there might be a little left. She'd tested herself last week when their cook, Mrs. Knapp, said she hadn't heard from her husband in twenty-five years. Didn't even know if he was alive or dead. "Twenty-five years," she had said. "Billy was seven, Margie only four. How do you find a man after twenty-five years to tell him he's a grandpa without hiring a private dick?"

She'd actually said private dick, making Eve think of old movies and men's genitals secreted in their shorts, and she'd grinned.

"Not funny, young lady," Mrs. Knapp had said sharply. "Not funny at all. Private dicks charge by the hour. How many hours do you think it'll take to find a man after twenty-five years?"

Then Eve had gotten the idea to test herself and gone upstairs to Mrs. Knapp's apartment in the west wing.

The door was unlocked. She slipped inside and looked around the little sitting room for something that might have belonged to the long absent George Knapp. There were framed photos on the mantel of Mrs. Knapp's Billy and Margie, at all ages. But one, half hidden behind the others, showed a young Mrs. Knapp and a good-looking man about the same age. He was shorter than Mrs. Knapp and very thin, with arms like sticks coming out of his wide shirtsleeves and elbows like knots in a tree branch. He was smiling proudly at the kids.

Eve slid the back off the frame and saw *June 1965* stamped on the back of the print. He must've seen this photo, maybe touched it, and it was his likeness.

Eve ran her finger over the glossy surface, then held the print against her chest and waited for the faint free-fall sensation that came with the visions, like standing up too quickly or missing a step.

She never got hot or cold, her flesh didn't creep or her hair stand on end—nothing so dramatic. Sometimes her ears felt stuffed as if she'd gotten water in them or were coming down with a cold.

She had waited for the feeling for ten minutes in Mrs. Knapp's sitting room holding George Knapp's likeness and nothing happened. Then she put the photo back, slid the backing into place, and on impulse kissed the picture and wiped away the faint smear her lips left on the glass.

Now she had to take another test. If it was gone, there was nothing to be afraid of; the scarf was just colored wool knitted in stripes. She reached for it. Her heart pounded so hard she was a little light-headed, and sweat beaded her upper lip. Her hand wavered. "Go on, Evie," Meg said in that seductive voice. "Go on. If it's really over, then that's just cashmere and lamb's wool. Nothing else. Go on, Eve."

She sank her fingers into the coil of wool. It was a little oily, probably from Tim's neck and a winter's worth of Hartford grime. Her fingers sank deeper into it; her heart thumped wildly but she didn't get that falling sensation, her ears didn't stuff up. Stupid, small-time symptoms, she thought. They should be grander; her eyes should change from brown to green, her face turn white and scraped-looking. Maybe there should be thunder and lightning or a wind that rattled windows and made tree branches creak.

Nothing happened.

She dug her fingers deeper into the scarf and felt the tabletop through the wool. Nothing. She picked the scarf up and wound it around her neck, tucking the soft wool under her jaw, and got a whiff of bay rum and a bready smell that must've come from Tim's skin. Nothing else.

Her heart slowed down; the sweat stopped running down her face. She unwound the scarf and put it on the table. "Nothing," she said to Meg, trying not to sound elated. "Absolutely nothing."

Then she leaned across the table and kissed Meg's cheek. "It's gone, Meggie. It's really gone."

"What the fuck are you so happy about?" Margaret Carpenter said bitterly. "For a while you were a woman with a power. Now you're just a helpless asshole like the rest of us."

● ●

On her way out, Eve stopped in the rest room alcove of the little roadhouse to use the phone. She tried the 518 number for Sam in case she'd dialed wrong before and got the same recording. Then she called Sam's mother, Greta, and asked if she could stop by.

• •

Greta Klein was short and plump with smooth, pink skin, even at seventy.

"Come into the kitchen," she told Eve. "I'm baking cookies for the bridge club tonight."

Eve followed her and sat at the table while Greta worked. She was wearing a white wraparound apron with bright red and yellow posies printed on it, and the kitchen smelled of butter and toasted nuts. She pulled a baking sheet out of the oven with light brown crescents with nuts sticking up in them like little quills, slid another sheet in, then set the timer and poured Eve a cup of coffee.

"Have a cookie?"

"No thanks." Eve sipped the coffee cautiously, afraid it would cause a resurgence of nausea.

"Drink, drink," Greta said, sitting across from her. "It's decaf."

"I haven't been feeling well," Eve said.

"Oh? That's why you're here?"

"In a way. I called the number Sam left me. It's disconnected."

"I know. He moved, doesn't have a phone in the new place yet. But it doesn't matter," Greta said gently. "He's not going to come back because you don't feel well, honey. I don't know what'll bring him back. Don't know why he left in the first place." She looked brightly at Eve. "He's crazy about you, you know. Was even when he left, which makes it even nutsier, doesn't it?"

Eve nodded.

"Crazy mad about you, probably from the first second he saw you. You're pretty, you know. Not drop-dead gorgeous, but I guess you know that too. But pretty, and after a while of looking at you, maybe better than pretty. And there must've been something else about you that made my boy fall for you. It worried me at first, because I was afraid if he couldn't have you he wouldn't ever want anyone else. But I didn't have to worry, because you fell for him too, didn't you?"

Eve nodded.

"So what happened?" Greta demanded softly. "How could you just walk away from each other—" She stopped herself, then amended, "How could he walk away from you and you let him go? How?"

"Something happened."

"Your mother died. Did that make you crazy or something?"

"Or something," Eve said very softly.

"That's not a reason. You don't leave the woman you love 'cause her mother dies. Parents are supposed to die and kids live on as parents, then they die too. You're not making any sense."

Eve didn't say anything. Greta fetched a huge sigh.

"Now you want to find him."

Eve nodded.

"He got a job in a bank in another upstate town and moved closer to it. Same kind of job he had here."

He'd been Trust VP at Bridgeton Trust; that was how Eve had met him.

Greta said, "He told me he doesn't want to be found by you unless it's desperate. And then—in the manner of men—he left it to me to decide what's 'desperate.' So now I gotta ask you, honey: Is it desperate?"

Eve nodded.

"You gotta be more specific. I think he's acting like a nebbish . . . need a translation?"

"No."

"But he's my son and I will respect his wishes. So you gotta be specific or I can't tell you."

"I think I'm pregnant."

Greta made a sound between a gasp and a chortle of delight and looked at her with glowing eyes.

"Do you feel sick? You look sick," she cried.

Eve nodded.

"Take one of the cookies. I swear to God it'll help. And I got some 7-Up in the refrigerator. Best thing for a stomach upset, 7-Up."

"That's what my Aunt Frances says."

"Your Aunt Frances always made me feel like a fart in a ballroom, but I never thought she was dumb."

Greta shoved a plate of fresh-baked cookies at Eve, then took a 7-Up out of her large, harvest-gold refrigerator. She popped the can top, poured the fizzing liquid out into a striped glass, set it next to the plate of cookies, and beamed at Eve. "Don't move, honey. I'll get the address and be right back."

Before Eve left with Sam's new address in a town called Raven Lake, Greta took her arm. "A word of advice, Eve. You look like a truck hit you, and my son loves you. If he *sees* you looking like that he'll come around. He could say no on the phone, but not to your face."

● ●

"BUT HE DID SAY *NO* TO YOUR FACE," FRANCES SAID. "HE WALKED out to your face." They were in the breakfast room, eating tuna salad with a casserole of noodles and cheese that Mrs. Knapp had left for them.

"I'm going, Frances. I'm packed and going."

"Raven Lake's in the Adirondacks, isn't it?"

"Yes."

"The family—the Tildens that is, not the Dodds—had a camp on some lake up there. I forget the name. We went summer, winter, and fall until our mother died. Never this time of year though, because of the flies."

Eve picked at the tuna salad, then forced herself to eat a forkful of the noodles.

"Good," Frances said. "Eat as much as you can. You've got a long drive ahead of you. Must be three, four hours."

"Four," Eve said. "But it's late. I'll find a motel halfway."

"No motels open this time of year . . . flies."

Eve put her fork down. "Forget the fucking flies, Frances. I'm going."

Frances looked down at her own uneaten food.

"I'm sorry," she said. "It's not really flies I'm worried about—you know that."

"I know."

Frances raised her head. She was a handsome woman somewhere in her fifties. She never celebrated her birthday; Eve wasn't even sure when it was. She did know that her aunt was . . . had been . . . a year or two younger than her mother. Eve had seen many pictures of them, of course, and of *their* mother, Olivia Dodd Tilden, who had been, to use Greta Klein's phrase, drop-dead gorgeous.

The sisters claimed an accident had killed Eve's grandmother, but Eve heard rumors from other kids and from Meg's mother that the beautiful Olivia Dodd Tilden had killed herself.

The sisters refused to talk about it, and Eve had given up asking years ago.

Frances had never married, never claimed a lost love, never

talked about herself at all except for a few reminiscences about her victories in swimming races in the fifties. Eve reached across the table and took her aunt's hand, but Frances eased it away. Her aunt had never hugged or kissed her that she could remember; neither had her mother. Of course her mother had been afraid that she'd *see* something about her daughter if she touched her.

"Listen to me, Frances," Eve said gently. "I *tried* to do it, really tried because poor Meg was so miserable. She had Tim's scarf and I put it on, hugged it, stroked my cheek with it, practically ate it. And I got as much about Tim Carpenter from that scarf as I would from probing the entrails of a goat. It's over."

"It was never over for your mother."

"Maybe she liked it, wanted to hang on to it. It could be . . ." Eve searched for a word and came up with *useful*.

"Not for her," Frances said. "It cost her her husband too. She hated it . . ." Frances paused, then mumbled, "I think she hated it."

They finished eating. Frances filled a thermos with coffee and took it out to Eve's car in the front of the driveway, then insisted on putting Eve's weekender in the trunk.

"Wish me luck, Auntie," Eve said.

Frances slammed the trunk lid. "You know I do," she said, then cleared her throat and stared critically at Eve's new little red LeBaron. "Can't imagine what possessed you to buy a car like that. It looks like a jelly bean on wheels."

"It's got an air bag," Eve said. "I might be driving for two now."

"Yes . . ."

"I read that two LeBarons collided at sixty, and the drivers walked away because of air bags."

Frances seemed to find the crushed stone of the driveway fascinating.

"I prefer the Town Car, of course," she said.

"Of course, Auntie."

"You don't need an air bag with a Town Car—whatever you run into is bound to be demolished."

"Yes, Auntie."

"Keep the doors locked, especially at stoplights."

"No stoplights on the Thruway."

"And call me."

"I will."

"And good luck, Eve," Frances said softly, then turned and went into the house, shutting the door firmly behind her. She was not the kind to stand on the terrace until Eve was out of sight. A few downstairs lights were on, but the rest of the vast, sprawling Tilden mansion was dark. Then Eve saw that Larry Simms's lights were on in his quarters over the garage. If Frances got lonely or frightened in the huge house she'd beep, and he'd come to her.

Eve climbed into her new little car, which did look like a jelly bean and smelled like new leather. She drove down the first curve in the drive and stopped to look back at the house. One end was now hidden by the trees, but most was still visible. The first time she'd brought Sam here, five years ago, they'd rounded this curve and he'd cried, "You *live* there?"

"Of course."

"In all of it?"

"We don't rent any out," she'd said tightly.

"Holy shit," he groaned, and she'd slammed on the brakes of one of Frances's cast-off "personal-sized" Lincolns. "Don't carry on like that," she snapped at Sam, afraid that the opulence of the house would put him off. "You're our banker, you know we're rich."

"Yeah," he had said softly, staring at the house through bare branches (it had been late November), "but seeing it on paper's one thing, seeing it in stone, brick, glass, and whatever else they used to make that pile's something else."

• •

FRANCES RINSED THE DISHES AND PUT THEM IN THE INDUSTRIAL-sized dishwasher, but didn't start it. Mrs. Knapp would do it after dinner tomorrow. Even then the washer would be more than half empty, since Eve would be in Raven Lake. Frances remembered the name from those summers in the mountains, but not the town itself. It was probably like most Adirondack towns, with shops that sold Swiss woolens and skis, sleeping bags and freeze-dried camping food, and mugs with the four circles, and LAKE PLACID OLYMPICS: 1933, 19—whatever on them.

Sam had gotten a bank job there like he'd had here, according to his mother.

He hadn't even stuck it out as long as her poor lost brother-in-law. No one had heard from him since 1963 except for a lacy card on Eve's twenty-first birthday in which the Hallmark bard had written, "Today's the day you're all grown up, but you'll always be the child of my heart," and Will had signed it, "Your loving father, T. William Leigh," as if he'd expected his daughter to forget his name. Or maybe he thought she'd never known it. But they were not the kind of people to try to expunge his memory or pretend that he was a bounder.

Bounder? Old age was making her positively Victorian.

They dealt with Will Leigh by not mentioning him. Eve asked questions, the subject was changed. She'd try to insist, but she had the Tilden-Dodd nonconfrontational genes and never forced an issue.

That was, until Sam left; that was one issue Eve *was* forcing. Frances didn't blame Sam. Living with someone who knew what you were going to do before you knew it must be agony. A whole new definition of intimacy, but not the kind anyone coveted or wrote about in self-help books on how to get closer to your spouse. Now Eve thought it was gone, and maybe it was. Maybe it slipped away as suddenly as it had materialized, and Eve would get her husband back.

Poor Sam, poor Will, she thought. They'd fallen for women with a gift, a talent, a curse, depending on how you looked at it. The second sight, Nanny Temple had called it, crossing herself whenever she mentioned it.

● ●

IT APPEARED IN ELLEN A MONTH AFTER THEIR MOTHER DIED. Ellen was nine, Frances seven. It was the last day of school, a hot day in June, and it happened in the schoolyard during recess. The kids were wild as crazed dogs, couldn't seem to settle on one game for long. They'd abandon the jungle bars for the swings, the swings for the teeter-totter, the teeter-totter for the slides, then back to the jungle bars or jump rope.

Later Frances—Franny then—decided it was the atmosphere of wildness that had made Lindsay Muir reckless and cruel enough to say the terrible things she did.

Lindsay was tall and skinny, with a long bony face and narrow eyes. Frances had heard she'd turned into a good-looking woman, but in those days she was gawky and plain and hated pretty, compact Ellen Tilden, with her well-covered bones and wide, dark eyes.

Lindsay had been whispering fiercely to her bosom buddy, whose name Frances had forgotten; they seemed to come to an agreement, nodded slyly to each other, and Lindsay slid off the bench and marched over to Ellen. She looked down at her with slitty eyes that were a little red-rimmed from the heat and schoolyard dust.

Franny knew something was wrong and left her place in the slide line to go to her sister.

Lindsay shuffled her feet, sending up puffs of dust that sparkled in the sunlight. There wasn't a hint of a breeze, and the girls' faces gleamed with sweat. Around the yard, in the shrubs and trees, the buzz of insects rose in a sawing wave, then sank, and in the relative quiet that followed, Lindsay Muir said in a ringing voice, "My daddy says your mommy killed herself."

The girls stopped what they were doing and edged closer to hear the rest (girls and boys had separate play yards in those days).

Lindsay raised her voice to be sure everyone could hear. "My daddy says your mommy locked herself in the garage, turned on the cars and could've gassed you all."

Ellen stood stiller than Franny had ever seen her stand. In fact Ellen Dodd Tilden, who was normally something of a fidget, seemed to have turned to stone.

Lindsay cried, "My daddy says killing yourself's the worst sin there is. Worse than being a whore and doing it for money. My daddy says . . ."

"It was an accident," Ellen said.

Her voice sounded peculiar, reminding Franny of the man at the carnival their papa had taken them to last summer. The man had a dummy with a huge red grin painted on its face and a hinged jaw that opened and closed as it talked. Franny had been amazed and wondered if she could get her own dolls to speak if she hinged their jaws, but their father explained it wasn't the dummy talking, it was the man, throwing his voice.

Ellen's voice sounded thrown, like the dummy's, with a deadly kind of tonelessness that scared Franny. In fact everything suddenly felt weird and scary. Franny's hair seemed to crackle around her head as it did in the dead of winter and her light cotton skirt clung electrically to her legs.

Then Lindsay chanted, "Soocide, soocide . . . your mommy's a soocide," and Ellen punched her. Not slapped her the way girls sometimes did; *punched* her like a boxer. The blow drove Lindsay back against the brick wall of the school building, and blood flooded out of her nose. It dripped off her chin and made splotches on her handkerchief-cotton dress that had little blue flowers on it. Frances could still see that dress, could have drawn it, even after almost fifty years.

Lindsay looked at Ellen in shock, then she yowled and wiped her face, smearing it with tears, blood, and snot.

"You turd," she screamed. "I'll tell my daddy. He'll beat you up. He'll tell everyone about your mother. He says your mother's worse than a whore, he says your mother's burning in hell." Ellen's hand came out slowly toward Lindsay and Lindsay stopped with a hiccup. Ellen's face was smooth and expressionless. As she reached out, Lindsay didn't flinch or try to get away since it was clear Ellen didn't mean to hit her again. Ellen's hand came toward her deliberately, fingers out, like a blind person searching. She touched the front of Lindsay's dress with its polka dots of blood, then wadded the fabric in her hand and said in that strange, 'thrown' voice, "It's *your* mommy that's the whore, Linny. Your mommy does it with Mr. Owen while your daddy's at work."

Lindsay whimpered and tears flooded down her face, mixing with the blood.

"Yes," Ellen said, "in the office in the garage, on an old leather sofa with a split cushion. And she yells a lot and he tries to shut her up in case there's a customer out front waiting for gas."

"Liar," Lindsay shrieked, then sobbed helplessly, and Ellen let go of her. The crackle seemed to die out of the air and Franny felt rivers of sweat run down her face and back, along her sides, tickling her ribs. Her nose, which had felt dry as sandpaper a second ago, started to run, her hair was limp and sweaty and felt chilly on her scalp. Poor Lindsay slumped against the wall, crying like a child much younger than her nine years. Lindsay had asked for it, but as their father said a lot, just because you ask for it doesn't mean you deserve it.

One day, Mrs. Larkin did walk in on Mr. Owen and Mrs. Muir in the messy office of the Standard Oil of New Jersey station (from which Mr. Owen was rumored to sell black market gas you didn't need stamps for). And before Christmas that year, it was all over town.

For a while, Franny was afraid of her sister because Ellen had known a lot of things she couldn't know. But Lindsay had known something too. A year or so later, their Uncle Albert Dodd got drunk at a family gathering and told the sisters that their mother, his sister, had stuffed cracks in the garage doors with blankets taken from one of the linen closets and turned on the motor of the prewar Continental.

"Temple found her," he told the girls slurrily. "She was still alive, but she died an hour or so later. Just as well, since the gas damaged her brain and she'd've been a vegetable if she'd lived."

He'd giggled giddily and shockingly, but there were tears in his eyes. "A sort of eggplant with hair," he'd said, staring into the dregs of his drink. "It was her visions. You know about the visions." They had known by then. "And voices too, I guess." He drained the last of his Manhattan, including the cherry, stem and all, without seeming to chew it up. "My poor sister . . . poor old Ollie, who'd been the belle of the nineteen thirty Casino Ball, the prettiest girl in Bridgeton, was crazy as a coot by the time she sucked that exhaust pipe, m'dears. Crazy as a fuckin' bedbug . . ."

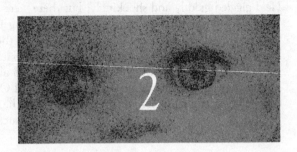

"It's the best pickup joint for a hundred square miles," the orderly said as the elevator ground its way up. Adam Fuller stared at the button panel, listening, but not looking at the other two men standing against the metal-coated wall.

"Broads're young," the orderly went on. He was Tom. Adam didn't know his last name. The other one was Tony, also no last name.

"And sometimes good-looking," Tom told Tony. "And they're looking for it. You're as likely to get laid as get in a fight. Pretty rare for the boonies."

"Yeah, only I'm getting too old and stiff in the joints to screw in the back of a car," Tony said.

"Not necessary," said Tom. "There's a motel rents by the hour in Echo Lake, next town over. About twenty-minute drive away. O' course, you'll find sand in the sheets—only sand if you're lucky—but you ain't there for the housekeeping."

"Fuckin' A," Tony agreed.

The elevator slowed. They were going to get off before Adam heard the name of the bar and he didn't dare ask. But as the elevator stopped, Tom said, "It's called Frank's on Raven Lake, just outside the town."

The door opened, the orderlies stepped out, and Tom said, "See you, Doc."

Adam nodded and the men went toward the nursing desk to pick up their roster for the morning shift. The elevator doors creaked closed and the metal-walled box, just long enough to fit a gurney, ground up to Four, the top floor of Glenvale General.

Frank's, Raven Lake. He didn't have to write it down; he wouldn't forget.

The doors opened, and he stepped into the hall, where Mrs. Warren and two interns who looked like they'd been up all night were waiting to begin rounds.

Rounds started at nine, and it was now exactly nine. Mrs. Warren, the floor's head nurse, introduced them and they went down the hall to Mrs. Trilling's room.

Mrs. Trilling's blood sugar was stable at last; Dilantin had controlled the seizurelike reactions to the wild fluctuations in glucose vs. insulin. Her feet, which had been chill on admission, were warm to the touch, the pulse in her ankles strong. She could go home.

He went over the case with the interns, then turned to her. She was fifty, a plain woman with clay-colored skin and a large doughy nose. Her thick lips were wet, her eyes dark and shiny as wet plums.

"Everything looks fine," he told her. "You can go home on Monday. Sorry to make you miss the weekend, but better safe than sorry, right?"

Her eyes filled with tears and she mumbled, "I thought I was going to die. I thought I'd never go home again." She grabbed his hand. He was afraid she was going to raise it to those thick, moist lips and he'd have to run to the toilet to wash or walk around with the slimy feeling of her saliva on his hand. But she just squeezed his hand in her own, which was, thankfully, dry, and let him go.

Next was Mrs. Boucher, whose stitches had been removed yesterday. Her bowel sounds were coming up nicely, and she was also a candidate for discharge on Monday. "As long," he said sternly, "as you keep walking . . ." down the hall to the window at the end that had a view of the mountains in the distance and a sill covered with struggling plants the patients left behind and the nurses tried to keep alive.

"No matter how uncomfortable, you must keep walking," he told her.

She didn't grab his hand or even thank him. She said, "The gas is terrible," and a crepitating sound came from under the covers. She blushed and mumbled, "Sorry." The interns blushed, too, but Adam laughed and said gently, "Feel better?"

"A little," she said. "Wish they could do something about the gas."

"It'll get better in a day or so," he said, and wrote Gas-X on her chart.

After Mrs. Boucher came Thomas Dorchester, who was losing his final battle with the final stage of lung cancer. Mr. Dorchester would not be going home Monday or ever.

Adam pulled down the clean woven cotton cover and crisp sheet over the man. The nurses were really good here—everything was clean as could be, with only the faintest odor—but nothing could conquer that smell of inner rot. Then he rolled up the white-and-blue-printed hospital gown to reveal the carcass. No other word could describe what was left of the still faintly vital Thomas S. Dorchester. His skin hung like the folds of a burst balloon; the genitals were crumpled paper.

Out of the corner of his eye, Adam saw the interns look away and felt a touch of satisfaction. He never looked away—even from the worst sights. He applied his stethoscope without bothering to breathe on it first. Tom Dorchester would not feel the cold.

The lungs had the texture of disintegrating sponge by now; they could not sustain life much longer. Dorchester would die tonight, tomorrow at the latest, though they could fool you and hang on for days, even weeks. Lots of things fooled you, he thought. His examination was gentle, firm, thorough, and pointless. But he went through it anyway, partly for the benefit of the interns, partly because it was the only kind of examination he seemed capable of conducting. As he went about it, he spoke softly to the two young men across the bed, but that was because of the atmosphere, not because Dorchester would hear him. He wouldn't.

"The chief resident wants to send Mr. Dorchester down to Albany, where they've got a newfangled ventilator."

"Then why's he here?" asked one intern, Chatterjee, a very skinny young man with dark skin and liquid brown eyes.

"Because the family won't have him moved," Adam said, looking up briefly from his examination. "They want him to die here in his hometown, where he'll see *their* faces at the end."

He rolled down the gown, rolled up the pristine white covers, and looked at the interns. "And the thing is, gentlemen, the family's right. Nothing the machines in Albany or we in Glenvale can do is going to save him. Better to give death its due," he said quietly, "and let his last sight be of his family, assuming he ever sees anything again, which is highly unlikely." He saw a glance pass between them and knew they thought he was wrong and sentimental. They still thought medicine was about never giving up. Adam had felt the same at their age, then had realized, suddenly and without fanfare, about three years ago, that it *wasn't*. That fighting death for someone in Thomas Dorchester's condition was futile and cruel, and he counted himself a physician from that time.

But these two were still in their control mode, and he knew nothing he said would jar them out of it. He straightened up and looked at Mrs. Warren. "Call the family," he said. "Tell them it'll probably be tonight."

"But *maybe*," said the other intern, Severensen, who was blond to the point of Albinism, with disappearing lashes and brows and weak-looking eyes.

"Sure," Adam said. "Maybe. But I think they'd rather have to make a couple of trips than miss saying good-bye."

Both interns looked down at the dying man, the dark one from India or Pakistan, Adam didn't know which, and the light one, who looked like his ancestors had been bleached by ten thousand years of sunless ice, and he saw that *look* in their eyes. He knew what it was, knew the word for it, just as he knew the word for quark even though he'd never seen one, never held one in his hands, never *felt* one. Never felt a quark, never felt the pity he saw in the eyes of the two young men looking down at Thomas S. Dorchester.

He straightened up, folded his stethoscope, and put it away, then went over the charts and said a few more things to them about pain control in terminal cancer, although Thomas Dorchester was beyond pain by now. Then they left the room and went on with rounds.

It was 10:00 A.M.; his shift ended at 6:00. Tonight was a full moon, and he'd go home, shower, and shave carefully, then change into the clothes he'd bought at the huge discount mart down in Sawyerville, don one of the el cheapo wigs he'd bought in the same store, and go to Frank's in Raven Lake.

● ●

FRANK'S WAS ONLY A FEW YARDS FROM THE LAKE. IT HAD LOG siding, long narrow windows, and a neon sign on the roof that threw strands of red light on the black water.

The lot was almost full. Adam parked next to a narrow sand beach and climbed out of the car, looked out over the lake, and got the disorienting feeling he'd been here before. He tried to remember when and couldn't. It was probably just one of those baseless sensations that people sometimes put down to experiences from an earlier life or some such crap. But it was very strong, and he stayed where he was, looking at the calm black water with the path of moonlight across it, trying to remember. Nothing came to him and then the roadhouse door opened, letting out a blast of noise, and the spell was broken. A couple weaved out with their arms around each other. They crossed the lot to a red pickup patched with orange rust and the man bent the woman back against the truck door and kissed her. His paunch made it hard for their lower bodies to connect, but the woman let out a phony groan of desire. Then the man climbed into the driver's seat, the woman staggered around the front of the truck and got in the other side, and they screeched out of the lot without stopping to see if any other cars were coming.

Adam watched the taillights straddle the center line as they headed for the main road, probably on their way to the motel in Echo Lake that had sand in the sheets (if you were lucky).

He shuddered. He would never take a woman there, would probably not be able to perform in such a place.

The truck's taillights disappeared and he wondered if they'd make it to the sandy-sheet motel before a trooper picked them up for DWI. Driving While Intoxicated killed more people up here than myocardial infarction. The rate probably rivaled that of northern Sweden or Siberia, though winter in upstate New York wasn't *that* bad; the sun didn't disappear in November and not show up again until March. But it was bad enough; it hit thirty below last January, and the cold found apertures in the doors and windows of his house and came right through the walls. He could stand dead atop the heating grate, practically frying his feet, and the rest of him would be cold. But it was beautiful too. The lakes froze solid; weasels, cars, and trucks with chains drove across them and there was a constant crackle in the air. The conifers looked like two-dimensional cutouts against the white sky, and maples, oaks, and beeches like line drawings of dead trees. Hard to believe they'd ever leaf out again, yet they were budding now and the snow that had come up to the windowsills on his first floor was gone except for a few blue patches deep under the spruces.

It was spring and warm and he was going to get laid. Really laid this time, not like last month when he'd tried to rush the season. Remembering still made him blush. He couldn't take the girl home or go to her house or to a motel. So they'd tried the car on a night when it was fifteen degrees and the full moon had looked like a circle of shaved ice; it had been a total bust.

But tonight he wouldn't need the heater; tonight would be perfect.

He'd told his shrink, Terence Bunner, about the fiasco with the last woman, because he knew Bunny would listen with total neutrality, under which Adam sensed partisanship.

Bunny was on his side.

"She was young," he'd told Bunny. "Even had a few residual zits. I like 'em young," he'd stammered. "But I couldn't do anything, maybe because she was wired, Bunny. Wired to the fucking teeth on coke, or crack, or God knows."

"Why'd you pick her then?" Bunny had asked.

Good question, and he'd searched for the right answer. He tried to lie to Bunny as little as possible.

"I guess maybe because she *was* wired, and I figured I could get her to do . . . things . . ."

"What things?"

"You know," he'd said, "and then she'd let me . . . you know."

"I guess I do." Then Bunny had laughed, bless him, and said, "I guess you wanted something besides the missionary position, right, Sport?"

Bunny had given him the first nickname he'd ever had and he liked it.

"Yeah, I guess," he'd said.

"You know what I'm going to say, don't you?"

He shook his head, and Bunny had said, "Yes you do, Sport. Just think about it a second."

He'd thought, then said slowly, "That it's like falling off a horse and I should get right back on."

"Or words to that effect," Bunny had said, smiling at him.

But he had to wait for warm weather and the moon.

Of course, Bunny would never have given him the old falling-off-the-horse advice if he'd known about the aftermath of Adam's lovemaking.

●   ●

HE OPENED THE ROADHOUSE DOOR AND WAS HIT BY A POSITIVE wall of that mindless, repetitious, cacophonous crap people called music. You couldn't listen to it; it wasn't meant to be listened to, it was music to work yourself into a frenzy by. It assaulted him and tore at his nerve endings and he wondered why they never played Bach or Handel in places like this. Fireworks Music was much sexier than this bilge, but then people tended to confuse sex and frenzy. They were wrong. Sex should be slow, deliberate, infinitely gentle. Nothing like the raucous screech coming through the roadhouse speakers.

It ended abruptly and, in the few beats of blessed silence before the next piece of atrocious shit started, he saw the one he wanted.

He was surprised because she wasn't young, and he usually liked them young. This one was in her late thirties or early forties, and the lines around her eyes and mouth showed up even in the rose-gel-covered lights of the place. She wore slacks and a pullover sweater with a crisp button-down blouse under it. Her dark hair had some gray in it and was soft and smooth, not moussed into those snakes around her head that made half the women in the place look like they'd just grabbed live electric cable. Her eyes weren't sunk in blue greasy gunk, her lips were just lip-color, not purple or brown or shimmering as if they'd been wrapped in foil. She was just a neat-looking, almost middle-aged woman with a light of intelligence (and maybe humor) in her dark eyes and she was drinking beer and a shot, not a Kyrrh or Lillet or some other faggy concoction. She felt him watching her, looked up, and smiled at him. It wasn't a coy or perfunctorily sexy smile. It was normal and direct, the smile of one adult making eye contact with another, and she was alone. With his heart pounding pleasantly with anticipation, he started around the crowded U-shaped bar toward her.

Everyone was too involved in themselves and their mating rituals even to look at him. But if they did, they'd notice the polyester knit jacket, cheap plaid shirt, patterned sweater (nylon), and the blond wig (also nylon). Even if someone more observant noticed and re-membered his face, he was not unusual-looking. There were probably twenty men in the place who fit his description.

• •

EVE PASSED THE ALBANY TOLLS, NEGOTIATED THE NORTHWAY interchange, and saw the first sign for Saratoga, where she meant to spend the night. But it was barely nine, she wasn't tired, and she was only an hour and a half or two hours from Raven Lake . . . and Sam. Suddenly she couldn't bear to put off seeing him just so she could sleep, and she decided to keep going. But her back ached, she needed coffee and something to eat, and the car needed gas. There were no service areas on the Northway, but a sign told her she could get gas, food, and a phone at the next exit. She took it, drove down a ramp to a two-lane road and a lit-up island of gas pumps with a diner next door.

She pulled up to the self-service pumps. Frances disapproved of pumping your own gas, but Eve enjoyed doing it, and when the lever on the nozzle popped, she goosed it up to fifteen dollars even like a pro, then went to the glassed-in booth to pay. A kid sat at a high desk with a girlie magazine opened flat to a beaver shot of a gorgeous blond. Eve cleared her throat, the kid saw her, blushed purple, and slapped the magazine shut.

"Sorry," he mumbled.

Another time she'd have blushed and stammered like the kid, thrown the money at him, and run away. But he looked so achingly young and upset, and she was only two hours from Sam and feeling better than she had in months.

She grinned at him. "Stuff like that'll ruin you for the real world."

"Tell me about it," he groaned and they laughed in sudden camaraderie. Then she asked him how the food next door was.

"Rad," he said.

She looked blank.

"As in very good," he said gently.

She thanked him and drove across the tarmac to the diner. It had a metal shell with spotlights on the roof to let people on the Northway know it was there. She didn't see a single fly in the beam. Frances had been a real Cassandra about the flies, or maybe the south wind, which kept the air mild, was holding them at bay.

She went inside. It was empty except for a trooper at the far end of the counter. He had on grays and a Sam Browne belt, a gun, cuffs, and a beeper, and a club hung at his waist. A campaign hat sat on the stool next to him. He was eating scrambled eggs sprinkled with what looked like fresh-chopped parsley. Pretty good for an all-night diner off the Northway, she thought.

He looked up, caught her staring, and they smiled quickly at each other and looked away. Just two strangers in a 1940s-type diner.

A month ago, she might have made the same innocent eye

contact and touched the counter he was leaning on, and *seen* things about him. For instance that he'd been passed over for promotion one time too many and had gotten bitter and started drinking and hitting his wife, and, this second, as he tucked into his off-hour dinner of scrambled eggs, fresh parsley, and rough-cut toast that looked like homemade bread, the wife was packing the kids into the car to leave him. Eve would have seen the wife's grim, anguished face, the bleary look of the children, who were up past their bedtime. She'd even have seen their little bungalow on a typical American street in one of the typical American towns around here as the wife backed the station wagon out of the drive to the street.

Eve would know that *he* didn't know, that he'd go home to an empty house and find his wife's note on the kitchen counter.

She'd have seen it in high relief; she'd have recognized the wife and kids if she met them, known the house if she drove past it. But tonight nothing happened except that she and the trooper exchanged brief smiles.

She was elated and suddenly starving.

The quilted metal door from the kitchen swung open and a waitress in a beige uniform came over to Eve. She was about fifty, with round rosy cheeks and sparkling brown eyes. Eve liked her, liked the trooper, liked the kid in the gas station. Liked the whole world.

"Two eggs scrambled, please," Eve said, "and coffee."

"Decaf or regular?" the woman asked.

"Better make it regular," she said. She still had 120 miles to go.

The waitress poured the coffee into a thick mug and set it in front of Eve, then went into the kitchen to put in the order. In the meantime, the trooper finished his eggs, picked up the crumbs of egg and parsley with a toast corner, and drained his coffee mug. He stood up, took the campaign hat, and came down the counter toward her.

Suddenly her stomach did a little flip, and she knew it was going to happen after all. She was going to see pictures about this man, know his deepest, darkest, most terrible secrets. Things even he didn't know.

She grabbed the edge of the counter and stared down at the clean Formica and waited. She felt a slight draft as he passed her, nothing else, and she risked raising her head.

He was at the cash register; the waitress had come out of the kitchen and was telling him his money was no good in here and he knew it. She called him Bill.

Eve looked directly at them.

The trooper had his hat on; he thanked the waitress, then left. The door swished open and shut, then she heard his cruiser start up and pull out of the lot, back onto the road that led to the highway.

Nothing else happened.

She slumped on the stool. It *was* over, she had to get used to it, and not verge on catatonia when anyone came within five feet of her.

The waitress came around the counter to her.

"Hey, you all right?" she asked.

Eve nodded.

"You look kinda green."

"I guess I need some food," Eve said.

"It'll be right out, honey. Bet I know what else you need."

"Not 7-Up," Eve said quickly.

The waitress laughed. "Naw, I was thinking of Alka-Seltzer. Good for what ails you. Fern—she's our cook—swears by it. Says if she ever slipped and cut her finger off, Alka-Seltzer'd probably make it grow back. Says it'd probably cure cancer if people'd give it a chance." The brown eyes twinkled. "Fern's a great cook, but she's a little . . ." She tapped her head with one finger. "But it's good stuff, even if it won't cure cancer. And maybe it'll put some color in your face. Whaddaya say? It's on the house."

● ●

HER NAME WAS ABIGAIL, ABBY, SHE TOLD ADAM. NO LAST names, they agreed. She had a good face, not exactly pretty, but certainly not plain. Her hair and eyes were the same shade, reddish brown, and except for the lines around her eyes and mouth, her skin was like a girl's.

She taught high school in Tupper Lake about thirty miles west of Raven Lake. Daren't be seen in a pickup bar around there, so once a month, she made the drive to Frank's. "To be with someone," she told him. "To drive away the dark . . ."

That was such a nice way to put it: *drive away the dark.* This wasn't cold and brutal as sometimes portrayed on TV and in movies, it was the best they could manage at this point in their lives to find warmth and contact . . . and drive away the dark.

Suddenly he almost cared about this woman he'd only known an hour, and who was about five years older than he was (she didn't volunteer her age, he didn't ask). He thought of the interns looking at the dying man this morning. If anyone could make him feel what he'd seen in their eyes, it was this kind, wise, almost pretty woman.

He asked her to go with him, and she said of course, as if surprised he had to ask.

He glanced quickly around the bar; it was hopping, as Tom the orderly had said, and everyone was involved in their own conversations. No one even glanced at him as he slid off the bar stool and followed her to the door.

They went through the cedarboard front door into the lot. It was still warm and windy, the wind coming from the south.

"Whose car?" she asked gently.

"Mine, if you don't mind." He had a new LTD bought last January.

They got to the LTD and he experienced that little burst of pride he still had in the car, with its long light-blue body and new-car smell people commented on.

He remembered the couple he'd seen when he'd arrived here and he moved her back against the car and kissed her, aware of the contrast between his lean, well-conditioned body and the paunchy redneck with the pickup truck. He eased her lips apart with his and reached into his pocket.

She strained against him as his fingers touched the cool steel handle of the scalpel.

They came out of the kiss, and he looked quickly around the lot. No one had come out, no one saw them together. He politely took her around to the passenger side, handed her in, then climbed behind the wheel.

● ●

SAM LIVED HERE IN THIS TOWN, ON LAKESHORE ACCORDING TO Greta. But Eve didn't know where Lakeshore was, and there was no one around to ask. The main drag of Raven Lake was about a block long, with one stoplight, no cars, and a string of dark shops. Even the gas station was closed and she hadn't passed a state or town police station. Only one building had a light on, a small Victorian house with a porch light illuminating the sign: RAVEN LAKE PUBLIC LIBRARY, FOUNDED 1937.

She didn't know what to do.

She dropped her speed even from what it had been on the curves and hills between the Northway and Raven Lake and drove up the street almost to the end, where it turned back into State Route 26.

She knew from the map that it curved back and recrossed the Northway north of where she'd exited, then went on to a tiny dot on the map on Lake Champlain where you could get a ferry to Vermont.

She started looking for an outside phone box to call an operator for help or dial 911 and risk their wrath when she just asked directions. Then she came abreast of a long low building with a lit sign, RAVEN LAKE LANES, and there were lights in the metal-framed window.

It was bigger inside than it looked from the lot. All the alleys were dark but one in which a man bowled while another hunched over a sort of lectern with a pad on it.

There was a small bar with a man with close-cropped red hair behind it arranging stemmed glasses in a pyramid. He heard the door and turned around.

"Can I help you?"

"I'm looking for Lakeshore," she said.

"Is that Lakeshore in Raven Lake?"

She nodded.

"I ask because every dinky, crapola town around here with a lake, and that's every town, also has a Lakeshore. Lakeshore Street, Road, Drive, Terrace . . ." He had a scoop nose, red lashes, light eyes, and skin freckled solid except for a few raw-looking pink patches.

"If I sound bitter," he said, "it's because I am."

"Hey, Mel, stop the bitching, already," one of the bowlers called good-naturedly.

He lowered his voice. "Been stuck in this godforsaken backwater two years. Got this place from an estate just outta probate. Thought I got a real steal. Believed them when they said it was a nine-month season. What a sucker. . ." His light eyes sparkled. "Wanna buy a bowling alley?"

"Uh, no thank you," Eve said.

"Of course you don't. Of course you don't wanna drive thirty miles to see a movie off season, and God forbid you wanna take your wife out to dinner. You got Bessie's, where you can get ham and eggs for breakfast, eggs and ham for lunch, and ham-burger any time until two P.M. After that, it's me here or Frank's, and all we got's cold sandwiches. Nine months, ha! Place's dead as my Aunt Fanny's Studebaker from October to December, and from March to July."

The ball racketed down the alley, pins clattered, and the voice of an invisible woman called, "Okay, gentlemen, that's it."

"Oh, my God," the bartender moaned. "That's it. Not even eleven on a Friday night, and that's it. In Albany we'd just be getting warmed up. You wouldn't be from Albany by any chance?" he asked longingly.

"Connecticut," she said. "Bridgeton, Connecticut."

"Sounds like another dink town, if you'll forgive me."

"I guess it is," she said. "But it's only eighty miles from New York."

"New York's the Devil's asshole," he snorted. "Long drive here from Connecticut?"

"About four hours."

"Well, your journey's almost over," he said kindly. "Lakeshore's three miles from here."

Three miles.

Journeys end in lovers' meetings, she thought. It was a phrase from a schoolgirl poem or one of the Gothic romances she'd read when she was young. She was in no condition for a lovers' meeting; she felt grubby, her hair was a mess, she needed a toilet.

"Can I use the ladies' room?"

" 'Course. Right through there, first door you come to. I'll give you directions to Lakeshore when you get back."

The ladies' room was small, clean, and chilly.

She used the toilet, washed at the little sink, and dried off with the rough brown paper towel. Her hair was tangled from the wind blowing through the car window and she wet it down and forced the comb through it. The circles under her eyes were almost purple by now, and her eyes were bloodshot from the glare of oncoming head-lights. Even so, she looked better—younger and more like herself— than she had in weeks.

"Three miles," she whispered to the mirror, then went back to the bar. The alley was dark; the bowlers had on windbreakers and were zipping their bowling balls into padded bags. Through the window, she saw the outside lights flicker off.

The men called good night to the bartender, nodded at her, and left.

"Want me to write the directions?" he asked her.

"Are they complicated?"

"Not at all. Just go out here, turn left, then bear left at the fork in the road about a mile up; keep going until you get to the lake. Looks like the road ends, but it doesn't. It's a T, and the road goes all the way around the lake except for a swampy patch you need a jeep to cross. But I assume you won't have to go that far."

"I hope not," she said.

"Okay, you get to the lake. To your right is Frank's Roadhouse. Definitely not a snazzy place. To your left is Lakeshore. There's no other roads, no nothing but mailboxes and driveways, houses and the lake. It's a gorgeous lake, lady. They call it Raven Lake because it looks black except in high summer when it turns the most amazing shade of gray blue you ever saw. Yeah, Raven Lake almost makes it worth living in this shit-kicking backwater—forgive the language. Raven Lake's got pike and trout, even some muskie. None of your little pan fish in Raven Lake. A he-man's lake . . ."

He loves this place, she thought suddenly, really loves it, and all the bitching and moaning is an act. She smiled at him, he smiled back and wished her luck.

The full moon was high; she almost didn't need headlights. She bore left at the fork and the road headed dead for the moon; then the moon and road seemed to bleed together into a long, rippling, confusing streak, and she slowed up, crept forward, and came to the lake, or what looked like a cove of the lake. To the right, strands of red and green neon blinked about a quarter of a mile away . . . Frank's Roadhouse. To her left, the road ran along the lake and into the trees. She turned left, passed a reedy hump of land making a small causeway across the neck of the cove, and then the black expanse of Raven Lake, cut by a rippling streak of moonlight, opened beside the road.

It was about a half mile across, with lights from scattered houses winking through the trees on the other side. Near shore was reedy, like the cove, and she heard peepers call and the plop of fish in the water.

The first mailbox she came to had the number 10 on it in beaded silver numbers and a driveway next to it rising up to a treed ridge from the road. As the numbers increased, the mailboxes got sparser. At number 210, the car heaved off the pavement onto graded gravel and she dropped her speed to twenty so gravel wouldn't spit up from the tires and nick the car. About half a mile later, she came to 300, the number her mother-in-law had written down for her.

Her hands trembled on the wheel; sweat popped out along her hairline. If she had any sense, she'd go back, find a motel, get a night's sleep, a good breakfast, and come back in the morning, fed, rested, calmer. But she was so close, she had to see him; she turned in and drove through a stand of birch and maple mixed with spruce. She smelled woodsmoke, then saw a break in the trees ahead and, a second later, pulled into a clearing with a small, neat, pretty house backed by the lake. She pulled around and stopped in three-quarter profile to the house. It had a stone chimney, front porch, and casement windows. Smoke came out of the chimney, the downstairs windows were lit, and she heard movie music. He was awake, watching a movie on TV. She reached for the ignition key and the porch light came on. The door started to open and her heart gave a giant thud that made her light-headed because it suddenly hit her that he might not be alone. He was handsome and separated, he had normal appetites, and there was no reason on earth for him not to bring a woman home. She jammed the clutch in, grabbed the gear-shift knob so hard her hand cramped. If she saw any sign of someone with him, she'd shove the car into reverse and back down the driveway fast, trying not to smash her pretty car into a tree. The door swung in and his figure appeared in the rectangle of light. She couldn't see his face, but recognized his height, the shape of his head and shoulders. He must have heard the car and come out to see who was visiting at this hour. He'd never seen the LeBaron, wouldn't know it was her.

No one came to stand next to him; the windows were blank. He seemed to be alone. She let go of the gearshift, turned off the motor, and opened the door. The interior light came on and he saw her. He leaped out the door and cried, "Eve . . . Evie . . ."

He sounded glad to see her—elated to see her. He must have missed her too, meant it when he mumbled that he loved her during those miserable phone calls. He was racing to get to her, and any second would step into the headlights and she'd see his face for the first time in almost two months.

He wasn't Greta's drop-dead gorgeous, no one would ask him to do cigarette ads, but he was tall, solid, with straight dark hair and dark eyes with Greta's long thick lashes, and a long face that had those indents that made him look rugged and sad at the same time.

She called his name too, swung her legs around, and boosted herself out of the car. She took a step toward him on the heavy uneven stone driveway and her foot twisted. She started to fall, reached out, and grabbed cold metal. It was a chain attached to a swing that hung from a tree limb next to the driveway. She hung on to it, righted herself, and felt that sudden, ridiculously small sinking sensation. Like missing a step, or going down too fast in an elevator, or any of the probably million similes she'd found for the onset of the *thing*: her mother's legacy to her.

The peepers shut up, a night bird was cut off in midcall. Wind blew the trees and her husband raced across the wood-slat porch in total silence. Then trees, house, clearing, and her husband disappeared and she was at the edge of another clearing. This one was smaller, ringed by old white pines that had left decades worth of their needles on the ground. A woman lay on them in a spreading pool of blood. She was naked except for a sweater and cotton button-down shirt (which would haunt Eve forever since she knew the woman had ironed that shirt a few hours ago so it would look crisp for tonight) pushed up under her arms. From there down she was bare, and her torso was slashed open from sternum to pubic bone. The flesh rolled open in layers, like a cutaway anatomy diagram, exposing a pulsing membrane over the ghostly shapes of her organs and intestines.

Eve let go of the chain, jerked back, hit the edge of the car door, and fell. The jagged stone cut her slacks and knee, but she didn't feel it. She screwed her eyes shut, trying to drive the vision away. But that only made it more vivid. The blood was glittering crimson, the woman's sweater was blue, the shirt was pale pink, and the layer of exposed fat running down her body was the color of new-washed wool. The pulsing membrane steamed in the night air; she was still warm, still alive. Slit open, almost bled dry, but alive and conscious. Her eyes rolled and seemed to look right at Eve with an expression of overarcing bewilderment. *How did this happen to me,* they seemed to be asking, *how did this happen to me?*

Then the pulsing stuttered, lost rhythm. The eyes, which seemed to see Eve across whatever barrier of time and space separated them, glazed, went blind, then froze in their sockets. The woman's jaw fell open, blood gushed out of her mouth and ran across her face into her hair, and Eve sobbed and pushed her knuckles into her eyes trying to drive the picture away. It was no use. They never stopped until they were ready to, and this one was still bright, though starting to fade a little at the edges, forming a border like a frame of film. A pair of men's loafers stepped across the border; they had tassels, were covered with blood and topped by pant legs that were also blood-soaked. Eve saw the figure from the back as it bent over the woman. A silvery rubber-gloved hand that looked leprous in the moonlight reached out and closed her eyes.

● ●

EVE HUDDLED IN FRONT OF THE FIRE SHIVERING LIKE A SICK DOG. Sam had wrapped a Hudson's Bay blanket around her, but she couldn't stop shaking. He sat on his heels in front of her for a moment, then got up and went to his new phone. It had been put in this afternoon and, thanks to her, his first call would be to the police.

"What do I tell them, Eve?"

"What I told you. That I saw a body in a clearing."

"*Saw?*"

"Found. Tell them I found her."

"Where."

"In a clearing," she stammered, "in the woods." Her teeth chattered.

"Honey," he said gently, "this is the Adirondack Park. There're millions of acres of woods and clearings. Did you see anything else?"

She had; she tried to recall what it was without having to see the dead woman again. There was the clearing, never mind the blood and corpse. Then there'd been the man wearing loafers. He'd walked away, and as he did her vision panned back just as it started to fade like the end of a sad movie. Fade to black, she thought the phrase was. She saw his back rushing into the trees, heard him in the underbrush, and saw . . . a shed at the edge of the clearing. It was log-sided, with one wall fallen in and crumbling green asphalt roof shingles. It could be a long-abandoned children's playhouse, but roof shingles were pretty elaborate for a playhouse, so it must have been an outhouse or tool or tractor shed.

"There was a shed," she said slowly, then described it to him.

"Anything else?" he asked. "Anything at all?"

She shook her head, and he picked up the phone and dialed 911.

● ●

THEY SHOWED UP A LITTLE AFTER 1:00 A.M. ONE WAS A HUGE man, much taller than Sam, who stood almost six feet. The other was small and slight, with dark hair combed back from his forehead and liquid brown eyes. Sam brought them into the living room, where Eve still huddled in front of the fire. They had ID cases out, must have shown their badges in the foyer.

The big one, who was not fat, just big, with arms that filled the sleeves of his jacket, crossed the room to Eve. The floor didn't shake, but she had the sense of something enormous coming at her.

He stopped and flipped the case open to show his badge and a laminated card in the slipcase next to it. He was Detective Lieutenant David Latovsky, Major Crime Squad, New York State Police.

"We found her, Mrs. Klein," he said quietly. "Right where you said we would. A few yards from Old Man Carlin's tractor shed. Lightning hit the Carlin house about ten years ago, place burned to the ground except for the foundation and chimney . . . and the shed. The Carlins threw in the towel and moved to Florida. State bought the land," he went on conversationally, pulling over a heavy oak chair as if it were made of balsa and setting it in front of her.

He sat down facing her, their knees almost touching.

His hair was thick, dark blond, and starting to recede in a widow's peak. His voice was gentle, but his dark blue eyes looked hard and smart in the firelight. He'd be hard to bluff.

He closed the ID case and slipped it into his inside jacket pocket.

"State left the land just as it was," he went on. "Stone chimney and foundation full of burned debris. But I guess you didn't notice that."

She shook her head.

"I see. Well," he said softly, leaning his enormous forearms on his thighs so his head came closer to hers, "why don't you tell me what happened."

Because you'll think I'm lying or crazy, she thought, looking at his large-featured, handsome face.

"I was lost," she said.

"Very lost, Mrs. Klein. The old Carlin place is a good eight land miles from here, around the other side of the lake."

"I was very lost," she said, forcing herself to meet his eyes. "I've never been to Raven Lake before, and all I had was the address, no directions."

"I see. But I thought *Mr.* Klein lives here." He looked at Sam, who was standing next to a long polished trestle table he probably ate at. Whoever had rented this place to him had kept it in tip-top shape, Eve thought. The wide-board floor shone, the smell of wax grew stronger as the room got hotter. The furniture was polished, the hearth swept. If Eve stayed here with him . . . if he'd let her . . . she'd keep it as well as the owners had.

"That's right," Sam said, looking helplessly at Eve. "I live here."

Latovsky turned back to Eve, eyebrows raised.

"We're separated," she said quietly.

"Ah," he said in a that-explains-it voice. "And you'd never visited before."

"No."

"Why now, Mrs. Klein?"

"I don't know."

"Were you hoping to reconcile?"

"Is that any of your business?" she snapped.

"I don't know," he said. "We've got a murder, Mrs. Klein, a very nasty murder. Not sure yet what's my business and what isn't. Uh . . . perhaps you'd like to have a lawyer present."

"For what?" Sam cried. "She didn't do anything."

"No. Of course not," the big cop said. "No question that it was a man who did the butchering."

Eve's stomach heaved.

"Now, where were we?" Latovsky said pleasantly. "You were lost."

"I took the wrong turn at the lake," she said hoarsely.

"Oh? And how did you find your way to the lake?"

She told him about the bartender in the bowling alley because the bartender might tell someone she'd been there, and that someone might tell someone else.

"So you *did* have directions," Latovsky said.

"Verbal directions. And I was nervous and got confused at the lake, and I guess I turned the wrong way."

"Confused," he said quietly. "Okay . . . then what?"

"I kept going, hoping I'd get to number three hundred or see lights from a house where I could ask directions or something."

"But you didn't."

She remembered the lights of houses across the lake. They'd been close to shore, probably hidden from the road by trees like this house.

"No," she said, taking a chance.

"But you did stop at the old Carlin place."

She nodded.

"Why?" he asked gently.

There'd been a path in the vision; it had been overgrown, but definitely a path that must've led from the road to the clearing.

"I saw a path," she said. "I thought it might go somewhere."

"I see. So you ignored the lit-up roadhouse and the driveways that obviously *did* go somewhere and picked an overgrown path in the middle of the woods, in the dark."

"I have a flashlight," she said, quickly. Frances insisted that Larry put flashlights in the cars' glove compartments and check them once a month. "In case," Frances had said. No one ever asked in case of what.

"A flashlight."

"That's right."

"But no other light. No indication of habitation," he said.

"Just the path."

"Yes, of course. The path. Pretty overgrown, that path . . ."

"Yes, but it's there," she said stubbornly.

"Pretty long way from the road to the clearing where we found her."

"Not so far," she said.

He leaned back; the chair creaked a little.

"Okay. You left your car, went up a path with a flashlight into the woods to the clearing that had once been Steve Carlin's cow pasture, saw the woman and the shed. But didn't notice the farmhouse foundation or the stone chimney . . ."

"No."

"Then what did you do, Mrs. Klein?"

"I don't remember. I was very upset."

"I can imagine," he said drily. "So you must've raced down that same path back to your car . . ."

She nodded.

"Then raced back the way you'd come. Presumably still lost."

"Yes."

"But you didn't stop at the roadhouse to call the police."

"No," she whispered. "But as I said I was very . . ."

"Upset."

"Yes."

"So you went back to the T of Old Rimer Road and this time took the correct turn."

"Yes."

"How long do you think all this took, Mrs. Klein?"

"I have no idea."

"Ballpark? Fifteen minutes? Half an hour?"

"I don't know," she mumbled. He had set some kind of trap, she felt it closing on her.

"Well, I'll tell you, Mrs. Klein. Without a helicopter that trip around the lake on Lakeshore—which is the only road—takes at least an hour, and even then you could break an axle. So it took you at least half an hour to forty minutes to get back to Old Rimer Road where Lakeshore T's and another ten minutes to get here. And on the way, you didn't just *pass* the roadhouse, Mrs. Klein, you crossed its parking lot because the road cuts through it. And Frank's is lit up like a Tokyo whorehouse. Town fathers've tried for years to get Frank to cool it on the lights: issued summonses, threatened boycotts, you name it. Nothing works; it's lit night and day, summer and winter. So you *had* to see it, *had* to figure they had a phone you could use to call for help. But you didn't."

Latovsky leaned forward so his head was only a few inches from hers. She leaned back, trying to put distance between them, but was trapped in the chair. She smelled the warm scent of his hair, a limey aftershave, and the starch in his shirt. It was almost two in the morning, he'd probably been sound asleep when they called him about the woman in the clearing, yet he'd put on a jacket, clean shirt, and tie.

He said, "The call from your husband to 911 came in at exactly twelve minutes after eleven. That right, Mike?"

"Right, Lieutenant." The little man grinned wolfishly.

"Eleven twelve," Latovsky said. "Fortunately, Mike—Sergeant Lucci here—was on duty tonight and knew exactly which green-roofed shed your husband meant, having lived on Raven Lake when he was a kid. Now, Mrs. Klein, we may be a bunch of rednecked shit-kickers up here, but we *do* have a helicopter, and in view of the fact that this looked like the fifth murder in our backwater serial—"

"Fifth!" Eve cried.

"That's right, Mrs. Klein. Four last summer and fall, now one this spring. Bastard seems to like warm weather. So, since this was the fifth, and everyone's understandably worked up, Sergeant Lucci got the use of the helicopter and was at the Carlin back pasture by . . . what, Mike. . . ?" He kept his eyes on Eve. "Eleven thirty?"

"Eleven thirty on the nose, Lieutenant," the smaller one said.

"And the woman was still warm, Mrs. Klein," Latovsky went on. "It was down to forty-five by then. Cools off fast here when it decides to, so it had gone from sixty to forty-five by eleven. But she was *still warm*, Mrs. Klein. Her blood was hot and liquid . . . her guts steamed . . ."

Eve's skin turned cold and slimy and she knew she was going to faint.

"The pine needles were sopping wet," Latovsky intoned.

"Stop it," Sam cried. "For Christ's sake, stop!"

Eve's eyes rolled back in her head. Any second now, she'd pass out and slide bonelessly out of the chair to the floor. *Let it be soon,* she prayed, *let him stop . . .*

But she stayed conscious and the big cop's voice kept battering her. "Even the pine needles were still wet with blood, Mrs. Klein, hadn't started drying even at the outer edges of the patch she lay on.

"Do you hear me," he snarled, "do you . . . goddamn it . . ."

Her eyes snapped open, looked into his, and saw utter contempt. She didn't get it. As far as he knew she'd gotten mixed up about the times and·hadn't stopped immediately to report the corpse in the woods. Wrong, silly, and maybe inconvenient for the police, but hardly contemptible. But he was looking at her as if *she* were the killer or worse. Then she put it together.

Warm blood . . . steaming guts . . . almost an hour after Eve had supposedly seen the body. They thought the woman had been alive when Eve found her and alive when Eve left her. Alive, alone, slit open, and dying, and Eve hadn't tried to save her, had passed the roadhouse with its phone and kept going because she was neurotic, spoiled, unimaginably self-involved. An icy bitch who wouldn't even take a minute to stop and call for help.

It was a horrendous indictment, but he'd have to think what he wanted. As far as she knew, being cold, neurotic, selfish—contempt-ible—was not illegal. Let him revile her all he wanted, get it out of his system, and leave her alone.

She must have mumbled it.

"What's that?" he snapped at her. "What did you say?"

"I said leave me alone."

"Not on your life, lady. You were there. You know a whole lot more than you're telling. And if I can't get you for depraved indiffer-ence . . ."

Depraved indifference?

"Then I'll get you for withholding evidence. Either way, I'm not going to leave you alone for a long, long time."

"I'm calling Del Kahn," Sam said. Del was the Tilden family lawyer.

"No, Sam," she said quietly. "It's all right."

"All right?" Latovsky choked. "You think it's all right? Well, just in case you're interested, lady, which I'm sure you're not—but I'm going to tell you anyway—her name was Abigail. Abigail Reese. Right now, someone back in Tupper Lake is telling her ten-year-old son that his mother's not coming home and someone down in Schenectady is telling her mother the same thing. And the mother'll have to come here tonight and get the little boy, because you can't leave a ten-year-old alone with strangers on the night you tell him his mother's been murdered. Now can you?"

Eve clasped her hands and stared at her laced fingers.

"Can you?" Latovsky boomed.

She didn't answer.

"Jesus Christ, lady. What rock did you crawl out from under?"

She raised her head to just the right angle and literally looked down her nose at him as she'd seen her mother do to servants. As three hundred years of Tildens must have done, and she said coolly, "I'm sure I don't have to take this kind of abuse."

"Oh, but you do," he snarled. "You're going to have to take a hell of a lot worse, because she's not the first, she's the fifth, and we're scared—terrified—there'll be more. Maybe withholding evidence on backwater serial murder won't cut much ice in the big town where you got more killers, rapists, and coke-head cocksuckers than we got trees, but here it's going to get you three to five, lady. Hard time, where you get fucked every night by some big black mama with a Coke-bottle dildo—"

Sam screamed something and went for him and Eve yelled, "NO—" then jerked her head back and said:

"I wasn't there."

They all stared at her.

"I was not there," she said, enunciating every word clearly. "I was here. I saw it, just like you think. But I was here in the driveway . . . on my knees in the driveway . . . when I saw it happen."

"Oh, Christ, no," Sam moaned, covering his face with his hand. "Oh, Eve . . . don't."

The little dark one stopped smiling the wolfish smile. Latovsky stared at her, then said, "What are you talking about?"

"I'll show you. Much easier than trying to explain," she said steadily, and reached out toward him. He flinched, but couldn't get away without leaping out of the chair like a scared rabbit, and he watched her hand come at him, palm out, fingers spread. It touched the front of his shirt, slid under his tie, and pressed itself flat against his chest. He shuddered, then looked up at her. She was smiling. The smile wasn't cold or mean . . . or happy or warm. It was the matter-of-fact smile of someone who knew exactly what they were doing, practicing a skill they had down cold. A crack mechanic might smile like that when he finally frees the valve lifter on your sixty Buick, or Itzhak Perlman when he picks up his violin. David Latovsky's mother had that look when she took a loaf of her locally prized egg bread out of the oven. A whole list of people who knew what they were doing and took quiet joy in doing it marched through his mind as the woman pressed her palm gently against him.

The touch wasn't cold. He'd shuddered because he didn't want her touching him, not because of any sensation that came through his shirt from her hand. In fact nothing much happened, except that she looked at him with her steady, grave, really quite mild dark eyes that had a moss-green undercast . . . pretty eyes . . . maybe beautiful . . . and smiled that little smile that had set off his train of thought. Then she said:

"Your wife's forty-two, same age as you, and you left—no—divorced her three years ago. You have a daughter you see two weekends a month. Your house is on a lake, it's got a front porch like this one, and it's too big for one person and hard to heat . . . heat . . ." She faltered, then went on in that perfectly conversational voice as if they were comparing the merits of Winey Keemum and Formosa Oolong tea.

"Heat costs you almost two hundred a month in the dead of winter, and you're afraid it'll go up much higher this year. You used to have a dog . . . a mutt with red fur . . . I can't see his name. You don't miss your wife much. You stopped loving her a long, long time ago. You don't love anyone now except your daughter and your mother and that worries you. And late at night . . ." She faltered again and her smile turned gentle. "But you don't want the others to hear that, do you? You love your work, sometimes think that in another time and place and with a little luck, you might have been one of history's great detectives. You're a good fisherman, use light line like a real sportsman, and last night you caught a six-pound trout for your dinner, right off the edge of your own lawn. And just now, I got a whiff of the fresh bread your mother bakes."

She wasn't waiting for confirmation. She *knew* and suddenly he knew she knew, and he jumped out of the chair like that scared rabbit he didn't want to look like and backed away from her. She looked at him steadily and said, "I don't *tell* the future, Lieutenant; sometimes I see it, sometimes I don't. But when I do, I never say so, because I'm afraid people will believe me and make sure whatever I tell them comes true."

● ●

ADAM HAD BEEN CAREFUL AS ALWAYS. HE KEPT LAWN AND LEAF bags neatly folded in the trunk of the LTD and he'd slit one open with his penknife and draped it over the front seat of the car to protect it before he got in wearing the bloody clothes.

Now he took the plastic bag carefully out of the front seat and carried it around the back of the house to the yard. The yard was ringed with trees and shrubs. He couldn't see the lights of other houses and the people in those houses couldn't see him, even though the moon was still high and it was more like dusk than the dead of night.

He rolled the bag up, stuffed it into another bag that he kept, also neatly folded, with a pile of others next to the garbage cans on the back porch. Then he stripped. It was chilly by now; he shivered as the cool air hit his bare skin, but there was worse to come. He put the clothes, shoes, underwear, gloves, and wig—everything but the scalpel—into the bag, then carefully tied the top and pushed it into the space under the back porch. He turned on the garden hose and directed the freezing spray at himself, starting at his head and working his way down his body until he was sure every trace of blood was washed away. He shivered and shook, his skin pimpled and shriveled, but he persevered.

When he was done, he took the scalpel, which he'd laid on the grass, and dashed into the house. He put a pot of water on the stove, added Clorox, and when it came to the boil, turned off the stove, put in the scalpel and left it there for a half hour. Then he put it back under the heating grate and finally took a hot shower, soaping carefully, shampooing his hair, then just letting hot water sluice over him.

He dried off, put on clean pajamas that smelled of fabric softener, turned out the lights, and climbed into bed.

He put his arms behind his head, looked at the streaks of light the waning moon made on the ceiling, and thought about tonight.

He'd done everything exactly as he had the last four times, but tonight's disappointment had been the greatest because he'd been sure this time would be different. He liked her more than the others, even liked the sound of her voice, and most women's voices set his teeth on edge.

He'd thought she'd know a good place, a clearing in the trees with pine needles and enough moonlight to see each other by. And she did. She must've been there before on one of her monthly forays to Frank's to make contact and drive away the dark. It was three or four miles from the roadhouse, up an overgrown path in a stand of ancient pines, with an old stone foundation and a log shed at the edge of the clearing that had looked elfin in the moonlight. The ground was covered with pine needles, flattened by the weight of last winter's snow, and they didn't need the blanket he'd brought in the trunk of the car along with the lawn and leaf bags. The needles were slick as silk and smelled sweet, sharp, clear. The cleanest smell there was.

It was starting to chill down and they'd undressed partially and quickly. He'd pulled off the wig and she hadn't looked askance as the other women had, but smiled and said, "I *thought* that was a rug. You're worried about being recognized?"

He had nodded.

"Running for Congress?" she asked lightly.

"I'm a doctor. I don't want one of my patients to see me . . ." He'd faltered, and she'd laughed and said, "Pussy-hunting in Raven Lake."

Why couldn't he laugh too, he'd wondered for the billionth time in his life. It *was* funny, his wearing a wig. Hilarious. So why couldn't he just laugh lightly and easily the way she did? He'd managed a stiff smile, then, to cover his lack of ease and humor, he'd kissed her. The sex part worked wonderfully, then he'd rolled away from her, leaving her lying on her back, legs bent, eyes closed. The moonlight and lovemaking smoothed out the wrinkles around her eyes and mouth, and she'd looked young and almost beautiful. He'd lucked out this time. This time it would happen.

She'd opened her eyes, looked affectionately at him, and saw the scars. They must look strange and terrible in the moonlight, and the other women had looked at them, then averted their eyes as if they were shameful. But she looked at them, cried softly, "God, what happened to you?" Then she reached out and ran her fingertips down his belly, across the ridges they made. The sensation was exquisite and he got an instant erection and made love to her again, then again, and they were both shaking when they got done.

"It's getting cold," she said softly. "We better cover up."

He heard the words with regret because he had to get it done before she put her clothes on; their time was up.

He'd grabbed his jacket, neatly folded on top of his other clothes, and reached into the pocket for the gloves and scalpel. He pulled on the gloves with his back to her and palmed the scalpel so she wouldn't catch the flash of metal in the moonlight, then he rolled back half on top of her and said, "Just one more kiss . . ."

"Greedy," she said fondly and let him kiss her. He moved his hand holding the palmed scalpel (so she wouldn't feel the cold metal) down her body. She thought he wanted more lovemaking, and she whispered, "My, you are something, aren't you?" He found the ridge of pubic bone he was feeling for, shifted to bare the front of her, and used the scalpel.

It was so sharp, he'd gotten so sure and fast with it, she didn't know what had happened at first. Her body jerked, she looked surprised, cried, "What was that?" then snapped her head up to see. He let her look past his shoulder at her own body, then leaned on her chest to hold her down so she wouldn't leap up and run into the woods streaming blood and guts and causing herself more agony. She screamed as all the others had, and thrashed wildly under him. But she was small—about 110, he guessed—and was already going into shock and he held her down easily and watched her face in the moonlight.

It ran the gamut of expressions as all the others had. Shock, pain, anguish, and anger, then horror, terror, self-pity, and finally, as she was dying in earnest, that bewilderment . . . and the question in her eyes: *Why did you do this to me?*

To heal myself, he'd have answered if he thought she (or any of them) would understand or give a shit what his motives were. So he kept quiet and watched her, waiting for *it* to happen.

He liked her, had made love to her and liked doing it, wanted to do it again, then did. Then again. He liked the look of her face and the sound of her voice, even when she screamed at him to help her as if she'd gotten confused about who'd done this to her.

He liked everything about her: the kind of clothes she wore, the smell of her hair and body, her finding that stupid wig he wore funny. Liked her enormously, and must—absolutely *must*—feel as much for this dying woman as those two interns this morning had felt for the dying, cancer-ridden Thomas S. Dorchester, whom they'd never seen before. He absolutely must feel as much for this woman as other people felt for friends and lovers . . . for their goddamn *dogs*, for shit's sake.

He *must.*

But nothing happened. He waited a long time, watching her face, but it was no use. And he'd finally rolled off of her so she could die without his weight on her and started to get dressed. Then he *did* feel something, but it had nothing to do with the woman dying on the bed of pine needles. It was a prickling feeling that made his hair stir and his skin pimple more than it would under the freezing spray of the hose. He felt someone watching him! He darted his eyes around the clearing, trying to see into the trees. The moonlight was bright enough to show up the hulk of a human figure, or even a deer, or fox, or coyote watching from the ring of trees. He didn't see or hear anything, but the feeling wouldn't go away and he'd rushed into his clothes, made sure she was dead, then put on the gloves and closed her eyes decently (the least he could do) and got the hell out of there.

Now he wondered what engendered that feeling of being watched since no one had been there.

He wished he could ask Bunny, but he'd probably say it was guilt. And Adam knew he had not felt guilt any more than he had love or pity.

He was hunting love, sorrow, pity, all the mysterious emotions he'd seen in people's eyes and body language, practically smelled coming off of them, and . . .

All he got for all his trouble was a hatful of rain.

That was from a movie that he didn't remember much about except that single line . . . all he got for all his trouble . . . his eyes slid closed; he started to fall asleep. He'd left footprints on the pine needles, and other clues. But they were useless unless they found him first. He had not left semen, had worn a condom . . . three condoms, now in his trouser pocket. But shoes and condoms and everything else that could link him to the woman in the woods would cease to exist a few hours from now.

He slept.

3

"MEL WRIGHT AT THE BOWLING ALLEY IN RAVEN Lake could've told her about Allison and Jo," Latovsky said. "Could have told her that my mother bakes bread for the neighbors, Bunny. She could've figured out the great detective part from the arrogant numb-nuts way I was acting. But she couldn't—*couldn't*—know or find out that I caught a six-pound trout last night on five-pound test line."

"She knew the line test?" Bunner said.

"She mentioned light tackle. Like a true sportsman, she said."

They were in the kitchen of Terence Bunner's quasi-mansion on the outskirts of Glenvale. Bunner and Al Cohen were the only two M.D. shrinks within two hundred square miles and they split the patients by age. Bunner got them over eighteen, Cohen under. They joked that they'd made the split at voting age. Bunner had a waiting list but never put off bad cases. The enemies up here were pretty impersonal, mostly the weather, and "bad cases" were rare. He did not treat alkies, figured AA could do a better job. Mostly they were alkies because their fathers or mothers were and they'd gotten the genes or the habit, and when they broke the habit, overcame the propensity, whatever term you wanted to use, the problem ended. Mostly.

He said, "So she knew you fished with five-pound test line, and that makes her psychic?"

"Sounds nuts put like that," Latovsky said, running his fingers through his hair.

"It *is* nuts, Dave. And you wouldn't say it or think it if you weren't exhausted. It's five A.M., and you're positively green. How about some coffee?"

Latovsky nodded, and Bunner got up from the table, wrapped his Indian-blanket robe tightly around his long, thin body, and went to the refrigerator, a huge new state-of-the-art thing with an ice-maker in the door. He opened it and peered inside. "We got decaf or regular."

"Make it regular."

Bunner took the can out and started spooning coffee into the drip maker on the counter. His wife had just finished remodeling the kitchen from a warm, cozy, slightly tacky fifties room with green linoleum and cedar cabinets to a space-age module with white tile floor, white composition cabinets, and pale gray polished-stone counters.

"Christ," he cried, lifting one slippered foot after the other. "Floor's like fucking ice. So's the goddamn counter. Can you imagine what it's going to be like in here when it's ten below out?"

"Cold," Latovsky said, grinning.

They were old friends, had grown up a block apart in the blue-collar section of Glenvale, had become buddies in kindergarten and stayed that way. They'd roomed together at SUNY at Albany; then Latovsky met Allison the end of his senior year and moved in with her. And Bunner went to medical school.

"Anything from the M.E. yet?" Bunner asked, pouring water into the coffee maker.

"No. But I don't need anything. Lucci was there first, got to look around before the troopers could screw everything up, and he said it's a mirror of the other four. She and the killer had sex, consensual or not—don't know for sure yet—but probably consensual, like the others. Then he slashed her open and left her to die. . . ." Suddenly Latovsky's voice choked.

Bunner looked at him. "Easy, Dave."

Latovsky laughed, but tears glittered in his eyes. "Four years at

Cornell Medical School, three years at Johns Hopkins, an M.D. and a Ph.D. . . . and all you can say is easy, Dave?"

Grinning, Bunner poured the coffee into the chipped, thick old mugs that he'd rescued before Mary gave them to the thrift shop along with all their old china and pots and pans. Clean sweep, she'd said. He hadn't minded except for the old mugs that he remembered his father drinking out of.

"He'd made love to her," Latovsky said. "Made love to her, Bunny. Must have felt *something*. How could he do it? How?"

"I don't know," Bunner said, bringing the mugs to the table.

"And why Raven Lake? Why not Echo Lake, or Blue Lake? Why not Plattsburg?" He pulled out a Xerox he'd made of the Adirondack Park map and smoothed it on the table. Red X's marked the murder sites.

"I did this looking for a pattern, and there isn't one. They're all over the place, like he opened the map, closed his eyes, and stuck a pin in it to see where he'd go next. Only two things are consistent. He does it on warm nights . . . you remember they stopped last October, and we thought the creep had moved on?" Bunner nodded. "And he does it at the full moon. Guy's a real nut."

Bunner didn't say anything.

Latovsky wrapped his fingers around the hot mug, trying to warm them. He'd been cold since he'd left the Klein woman at the little house on Raven Lake. That spring cold that ate through your bones, he thought. Bunny was right about his new kitchen; the hard slick surfaces would soak up the cold and send it back into the room. It'd cost them three hundred a month just to heat the kitchen.

"She knew what my oil bill was last winter," Latovsky said quietly.

"Stop it, Dave. Just stop it."

He sipped the coffee and burned the roof of his mouth, and suddenly had an even worse thought than the ones that had been torturing him since Lucci called him about the dead woman. He raised his head and looked sickly at Bunner. "Warm nights, full moon," he said slowly. "We could have one a month every month until *next* October."

"Maybe."

"Why?" Latovsky cried. "Why does he care what the temperature is?"

"Because he wants to be outside where no one can hear them

scream, and he doesn't have to worry about your finding fibers on carpets or furniture. Hard to pick out a couple of hairs in a bed of pine needles."

"Okay. And why the full moon?"

"To see by."

"See what by?"

Bunner looked into space and said softly, "Maybe their faces."

"So we'll have a dead woman for every full moon?"

"I don't think so," Bunner said suddenly. "He'll skip May and June."

"Why?"

"Fly season," Bunner said, standing up.

"Jesus, you make him sound rational."

"But he probably is, David. Be much easier to get a nut."

"You telling me the son-of-a-bitch is sane?"

"No. But he's not crazy either." Bunner slid the carafe off the heating element and brought it back to the table to refill their mugs. "There're lots of shrinks would tell you *anyone* who kills is crazy. And anyone who slashes open five women and leaves them to die in the woods is off-the-wall out of his skull. But I don't buy it. And neither should you, because it'll send you looking for a nut and there *is* no nut. This guy's probably perfectly normal on the surface, maybe good-looking, doesn't have any apparent problems with women. Some serial killers have been married men with kids. Some held down good jobs, were professionals." Bunner grinned. "He could be a shrink. The hallmark of this guy is the total unlikelihood of his being what he is."

"You mean he's just like everyone else."

"With a glitch."

"You call killing five people a *glitch?*" Latovsky cried.

"Yes, Dave, because that's what it is. Stop thinking *raving maniac* or you're never going to get him. Look for a regular guy, a good neighbor. Not old, not real young. Just a regular guy . . . with a glitch."

"Anyone you treat fall into that category, Bunny?" Latovsky asked suddenly.

"We've been over and over this, Dave. If anyone did, I'd tell you. If I set patient confidentiality over the deaths of five women—or even one—I'd be the crazy one. But the point is I could see the bastard every day and not know it's him."

"Because he's not crazy."

"That's right."

"Okay, Bunny. Then what is he?" Latovsky demanded.

"Evil," Bunny said firmly, and Latovsky felt the hair on his arms stir.

"Getting kind of cosmological here, aren't we," he said, trying to sound nonchalant.

"No one ever said the truth had to be mundane."

"Okay, as long as we're pissing on the mundane," Latovsky said, feeling himself start to blush, "how about my psychic?"

• •

LATOVSKY BROUGHT HER INTO BUNNER'S OFFICE AT 10:00 A.M. IT was Saturday morning, the phone was quiet, no patients went in or out, Mrs. Meeker was not on the front desk wearing her pink cotton cardigan over one of her starched blouses, and for the first time since Terence Bunner had opened this office eight years before, the place looked dismal to him.

He hadn't realized the carpet and furniture had gotten so worn, or that the drapes needed cleaning. Mary had picked the fabric, which was off white with bright green vines of some kind trailing down it. But the green had faded, the off-white was a greasy-looking yellow. The windows were grimy and his desk could use refinishing.

He saw all this for the first time, and the woman sitting across the desk from him didn't brighten things up any. Her face was gray; there were circles under her drab brown, slightly bloodshot eyes. He thought she must be about thirty-five, but she could have told him fifty and he wouldn't have been shocked. She looked exhausted, and something else that he didn't like to say because it wasn't very scientific: She looked heartsick.

Dave Latovsky's psychic.

Bunner had trained himself to really look at people, take in details and remember them. He looked at her now. Her clothes were good, but her purse was the real tip-off. It was large, black leather, with a discreet F on the small gold catch—Fendi or Ferragamo, which meant that the purse probably sold for eight hundred to a thousand. She was wearing flat shoes with rubber soles, not sport shoes like LA Gear or Nike or any of that crap, just plain rubber-soled flats. Old ladies' walking shoes with a thousand dollar purse. And the little bird pin on her sweater was heavy gold, with a half-carat diamond for the eye.

She was rich. Or her husband was. Her wedding ring was a plain

gold band, the heavy kind you bought at Tiffany or Van Cleef &
Arpels. Her slacks were good wool, well worn, with the knee torn out
of one leg, and he got a peek at a large flesh-colored Band-Aid. She
had fallen and skinned her knee like a six-year-old.

Latovsky had told her Bunner's name, but not the other way
around. Bunner took a fresh tape out of the desk drawer, labeled the
time and date, May 8, 1993. Then he said, "I'd like to record this, if
you have no objection, Ms. . . ." He waited for her to say her name.

"It's Mrs.," she said. Her voice was low-pitched and pleasant, the
only pretty thing about her.

"I have no objection as long as you don't use my name," she went
on. "I don't even want you to know it."

Bunner nodded, slid in the cassette, and pushed the record button. He said, "I heard most of the story: You claim you were in front
of a house when you 'saw' a woman die miles away. Is that right?"

She nodded.

"You were nowhere near the site?"

"No."

"That's confirmed," Latovsky said. "Mel Wright says she left his
place at quarter to eleven. He remembers the time because he was so
bitched off about not having enough business to stay open. She
couldn't have covered all that ground and called 911 by eleven twelve.
It's not possible."

"I see," Bunner said. Pretty slim evidence for Latovsky to suddenly start believing in psychics.

He took her slowly through the story. It ended in the driveway,
with her on her knees in the gravel (which explained the torn slacks
and Band-Aid). She'd seen the woman, seen blood soaking the pine
needles, seen the man's shoes and the cuffs of his trousers, then seen
his back as he rushed down the path through the woods.

"Probably to the road," she told Bunner.

"Probably? You didn't 'see' the road?"

"No."

"But you saw everything else. The woman, the man's feet and
back, the trees, the shed. Even though you were miles away."

"That's right."

"But not the house foundation, not the road."

"No. They were outside the . . . frame."

"Frame?"

"The frame of the picture."

"Hmmm." Bunner didn't think she was lying to weasel out of having left a woman to die. But that didn't make her psychic either.

"You really *saw* all that?" he said.

"Not just saw it. Heard it, smelled the pine needles and . . ." She hesitated.

"And what?"

"The blood," she said looking down.

"I see." Bunner fiddled with a pencil because he didn't know what else to do. The tape hissed slightly in the machine as it recorded nothing.

He looked up at Latovsky. "I don't know what you want me to ask."

She said in that lovely voice, "He wants you to confirm what he can't get himself to believe or not believe. I don't think you'll do it with questions, Doctor. I'm not crazy, I won't act or look as if I am. But not being crazy doesn't mean I saw a woman die from miles away either, does it?"

"No," he said, "it doesn't."

"Then why don't we stop wasting time. You don't know my name, the lieutenant's given me his word that he'll never tell you, so . . . hold out your hand."

Something started beating wildly in Bunner's middle.

He didn't move.

She said, "I won't hurt you."

He raised his hand from its resting place on the desk and looked at it as if he'd never seen it before. She waited patiently, then smiled at him, and he realized she'd probably be pretty after a few hours of rest. Very pretty: the kind who's beautiful on some days, so-so on others, and very drab on days like this. He looked intently into her tired brown eyes and didn't see anything at all to frighten him. And he grinned and thought, *Okay, big-time scientist, M.D., Ph.D., third in your class at Cornell, give the lady your hand.*

He stretched it out toward her and she reached for it with a pale hand, with tapering fingers that looked almost like a child's. She was younger than she looked if he could believe the evidence of the hand reaching for his. He felt himself tense, the way he sometimes did when crossing a rug in winter to turn on the light, knowing a shock was inevitable. Their fingers touched; nothing happened. Her fingers slipped along his, and she took his hand in hers, then let him go and sat back in the chair.

Nothing happened.

"I'm sorry. I'm very tired," she said, and he relaxed. It was an excuse, the great grandaddy of all excuses. I'm tired, Harry, I've got a headache. No fuckee tonight, Harry. He had gotten an excuse, not revelations from beyond the normal confines of time and space, and he was immensely relieved.

Then she said, "There's one you're most worried about." Her eyes slid closed like a kid who can't stay awake any longer. "I can't get his name, but you probably don't want me to know it anyway. He tried to kill himself last spring. You were his doctor then, you're still his doctor, and you're afraid he's going to do it again. It was the real thing last spring. He slashed the undersides of his arms from wrist to elbow. It wasn't a plea for help, a cry for love, attention, and understanding—he really wanted to die. He still really wants to die, and as the days get longer, the water changes color on the lakes, and the mountains start to green up, dying is all he can think about.

"He'll try again. This week or next, toward the end of the week. Thursday, Friday, close to the weekend, because it's spring, and he can't believe he has the right to see another spring, enjoy another weekend with his wife and little girls. And you can't understand what's behind it. You've been at it for months trying to dig it out of him. He knows, of course, but he doesn't know. Half forgot it ever happened. He can't allow himself another spring, another weekend, because he killed his mother."

Bunner heard his ragged breathing turn to a groan of terror. She opened her eyes and looked through him. Through the wall, he thought, over the parking lot, and God only knew what she saw; not him, not this office, but then she told him. She saw Ken Nevins's mother.

"She has blond hair—I think it's dyed. She's sick. Been sick a long time, only gets out of bed now to shower and use the toilet . . . and dye her hair. She smokes.

"They can't leave her alone, but his daddy's got to go someplace, don't know where, and he wants to take his older brother, but not the younger boy. He's got to stay home with her. Sit with her in the fusty bedroom while she smokes and reads or watches TV. He can't go outside to play, or listen to the radio, or watch any of the things he wants to on TV. It's spring, like it is now. Like it was when he slashed his arms open last year. The window's only open a crack because she can't stand drafts. Not enough to clear the air, only enough so he can hear the other kids out in the yards playing and laughing because they feel great because it's getting warm and school'll be over soon. He wants to be out there with them. *Longs* to be. But he has to stay here with *her*, while she smokes and reads and stares into space. She has on a thing . . . it's a negligee, but he doesn't know the right word for it—calls it a robe. It's light blue and filmy, made of nylon.

"Oh, God . . ." she cried, "oh . . . my God—"

She bowed her head so suddenly her neck bones crackled, then it was totally silent. He didn't know how long it went on; he couldn't move his head to look at Dave or the clock. Couldn't bring himself to pick up his pencil to fiddle with to pass the time or to move his lips to say anything. He just sat there, staring at the top of the nameless woman's head. Her hair was short and reddish brown, curly, with the part making a pale line across her scalp.

Then she looked up at him and said, "Get him to show you his hands, Doctor, the *palms* of his hands. Then he'll tell you."

"*You* tell me," Bunner cried. His voice sounded like he'd been crying for a week. He cleared his throat hard.

"It's not up to me. Besides, he's the one who's got to remember what happened, not me. I don't want to die. *He* does."

● ●

BUNNER LOOKED BACK AT THE SILHOUETTES IN THE CAR, Latovsky in front, the woman in back. Latovsky had turned around and slung his arm across the back to say something to her.

Bunner wondered what it was, what anyone could have to say to her, how his old friend even had the guts to sit in the same car with her. And there was a husband—talk about profiles in courage—some amazingly gutsy fool had actually married her!

He turned back and rang the bell. It chimed inside, then he heard footsteps, inhaled, held it, and the door opened. It wasn't Ken, but his wife, Jenny.

She'd come to the office a few times to pick up Ken on days when she'd needed Ken's car and Bunner had met her then. She was a lanky woman, a few inches taller than Ken, almost as tall as Bunner (but still a good head shorter than Dave) and she had a long bony face with large, androgynous features. She'd look like a man with the right haircut, except for her large gray eyes, which were lovely and feminine.

She raised her heavy straight eyebrows when she saw him, but in surprise, not alarm. She wasn't afraid he was bringing bad news about her husband, so he must be home.

"Dr. Bunner, this is a surprise."

"Hello, Jenny. Is Ken home?"

"Why, yes. Watching the game. Don't ask me which game." She smiled. Her eyes really were magnificent. He hoped the two girls, whom he'd never seen, had inherited those eyes, along with Ken's fine features and smooth skin.

"I guess it must be important for you to come here on a Saturday morning," she said doubtfully.

"It is to me. Is there a problem?"

"Only that Saturday morning's his quiet time. I keep the kids out of his way, don't make him go to the dry cleaners or mow the lawn or any of that garbage until afternoon. And he sort of prizes these few hours."

He could hardly say, *I'm here because a woman who looks like an unemployed nanny (except for jewelry worth about thirty thousand dollars) claims to be psychic and told me he's on the verge of another suicide attempt, and I've got to look at the palms of his hands.*

He didn't know what to say, so he kept quiet.

She looked at him a moment, then opened the door all the way. As he passed into the small foyer, which had fresh flowers on a table against the wall, she looked past him out the door.

"Are they with you?" she asked, nodding toward his Caddy at the curb.

"Yes."

"Do they want to come in?"

"I don't think so," he said. "I won't keep them—or Ken—long."

He was sure he wouldn't, because he didn't believe the exhausted-looking woman who claimed to be psychic. Glenvale was larger than the towns in the Park, but still not very big. Half the people in it knew about Ken's attempted suicide; it wasn't such a stretch from that to her figuring he was a patient of Bunner's since Terence Bunner was the only M.D. shrink for adults between Glenvale and Malone.

Dave said she had never been up here before, but he had only her word on that. So she could've heard about Ken and put the rest together with a combination of luck and savvy.

"Let me just tell Ken," said Jenny Nevins. "Don't want to just spring you on him."

She closed the door, led him into a small sitting room with

comfortable-looking chintz furniture and a tiny fireplace stuffed full of a shining black woodstove. "I'll just be a second," she said, and left him alone.

She was back quickly, motioning to him from the doorway.

"He's downstairs. We finished the basement a few years ago"— she led him deeper into the house—"and it looks okay, but it's still got a chill to it, no matter what the weather. But he likes it down there. Maybe because it's quiet and he can be alone." Then she must've seen the look Bunner shot at the door they were approaching, and she dropped her voice. "He didn't do it down there, Dr. Bunner. It's carpeted and that'd make it hard to clean." There was a flash of tears in her eyes. "He did it in the bathroom, where it's tiled. He's the most considerate man on earth."

Slashing your arms open in a tiled bathroom to keep from spoiling the rug in the finished basement was a whole new definition of considerate, Bunner thought. He wondered if the woman waiting with Dave out in the car had *seen* Ken use that mat knife. Another mark of deadly (accent on *deadly*) seriousness, using a mat knife instead of a razor blade.

But she hadn't *seen* anything, he told himself firmly. He was here because he was thorough and conscientious, not because he believed the woman in the torn slacks had seen anything in his office half an hour ago except the gaily colored drapes that needed cleaning.

They stopped at the door, and Jenny Nevins gave a crooked, mannish-looking grin and said, "Don't keep him too long. He loves his bit of solitude." Then she opened the door and said in a louder voice, "Can I get you some tea or coffee or a soft drink?"

He shook his head, said, "Thank you," then descended into the Nevinses' finished basement.

Chill came up the stairs to greet him; the steps and floor were carpeted, the cement or other foundation material was covered with good tongue-in-groove paneling, but it still felt like a basement, with windows high in the walls letting in thin streams of grayish light.

Ken Nevins stood in front of a chair upholstered in plaid wool. On the TV was a preseason exhibition baseball game with the sound off. A cooler sat next to the chair, a bottle of beer on the side table.

"Hi, Doc," Ken said. He looked fine, rosy-cheeked, well rested. Nothing like he had last year before the suicide attempt. The woman Dave had brought him was not only a fake, she was a cruel fake.

"Want a beer?" Ken asked. He was shortish with very regular

features, wide brown eyes, and straight, thick, dark hair. He was good-looking, almost pretty, on the verge of effeminate. But a year's worth of delving had convinced Bunner that Ken Nevins had not tried to kill himself because he was a repressed homosexual. Bunner didn't think he was, though it was next to impossible to be sure. Everything in his work was next to impossible, he thought suddenly. He should have taken his family's advice and become a surgeon or an airplane mechanic, he thought wryly. Dangerous work, with a terrible responsibility he couldn't imagine shouldering because, as Dave had observed once, if you fucked up, you could kill someone. But this was the same too, wasn't it? He'd fucked up once, and Nevins had almost died. If he fucked up again . . .

Goddamn that woman, he thought fiercely.

Bunner said no to the beer, and Ken sat back down in the plaid chair.

"Need an invitation?" Ken asked pleasantly.

Bunner shook his head and sat on a matching couch. On the TV a bat cracked a ball and the crowd roared in silence.

"Just like to watch?" he asked Ken.

"I figured you'd come to talk about something," Ken said, "not see the game."

"Yeah . . ." He hesitated, feeling as foolish as he ever had in his life, and then he lied to Ken Nevins, something he almost never did to his patients.

"Just decided to see you, Ken."

"Oh?"

"Yeah. Try to visit all my patients at home at least a few times." Another lie.

"First I've heard of it," Ken said suspiciously.

"Do you mind?"

Ken shrugged and looked at the silent game in progress on the twenty-one-inch screen.

"Well, you've come and seen. I guess you can go," he said coldly. "Unless you'd like the house tour. The girls are at a kiddy birthday party and they had a sleepover last night. But Jenny's a good housekeeper, the beds're probably all made by now . . . and the rest of the debris taken care of." His voice got colder with every word until *debris* sounded like ice cracking, and Bunner realized he was tampering with trust he'd spent a year building.

He wasn't going to let this happen and he said quickly, "I'm sorry, Ken. That's a load of shit I just gave you. I never visit my patients unless they ask me to for some reason. I'm not a social worker."

"I thought as much," Ken said quietly. The icy edge left his voice. "So . . . what's going on, Bunny?"

"I can't tell you. It's too nuts. But . . . Ken . . . can I see the palms of your hands?"

Ken Nevins's normally rosy, almost girlish complexion went white, then gray.

"Why?" he choked.

Bunner was startled at his reaction. "It's . . . it's . . ." he stammered. "More of the same silliness. At least I thought it was. Ken," he said, forcing himself to speak slowly, clearly, "Ken, show me your hands."

Ken clenched his fists reflexively. "You've seen those scars, Doctor. Everyone's fucking seen those scars."

"Your *palms*, Ken, not your arms."

"Fuck you."

With all the gentle, confident command he could muster, Bunner said, "Ken, show me," and he held his hands open and out to Ken Nevins. Ken hesitated, and Bunner knew he'd played out all his line. If Ken wouldn't do it, he couldn't ask him again. At least not now. But then slowly, barely an inch at a time, Ken Nevins raised his clenched fists off the arms of the chair and laid them in Bunner's waiting hands.

Then he opened them, and Bunner choked down a gasp that rose like a flash fire in his throat.

The skin of Ken Nevins's palms was riled, ridged, runneled, and twisted, and in a few places stretched taut and shiny. It looked like he'd taken a meat grinder to his palms a long time ago, and they'd healed into these writhing scars. But you wouldn't try to kill yourself by grinding up the palms of your hands, no matter how crazy you were. Besides, the scars were at least twenty years old. And then Bunner realized they were burn scars. When Ken Nevins was a kid, he'd burned the palms of his hands horribly. He'd put his hands, palms down, on a hot stove, or turned over the skillet of french fries his mother had left unattended on the stove—only his mother had never made french fries. She'd been an invalid, he'd known that from Ken . . . that woman had known it, too, God knows how. And God knows how she'd known about these poor scarred palms.

Both men were quiet for a long time. There was a break in the game, and out of the corner of his eye Bunner saw a clump of rugged-looking male models toasting each other with beer bottles. The advertisers must think only pansies used glasses.

More time passed while Ken let him hold his hands, excoriated palms up.

● ●

BUNNER SAID, QUIETLY, "I SHOULD'VE SEEN THEM BEFORE."

"Naw, you shouldn't. It's easy to keep your palms hidden, Bunny. You put 'em face down on your thighs . . . like this." He demonstrated. "Or keep your hands folded and everyone thinks you look sort of prim. Or nervous if you clench them. It's easy."

"What about in the hospital?" Bunner was asking easy questions, building to the hard one.

"You weren't in the ER that night, Bunny, and trust me, no one gave a shit about my *palms.*"

Now for the big one, Bunner thought.

"How'd it happen, Ken?"

He looked up and saw tears swimming in Ken's eyes. He'd never seen Ken cry before, even the morning after a suicide attempt had left his arms slashed almost to the bone. But he was crying now. Silent tears streamed down his face and dripped off his jaw and he pressed the runneled palms to his eyes.

After a moment, Bunner said, "Can you tell me what happened?"

"I killed my mother," Ken said.

● ●

BUNNER GOT BACK INTO THE CAR WITHOUT SAYING ANYTHING and started the motor. Latovsky looked questioningly at him, but Bunner shook his head and drove away from the Nevins house. The woman sat silently in the back seat.

He didn't know where to go. Stopping at Ray's or Tony's or any of the town coffee shops or restaurants or one of the dim little smokey bars that would also have the rushing-the-season baseball game on a huge screen and trying to talk about . . . what he had to talk about . . . was ludicrous.

He couldn't take them back to his chilly kitchen that might pay for itself with savings on air-conditioning—except you almost never needed air-conditioning up here—because he did not want her near

Mary and the kid, who'd be home from the school soccer game by now, because she might see *things* about them. The thought actually made him queasy, and he kept driving.

Glenvale was a large town, almost a small city. There was a proper business district—the usual dirty stone buildings with old signs painted on the windows for lawyers, dentists, and so on. His office was in one of the few new buildings in town, but most of the rest of the professionals had to put up with musty carpeting, cracked granite floors, and walls that bulged under greasy-looking enamel in drab colors. But they could open their windows, didn't have to have hot or cold air blowing out of registers all the time.

He drove slowly down Main Street, past the Glenvale Cinema where he and Dave had gone to Saturday afternoon movies back in the days when Audrey Hepburn and Marilyn Monroe were considered the most beautiful women on earth (depending on whether you liked women lean or lush) and the good old guys like Tracy and Bogart and his all-time favorite, Robert Mitchum, were still making movies.

He kept going. It was Saturday, pushing noon; traffic was heavy, and the trip along Main took ten minutes. It was a warmish day for early May; sun beat down on the car as he stalled in line after line of cars waiting for parking places, and he started to sweat. He noticed that Dave's face was shiny and he looked in the rearview mirror at the woman. She sat with her head bowed slightly and seemed to be looking at her hands. She wasn't nervous about whether he'd found out she was a fraud; she knew he had not.

She was also sweating a little, and the sheen on her skin improved her looks, made her almost pretty. Then he realized she *was* pretty, had a nice, nonthreatening kind of prettiness that would take you a while to notice. Nothing blatant about it, any more than there was about the little gold bird pinned to her sweater, unless you just happened to have the kind of sharp eyes that could differentiate solid gold from yellow crap and real diamonds from glass.

The line of traffic broke a little and he picked up speed. They were away from the town center now; they passed the IGA where Mary did most of their shopping and where Jenny Nevins probably bought her family's food. Then they entered a residential section of small houses, not far from where his folks and Dave's once lived. Then they were out of town, and he finally knew where he was headed. Ten minutes later, he pulled up at the abandoned gravel quarry, now full of milky water, with the old ten- or fifteen-story crusher that looked like a monstrous funnel standing next to it.

He pulled up at a strip of brown weeds that were showing the first signs of life in response to the warmth and sunshine.

No one ever came here except kids who'd been warned how dangerous it was, and never under any circumstances to go near the water or the crusher, and certainly never to climb the crisscross metal frame supporting the huge funnel. It was just made for climbing, of course, and the water for swimming, and he and Dave had done both.

The Caddy idled smoothly for a moment, then he shut it off. The woman looked up; Dave turned to him.

"You don't need me to tell you, do you?" Bunner said, looking at her in the rearview mirror. She shook her head.

"But *you* do, don't you, David."

Latovsky nodded.

"His palms are solid burn scars, third-degree burns. Must've been very bad, unbelievably painful. They should have done a much better job with the skin grafts, but it was almost thirty years ago.

"He *was* in the room with his mother that day, May tenth, he thinks, but he's not sure. Doesn't want to be sure, and I don't blame him. Anyway, he was left alone with her in that room, with the window open only a crack, and the TV on, and the room full of smoke because his mother was a chain smoker or next thing to it. And she had on that . . . negligee . . ." He almost choked on the word.

"Blue synthetic," he went on, and he got hold of himself. "Just as you told us. Maybe it was nylon, but whatever it was, they didn't make fire-retardant fabric in those days, at least it wasn't a law like now, or something. I don't know. And it doesn't matter anymore, does it?"

She shook her head a fraction, then looked out the window at the standing water in the old quarry. She knew what he was going to say, didn't have to listen, and he hated her.

He cleared his throat. "Doesn't matter what it was made of." He raised his voice and she looked back. "Because it went up like tinder, didn't it?"

"Yes," she said softly.

"Ken had fallen asleep in the chair by the window. It was warm and he was just a kid, and the other kids' voices outside must've lulled him, or maybe it was the TV. He fell asleep, then she did too with the cigarette in her hand. Just nodded off over a book or something, and the crackle woke him up. That's what he told me. The crackle of the fire woke him up, and he saw his mother lying on a bed of flames. Still there, still recognizable under the veil of fire. But the whole bed was burning and she must've been unconscious from the smoke by that

time, or even dead. But he was only seven, he didn't know that, and
he tried to save her. She was too big for him to drag out of the bed,
he didn't have the strength or leverage, so he tried to beat out the
flames with his bare hands. The burning nylon or whatever shit that
robe was made of stuck to his palms and kept burning, but he didn't
stop. Finally he ran out of the room looking for something big enough
to throw over his mama and smother the fire. He was smart enough for
that, and to know that the sheer curtains in the bedroom wouldn't do
the job. He pulled down the drapes in the dining room—green brocade, he just told me. Put me in mind of the drapes in *Gone With
the Wind* that Scarlett made a dress of . . . only that was velvet,
wasn't it?"

She didn't say anything.

"Anyway, he tugged the drapes down somehow; the palms
must've been black by then, burned to the bone, and the flesh would
have come off on the brocade. The pain would have been excruciating, but he did it and ran back with the drapes to try to smother the
flames. An adult would have known it was hopeless, would've given
up by then, and of course had the sense to call the fire department. But
he was only seven, remember. He got back to the room. The bed was
still burning. The fire didn't spread. But the bed was turning black,
and under the flames, he saw his mother was too, and her face had
melted—like candle wax, he said. Of course, it really hadn't. That's
just his memory. It would be crisp and turn black like the rest of her;
meat doesn't melt when it's burned, after all. It chars . . ."

He took a long shuddering breath and glared at Dave Latovsky;
he'd never seen his old friend look so sick. He went on. "Anyway, he
threw the drapes over her, and that probably helped some, but it was
way too late by then. And then he heard sirens, and he knew someone
was coming to help. And that's all he remembers. Didn't even remember that much until I helped him along, after you helped me
along," he said, looking at her again in the rearview mirror. She
nodded in silence. Was she ever happy? he wondered suddenly. Could
she laugh? What incredible horrors lived in that head of hers?

"He knows some of the rest, not because he remembers, although
with time and work I believe he will, but because his older brother told
him. He was curled up on the floor when the firemen got there. Fetal
position, I imagine. That fits, because according to his brother, it took
him over a week to straighten his legs out and walk, and during that
time his older brother and his father had to take turns carrying him to
the crapper."

He took another long breath and let it out shakily, then said, "So, whatever your name is, that's the story and the secret. And now that I know, and he knows, at least sort of . . . now maybe I can save his life.

"Ken should be grateful to you. So should I. But I'm not. Maybe because you just shit all over my ego, did in forty-five seconds what I haven't been able to do in a year of digging. That hurts. Of course, I shouldn't put my ego over a patient's welfare, and I don't. And I know I should thank you from the bottom of my heart, and I do. But lady, you just shit on a whole lot more than my ego—you shit on everything I and most of the people I've ever known believe, would stake their lives on probably. Which is, there ain't no such thing as what you are, and no one can do what you can. So you'll understand that I'll be glad to see the last of you. Most people would be."

"Oh," she said softly, smiling slightly at him, "some people find me quite . . . useful."

He didn't answer that. He twisted around to face Latovsky and said, "She told the truth, Dave. She did see it, but she wasn't there. She's not withholding evidence, isn't guilty of depraved indifference. Let her go."

He faced front, started the car, and drove them back to his building's parking lot. It was empty at 1:00 P.M. on a Saturday except for Latovsky's dinosaur Olds, which he'd bought before his divorce and now, with alimony, couldn't afford to unload for a new, more economical car. Next to it was a bright red, new LeBaron that avoided the Greek diner look of the bigger Chryslers.

As he pulled into the almost empty lot, he noticed how shoddy the professional building of Glenvale looked. It was at least eighty years younger than the buildings downtown, but the cement facing was streaked with yellow, all the fixed windows needed washing, and the metal around them, which had started out gunmetal gray, had a yellowish look as if it were coated with grease or on the verge of rusting. Suddenly, for the first time, everything in his life—his office, and the building, and his freezing kitchen—seemed shoddy to him.

He pulled up next to Latovsky's car. She asked, "I'm free to go?"

Latovsky nodded, and she opened the back door and started to slide out, putting her hand on the back of the front seat for leverage. As she did, her knuckles grazed Bunner's collar and she suddenly stopped moving and sat stiffly on one haunch, with one leg halfway out of the car.

"Doctor," she said quietly.

"What?" he snapped.

"You're supposed to go to a party tonight. . . ."

The Spring Fling dinner dance at the country club. He'd almost forgotten about it, but Mary had bought a new dress and sent his tux to the cleaners for the occasion.

"What about it?" he asked. His voice had scaled up at least an octave and sounded almost pubescent.

"Don't go," she said.

"Why not?" he cried in that shameful adolescent voice.

"I don't know," she said. "I just knew there was a party and you were going . . . and shouldn't. Well . . ." She smiled feebly. "If that's all . . ."

"Of course that's all," he croaked, and noticed Latovsky didn't say anything. Was probably thinking about some way to make use of her to get the son-of-a-bitch who'd murdered five women and seemed to be laughing up his sleeve—up his cupcake, Mary would say (it was one of her favorite phrases)—at all of them. Dave was a fool, Bunner thought. This woman was a jinx, should wear a red P on the front of her clothes. For Pariah.

Real scientific, he thought. His old prof, Arthur Gibson, who'd done some of the original work on the biochemistry of schizophrenia, would really love that one.

She climbed out of the car and went to the red LeBaron. She should sell that pin and buy herself a Porsche, he thought. But she probably didn't have to. Could probably buy five Porsches, peel off the two hundred thou in big bills and never miss the cash.

Bitter, he thought. Very bitter, and not like him. But he couldn't help it. He hated her.

Latovsky started to get out too.

"You're going after her, aren't you?" Bunner asked.

Latovsky nodded. "Maybe she saw something . . ."

"Who sups with the devil needs a long spoon," Bunner said sententiously. At least his voice had stopped squeaking. Latovsky settled back in the seat and looked at his old friend. "You know," he said quietly, "you doctor types are all a bunch of egomaniacal control freaks, and the second someone else gets a little power, you fucking go to pieces."

"That's a shitty thing to say."

"Yeah. But true, and you know it. You're too decent and honest at heart not to know it. Maybe she 'saw' something"—he managed to put quotes around the *saw* with his voice—"maybe she didn't. I don't think she did, or she'd've said so by now. But I'd be an asshole not to ask, now wouldn't I?"

Bunner nodded morosely, and Latovsky said, "There *is* a party tonight, isn't there?"

Another nod.

"And you're supposed to go," Latovsky said.

"Yes."

"If I were you, I'd stay away from it, Bunny."

"But you're not me," Bunner said, and he reached across Latovsky and popped the Caddy door open, wanting Latovsky out of there before Bunner said something that might damage their friendship. He liked and trusted Dave Latovsky more than anyone he knew; besides, causing trouble between them would be like giving that shabby bitch climbing into the red car even more power.

Underneath his pointless, irrational anger, he sort of knew he'd forget about her before long, or be able to put what had happened today into some kind of perspective. Maybe even wind up being interested in her, wishing her well, or something a lot more benign than what he was feeling now. But his feelings never had a chance to mellow because he ignored her advice and went to the party that night.

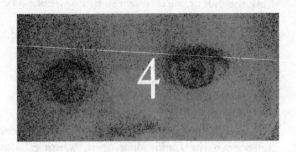

4

THE RED LEBARON WAS IN THE DRIVEWAY NEXT to the beige Civic that must belong to the husband. Latovsky parked next to it, then went up the porch steps and rang the bell.

Klein didn't look happy to see him.

"She's been up all night, just like you have, Lieutenant."

"I know. This won't take long."

He had one question and he couldn't rest until it was answered, if there was an answer.

Klein sighed, then stepped aside to let him in.

"She's in the kitchen," he said, "making tea. We're going to drink tea and talk about our lives, Lieutenant. May not mean much to you, but it does to us."

"I said I'd make it fast. Where's the kitchen?"

She was at the counter holding a steaming kettle in one hand and looking up at the ceiling. Two thick mugs with teabag tags trailing out of them sat on the counter.

She glanced at him, didn't seem surprised to see him, then looked back at the ceiling. He followed her eyes and saw an old device screwed into the ceiling next to the light fixture.

"What is that?" she asked.

It had been painted over so many times the details were lost but he knew what it was.

"A pulley," he said.

"For what?"

"You're not a country girl."

"We live in the country."

"Not on a farm."

"No. It's not a farm."

"This house must've been converted from a barn. Lots of houses around here were and the pulleys were used to raise sacks of grain or feed. It was usually bolted through a beam, or the ridgepole in some cases. Beam in here, I'd say from the height of it. Anyway, when they did the remodeling, they didn't want to weaken the beam by unbolting the pulley, so they just painted it and left it."

"I see." She shuddered.

"Something wrong?" he asked.

"I hate this room," she said, and he looked around in surprise. It was just a nice old-fashioned kitchen, mostly white like his mother's kitchen.

She looked away from the pulley. "Want some tea?"

"Why don't you go sit down. I'll make it," he said.

"I don't have any more to tell you."

"Just one more question. Give me the kettle."

She handed it to him, their fingertips brushed, and he jerked back suddenly, almost dropping the kettle.

"Don't worry," she said softly. "I didn't see anything."

"It's not that."

"Oh, I think it is. There's sugar in the bowl on the table and honey next to it, if you want. Sam and I take it straight."

She left the room and he brewed the tea, letting it steep an extra minute because the Kleins looked like they needed it strong. Then he found a small tray in a cupboard under the counter and brought in the mugs.

They sat on opposite ends of the room, not talking about their lives. But they couldn't say what they had to with a stranger in the house, and he'd make it as fast as he could and get out.

He handed her the mug, half hoping their fingers would touch again to prove to her that he wasn't afraid, but they didn't. He gave Klein his cup, then settled in the same chair he'd sat in last night.

Last night he'd have said second sight was bullshit and psychics were on a par with the carny morphadite and two-headed lady.

He gave her time to sip the tea. She was very pale; the skin under her eyes looked bruised. She must be as exhausted as he was, but she had not whined or given Bunner a bad time in return for the snot he gave her. She had conducted herself like a lady, his mother would have said, and he realized he liked this peculiar, amazing, half-frightening woman. Liked her very much and hoped that the handsome husband, who would probably be a lot handsomer if he got some sleep and smiled once in a while, would go back to her if that's what she wanted. If that's what was best for her.

He wondered.

"Mrs. Klein." He put the cup down on the table next to the chair and saw her brace herself, but he went on doggedly. "Last night, you knew about . . . me . . . when you put your hand against my chest; today you knew about Ken when you touched Bunner. Then later, your hand brushed Bunner's back before you told him to stay away from that party."

She nodded.

"Then what did you touch last night to 'see' what you saw?"

● ●

THE SUN WAS GONE, THE AIR HAD A GREENISH TINGE, AND IT WAS colder and starting to rain. Eve stood in front of the swing, with Latovsky next to her; Sam stayed on the porch, keeping his distance.

Eve looked up at the heavy chain bolted through the limb that was as thick as the trunks of some trees. The chain was still solid, but the wooden seat had cracked and blistered through the years. Abigail Reese must have touched the swing, maybe played on it when she was a kid—or the killer had.

"She ironed her blouse," she said quietly.

"What?" Latovsky asked.

"Never mind." She looked at him. "It doesn't always work, you know. I might see nothing, I might see lots of things about anyone who's ever touched it or played on it."

"I understand."

She stared at the chain, praying she wouldn't see that woman die again, then she reached out and grabbed it.

The metal was cold and damp from the drizzle and felt slightly greasy.

Nothing happened; Latovsky waited tensely a few feet away, Sam came to the porch railing, the porch slats creaked under him. She looked up at the sky; the tree branches were still bare but she could make out buds on them. The sky had gotten low, the clearing felt closed in . . . and a wave of water came at her. It stopped short, receded into foam, and she thought it must be the lake or ocean, but it was bright blue and she was surrounded by sweating white tile walls. Someone was swimming toward her, doing a splashing butterfly stroke. The swimmer reached the end of the pool, grabbed the railing, heaved himself up, and pulled off his goggles. It was Tim, Meg's husband; *the thing* was clearing up old business and she was seeing what she'd been "supposed" to see yesterday when she wound Tim's scarf around her hand.

Tim passed her and she followed without wanting to. He left the pool chamber, the smell of chlorine changed to piney disinfectant, and they were in the shower room, only the two of them. Only Tim, really.

He turned on the water, stripped off his trunks, and Eve tried desperately to look away because she'd see him like this across the dinner or bridge table and want to die with embarrassment. But the picture turned with her as it always did—her own version of surround-a-vision—and she saw her best friend's husband naked. His body was comfortable-looking, a little soft in the middle, and he came here (wherever *here* was) to lose weight, and get into shape.

Then they were in the locker room; he had his underwear on (thank God). He was putting on his shirt . . . and a little boy cried, "Higher, higher."

Tim had dried himself carefully, but his shirt still got damp when he put it on. His suit was wrinkled from an hour in the locker, his tie a wreck.

"Higher . . . higher . . ." the little boy squealed. "Push me higher."

Tim *did* take off his clothes and put them back on some nights, but he did it to swim laps, not boff some bimbo from the office. She couldn't wait to tell Meg.

"Higher . . . higher," squealed the boy, and she was back in the clearing. Only it was summer. Trees in leaf and jagged pieces of sky flashed over her head.

"Higher"—desperately. "Higher . . ." The boy on the swing was about five or six. A boy about twelve was pushing him.

"Higher!"

"Any higher and you'll fall on your fool head," the older one said.

"I won't! I won't." The little one clutched the swing chains so hard his knuckles were white. "Higher," he screamed.

" 'Nuff." The older one stepped back and the swing started to lose momentum.

"No! I was almost there," the little one moaned.

The big one laughed. "You weren't almost anywhere but about to fall and crack your skull. Look, I gotta go, I told the guys."

"No! Don't leave me!" He sounded terrified. This wasn't just a little boy wanting a big boy to keep playing with him; something else was going on.

"Gotta," said the big one. "I promised."

"Take me with you," pleaded the little one. He was very pale and tears filled his eyes.

"The other guys don't like you tagging along. You know that. C'mon, don't kick up a fuss now," the older one said gently. "Tell you what, I'll come early and we'll take the boat out, okay?"

"Please, please." The little one sobbed, "Please . . ."

But the big one was already heading down a path that was no longer there. It must have led back to the road and had been allowed to go back to the woods since this happened.

The older one disappeared. The little one ran to the path and wailed, "Don't leave me . . ." The wail died away, the clearing was silent a second, then a voice called, "But he *has* left you, Sonny."

The boy froze, facing the path.

"Come on, now." The voice was wheedling, half chanting, with a sickish thrill in it. "Come on . . . come on *now* . . . don't make me wait. Gotta get it all cleaned up."

Tears and sweat ran down his face.

"Time," the voice called. "Time . . . NOW! It'll only be worse if you make me wait."

The boy turned and faced Eve. His little face was almost as white as his shirt and his eyes were sunk in dark holes, but he was still a beautiful child, with light brown eyes and thick, straight, light brown hair—*like the killer in the woods*. But it couldn't be; this was just a sweet little boy who was frightened and vulnerable, and lonelier this second than any child on earth.

Poor thing, Eve cried inwardly, *Oh, God, the poor little thing. What waited for him in that house? What was the owner of that voice going to do to him?*

He took a step toward the house.

Don't, Eve begged silently, *don't go in there. Run away!*

He took another step, then stopped and sobbed softly. Eve wanted to scoop him up in her arms and carry him away, or face down whoever was waiting for him.

"Now!" the voice bellowed. It was deep but feminine, harsh with excitement, and Eve knew she was looking forward to whatever was going to happen. Eve's skin crawled, the hair on her neck and arms stiffened; she couldn't let this happen.

But it *had* happened. It had been over and done with long ago. The boy was a man.

"Hurry," the woman yelled. He was almost to the porch, and the woman said softly, with hate and longing, "Good boy! Two more steps . . ."

Eve yelled, "No!" and made a grab for him. Her hand sliced through his back, which had a spreading sweat stain on the little white cotton shirt, and hit Latovksy. He cried, "Hey, easy," and she was back.

She shivered uncontrollably and he pulled her to him and put his arms around her. She was enveloped in his jacket and the faint smell of his sweat, but she knew the little boy was still there, beyond Latovksy's bulk, and she pushed. It was like pushing a sequoia, but he gave way and she darted around him. The clearing was empty, the path overgrown again.

● ●

"Two BOYS?" LATOVSKY SAID.

"One about twelve, the other about five, and terrified."

"Of what?"

"The woman, I guess. I couldn't see her—she was outside the frame."

"What about *him?*"

"He was just a pretty little boy, very thin and pale, with big eyes . . ." She stopped because she was betraying that terrified child.

"Why did you see *that* boy?" Latovsky asked softly. "Why not some other kid who'd played on the swing?"

"I don't know."

"Was it *him?*"

She kept quiet.

"C'mon, Eve. Five women are dead—there'll be more. Was it him?"

She nodded.

"How long ago?"

"I don't know. He was such a little boy, five . . . maybe six, no older. He was just a little boy." She was pleading for him.

"Not anymore," Latovsky said quietly.

He turned to Klein. "You rent this place?" He took out his notebook and pen.

Klein nodded.

"Who from?"

"Mrs. Alan Rodney, 85 Greener in Glenvale."

Latovsky wrote quickly, then turned back to Eve.

"And where can I find you if I need you again, Mrs. Klein?"

"You won't need her again," Klein snapped.

"I'll get it from your license plate," Latovsky said. "Telling me'll just save computer time."

"Tilden House, Old Warren Road, Bridgeton, Connecticut," she told him.

"Street number?"

"It doesn't have one."

Must be a condo complex big enough so everyone in town knew where it was, he thought.

"Okay." He flipped the book closed and looked at Klein, who was on the far side of the room.

"And you, Mr. Klein. You'll be here if I need you?"

She paled, Klein looked away, and Latovsky realized he'd just asked the big question: Would Sam Klein of the unromantic name stay on Raven Lake or go home to the lady with something extra inside her skull? Tune in next week, he thought.

Klein took a deep breath and looked at his wife. "You can find me there, too. It'll take me a couple of days to clear up here, then I'm going back."

Color rushed to her face, the greenish-brown eyes lit up, and Latovsky wondered how he'd ever thought she was plain.

●   ●

"Rodney residence," a woman answered.

"Mrs. Rodney?" Latovsky asked.

"Who's calling, please?"

He told her. A pause, then she said, "One moment, please."

He was in the kitchen; the other two were in the living room whispering to each other.

Another woman, who sounded older than the first one, came on the line.

"This is Mrs. Alan Rodney."

He identified himself again and asked if he could see her this afternoon.

"I suppose, but I don't know what I could possibly tell—"

He interrupted. "It'll take me about an hour to get there, maybe a little longer. In the meantime, there's something you can do for me, ma'am. Save us both time." He told her what he wanted, hoping she wouldn't argue with him or demand a reason on the phone. The whispering in the living room stopped and he wondered if they were kissing. Then Mrs. Rodney said, "*All* the names?"

"Yes, ma'am. I know it's an imposition and I wouldn't ask if it weren't important."

"Very well, Lieutenant. But please don't be later than three thirty and be sure to have your badge or whatever with you."

"Yes, ma'am," he said meekly, then hung up and went into the living room. They looked at him, then back at each other, and he knew they'd be in each other's arms the second he got out of there.

He made his good-byes quickly and left the house, quietly closing the door, although he wanted to slam it. He hesitated on the porch; it was quiet inside and he knew they would be in bed by the time he got down the drive to the road.

Music up, he thought with a bitterness that startled him, *Roll credits.*

He was on 128 heading east for the Northway when his beeper went off. He pulled over into a lay-by with a wood-burned sign, WRIGHT POND, SIX MILES. The rain was getting heavier, the sky was low and thick, no one was making the trek to Wright Pond, and the lay-by was empty. He tried to call in, but static from the mountains or rain made it impossible. He gave up and pulled the batteries on the beeper so it wouldn't keep going off on the trip back.

● ●

"FORGIVE ME FOR NOT GETTING UP," MRS. RODNEY SAID. SHE WAS as old as she'd sounded, with thin, crinkled skin and iron-gray hair pulled back in a meager bun. But her dark eyes were bright and smart.

"May I see your badge, please?"

He'd shown it to the maid at the door, he showed it again, and she examined it carefully, checked his face against the photo in the ID card. Then she handed it back and held out a gnarled bony hand that felt like a leather bag of twigs when he shook it. She smiled and suddenly looked twenty years younger.

"Please sit down, Lieutenant."

He sat across from her in a wing chair facing a set of rain-streaked French doors that opened to a garden of azaleas and rhododendrons lashed by wind. The storm was getting worse; he was glad to be off the highway.

The maid came in carrying a silver tray with a heavy carved silver tea service on it and set it on the table in front of Mrs. Rodney.

"I ordered hot tea," she said, "thought it would be welcome on a day like this. Thank you, Alice." The maid withdrew and Latovsky wondered how she'd handle the heavy pot with her gnarled hands, then saw it was on gimbals. She added the sugar he asked for (no milk) and set the cup and saucer on the tray. "Would you mind taking it?" she asked. "I don't trust these hands and I've had disasters before."

He took the cup and saucer off the tray and held the elegantly thin china gingerly, half afraid it would burst spontaneously in his hand. He drank quickly, burning his tongue, then put it back on the tray.

"More?" she asked.

"No thank you."

The fire toasted his face, his eyes burned, and he had trouble keeping them open.

"You're very tired, aren't you, Lieutenant?" she said gently.

"Yes, ma'am."

"Last night must have been horrible. That poor, poor woman. It's been all over TV and radio this afternoon. Your captain just held a press conference."

So that's why they'd beeped him; he always stood in for Meers with the press.

"He doesn't exactly inspire confidence," she said quietly. She was being polite. Lem Meers was kind, smart, totally loyal to his men, the best detective Latovsky had ever known, the best captain he'd ever had, and a disaster in front of a mike. He jiggled and jerked, cleaned out his ears, picked his nose, couldn't find two words that went together, and generally came off like an autistic hillbilly. The hillbilly part was true. Meers was from a tiny town at the northern edge of the Park, almost to the border, and he'd once told Latovsky that he had not worn store-bought clothes or watched TV until he was grown.

"He's shy but competent, Mrs. Rodney," Latovsky said.

"Oh, I daresay. It's the smoothies you have to watch out for, isn't it?"

They smiled at each other.

"But something he said confused me, Lieutenant. He made it clear, as clear as he made anything, that is, that last night's murder was committed on the east shore of the lake, and our cabin, which you said was germane to your investigation, is on the west shore."

Her head tilted as she waited for an answer.

Careful, he thought. She was a bright old babe, she'd see right through a dumb lie, and he was too tired to think of a smart one. He tried a little truth.

"A piece of information came our way, Mrs. Rodney. The source is admittedly, uh, unconventional . . . the sort of source we usually ignore, but we've got five murders and no leads, and we can't afford . . ."

Exhaustion swept him, he ran out of words in midsentence and stared at her with his mouth open.

"To ignore anything?" she prompted.

He collected himself. "Yes, to ignore anything no matter how farfetched. The information suggests that one of your tenants, maybe from a long time ago, is connected to the killings."

"That's impossible. All our tenants have been families."

"Killers have families, Mrs. Rodney."

She looked startled, then smiled. "Of course they do, Lieutenant. Forgive me—getting old makes you forget the obvious."

He wondered how old she was.

"I prepared the list you asked for on the phone. It's on the desk by the doors. Would you mind?"

He went to an antiquey-looking pulldown desk next to the French doors. The polished top was clear except for a single folded sheet of heavy, off-white paper with her name engraved at the top and a list of names and addresses in looping Palmer penmanship. If Eve was right (and he was here because he knew she was), the killer's name was on it. He picked it up, tucked it in his pocket, and went back to the chair next to the fire.

"I won't keep you much longer," she said. "But I thought you should know a little about the house, in case it's important for some reason. You never know."

"You never do," he said, hoping he could stay awake through whatever she had to say.

It had been a dairy farm when her father bought it back in the forties, she told him. "A very small one, with a house and barn. The house was beyond repair, but the barn had a solid stone footing a couple of feet thick, and my father had it remodeled."

And left the pulley in the kitchen ceiling, he thought.

She went on, "He used it as a fishing and hunting camp for himself and his friends. He used to try to get my mother to go up there, but she loathed the great outdoors in general and the Adirondacks in particular. About the only thing my mother and I ever agreed on. People wax rhapsodic about Whiteface; to me it's a worn-down, malevolent-looking hump."

"I'm in the rhapsodic camp," Latovsky said.

"Most men are. Anyway, when my father died, he left the house to me. A good thing too, since my son adores it, uses it as soon as our summer renters leave and all through the winter. He *fishes*." She laughed softly. "I make it sound like child-molesting, don't I?"

"A little."

"Do you fish?"

"Yes, ma'am."

"Pike, muskies . . ."

"Crappies, bass, perch, trout, anything I can hook."

"Just like Alan Junior. Anyway, it's been his much more than mine. And I got his permission before I rented it to Mr. Klein, since there was a chance he'd be there all year and my son would miss his ice fishing. They build a shack, you know. Out on the frozen lake. Quite elaborate some of them, with stoves and so on." She stopped herself, then said, "I'm rambling and I'm sure you want to get some rest before you begin following that farfetched lead. I should tell you, Lieutenant, we've been renting the little house since the fifties. Many of the families on that list have certainly moved, some may have died out."

● ●

IT WAS FOUR BY THE TIME LATOVSKY OPENED THE SIDE DOOR to his house and went down the hall to the kitchen, shedding his coat and jacket. The message light blinked on his machine and he played the tape as he stripped off his shirt and tie and left them on the kitchen chair. He was usually compulsively neat and put everything away (something his ex-wife had liked about him), but not today.

Lucci's voice came through the speaker.

"Dave . . . where are you? The press's at our throats, Meers is shitting cinder blocks." Then some clicks and another message from

Lucci. "Only fifteen minutes to go, Dave. Please . . . please . . . where are you?" There were no other messages.

He gulped orange juice straight from the carton (his ex had hated that), reset the machine, turned off the phone bell, then stripped and showered and staggered into the bedroom. He never slept in his underwear because he thought it was disgusting (the only other thing he and his wife had agreed on) but was too tired to put on pajamas, so he lay down naked and pulled the comforter over himself.

Sam and Eve Klein must've worn themselves out making love by now. He wondered if she'd drive to Connecticut tonight or stay in Raven Lake. Rain roared on the roof; a branch of the old ash tree smacked the kitchen window. It was a rotten night for a long drive; he hoped she'd stay put, then hoped she wouldn't.

What an amazing, terrible, wonderful thing she could do . . . if you believed, and he did. But if he believed she'd seen Abigail Reese from across the lake and the little boy who'd grown up to kill her, he also had to believe she'd seen something happen to Bunner at that party.

Don't go, she'd said. Latovsky should have asked her why.

He made himself sit up and call Bunner.

"Hi," said Mary Bunner's taped voice. "We can't come to the phone right now . . ." He waited for the beep, then said, "Bunny, it's me. Call me at home. Call me—it's important."

He hung up, set the clock for six to give himself two hours' sleep and enough time to get hold of Bunner before they went to the dance, then he flopped back on the pillow and fell asleep.

Higher, . . . push me higher.

The boy zoomed back and forth on the swing with jagged shadows of leaves flashing across his face. The face was intact, but the body was slit open from throat to crotch; blood streamed out behind him as he swung. His organs glittered in the sun. . . .

Latovsky woke up with a jerk. His face and hair and the pillow under him were drenched with sweat. He lay frozen, afraid to close his eyes and fall asleep again in case the dream recurred. Then exhaustion dragged him under and he slept deeply and dreamlessly until the alarm went off.

● ●

"Come in, son, come in . . ." Donald Fuller said heartily. They went into the living room, where the arms of Adam's mother's green velvet sofa were threadbare and the straight velvet skirt that hid the legs was streaked with heel scuffs.

The house was not dirty. Mrs. Longmire, who lived in the next block, still came every week to clean. But it looked sad, especially this room, which had been his mother's favorite. She'd made sure there were fresh flowers every week, and the silver dish on the coffee table had been polished and filled with candy on a doily. Now the little stemmed dish was tarnished and empty, there were no fresh flowers.

He and his father always started in here. He sat on the couch, his father on the chair on the other side of the small hearth, and they tried to make conversation.

His father told him that his brother Mike was doing okay, the kids were fine, Claire was skinny and nervous as always, and her cooking was going from bad to worse.

"Kee-rist, last Sunday's chicken was cooked so hard you couldn't tell where meat ended and bone started."

Adam didn't defend Claire because he disliked her. In fact he thought if he ever felt anything for a member of his family, it would be hatred for his sister-in-law.

The old man railed on about her and her cooking for a while, then asked Adam, "Got a girlfriend yet?" as he always did.

"Not yet."

His father looked at the little mantel clock. The half hour they forced themselves to spend in this room was up. "What say we pop a few in the kitchen before they get here?" he said. *"She,"* meaning Claire, "always looks at me like I'm an old bum when I drink out of the bottle. Not dainty enough for her highness, I guess."

He followed his father down the narrow hall to the kitchen. The carpeting was worn through the nap. "Need new carpet, Pop."

He said the same thing every month, his father gave the same reply. "Fuck it."

His father entered the kitchen, but Adam hesitated. This room always made him uneasy and he had to make himself step over the threshold. His father opened the refrigerator to get the beer, and Adam took a deep breath and went in. The kitchen was as dismal as the rest of the house, but maybe it bothered him more in here because this had been the heart of their home when his mother was alive, full of smells of baking cookies, roasting meat.

The old man clicked on the little Sony Adam and Mike had chipped in to get for him, and they settled down to a baseball game— Red Sox and someone, Adam didn't pay attention.

Their silence was more companionable than their attempts at conversation and Adam dozed a little, woke, then dozed again.

It had been almost two when he'd finally finished cleaning up last night and gone to bed, and he'd had to be up and out by eight to make the once-a-month, three-hour drive to Sawyerville to see his father.

"Hey, Adam."

His eyes snapped open.

"They're here."

Tires ground over the gravel in the driveway. A moment later, a child's voice piped something Adam didn't get and there was a knock on the back door. He sat up and rubbed his grainy, burning eyes. He had to keep his guard up in spite of his tiredness because of Claire, who was sharper and smarter than his brother or father could ever be. As smart as Adam, maybe. And she disliked him as much as he did her.

The kids burst into the kitchen and threw themselves at him. He tolerated them.

"What'd you bring us, Uncle Adam, what'd you bring us?" the boy who was seven yelled, dancing on feet that looked huge in their cloddy shoes at the ends of his skinny legs.

"What'd you bring us?"

The little girl was four and she clung to the sleeves of Adam's jacket and stared up at him with Michael's large dark-blue eyes that looked black in the overhead light.

"Something good," Adam said. A huge hand stuck itself into his sight line to shake; it was his brother, Michael, who'd taken over the old man's small, not very profitable contracting business. He'd been the one to stay home to make money to pay for Adam's living expenses at Dartmouth (Adam had gotten full scholarships for tuition). Mike had never gone to college, had only been out of Sawyerville a few times in his life—to Niagara Falls for his honeymoon, a few other places, mostly on hunting or camping trips. But he'd never shown the slightest envy or resentment and Adam knew he should be grateful. Would have been grateful if he'd known how. Then his sister-in-law's long thin shadow fell across the table in the light coming through the window over the sink.

She was almost as tall as Adam, who was almost as tall as Mike, and she was very thin. An arrow of a woman with a square jaw and a shock of curly dark-brown hair that looked too heavy for her birdbone neck.

"Hello, Adam," she said coolly.

"Hi." He tried to dredge some warmth into his voice and failed.

She carried a large plastic container covered with foil.

"Good to see you," he said.

She nodded, but didn't lie back that it was good to see him. She started rummaging in the cabinets for a pot to heat the contents of the container in. "Brought some chili," she told the old man. "It's getting cold out, thought it'd warm us up."

Adam looked quickly out the window. The sky had a whitish look that meant frost back in Glenvale, snow up in Raven Lake.

Raven Lake. What had been so familiar about Raven Lake?

Maybe the old man knew but Adam couldn't ask without admitting he'd been there.

"Get the presents, Uncle Adam," Mike Junior screeched. "Get them!"

"Sure thing," Adam said.

He went out the back door, down the steps, and round the house to the front where he'd parked the car. Mrs. Van Damm, who lived across the street, was watching from her front window as usual.

He took out two packages with pom-pom bows they'd put on them at the Walgreen's in Saugerties. He'd bought his nephew a cap gun, which he'd probably shoot incessantly, driving his mother nuts, and for his niece, a tropical Barbie Doll with a sarong.

● ●

CLAIRE SERVED THE CHILI, WHICH TASTED LIKE THE OLD JOKE about throwing away the beans and eating the can. Mike ate with gusto, Adam and the old man picked at the mess. The kids ate, then went out in the yard, and Mike Junior started shooting at May with the cap gun. *Snap, snap,* jarringly loud, and she screamed.

"God damn," Claire cried, and raced out. Mike and his father were engrossed in the game; Adam looked at his watch. It was after four, and he had to be in Glenvale early tonight.

Claire came back in with the cap gun and gave him a filthy look.

"Stupid fuckin' present for a seven-year-old." She dropped the gun on the table. Adam stared at it in a daze of boredom. It looked amazingly real, a little like his father's Colt.

The Colt must still be upstairs on the shelf in the master bedroom closet, and all at once Adam wanted it. Maybe because of the feeling of being watched last night.

" 'Scuse me." He stood up; no one paid attention.

He went quietly up the stairs and down the musty-smelling hall to the master bedroom, another room in the house he didn't like going into. When his mother had been alive, the candlewick spread on the bed had been blinding white, perfectly smooth. Now it was yellowed, the fringes unraveled or gone.

He stood in the doorway.

This was almost as bad as the kitchen, maybe because he hadn't been in here for so long. He'd have to tell Bunny, "Hated going into my folks' bedroom, Bunny. Must be all sorts of symbolism there."

"Why *did* you go in there?" Bunner would ask.

"To get my father's gun."

More symbolism, Adam thought, smiling to himself. He wouldn't mention it after all.

He opened the closet; his mother's clothes were long gone, but he still imagined a lingering odor of talc and laundry starch that he associated with her. The smell filled his nostrils even after all these years, and he started to sweat. Quickly, he reached up, felt along the shelf, and found the old shoebox his father used to keep the Colt in. It was very heavy—the gun was still there. He lowered it, backed quickly away from the closet, shut the door, and opened the shoebox.

The Colt was wrapped in chamois; it was cleaned and oiled, the only thing his father owned that he'd ever taken care of. He rewrapped it, put it in the box, carried it downstairs. The TV was blasting; no one would hear him. He slipped out the front door and went to the car. He opened the trunk and saw the curtains over Mrs. Van Damm's window twitch. But she'd only see him stashing a shoebox. Cobbies for Colt, he thought, and he grinned and waggled his fingers at the window. The curtain twitched again, then hung still.

He closed the trunk lid and, as he did, got a sickly, coppery-sweet whiff of rancid blood from the plastic trash bag.

● ●

"Gotta get going," Adam said.

"So soon?" his father said.

"Yeah . . . got a date."

That brought them to attention.

"What kind of date?" his father asked.

"With a woman, Pop. A doctor in fact, head of pediatrics at the hospital."

Claire watched him with her narrow gray eyes.

"Lady doctor's gotta be over thirty," his father said disapprovingly.

"So'm I, Pop. Way over. Got the trash ready?"

He took a week's worth of his father's trash to the dump on his monthly visits, had been doing it since the first woman, Eileen Hale. It had become, as he'd wanted it to, an established habit no one paid attention to.

"All ready. Over there by the cellar door," his father said.

"Where're you taking this lady doctor?" Claire asked.

He was glad he had something impressive to tell her. "To the Spring Fling dance at the Glenvale Country Club. I joined last month."

• •

SEAGULLS SCREAMED OVER THE DUMP, THREE HUNDRED MILES from the ocean. When Adam was a kid, bears used to come here to forage, but they were long gone; nothing left but gulls and rats and the sickening old man with matted hair and one eye with a milky haze over it who guarded the dump.

He watched as Adam put the neatly tied bundles on the conveyor belt sliding toward the maw of the incinerator. Huge stacks that were supposed to keep particulate from falling back on the town belched out black smoke that blew north and east, back to the mountains, where it fell as acid rain and killed the trees and lakes. His clothes, stiff with Abby's blood, would be part of it.

He watched the bundles. The old man watched him with his good eye.

The gulls screamed. Adam looked up, watched them wheel, then looked back. The bundles entered the incinerator and he nodded at the old man and trudged up the rise from the dump to the car. He opened the trunk. The smell was already fading; a stick of solid air freshener would get rid of it by morning. He took the shoebox out of the trunk and set it on the passenger seat.

5

THE MESSAGE LIGHT WAS ON AGAIN WHEN Latovsky woke up. He listened, hoping it was Bunner, but Lucci's voice said despondently, "Meers did it, Dave. He met the press and sounded like a retard on smack. Where the fuck were you?" and the message ended. Poor Meers; he'd call him later, tell him he was sorry.

"S'okay," Meers would respond. "I should be able to sound coherent in front of those assholes on my own, Dave. Don't apologize."

The next message was from George Rule, the circuit medical examiner who did their autopsies.

"Hi, Dave. It's five thirty and I'm still at Glenvale General. I'm done with Reese and I'll wait for you to call or the rain to let up, whichever comes first."

It was after six and still pouring. Rule probably wanted to get home to Glens Falls and salvage something of his Saturday night. Woman-in-the-Woods was screwing up everyone's weekend.

Lousy label for it, Latovsky thought. He was surprised the press hadn't come up with something catchier by now.

He called the path lab at Glenvale General and Rule was still there.

"Had my coat on," he said. "Hope this crap doesn't turn to sleet."

"Hope not," Latovsky said, though it probably would.

"You want highlights, or chapter and verse?"

"Highlights. I'll read the rest on Monday."

"There aren't any highlights," Rule said morosely. "It's exactly like the other four, with one possibly notable, possibly meaningful exception."

Latovsky waited.

"I found more condom lubricant, Dave." Rule made it sound important.

"So?"

"So, more lubricant suggests more condoms, more condoms suggests more contact. They got it on at least twice, maybe three times. The lady turned him on, Dave. Really turned him on . . ." Rule choked off, then came back. "How could he? He made love to her, wanted her enough to do it maybe three times in maybe half an hour . . . you'd think that'd give him pause, make him want to keep her alive to do it again the next day and the next and . . ." He choked off again. His voice was lower, calmer when he spoke again. "Same brand as before: Trojans—which you can only get in fifty million drug stores. Same kind of instrument, too. Short, extremely sharp, probably excellent steel."

"Scalpel?"

"Maybe, as I've said before. Or maybe a good vegetable knife, or whittler, or hobby blade. And maybe he's a doctor or a nurse or orderly . . . or someone who buys good steel knives at Bloomingdales at the mall."

"Okay, okay. What else?"

"She was healthy, had all her teeth, and gave birth to at least one child. She ate about seven last night, drank several ounces of sour mash and beer from about nine to about ten . . . then died. I'd say about ten minutes before Lucci got there, from what he found. The slice was good, clean, fast, and precise, just like the others, and it took this one . . . it took . . ."

He faltered; they all faltered when it came to this part, because it seemed . . . it looked . . . the evidence suggested . . . that the cuts were deep enough to kill, shallow enough to keep the women alive as long as possible.

Rule collected himself again and went on. "Took this one maybe twenty minutes and she died of shock and loss of blood. Twenty minutes, Dave—for twenty minutes she lay on her back, watching her guts dry out. . . ."

While he watched her face in the moonlight, Bunner had said in his kitchen this morning.

"Twenty fuckin' minutes!"

"Easy, George," Latovsky said.

"Sorry. I just can't get used to it. You'd think I would by the fifth one . . ."

His voice was high and tight, and Latovsky said firmly, "What else, George?"

"Else? Nothing else. We found polyester fibers from some cheap blue jacket, the kind you buy at K Mart. Meecham's checking but we both know it's a dead end. We'll have tox studies by Tuesday, but she didn't die of poisoning. Oh, and she was HIV negative."

"Too bad."

"Yeah. Be nice if she gave the bastard AIDS. And that is that, David, except . . ." He hesitated. Latovsky waited again, then Rule said, "I've got to say this. It's not medical or scientific, or even very forensic, I guess, but I've got to say it because it might matter."

"I'm listening."

"These cuts he makes are very clean, very precise—"

"Like a surgeon," Latovsky's voice leaped.

"No. They don't take special knowledge, just special . . . coolness. He doesn't come when he cuts. The cutting's not the fun, the killing's not the fun, something else is. He kills coolly, dispassionately, *then* has his fun, whatever it is."

"Sex after death?"

"Don't know, but I don't think so. And these're not rapes. All evidence says the sex is totally consensual. There is no violence of any kind, no beating or extra slashing or torture or anything except that single cool, precise, and killing cut. So he's not killing to get off. Something else is going on."

Rule's voice was heavy with significance, but Latovsky knew something else was always going on. Inner motives were crap unless you lucked into one who killed for money or revenge, to relieve a burden . . . or get her daughter on a Texas cheerleading squad. That one had to take the gold cup.

"I see," he said. He didn't want to discourage Rule, but the truth was he had a better chance of finding the Woman-in-the-Woods killer from Lydia Rodney's list, generated by the vision of a psychic, than from the inner workings of the killer's mind, even if he knew them.

"Point is," Rule said, "if that's the case, if the killing's only a means to some other end, then he isn't gonna get sated with it and stop like I've read some of them do. He's going to go on and on until he achieves that end or gets too old to get it up."

"Or we get him," Latovsky said.

It was quiet on the other end.

"I guess you don't think that's going to happen, George."

"He's cool and careful and I have my doubts," Rule said.

They said good-bye and hung up. Latovsky tried Bunner, got the tape again, then made himself a cup of instant coffee and unfolded the thick cream-colored sheet of stationery with *Mrs. Alan Rodney* engraved at the top.

The names on the list were standard American: Forbes, Fuller, Rice, Everett, even a Smith with the letter J, probably for John.

The list started in 1955 with the Forbes family.

Multiple intercourse, maybe three times in half an hour, meant the killer was young, early thirties at the outside, Latovsky thought. Abigail Reese had been forty and a school teacher. Maybe she'd liked them young, but Latovsky doubted she went for the acne set and he drew a line between 1960 and 1970. After '70 the killer would have been too old to play on swings. That left six names, starting with Fuller in 1960.

He went back to the phone, put the list on the counter, and called Ruth Renssalaer, his contact at the phone company.

It was Saturday night, but she was home.

"Hope you got something for me to do," she said. "We're baby-sitting the grandkid. He's sleeping and the hubby's watching play-offs."

He told her what he needed, then read the names, dates, and addresses on the list.

"Can you do it before Monday?" he asked.

"Maybe. I got a terminal here, and I can get the ones who're still in our territory. It'll have to wait for Monday if they've moved to the Sunbelt or gone with one of those baby-butchering break-offs that're trying to cut our hearts out."

Ruth was AT&T and loyal to the core.

"Where can I find you if I find them, Dave?"

Rain streamed down the window, obscuring the lake; cold seeped

through the glass. He could stay here warm, dry and alone or call
Jeanne Hinkley and stay here with her. She was falling for him—she'd
find a baby-sitter and come. But then he'd have to make love to her
and he had an awful feeling that, at the moment of crisis, he'd see the
face of the psychic behind his closed lids.

"I'll be in my office," he said.

●   ●

THE MACHINE ROLLED THE TOLL TICKET. EVE TOOK IT, TUCKED IT
in the sunvisor, and headed out on the plaza. The pavement smoked
in the rain under the vapor light, then the lights ran out and the road
was a glistening black smear with rippling puddles hiding the shoulder.

She followed the signs for South, Albany, New York, New England.

She'd planned to be home by ten, but it would be more like
midnight at this rate. Frances would still be up and Eve would make
her a cup of cocoa, bring her whatever Mrs. Knapp had baked for the
day and tell her a little about what had happened, then give her the
news that Sam was coming back. Frances would say, *How nice*, which
was about as effusive as Frances could get.

She tried to stay at sixty in spite of almost zero visibility, trying
to put distance between herself and Glenvale . . . and Terence Bunner. Her knuckles had just brushed his back; no more than a feather
touch, but she'd suddenly seen a ballroom with people dancing in
candlelight and music playing off speed and she'd known he was going
to a party or dance . . . and shouldn't. That's all. No big disaster that
she could see, just a tiny voice in her head with a warning meant for
him—*don't go*.

She'd told him and he'd looked at her the way he would at a rabid
dog that had appeared *de novo* in his back seat. He wasn't going to
listen to her warning or anything else she had to say because she'd
been right about the man with the scars on his hands, and he hated
her for it.

"Fuck you," she muttered.

A truck thundered past. Her wipers couldn't keep up with the
backsplash and the road disappeared. A transparency of the same
ballroom blossomed on the windshield. Music played, candlelight
flickered on the women's jewels, on the crystal and silver on the table
and on the long-stemmed empty silver dishes in which they had served
ice cream.

Bunner was alone at a table, wearing a tux and staring lugubriously at a bunch of flowers. He was drunk . . . and she could be driving off the end of the earth and not know it. She had to get off the road.

Then, under the diaphanous picture, through Bunner's tux shirt, her headlights hit a sign, SERVICE: ONE MILE. FOOD PHONE GAS . . . NEXT SERVICE THIS SIDE THIRTY MILES.

She put on the blinker and Bunner called, "Hey, bleep, over here." Names were bleeped out of the visions like dirty words on TV. She had the feeling she might get them if she tried, but she didn't want to try. Bunner called again and another sign said, SERVICE, HALF MILE.

A car honked and plowed around her, sending more water against the windshield, but it didn't affect the scrim of Bunner and the ballroom on her windshield and a black-coated back appeared inside the frame of the picture.

SERVICE, THIS EXIT loomed through the rain. Eve hit the brake and the car skidded. She thought she'd miss the turn and plough up the grass embankment, but the wheels gripped the pavement, the game little car made the turn, and she was on the ramp, headed for the service area as the whole back of the man slid into the frame and she saw a head of crisp, thick, light brown hair.

Bunner held a bottle up; a smeared sign behind it pointed buses one way, cars the other. She took the car road and pulled into a lot, sloshing through puddles slicked with rainbows under the vapor lights. She stopped in the rank closest to the building and killed the motor as the killer in the woods sat down at Bunner's table.

● ●

EVE RAN THROUGH THE RAIN. SHE SMASHED OPEN THE DOOR INTO the service building and slid on red tile smeared with muddy footprints. She caught herself on the wheelchair rail against the wall, then composed herself a little and went into the lobby.

It was empty except for a woman with thick frizzy red hair and almost as many freckles as the man in the bowling alley in Raven Lake.

She was behind the counter of a "newsstand" that sold cigarettes, maps, lap games, mugs with ALBANY and THE ADIRONDACKS on them, T-shirts with cutouts of the mountains, stuffed animals, and a few sodden-looking newspapers.

Eve searched her change purse and found thirty cents. She pulled out a ten and went to the counter to get change. The woman smiled, showing tiny teeth and lots of gum.

"For the phone or vending machines?" she asked Eve.

"Phone."

"I ask 'cause the vending machines are fussy, quarters only, but phones'll take anything, won't they?"

Eve hadn't used many public phones, but she nodded.

The woman given her ten dollars assorted change, and Eve rushed to a bank of phones between the rest room doors. A kid came out of the restaurant and went to a wall of video games.

It was quiet except for the faint clink of dishes and silver from the restaurant. The air smelled of wet wool and a little of sweat and a conglomeration of women's perfumes as if a crowd had just left.

Eve got a whiff of cooked meat from the restaurant and her mouth watered. She wasn't sure when she'd eaten last. She'd get something here after she talked to Bunner, *if* she talked to him.

She was still in the 518 area. Information gave her Bunner's number and she dialed, then deposited what seemed like enough money to call Moscow. As the phone started to ring, she rehearsed what she'd say. It'd have to be fast and to the point or he'd hang up on her. "I know you hate me and what I can do," she'd say. That might make him pause, and she'd go on, "But I was right about the scars, I'm right about this. Don't go to that party tonight—don't go—for your sake . . ."

And mine.

The thought came out of nowhere and for the first time in her life, she put her hand protectively across her belly.

The phone rang and rang; she banged her fist against the unit and the woman behind the counter looked up at her. The kid at the video screen was intent on the game.

A woman finally answered in Glenvale. "Dr. Bunner's answering service."

Of course it was a service this time of night; she should have planned on it.

"Doctah Bunnah," she said in the snobbiest accent she could manage, eliding R's the way Frances did.

The woman didn't sound impressed. "Dr. Bunner's not here now. But if you leave your name . . ."

"I've got to talk to him."

"And number," the woman went on, "he'll call you back."

"This is an emergency."

She'd never used those words before in her life.

The woman hesitated, then said gently, "Dr. Cohen's on call. I'll have him—"

"It's got to be Dr. Bunner. Please, it's extremely important."

"I'm sure it is, and I'm sure he'll get right back to you. Please, give me your name—"

"He doesn't know my name."

Longer pause, then the woman said, "Aren't you a patient?"

"No. I'm a friend of a friend of his. A police lieutenant." That should cut some ice. "Look, it's imperative . . ." She looked at the wall clock over the video screens where colored lights and glowing fantastic figures zoomed across the kid's screen. It was seven; Bunner must be home getting dressed, putting on his tux for the party.

"If you'll just give me his home number . . ."

"Of course that's impossible," said the woman.

"But it's an emergency." Eve's voice scaled up; she sounded nuts even to herself. The woman behind the counter listened openly.

"I understand," the woman said soothingly, "and I know he'll call—" She was humoring Eve.

"Nooo," Eve almost screamed. Even the kid's attention was distracted. She lowered her voice. "Look, I don't expect you to get yourself in trouble—"

"Big of you," the woman muttered.

"But *you* can call Dr. Bunner at home, can't you? Can't you?"

The woman didn't answer.

"Then do it," Eve went on. "Please . . . do it. Tell him the woman from this morning—he'll know who it is—the woman from this morning says don't go. Something terrible will happen if he goes."

To both of us, she thought.

Her hand was on her belly again and she felt a searing burst of rage at the *thing.* She was supposed to be psychic, to see all past and present, with tiny, tantalizing, and, in this case, terrifying, glances into the future—a dyed-in-the-wool, go-to-hell psychic who had watched a woman bleed to death from miles away . . . and she didn't even know if she was pregnant.

"Go where?" the woman asked gently, still using that humoring tone.

"Uh . . . to a party."

"What party?"

"I don't know. But he will." She sounded utterly insane. "Please, I know how this sounds, but please. Just call him."

"Of course, dear."

"Don't sound like that," Eve shrieked, and across the room the kid hit a jackpot or something and yelled, "Hot shit!"

"I beg your pardon?" the woman said, and Eve clamped her jaw so hard it hurt to keep from breaking into wild laughter.

● ●

THE PHONE RANG IN BUNNER'S DEN AND UPSTAIRS IN THE BED-room. Mary Bunner reached to answer it.

"Don't," Bunner said. "Let the machine get it."

She drew her hand back, the machine downstairs kicked in, the ringing stopped.

"Why?" She asked.

"It's Dave, trying to keep us from going tonight, and I don't want to argue with him."

"Why should Dave care where we go tonight?" Mary asked.

He couldn't tell her about a session with a psychic in the office this morning, a psychic who'd seen scars on Ken's palms and a dead woman from across a mountain lake. He certainly was not going to tell her about that absurd *don't go.* He *was* going, would get drunk and dance until he dropped and have the time of his life.

Then he'd call Dave in the morning and tell him the lady with the ESP was full of shit. Not just a fake, but a vicious one.

But she'd known about the scars on Ken's hands.

"Bunny, why does Dave care where we go?" Mary asked again.

"Because he hates the club, thinks they're a bunch of tinhorn, shit-kicking snobs."

"Well, he's got that right, doesn't he?" she said lightly.

Downstairs the machine recorded the message and turned itself off.

● ●

LATOVSKY HUNG UP. BUNNER STILL HAD THE MACHINE ON; HE was avoiding Latovsky. Latovsky would have to go there, confront him at the club, and get him out of there.

Bunner was stubborn, but Latovsky would be stubborner. "Bunny, I haven't asked you for a favor since you gutted that cat for me in high school biology," he'd say. "I'm asking now. Come with me."

And go where? Where would he take Bunner and Mary?

The Loft.

"The Loft," he'd say. "Steak and martinis on me." Better than the institutional crap they'd get at that club.

It was seven. He'd show up at eight, before they started dinner.

He went back to his paperwork for the feds. He'd fax it on Monday, as soon as he got the postmortem from Rule.

He left the office to get a candy bar from the vending machine and some coffee. The squad room was almost empty; even five murders, the last less than twenty-four hours ago, couldn't interfere with everyone's Saturday night plans. Dillworthy was on the phones; he gave Latovsky a sour look as if it were Latovsky's fault he'd pulled Saturday night. The men always blamed Latovsky, never Meers. Meers was their idol, the Teflon Captain, and that's the way it should be, Latovsky thought.

He grinned at Dillworthy and went out into the long stone-floored hall that held on to faint echoes even when the building was almost empty.

Only Mounds were left in the candy slots; he didn't like Mounds and settled for a Ring Ding and the coffee. He carried them back to his desk and went back to work, sipping the sour, scalding liquid, eating the supersweet little cake. The sugar gave him a jolt and he finished the report quickly, then neatened the stack of papers, brushed crumbs off his desk, and closed the folder with WOMAN IN THE WOODS printed across it in Flair pen.

He took his damp coat off the hook on the closet door, turned off the lights, and left the office.

Dillworthy was staring into space, with a scrawl of doodles on the pad in front of him.

Latovsky went to him. "I'll be home in a couple of hours if you need me."

"You won't turn your beeper off in between, will you?"

"No."

"Swear? I mean what if the president gets offed in Ticonderoga?"

Latovsky grinned and raised his hand. "I swear."

He started for the door and the phone rang. He went a few more paces and Dillworthy called, "For you Dave. Ruth Renssalaer."

He went back to his office, pulled out the list and his pen, then picked up the phone. He started to sweat inside his coat, should have taken it off.

"Ruth?"

"Got 'em, Dave. Can you believe that? Got 'em all except a couple named Coombes. But I'll get them on Monday unless they moved to Mars. The rest are wherever they used to be. Rice in Schenectady, Fuller in Sawyerville, Everett in—"

"Okay, okay . . . take it easy."

But her excitement was infectious and he found his hand trembling as he went down Lydia Rodney's list with her.

At eight, with a Xerox copy of confirmed addresses, he left the squad room and went down the worn stone steps to the lobby. Even the press was gone by now, leaving behind muddy footprints drying to dust in the hot air blowing out of the registers.

He pushed through the side door to the parking lot.

The rain had almost stopped; drizzle made shimmering clouds around the lights in the lot. The Olds hated wet weather and he prayed it would start. He would be late getting to the club; they must have served dinner by now.

He sloshed through puddles toward the car, was almost to it when a huge Ford, almost as old and beat up as the Olds, pulled in. The headlights caught him, the Ford's brakes squealed, and Jim Riley yelled, "Stop, David. Goddamn it, stop right there."

Latovsky stopped.

Riley leaped out of the Ford and raced toward him through the puddles.

He was a staff writer for the *Albany Register*. Latovsky had known him since grammar school and they had a kind of tacit pact as adults. Riley never went behind Latovsky's back, never made the squad look bad unless they really screwed up, and Latovsky never lied to Riley or sent him chasing his own tail.

"Where the fuck have you been?" Riley snarled.

"What ever happened to 'Hello, how are you?' "

"Hello, how are you? Where the fuck have you been?"

"Why?"

"Why?" Riley cried. "Why! We got five murders, fuck-all to write about, and you ask why!"

"You had a briefing," Latovsky said mildly.

"That wasn't a briefing, it was a hyperactive animal act."

Latovsky looked down at the puddle around his feet; wind from the high peaks forty miles away riffled the surface. The temperature was starting to drop.

"I guess it was pretty bad," he said.

"Bad! It was horrible. Your leader cleaned out his ears, picked his nose, scratched his ass, almost stuck his foot through the lectern and—get this, Dave—he farted."

"Farted . . ." Latovsky swallowed a guffaw.

"That's right, farted, in front of God and every stringer between Kingston and Albany."

"Farted." Latovsky's voice shook.

"You got it. If he'd been sitting, I swear he'd've raised a cheek. Satellites must've picked up the titters . . . and the smell."

"Sorry . . . I . . . missed . . . it." Latovsky could barely talk.

"No you ain't. That fart had a liquid center." Riley giggled and they broke up and laughed wildly and helplessly. Tears mixed with the drizzle on their faces and they rolled back against the fender of the Ford, clutched their ribs, rocked back and forth until their throats burned and their sides ached. They quieted down and Latovsky slumped against the car and wiped his face with his hand. Little snorts burst out of Riley for a moment, then he got control of himself. "C'mon, Dave. Let's get a beer and you can tell me what Meers tried to."

"Can't," Latovsky said.

"Got a date?"

"Just can't." Gotta save a friend from a dinner dance, he thought, and suddenly felt ridiculous.

"Tomorrow then?"

"Maybe," Latovsky said evasively.

"Dave, it's got to be tomorrow. I've got to have something if I'm going to even pretend not to knock you guys. Meers looked like a maniac, like *he* was the killer. Tomorrow."

"Maybe," Latovsky repeated and headed for the Olds. They must be clearing away the first course at the Glenvale Club by now: canned fruit salad with melting, flavorless red sherbet on top.

"I'll be here at ten A.M." Riley said. "You bring the Danish."

Latovsky climbed into the Olds without answering. He turned the key and held his breath. It started with a gurgling roar and he patted the steering wheel.

Riley called after him, "I'll be here, Latovsky."

● ●

THE MAITRE D' AT THE GLENVALE CLUB LOOKED LIKE THE PILLS-bury Doughboy. The top of his head came to the knot in Latovsky's tie; he was wearing white tie and tails and had a round compact paunch that pushed out the front of his white piqué vest.

"I'd let you in there if it were up to me, Lieutenant," the little man said, "I swear I would. But it's members only—no exceptions. And if I make one for you, there'd be no end. Not to mention that I'd lose my job—unless you've got a warrant." The maitre d' looked pathetically hopeful. Latovsky raised empty hands, palms out.

"Oh, dear," said the little man, "oh, dear." Then he brightened a little. "I could bring Doctor Bunner a note if you think that will help."

It might, Latovsky thought, and nodded. The little man hurried to a counter behind which a blonde with dark roots and three earrings per ear chewed gum and watched intently. Latovsky wondered if they let the receptionist at the Shinnecock Club in Southampton chew gum. The maitre d' brought back a memo pad with *Glenvale Club* and a tennis racket and golf club crossed next to it. Latovsky took out his pen and used the counter to write on. The woman's cologne was heavy and sweet; a couple of minutes of it would give him a headache.

He thought a second, then wrote, "Bunny, I'm out in the lobby tilting at the Pillsbury Doughboy. Rescue me. Steaks at The Loft—my treat. I'll call Jeanne to come, too. Help! At least come out and talk. It matters."

A little humor, a little pleading. He thought it would work.

He folded the note and handed it to the maitre d', who carried it through double doors quilted in vinyl. As they swung open, Latovsky got a glimpse of the surprisingly beautiful room, with chandelier and candlelight shining on silver, crystal, the women's hair and jewelry.

The door swung shut, and he tried to settle down to wait. It was very warm in the lobby; his coat started to steam, his shoes were stiffening up. He walked along a wall with pictures of club members playing golf or tennis or holding up trophies. One cutie in a tux was shaking hands with Cuomo and trying not to look thrilled.

The receptionist watched every move he made as if she expected him to pocket an ashtray. He sat on the banquette along the wall, then realized his coat would get the upholstery damp and stood up again. He was very edgy and sweat was running out of his hair by the time the maitre d' came back, looking stricken. "He wouldn't come, Lieutenant. I'm sorry, he just wouldn't. He said to give you this."

It was Latovsky's note, refolded. On the bottom, Bunner had written in his M.D. scrawl, "I'm having a ball; no one's tried to garrote me or get me to drop my pants in the men's room, so get stuffed. See you tomorrow. Love, B."

Latovsky looked up at the quilted doors. The maitre d' dabbed his lips with a handkerchief and Latovsky mentally played a scene in which he smashed through the doors and dragged Bunner out, with Mary yelling furiously and Bunner fighting him every step of the way. It was almost as funny as Riley's description of today's news conference.

"Lieutenant?" the maitre d' said faintly.

Latovsky looked at him, then at the doors again, and felt the urgency disengage. Eve had tried, he had tried; Bunner wasn't buying and Bunner was a big boy.

He smiled at the maitre d', said, "Thanks for trying," and left the club.

● ●

INSIDE THE BALLROOM, BUNNER SAW ADAM FULLER COMING BACK from the men's room. He didn't know Adam belonged to the club, and he straightened up in his chair as much as he could, raised his hand, and called thickly, "Hey, Adam. Hey, Sport . . ."

A compadre at last, he thought. A man who could talk about something besides golf and the stock market.

Bunner was alone at the table; everyone else was dancing or table hopping. Mary was across the floor in that new beaded creation that probably cost five hundred bucks. Five hundred bucks to go to a jerkwater country club dance in the town time forgot. She was dancing with Bill Apted, a Yuppie asshole who pretended he was a satyr. Probably a repressed fag, Bunner thought. Apted's hand was way down on Mary's back—another couple of inches and he'd be feeling her ass.

Adam sat down. "Hi, Bunny," he said pleasantly. *God*, Bunner thought, *he is such a pleasant young man.* Too pleasant, too calm, too much in control of everything, except when it came to women, and even then his lapses were perfectly normal, perfectly understandable in a man who'd spent most of his adult life getting an M.D. at Dartmouth. Perfectly normal, Bunner thought. The only normal person in the place and he should like him—*did* like him, he told himself. They were patient and therapist, doctor and doctor, and they had something more in common: their interest in Adam's adjustment to the world, which was excellent, all things considered.

Or looked excellent. Then why did he come to see Bunner once a week, and why did Bunner let him?

Deep questions that should be asked another time, Bunner decided. When he was sober.

He grinned at Adam. "Lemme get you a drink." He emptied some ginger ale out of Mary's glass into the flower vase on the table and picked up the bottle of scotch. He poured a couple of fingers for Adam, filled his own glass to the brim, and sipped daintily. As long as he was dainty no one could accuse him of being really drunk, though he was getting there—definitely getting there. He'd started with martinis, always a bad sign. Eaten some very dry meat that had been billed as filet, covered with gummy gravy with chewy foreign objects that might have been mushrooms or twigs.

Suddenly the dinner he'd consumed a couple of hours ago wasn't sitting well.

"Bunny?" Adam said, sounding concerned.

Interesting. There was no missing the concern in his voice, but it didn't reach his eyes. Nothing ever reached Adam Fuller's large, brown, almost beautiful eyes. Nothing at all.

"Yeah, Sport?"

"You okay? You look a little pale."

"No, as a matter of fact, I am not okay. I am plastered," he said, eyeing the glass of scotch with sudden loathing, "and if I don't get some fresh air in about ten seconds, I'm going to throw up in my lap . . . or yours."

Adam grinned; it was such a pleasant expression, perfect for the circumstances, Bunner thought. A little amused, a little worried. The mouth knew exactly how to form it. But nothing happened behind those eyes.

Adam put his hand under Bunner's arm and lifted. Meekly, Bunner rose to his feet.

"Where're we going?" he asked. He was actually slurring his words. He didn't think he'd been this drunk since the night twenty-two years before when he'd finally gotten the precious M.D. and he and Dave celebrated. Tonight's drunk was Dave's fault for bringing that woman to see him. Then sending in that stupid note. He hoped Dave had gotten some sense and gone home.

"We're going outside to get you some air," Adam said. Even his intonation and the pitch of his voice were perfect. Perfect Adam.

"What about your date?" Bunner asked.

"Oh, she'll be okay."

"Who's *she*?"

"Naomi Segal, from the hospital. She's over there talking to some people. She won't miss me for a while."

Bunner had to force himself to focus. He knew Naomi Segal, head of pediatrics. She was short and plump, with a huge mass of dark hair, fat rosy cheeks, and bright brown eyes that almost disappeared when she smiled. She was wearing a gown of royal blue satin with lots of gathers across the front that made her look even fatter, darker, jollier.

She was deep in conversation with two other women who had their backs to Bunner.

"You gonna lay her?" Bunner asked as Adam led him away from the table toward the sliding glass doors that took up all of one wall.

"Gonna try," Adam said cheerfully.

Cheerful Adam.

Adam slid open one of the doors and half led, half pulled Bunner out onto the clubhouse's flagstone terrace. It had stopped raining; the air was clear, cool, and damp, and it hit him like iced white wine. He reeled, grabbed for the door frame, and missed. Adam held him up easily. He must be very strong, Bunner thought; his fingers were like iron bars on Bunner's upper arm, and Bunner felt solid muscle as he leaned against him.

"Here," Adam said. "Sit here, it's dry."

Bunner collapsed on a stone bench. It *was* dry, but very cold; the chill went right through his trousers to his butt. It would play hell with his hemorrhoids, but he couldn't get back up on his feet. He sat still and breathed in fresh, sharp, almost metallic air. The clouds were gone, stars pricked the sky, and the moon still looked full.

Night of the full moon.

The moon and lights from the clubhouse and along the drive to the road lit the golf course, turned the perfect lawn to a slightly heaving, immense expanse of smooth felt green.

He breathed in again; his head started to clear.

"Better?" Adam asked.

"Infinitely. Don't think I'm gonna lose my lunch. Dinner, actually. Not that it would be much of a loss. Rotten dinner. Seventy-five bucks a head and the best they can do is shaved, re-formed unidentifiable meat and the only canned gravy that *does* have lumps."

"I think the lumps were mushrooms."

"Mushrooms," Bunner said faintly. "Let's not talk about it."

They were quiet. Then Bunner said, "Thanks, Sport."

"For what?"

"For helping me."

"You help me," Adam pointed out. Tit for tat in his mind; such a neat young man. So excellent, ordinary, normal. So why was he Bunner's patient? What was Bunner supposed to do for him?

Get some expression into those handsome eyes, Bunner thought.

"*Do* I help you?" he asked, feeling slightly maudlin. "Do I help anybody?"

"Of course you do."

Bunner started to shake his head, felt the solid stone bench sway slightly under him, and he stopped moving. "Didn't help Ken," he mumbled.

"Who?"

"Ken. No last names, please. But you know who he is, Sport. He wound up in your emergency room just about this time last year."

"Oh. That Ken."

"That Ken. Didn't help him. Dug around in that truly nice man's head for months and got zilch. Total fuckin' zilch, Sport. Then *she* comes along and does it all in ten minutes. Not even . . ."

"Who does what?" Adam asked gently.

It was exactly the right tone, if only he could get a matching expression into those empty, empty eyes.

Bunner said, "A psychic—that's psychic with a P, Sport. A psychic saw the scars on Ken's hands."

"Scars . . ." Adam's voice was suddenly as bleak and empty as his eyes. But Bunner wasn't to be stopped. He'd started and had to keep going; trying to force this back down now would be like swallowing sewage sludge.

"Scars . . . from when he was a kid."

Adam was backing away from him. Bunner expected him to slip back through the doors to the happy folks having a good time inside. Only they weren't happy, he thought; they were a bunch of middle-aged assholes trying to do some tribal-rite dance without knocking their backs out of whack.

But Adam didn't go inside, he just backed into the shadow cast by the wall so Bunner couldn't see anything but the smear of gray his shirt made and the shine on his patent-leather dress shoes.

"Scars . . ." Adam said, in that stone-dropping-down-a-well voice.

"Scars," Bunner repeated, suddenly drunk-annoyed. "We got an echo out here? I said scars. She saw the scars Ken got when he tried to save his mother from burning to death. At which he failed, by the way. Or no—he didn't fail, I mustn't think like that. There was never any chance of saving her.

"I should've gotten it out of him, should have seen those scars myself, but I didn't—*she* did. And that's not all the little lady with something extra saw, Sport. She says she saw the man who killed the woman in the woods last night."

Not a sound from Adam.

Bunner grinned, but the grin felt sly and mean; he wiped it off his face but it came right back as he said, "From the back only, of course. Know why she only saw that murderous prick's back, Adam, old boy?"

"Why?" Adam's voice was even bleaker than before; if a glacier could talk it would sound like that, Bunner thought. But he was past caring how Adam or anyone sounded—he was into it, telling it, getting it out of his system. "Because if she saw him from the front, she'd have to describe him, and she can't because she didn't 'see' him or anything else."

"Except Ken's scars," Adam said in that glacial voice.

"Except Ken's scars," Bunner intoned.

"And if she saw that . . ." Adam waited, but Bunner didn't respond. "What else did she see, Bunny?"

And Bunner told him; he described the office visit with Latovsky and *her* without names, of course. "She claimed to see the killer's back; she said he was wearing a blue blazer, lighter-colored slacks."

"Like half the men in America on Friday night."

"Right," Bunner said, eagerly. If he could discount that part of it, maybe he could find some rational explanation for her knowing about Ken's scars. Then he could consign her and her "gift" to oblivion and the universe could go back on its normal track where everyone was bound by the same limits of time and space. He wouldn't have to change his ideas of the possible. No one liked to do that, except malcontents whose lives were so dull and intellects so lazy they got their notions of "possible" from supermarket tabloids: Baby with three heads. Eighty-year-old woman bears twins.

"She also said he wore tasseled loafers."

"Tasseled loafers!" Adam sounded a little riled by that and Bunner understood. The blazer and slacks anyone could figure, but tasseled loafers . . .

Bunner ignored that and went on to her holding out her hand to Bunner. "Like being offered a nest of maggots," he said; then told of taking the hand anyway, of going to Ken's and seeing the scars for himself, and finally of the trip to the quarry because he couldn't stand being inside four walls with her, "because I hated and feared her," he mumbled.

"Was she fearsome?"

Bunner went on, without answering, "And just to show you what total bullshit I had to listen to this morning, she also told me not to come here tonight."

"Oh . . ."

"Didn't tell me why of course, just said *don't go,* in that creepy voice. And look at what a wonderful time I'd've missed if I'd listened to her," he said bitterly.

Adam made a funny sound that could have been a giggle and asked, "Then?"

"Then . . . nothing. She drove away in a little red car I swear cost less than that dumb pin she was wearing and disappeared. The End." Bunner threw out his arms dramatically, which was a mistake because he was still drunk and the world started to swirl around him. He dropped his arms, gripped the edge of the freezing bench, and everything settled down. Then Adam said quietly, his voice coming out of the shadow next to the wall, "But she didn't see his face."

It was an odd detail for Adam to fix on, that the woman had not seen the killer's face, and Bunner tried to look at the other man, but the shadow hid him.

"You haven't been listening," Bunner said testily. "She didn't *see* anything."

"Except the scars on Ken's hands," Adam said.

He sounded convinced! He was a colleague, had an M.D. from Dartmouth, was board certified in internal medicine. That didn't make him a scientist, but surely the next thing to it. Surely he couldn't believe this horseshit.

Then Adam asked the question one physician should never ask another, but he asked it anyway.

"Who is she, Bunny?"

He tried to make it sound supercasual, but Bunner knew better, and he again gripped the edge of the stone bench. The puddles were drying, white at the edges. There'd be hard frost by morning, but that was fine because it'd keep the flies at bay another day. What a god-forsaken place this was—they were probably getting their bathing suits out of storage in the Carolinas.

Who is she? was the dead wrong question for one physician to ask another and Adam knew it, but he'd asked anyway.

Bunner tried to make a joke of it. "Why, Sport? Want to know if you're going to meet a tall dark stranger?"

"Could she tell me?"

Bunner didn't answer.

"C'mon, Bunny. Could she? Did you . . . do you believe her?" No answer.

"Do you?" Adam demanded with more urgency than Bunner had ever heard in his voice, and the truth just fell out of Bunner's mouth, like the hoptoad in the fairy tale fell out of the mouth of the fair maiden, he thought, and said, "Yes."

• •

THE MESSAGE LIGHT WAS BLINKING WHEN LATOVSKY GOT HOME and he played the tape.

"Lieutenant . . . Dave . . . it's Eve Klein. I tried to get hold of Bunner and couldn't. Dave, you've got to stop him. He mustn't go to that party."

A couple of clicks, then her voice again with the same message.

He turned off the machine and called the 203 number she'd given him. A gruff-sounding man answered on the third ring.

"Tilden House."

"Is there a Mrs. Klein there? Eve Klein?"

"Mrs. Klein's not here at the moment. Can I take a message?"

Very professional-sounding, Latovsky thought. Like the secretary of a corporate executive officer. He said, "Tell her Lieutenant Latovsky called."

"Lieutenant . . . ?"

"Latovsky. New York State Police. Please tell Mrs. Klein I tried to stop him, but it was no go."

"That's a very cryptic message, Lieutenant."

"She'll know what it means." Latovsky hung up before the man could ask questions. He started to strip off his wet coat, then thought about it. He was cold, hungry, exhausted, and starting to tremble. He thought about his warm bed with longing, but he left his coat on and went back out into the night.

The wind had picked up; the temperature was dropping by the minute. The lakes up north would be skinned with ice by morning. He got into the Olds and fifteen minutes later pulled back into the parking lot of the Glenvale Club.

He wasn't going to confront the poor maitre d' again; he didn't know what to do except stand watch like the fairy godmother making sure her charge got home from the ball in one piece.

He waited, cycling the heater on and off so he didn't fall asleep and freeze to death. At midnight, people started leaving and he came out of his semistupor. At twelve thirty, Bunner lurched through the front door, supported by Mary.

His old buddy had gotten shit-faced.

They made it to the Caddy. Mary guided him into the passenger seat, and Latovsky saw Bunner's head sink against the side window. He actually heard a faint thunk, even from here.

Mary'd probably had a few too (although Latovsky had never seen her even vaguely drunk).

It was Saturday night, when construction crews and rangers came down for a little fun. Mary drove carefully, making full stops at every sign, always letting the other car have the right of way in case the driver was as plastered as her husband.

Latovsky followed them home, keeping a few car lengths back. The Caddy was huge, and Bunner had scraped the sides more than once on the narrow garage door. But Mary slid the car in without mishap, the automatic door ratcheted down and a few minutes later Latovsky saw lights on the second floor.

Bunner had ignored the psychic's warning, gone to the party, and come home unscathed, except for getting drunk, and you didn't have to be psychic to know that was going to happen.

● ●

"I'VE HAD ENOUGH TO DRINK," ADAM TOLD NAOMI SEGAL.

"Me too." She patted his arm. "Why don't I make us some hot chocolate."

With whipped cream on top that would coat his mouth, and a poisonously red maraschino cherry on top, he thought. He'd have to drink the crap, then make love to her. That was going to take some doing because she was so round, oily, jolly, like Santa without the beard. He wasn't sure he could manage, unless he thought of someone else.

Abby in the moonlight, naked from the waist down, lying back on the pine needles, holding out her arms to him . . .

But he'd just heard something amazing, and he had to think about it, not Abby or Naomi or how to get it up for a female Santa Claus. He had to understand what it meant to him—if it meant anything.

Naomi waited for his answer with her head tilted, and he saw longing in her eyes. She was head of pediatrics, it wouldn't do to hurt her feelings. He didn't want to anyway, because she *was* jolly and kind and he liked her.

He said, "I'd love some hot chocolate. Uh . . . where's the john?"

"Just down the hall. First door you come to." She gave him a glowing smile and took herself off to make the hot chocolate.

The washroom had a sloping ceiling, pink tile, pink sink and towels. Even the commode was pink, and the rosy glow of the pink bulbs in the light fixture over the mirror made him almost handsome.

She had not seen his face.

But if he were the cop who'd brought her to Bunner, he'd keep at her until she did.

It wasn't a very distinctive face. A description of it would fit the faces of half the men under fifty in the state. But they'd get an Identikit or whatever they called it, use computer imaging under her direction, and they'd get a likeness. Sooner or later, someone would notice that the killer in the woods in the posters looked a lot like the nice young internist at Glenvale General.

He had to do something.

"Do what?" Bunner would exhort him. "Say it, Sport."

Find her and kill her before she sees my face, the way she saw my back in the woods, and the scars on Ken's hands . . .

Scars.

Two scarred men; what a remarkable coincidence.

She had seen Ken's scars . . . Abby had seen Adam's.

"God, what happened to you?" Abby had asked, and he'd made up a tale about an automobile accident when he was a kid, and getting cut with flying glass. It was a lie; there was no accident that he knew of. The truth was, he didn't know how he'd gotten the scars any more than Ken had known until *she* showed up.

He undid his cummerbund, pulled up his shirt, then pulled down his tux pants and shorts and confronted them in the mirror for the first time in years. Hundreds of them crisscrossed his belly from his navel to his groin. Some were thin, pale lines, others had keloided into fat pink welts like bloodworms. They were cuts, not burns, and they looked as if someone had played tic-tac-toe all over him with a razor.

"Aaaaaddaaam," Naomi called.

He started guiltily and pulled his shirt down to cover the scars. Then he flushed the toilet, redressed, and rehooked the cummerbund. After he drank the hot chocolate, he'd have to unhook it again and get a hard-on for Naomi Segal.

He'd manage, he thought, and she'd be perfectly safe with him because he could never feel enough for her to make it worth doing the . . . other.

"What other?" Bunny would chide. "Say it."

To make it worth slicing her open to watch her die in the moonlight while I try to feel love, sorrow, pity . . . something. That direct enough for you, Dr. Bunner?

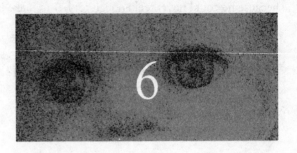

6

M ARY BUNNER WAS DRESSED, HER HAIR WAS
combed, and she looked like she'd gone to
bed at nine last night. She had that gift, Latovsky
thought.

"Hi, Mare, I guess it's kind of early," he said.

"Well, maybe just a tad on the Sunday morning after the big dance, but come in."

"Can't, I've got to hit the road."

He had four hundred miles of driving to cover the people on Lydia Rodney's list. He could just make it if he started now.

"I wanted to know . . ." He was not sure how to ask.

"You wanted to know . . ." she prompted.

"Uh . . . how everything is. Specifically . . . Bunny."

She stared at him and his heart lurched. "Mary, is he okay?"

"You're the second person to ask this morning, and it's not even nine."

"Is he . . ."

"First Isabelle on the service, sounding about the way you look. She got me so worried I sneaked back upstairs and watched him snoring."

"Mary, is he . . ."

"He's fine. If you discount the fact that he's

hanging over the toilet as we speak, puking up about two quarts of Chivas and Beefeater, mixed with the clubhouse red that's about two weeks from turning to vinegar. In other words, he's as fine as he's got any right to be. Now what's this about?"

"Just wanted to know."

"Suddenly you and Isabelle just want to know if Bunny's okay?"

He swallowed and felt his Adam's apple bob. Mary was a tall, solid woman with a fearsome temper and he could see she was starting to lose it.

"Ask *him* about it, Mare."

"Oh, you can be sure of that!" she said tightly.

"But don't blame him. It's not his fault."

"*What's* not his fault."

"Sorry, gotta run." He hurried across the lawn to the Olds.

"Dave . . ."

He gave her a big, dumb grin and waved. "Tell Bunny I'll be back for the game."

Everything back to normal, he thought as he climbed into the car. He'd come here for Mary's good Sunday dinner, because it was not his weekend with Jo; he and Bunny would watch whatever game was on, then he and Bunny's son Pete would shoot baskets in the long twilight. Then he'd go to Jeanne's for a quickie or a longie, depending on how late it was.

A typical Sunday in Glenvale; familiar, static, and as comforting as a Norman Rockwell painting.

Mary called again, but he started the car, and waved as if he didn't hear.

● ●

BUNNER CREPT DOWNSTAIRS, CLUTCHING HIS BATHROBE AROUND him with one hand and the banister with the other, trying not to jar his head.

The house was quiet; whoever had rung the bell hadn't come in, thank God, and Pete was still at the Cohens', where he'd spent the night. No size-ten Nikes pounded overhead, no artillery-attack music blasted out of the stereo.

He went to the kitchen.

Mary was showered and dressed in pressed slacks and a clean blouse. Her hair was combed and shining and she looked good enough to address the PTA.

"I hate you." He spoke softly to keep the noise level down.

"Should hate yourself." She also spoke softly, bless her. "Don't know what you were trying to prove last night, Bunny, but I hope you proved it."

He had; had proved that he could be as irrational as a fundamentalist preacher when something struck at his core beliefs. But they'd probably have the sense not to get plastered.

He eased himself into one of the cold white vinyl chairs and leaned on the cold tabletop; he was going to choke that fucking decorator.

Mary set a plate of dry toast and a cup of tea in front of him.

"What's this?" he croaked. "I need aspirin. I'll die without aspirin."

He really needed that hair-of-the-dog drink. But just the thought made him dizzy and nauseous all over again.

Mary said, "Aspirin's acid, Doctor, and you consumed enough acid last night to eat through a vault. It's time to soak some of it up. Eat the toast." He bit into it gingerly, chewed for a long time and swallowed. It felt like it would stay down and he took another bite.

"Try some tea," she said. "I put honey in it."

He did, then another bite of toast. Mary sat down across from him.

"I've had a very strange morning, Bunny. Isabelle from the service called at eight thirty to make sure you were okay. Seems a nameless woman called last night and again this morning, saying something terrible was going to happen to you. Isabelle's not a fanciful woman, to put it mildly, but the woman spooked her, and Isabelle finally spooked me. Then Dave showed up, wanting to know the same thing."

"What time's Pete coming home?"

"Don't change the subject. What happened?"

A woman who claims to be psychic made a dire prediction. But the prediction had not been dire; she'd merely said, "Don't go." Maybe she knew what shape he'd be in this morning.

"Bunny, what's going on?"

"Change of season makes everyone a little nuts," he said.

"What an incisive psychiatric diagnosis, Doctor."

She got up, put another slice of bread in the toaster, and the phone rang. The sound ripped through his head and he gagged and put his hands over his ears. Mary leaped up and grabbed it as it started its second ring and he uncovered his ears.

She kept her voice low so he could barely hear her and his innards calmed down. No, she told the caller. Dr. Bunner couldn't come to the phone right now. He wasn't feeling well, try the office in the morning and so on. Then he realized that she was repeating herself, arguing with whoever it was. Stick to your guns, Mare, he urged silently. Please stick to your guns.

She did for about five minutes, then she took the phone away from her ear, covered the mouthpiece, and looked at him. "He won't take no for an answer, Bunny. And he sounds . . . agitated. I'm a little afraid to just hang up on him."

Hang up on him, Bunner thought, *hang up on the slimy nut. It's Sunday morning, I've got a hangover . . . I've got a life, too.*

"He sounds weird, too, Bunny. As if he's got something in his mouth or something. I think you better . . ." She held the phone out. He struggled to his feet and made his way along the counter. The top was freezing—he was going to sue that pansy decorator for every extra cent it cost to heat this Bauhaus monstrosity next winter.

He took the phone from her. It was pleasantly warm from her touch and he nestled it against his ear.

"This is Doctor Bunner," he said. His voice sounded as if he'd been swallowing sand.

"Bunny . . . oh, Bunny, thank God!" He didn't recognize the voice, but whoever it was knew him well enough to call him Bunny.

"Who is this?"

"I can't tell you, don't make me tell you. I can't—please, don't make me." A low quivering sob came through the phone. It sounded real enough but he suddenly thought of Olivia De Havilland in the *Snake Pit.* He said, "You've got two seconds to come up with a name, or I'm hanging up."

"Whoever I am, I need help, Bunny. Your help."

Someone's help, Bunner thought. The voice was muffled and garbled as if he were talking through a mouthful of marbles into a receiver with a handkerchief over it to disguise his voice. But that was pretty paranoid, even for a shrink with a hangover.

Then he thought of *her* and wondered if she could possibly disguise her voice to this extent. But that was worse than paranoid. She had shown no interest in tormenting him and the voice was definitely masculine.

"Please," the caller moaned, "I've got to see you now." The madness might be feigned, but not the need, and Bunner felt the tug of that compassion that was his greatest weapon against the sadness, confusion, fear, and sometimes terror that afflicted his patients.

But he didn't want to feel compassion or anything else now. He wanted to eat more toast, take a shower, put in more sack time. He felt it anyway, and gently said, "Look, whoever you are, I've got the hangover from hell and I'm in no shape to see you or anyone else. Call Mrs. Meeker in the morning, tell her I said to fit you—"

"Nooooooo!" the caller shrieked, and Bunner dropped the phone. It hit the freezing stone counter, bounced off, and dangled at the end of the cord. Bunner bent to get it, and ice shards of pain slashed through his head. He staggered and grabbed the counter to keep from falling. Mary leaped forward to help him but he waved her away, reeled in the phone, and put it back to his ear. Now he was furious; "Listen to me, you son of a bitch—I said not today, I am sick today. I'm a person, too," he raged softly. "People get sick and you can call Mrs. Meeker tomorrow or you can sit on it. You got that?"

"Oh, yes," the muffled garbled voice said slyly, "I've got it. Now you get this, *Doctor* Bunner. I'll be at your office door in exactly an hour and a half. You can be there too and give me the care and succor a physician is supposed to give his patient, or you can stay home and nurse your hangover. But, if you do, I'm going to jam a gigantic gun in my mouth—I'm looking right at it—and blow the back of my head all over your office door. You got *that*, Dr. Bunner?"

Then came a click, then silence. Bunner kept the phone to his ear, not believing the bastard had hung up on him until the dial tone kicked in. Then he put the phone down and looked at his wife.

"He said he'd kill himself," he said wonderingly.

"Oh, Bunny."

"Said he'd blow his head off if I won't see him."

"Did you believe him?"

"No . . . yes . . . I don't know."

• •

THE LOT WAS EMPTY WHEN BUNNER GOT THERE, BUT IT WAS twenty of, and the caller wasn't due yet. Bunner let himself into the lobby and left the door unlocked so the caller could get in, then he rode up to the fourth floor, past the silent floors of the office building. No one was there on Sunday except Marsh Todd in his watchman's cubbyhole in the basement.

The doors opened on four and Bunner got out.

They'd turned the blowers off for the weekend, none of the windows opened and the air was very stale. You couldn't even breathe in here without using oil, gas, electricity, or whatever fired the works in the basement. At least they could build these monstrosities with windows that opened. The decorator, or whatever he called himself, had tried to put fixed windows in the new kitchen, but Mary had put her foot down. When Mary put her foot down, you didn't argue. The decorator would have totally ignored Bunner.

He reached the jog in the wall that hid his office at the end of the hall, and got a sudden attack of what his mother used to call the screaming meemies.

He stopped dead.

What if the caller wanted a spectator, not a savior? What if he was waiting around the jog with the gun in his mouth, and when he saw Bunner, he'd pull the trigger?

BLAMMO . . . blood and brains all over the walls.

Or maybe the caller had it in for Bunner for some reason, and he'd called, then come here and pulled the trigger, and when Bunner rounded the jog, he'd slide in a slick of gore . . .

He leaned against the wall and a vicious, burning belch rose in his throat, leaving the taste of vomit, and he thought *Happy Sunday* and chewed a couple of the Rolaids he'd brought with him. He swallowed, took a deep breath, and rounded the jog.

The hall was empty.

He let himself into the office, sat down at Mrs. Meeker's desk, and turned on the little fan she kept to move air when the system was on the fritz.

The caller had manipulated him shamelessly. Bunner had pleaded that he was sick and helpless, which would have stopped most people. They'd say they were sorry, that they'd call Mrs. Meeker in the morning, or ask him to tell them who else to call if things were really out of hand for them. But the caller had just kept at him with the utter self-absorption of a psychotic.

Only none of his office patients was psychotic. The only psychotics he saw were in Duyvilskill (Devil's Brook), the state hospital north of Albany.

What if one of those poor, sad, sick sons of bitches had broken out, wangled a gun, and was on his way here?

Bunner's mouth suddenly dried out, the undissolved grains of the Rolaid in his mouth felt like gravel, and sweat popped out all over him. If one of *them* was out, *he* was getting out. He'd call the cops from a pay phone on his way home.

He grabbed the phone and dialed fast; it rang and rang but someone had to be there even on Sunday. He looked up at the wall clock over the door. It was ten to twelve, ten minutes to go.

Finally the main switchboard picked up. "Duyvilskill."

"It's Dr. Bunner. Get Charlie Perkins on the line, fast."

"Just one moment, Doctor."

A click, then dead air. The hand on the clock clicked to eight of, then six of.

"Bunny?" It was Charlie.

"Charlie, are they all there?"

"Of course, they're all here. What makes you think—" Charlie stopped, then said a little shakily, "Hold on, I'll check."

More dead air. It was two minutes of; Bunner found himself listening for the elevator. The building was silent; nothing moved except the sweat running down his face.

At two minutes after, Charlie came back.

"All present and accounted for. All in the lounge watching *The Dirty Dozen* for the fiftieth time. It's their favorite, especially Telly Savalas as the nut. What made you think—Jesus, Bunny. What made you think . . ."

"I got this weird phone call."

"Yeah, well, you scared the shit out of me."

They were not men you wanted walking around loose.

"Scared the shit out of myself," Bunner said.

They hung up and Bunner went into his inner office. It was ten after. The caller had changed his mind or gotten stuck in traffic past the mall. Shop until you drop, even on the Sabbath. Especially on the Sabbath, Bunner thought.

He'd give him ten more minutes, then go home.

It was a good chance to go over the journal tables of contents he'd gotten behind on; he pulled one out of the stack and noticed the recorder with the tape of *her* still in it. He'd rewind and record over her, because he never wanted to hear her voice again. He reached for REWIND and heard the elevator mechanism inside the wall. It was a sound he'd never notice on a normal day with people's voices in the other offices, phones ringing, the coffee cart rolling up and down the hall. But it was almost loud in the silence around him.

He had an impulse to run; he could be down the hall, out the fire door, down the stairs to the parking lot before the caller stepped off the elevator.

But doctors didn't run from sick people any more than firemen ran from fires. And this poor bastard was sick, no matter what else he might be. Sick and in pain and crying out for help in the only way he knew how.

That compassion again, Bunner thought; it was really going to do him in some day.

He sat still, his hands resting loosely on the desk blotter. The blotter was stained with coffee, crumpled at the edges, with doodles all over it. Mrs. Meeker had been after him to change it or let her do it, but that meant moving everything on the desk.

He heard the hiss of the elevator doors opening. The hall was carpeted; he didn't hear footfalls, but imagined he could feel them reverberate as the caller came down the hall . . . around the jog . . . to the door of Suite 44.

The outer door opened and a long thin shadow sliced across the floor, looking absurdly sinister in spite of the sun coming through the fixed windows. The shadow shortened and fattened as it came closer, then it slid into the office and Adam Fuller appeared in the doorway.

"Sorry about the histrionics, Bunny," he said apologetically.

● ●

FULLER. THE NAME WAS TAPED ABOVE THE LETTER SLOT IN THE door. Latovsky rang the bell of the house on Barracks Lane (probably named for long-gone barracks of the Grand Army of the Republic), then stepped back and looked at it. It needed paint; the shades drawn in the front windows were yellow and crumbling at the edges, the porch tilted, the slats underfoot creaked.

All the houses on the block were small and a little mean, but this was the most neglected-looking.

No one came and he rang again, then used the knocker.

He could have called and made an appointment. But then they'd be ready for him, have their faces composed to show nothing, no matter what he asked. The questions would be neutral. Did they rent the house on Raven Lake? Did they have a son? Had their son played on that swing?

He couldn't ask what he really wanted to know: Was there something a little odd, a little cruel about the boy? Did he pull the wings off flies? Set cats on fire? Did they think he could graduate from small-animal torture to murder?

They'd know the answers even without the questions, and whatever they felt or feared would show in their faces if they weren't prepared.

But they weren't even home and that was the downside of trying to catch people off guard.

He raised the knocker again.

"Looking for Don Fuller?"

He turned and saw a woman at the bottom of the porch steps looking up at him. She was in her seventies, with skin like a dry stream bed, hair like a sprung broom, and the brightest, clearest, bluest eyes he'd ever seen.

He crossed the creaking porch and went down the stairs to her.

"Yes, ma'am. Do you know where he is?" he asked.

"Might. Who's asking?"

He gave her his card and her eyes brightened with delight. "Cops," she cried. "Always knew Don would get into real trouble one of these days."

He was not shocked by her malice; there were lots of malicious old ladies in these towns. Their husbands were dead, their kids had moved to the cities, and the women got by on meager pensions, bottom-of-the-line Social Security, and whatever their children could spare. They subsisted on beans, bacon, and potatoes, government handouts of surplus cheese . . . and malice. They never ate fresh fruit, never heard of oat bran or high fiber, wouldn't jog unless their skirts were on fire . . . and most of them lived to be ninety.

Someone should do a study of the role of malice in longevity, he thought.

He took the card back and said, "He's not in trouble, ma'am. I just wanted to ask him and Mrs. Fuller a few routine questions."

"That right? Well, you can ask *him* when he shows up, but you'll have to wait for the last trump to ask *her*. Barbara Fuller's been dead near on to thirty years. Got hit out on Route Six, coming from Coleman's Dairy. They put up a light afterwards. Always do . . . afterwards. But then it was just a stop sign, and I know *she* stopped. Barbara Fuller'd no more run a stop sign than she'd show her drawers on Main Street at high noon. She was the neatest, best organized, carefulest creature God ever made. Kept the cleanest house, baked the best cakes and pies, and brought 'em to church suppers and bake sales wrapped in enough plastic to go twice around the earth. Unholy bitch, of course. Takes more'n clean toilets to make a human being. But she stopped at that sign, bet on it, Officer—*she* stopped."

"But?" he asked.

The iridescent blue eyes looked past him. "But the kids coming the other way didn't and they broadsided her at eighty and drove the whole side of the car into her. Heard there was so much glass stuck in her she looked like Christmas tinsel and her ribs broke through her skin and cracked, oozing marrow. Heard there was a hole in her skull big enough to see her brain through—"

"Mr. Fuller." He jumped in to shut her up.

"What about him?"

"You said . . ."

"I know what I said." The amazing eyes drilled into his. "He's in a bar. Only about ten in town so you'll find him if you look. He's a tall fellah, skinny as a coat hanger. About as old as me, with sandy hair that barely covers his skull anymore. He'll have on corduroys, most likely, and a button-down sweater with some of the buttons missing, and he'll be soused, or on his way to it."

She'd just described about ten billion old men, Latovsky thought.

He might find him anyway, but it could take half the day. He'd be better off heading for Utica to see the Everetts. Get as much of the list covered as he could.

He turned over the card and put it on the porch rail to write on.

"Does Mr. Fuller have a son?" he asked as he took out his pen.

"Two sons. Likely enough fellahs. One's in his thirties, and Mike . . . Lord save us, Mike must be over forty by now. Time does fly."

Latovsky wrote, "Mr. Fuller, please call the underlined number as soon as you can. Important. Thank you. DL." He went up the steps to put it through the letter slot.

"Don't do that!" she cried.

He stopped and she hobbled up the stairs to him.

"Not if you want him to see it anytime soon," she said. "He don't even use that door. Be too drunk to notice an itty-bitty card like that anyhow and it'll lay there 'til Wednesday when Frieda comes to clean. Frieda's only one that keeps him from rotting away like an old stump. Give it here. I'll see he gets it."

The blue eyes challenged and pleaded at the same time. Something out of the ordinary was happening on her street, and she wanted in on it, even for the few hours until she had to part with the card.

Part with it she would, Latovsky thought. These old town women had the compassion of sharks but the sense of honor of Cyrano, and she'd do what she said she would; you'd have to hack her to pieces to stop her.

He handed her the card; she bobbed her head in acknowledgment and stuck out her other hand. "I'm Ida Van Damm, by the way. Pleased to meetcha."

They shook and he went down the porch steps to the Olds. He looked at her, and wished he had a hat to tip because he could see from the bones under the desiccated skin and those remarkable eyes that Ida Van Damm had once been a knockout.

● ●

ADAM'S SMILE WAS WIDE, EASY, RELAXED. HE WAS WEARING A plaid sport shirt, light poplin jacket, and freshly pressed cords. He looked like what he was: young physician on top of the world on his day off.

"You're not suicidal," Bunner choked, trying to control his rage.

"No. And I do apologize, Bunny. But I had to get you here without anyone knowing it was me."

Without anyone knowing?

Adam Fuller was in much, much worse shape than Bunner had figured. He should have known that such total neutrality must hide agony but he hadn't, any more than he'd known about the scars on Ken's palms. He should go into another business, he thought with self-loathing. Maybe get a job with a pharmaceutical company as one of those jerk-off M.D.s who vet drug ads. He'd let his patient go on like this for months and now poor Sport was on the edge and Bunner had to pull him back somehow, because a trip down that particular rathole was a journey to hell. He'd rather have his leg amputated without anesthetic.

All his anger evaporated and that good old compassion that made his eyes burn and his throat tight took over.

"Why couldn't you tell me it was you, Sport?" he asked gently.

"Because I'm not suicidal and you know it and wouldn't have come."

Mad, but logical. Another instance where logic and reason had nothing to do with each other.

"But why did you have to get me here at all, Adam?"

"Why . . . to find out who *she* is, of course."

"She?"

But he knew exactly who Adam meant and the next obvious question was why Adam Fuller had gone to these lengths to find a woman he hadn't even known existed before last night. A dreadful, terrifying answer that Bunner couldn't bear to contemplate came to him. But he contemplated it anyway.

Last night, he'd gotten blotto and blown his cork about a "psychic" who'd claimed to have "seen" the killer in the woods. Now Adam Fuller had pulled out all the stops, disguised his voice, risked Bunner's wrath and his own credibility to find out who she was. Bunner tried not to know why, tried to force the knowledge down with all his might, but it came right back up again like rotten food and he knew Adam Fuller wasn't losing it or going over some edge. He was behaving with the undisputable reasonableness that dictated he find the woman before she ID'd him for five murders.

Insane, absurd, ridiculous.

But it wasn't, and the instant Bunner thought it he knew it was true.

The only question left was what to do next.

He wanted to play for time; to insist *Who . . . what woman . . . I don't know what you're talking about.* He'd been drunk, Fuller might fall for it, but he doubted it; besides, he didn't need time, he needed help. They both did.

"We need some help here, Sport," he said quietly.

Maybe something could be salvaged if Fuller said, "I know we do." But he just looked at Bunner with eyes that were so empty Bunner wouldn't have been shocked to see the hunting print on the far wall through them.

Bunner kept his voice low and soothing. "Al Cohen might be able to help us out here. You know Al. I'm going to give him a ring."

Sure, and say what? *Al, I've got a quinti-killer in my office, what do you advise?* And Al would answer, *Get the fuck outta there and call the cops.*

He wouldn't call Al after all, he'd call Dave and say, "Al, I'm in the office and need a little help here. Think you can come over?"

Dave would get the pitch and be there in five minutes—a long five minutes, but he and Adam would get through them somehow.

"Sit down, Sport," he said quietly. "Pull the chair out . . . they always cram it against the desk when they vacuum. Sit down and we can talk until Al gets here."

He reached for the phone; Adam reached under his jacket and pulled out of his belt an enormous gun with a chrome body and Bakelite handle; a Dirty Harry gun that would blow Bunner's head clean off his neck.

"Don't touch the phone," Adam said quietly.

Bunner dropped his hand to the desk. He'd never faced the business end of a gun before and the effect was remarkable. His nervous system shut down except in his gut, where ten-pound moths butted and fluttered. Adrenaline spurted through him, but it didn't make him sharp or ready; it made him helpless. His bladder let go; a few drops splotched his shorts before he could get his muscles clenched again, and his voice failed him utterly. He tried to say something, he had no idea what, but a sick, thick croak was all that came out.

"Water," Adam said solicitously. "This is a shock, I know. You need some water, Bunny."

He went to the water cooler, tucked the gun under his arm and pulled down one of the paper cups. This was Bunner's chance, his only chance, because he knew as surely as he knew that he'd give his testicles to see David Latovsky come through the door this minute that Adam Fuller was going to kill him.

He had to get around the desk to the door, across the outer office, down the hall and out the fire door. It was a long shot, it seemed impossible, but he knew the way; Adam didn't.

He had a twenty-eighty chance if he tried; zilch if he didn't.

He tried to stand, but his legs felt like melting rubber, the distance to the door was endless, and he felt the odds hit zero. The water cooler burbled; Adam turned with the cup in one hand, gun in the other. He'd let it droop, but now he raised it to the middle of Bunner's face.

"Dumb Bunny," he said almost fondly. "No way out of this except what I have to offer. It's not much, but it's the best I can do under the circumstances. First, drink the water." He brought the cup to Bunner and Bunner tried to take it. His hand shook wildly; half of it spilled on the blotter.

"I can hold it for you while you drink," Adam said.

Bunner tried to shake his head and couldn't. He put all his concentration into holding the cup, finally got it to his mouth, and drank what was left. The cool, sweet water hit his throat like oil on a seized engine, and he croaked, "She didn't see his face, I told you she didn't see his face."

"But she will. I'm not psychic, but I *know* she'll keep trying until she does. I wouldn't worry if this were Boston or New York, but it's not. They'll get a sketch and someone'll recognize me. They'll get me and stick me in the deepest darkest hole they can find. And then . . . it'll never happen, Bunny."

"What?" It took a long time to choke that word out.

"I'll never *feel* anything. God, how silly it sounds when you just say it. But it's not silly; it's why I've done everything in my life. I went to med school figuring sick people would be pitiful, vulnerable, most likely to stir something in me. Turns out they can be bitchy and vicious too, but it doesn't matter. Gallant or strong, whiny or cruel, I don't hate or love or feel anything for them."

His voice dropped; he concentrated on the gun in his hand. "Same with the women, Bunny. What could be sadder, more pathetic, more deserving of pity and sorrow than a woman who should live another forty years, slit open and dying in the moonlight and not knowing why this happened to her. A woman you just made love to, a woman you *liked*. But that didn't work either. Maybe you could've done something if I'd been up front with you, told you about *my* scars."

Bunner tore his eyes away from the gun and looked at the hand at Adam's side. It was unmarred from what he could see.

Adam smiled. "They're not on my hands, Bunny; not just on my psyche either; they're on my belly. They're cuts, not burns like Ken's, and there must be a couple of hundred of them, running every which way. Looks like I belly flopped into a net of knives. I asked my old man, of course, and my brother, but they didn't know what I was talking about.

"I *should've* told you about them and maybe we could've found out together how I got them. It's too late now and I'm sorry. At least as close to being sorry as I can get."

It finally pierced Bunner's haze of terror that this degenerate son of a bitch had killed five women to try to pity them! But why not? Madness came in more flavors than Ben and Jerry's ice cream, which even had one called Monster Mash. Bunner almost grinned, but his lips trembled wildly and he came within a hair of laughing. If he laughed, he'd cry, and hysteria wouldn't help him. Nothing would, except a *deus ex machina* in the form of someone coming in for a little extra work on the weekend. He listened with all his might for the elevator, a phone, footfalls in the hallway.

It was silent.

He turned his head to the window, away from the sick bastard with the gun. There was his ostentatious and beloved Caddy and a light blue Ford that must belong to Fuller. Nothing else; no one passing with a dog on a leash or even driving by. No one would hear if he banged on the window or risked throwing the tape recorder through it.

The tape recorder.

With her voice saying the last thing this prick wanted to hear. Fuller was in for a shock and Bunner was going to deliver it. He looked forward to it, because it was the last thing like fun he'd probably have for all eternity. The thought unmanned him; his throat filled, tears burned his eyes, and more hot urine leaked into his shorts. But he was not going to weep, wet his pants, and beg this monstrous shit for his life. He was not—

"Are you listening to me?" Adam demanded.

Bunner looked back at Fuller. He'd seen livelier eyes in the heads of anatomy-lab cadavers. But the rest of Adam's face was composed into an expression of anticipation. He had more to say. This was going to be their last session, free of charge, Bunner thought, and the hysterical laughter that would turn to craven sobs almost got away from him. He choked it down.

"You should listen to this part, Bunny. It's important to you."

Wrong, Bunner thought. *Nothing is ever, ever going to be important to me again.*

"See," Adam said, "if I don't find her, stop her . . . if they find me first, and I'm never cured, then all this"—he waved his free hand, meaning the five dead women and Bunner's imminent death—"will be for nothing."

Cured? He made it sound like a genuine disease, like cancer of the emotions. But maybe Fuller had *never* felt anything, and undescended emotions, like undescended testes, might be more apt. Bunner tried to say it, but his voice was still among the missing.

Adam went on, "Of course I don't expect you to care if I'm cured, if I ever love a woman, pity a patient, mourn my mother—"

He stopped. "My mother. Now why did I mention my mother?"

Hey, why not? Bunner thought. *Your mother . . . Ken's mother . . . mothers are the weekend special.* That laughter threatened again; he was on the verge of losing it.

"I guess because I never cried for her," Adam said, "never felt the slightest twinge when she was killed. It must have shown, because the troopers who came to tell us about the accident wound up looking at me as if I were something smelly smeared on their shoes. Water under the bridge, my mother would say. She had a million little sayings, each more banal than the last. But I remember them; they're about all I *do* remember about her.

"I don't expect you to care about any of that, Bunny. I'm the one who killed you—will kill you. Why should you care about the state of my future mental health? But one thing should matter to you, Bunny. Matter mightily.

"If you don't tell me who she is, where she is on your own, I am going to . . . kneecap you." Then Adam chuckled, actually chuckled! A light rippling sound that was almost pleasant to the ear. "Jesus, how Hollywood Mafia. Didn't think I could get it out with a straight face . . . and I couldn't. But I'll do it, straight face or not, and I leave it to you to imagine what that will be like."

Bunner did: flesh, bone, tendons smashed to mush by a slug from that enormous gun. More urine leaked into his drawers; he couldn't stop it. The relief of letting go would be wonderful: cry, piss your pants, then faint, he thought. Draw the curtain on this little horror show—but not yet, not until he played that tape and watched Fuller's face when he realized that he'd lost.

"Or I could do your jaw," Adam said calmly, "or genitals. The point is you'll tell me sooner or later. You know it, I know it. So why not just do it, save yourself the agony and your family the horror of knowing how you suffered?

"Who is she, Bunny?"

Bunner reached for the recorder and Adam cocked the gun. Bunner tried to tell him it was his turn to listen, but he still couldn't talk. He shook his head and Adam seemed to get the message; at least he didn't pull the trigger, and Bunner pushed REWIND with a finger so shaky it almost didn't work. The tape hissed softly across the heads until it reached the point he thought he wanted. He pushed STOP, then PLAY, and her low, woolly, lovely voice came through the little speaker.

"But not being crazy doesn't mean I saw a woman die from miles away either, does it?"

"No, it doesn't," Bunner's taped voice said.

Her again: "Then why don't we stop wasting time. You don't know my name, the lieutenant's given me his word that he'll never tell you."

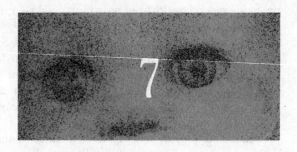

"YOU AGAIN!"
The same woman was still on the service, must have been on all night, and her voice was ragged. "You upset me so much last night I called there this morning and woke Mrs. Bunner up."

"Is Dr. Bunner . . . ?" Eve asked.

"Mrs. Bunner was very nice about it; she told me they had a marvelous time and Dr. Bunner is just fine, thank you very much. Nothing 'terrible' happened to him or anyone else. Now I'll thank you not to call this number again, except at regular office hours," and she hung up, leaving Eve listening to dead air.

Eve put the phone down and stared stupidly at it.

He was fine, a vision had been wrong at last; the killer hadn't sat down with Bunner, the dread that had chased her down the highway, kept her awake, was still with her, was an . . . artifact . . . or the result of the emotional swings of pregnancy.

If she was pregnant.

She left her mother's suite, where she'd spent the night, and went down the gallery to the stairs. On the way, she passed the suite that had been her's and Sam's and would be again day after tomorrow. The door was open, the vacuum was going, the cushions were off the couch, and Laura was vacuuming the drapes. The air smelled of furniture polish, and the old TV and stand were pushed to the side. Eve had to call Barker's Electronics in Torrington and browbeat them into delivering a new one tomorrow.

But first, she called Meg from the phone in the drawing room. Frances stuck her head in while it was ringing.

"Mrs. Knapp's making Eggs Benedict."

Eggs Benedict—poached eggs with quivering yolks covered in yellow sauce—Eve's gorge rose. George, the Carpenters' butler, answered the phone and she asked for Meg, then covered the mouthpiece.

"I don't think so, Auntie. Just some cereal, tell her. Corn flakes?"

"You've got to eat more—"

Meg came on the line.

"Meg, can you come over? I've got something to tell you."

"Why not tell me now?"

Frances was still in the room; Tim or Tim Junior and the nanny or all of them including Meg's mother were probably in the room with Meg.

Eve said, "Better in person."

"Okay. Is one okay?"

● ●

MEG GOT THERE AT TEN OF. FRANCES WAS CLOSETED WITH MRS. Knapp planning Sam's coming-home dinner on Tuesday. Greta would be there, as would Meg and Tim; Larry might even condescend to eat with them.

Eve had called the store in Torrington and told them she'd buy the most expensive 27-inch TV they had if they'd deliver it tomorrow. The salesman said, "Twelve hundred expensive enough for you, lady?"

"Twelve hundred's fine."

"I'll have it there by three tomorrow."

Now she and Meg sat across from each other in the drawing room. Meg had a glass of sherry; Eve was drinking club soda, afraid anything else would make her sick. She still couldn't shake that dread, had managed to choke down only a couple of spoonfuls of cereal. Maybe she was coming down with something.

She told Meg about the vision in the clearing when she'd finally "seen" Tim at a health club somewhere between Hartford and Bridgeton. Not in a cheap motel screwing the "other woman" who didn't seem to exist.

Meg tried to appear unaffected, but she paled, then blushed. Her hand shook as she raised the glass, and sherry spilled on her skirt and the couch.

"Shit!" She slammed the glass on the table, spilling more sherry and cried, "Fuck!" They started to laugh a little wildly.

"Didn't have to be a *cheap* motel," Meg gasped. "Tim's got some money . . ." and they laughed harder. But both sensed an edge of hysteria and got themselves under control. Eve swigged the soda, the bubbles went up her nose, and she choked. Meg came over and clapped her on the back . . . spilling more sherry. Then she topped off her glass from the decanter and went back to her place.

There were still tears of laughter in her eyes, but her expression was serious. "I still don't get it," she said. "Why would Tim go to some mingy little place, God knows where, when we've got a nice club right here with an indoor pool and a gym? And why . . . oh, Evie, *why* couldn't you tell me this on Friday and save me a stupendously rotten weekend?"

"I tried, I did, Meg. But I just couldn't . . ."

It was saving itself to show her the woman slashed open in the woods, and that terrified little boy on the swing who'd grown up to kill five women and shoot Bunner in the face . . .

Shoot Bunner in the face.

"I hope you're not just saying it to make me feel better," Meg said. Then her voice stopped, although her mouth kept moving. Behind her, in utter silence that almost pounded it was so absolute, the heavy drapes over the half-open windows billowed in a spring draft . . . then they disappeared and Eve was in Bunner's office.

He was behind his desk, the man with the light brown hair was in front of it. He had on a beige poplin jacket and something in his hand at which Bunner stared fixedly. Eve couldn't see the man's face or what he was holding, but she knew it was a gun.

Bunner's eyes were round and blind as wet stones and his face was the color of sour milk. His eyes moved away from the gun to his hand resting on the recorder he'd made a tape of her with on Saturday. But they moved with sickening languor as if they couldn't obey commands from his brain anymore.

He seemed to try to move the hand, but couldn't, then his eyes made their sluggish way back to the gun, and the other man said, "Sorry, Bunny."

The back of the jacket pulled as he raised his hand. Bunner's eyes crossed and rolled back and he seemed to lose consciousness. His body sagged, started to fall forward, and the gun went off. For a second, nothing happened; Bunner was still there, with his body beginning its fainting slump . . . then his face disintegrated, and a blob of blood, pulverized flesh, and other matter smacked the windowpane. Smoke hid him for an instant, then his body toppled through it and she saw a mass of red pulp where his face had been.

She screamed and Meg screamed back, "Eve . . . Evie . . . my God . . ."

The office snapped out and she was back in the drawing room. The drapes billowed, she smelled spilt sherry instead of cordite and was looking into her friend's round, frightened eyes. And Bunner was dead . . . or about to be in the next second . . . hour? Day? She didn't know.

She grabbed her purse and started tearing through it looking for Latovsky's card. She knew she had it; she'd used it last night to call from the service station and leave a message on his machine. But then she'd just dropped it back into the purse instead of putting it into the zipper compartment and now she couldn't find it.

She upended the purse and everything—her wallet and keys, her change purse, and the little pink-and-blue box of the pregnancy test kit she'd bought, then didn't have the nerve to use—fell out on the table. The card floated free and she grabbed it.

● ●

LATOVSKY WAS AT A TRUCK-STOP COUNTER WHEN HIS BEEPER went off. A couple of truckers along the counter glanced at him, then went back to their food. He turned off the beeper, left half his sausage grinder, and went to find the phone.

The trip had been a bust so far. Fuller was not home, the Everetts had two daughters, no son. The Rices had a son, but he was stationed in Germany with NATO. He was coming home next month, his mother had said exultantly in the tiny living room with flowered carpeting and a huge TV, and Latovsky had thought, World War Two was finally over.

The Lyons had a son too, and *he* was in Anchorage with the Alaska State Hospital Administration. The Dryers, next on the list, probably also had a son and he'd be at a weather station in Antarctica.

It'd be funny if it weren't so pitiful.

He'd check on the Rice and Everett sons, but knew they were

where their parents had said and neither had flown six thousand miles to murder Abigail Reese on Friday.

The phone was in an alcove with the restrooms and he called the squad and got Barber.

"Lucci was beeping you," Barber said, "but he just ran outta here like a rabbit with his ass in flames. Broad called a little while ago for you. I took it and she said a Dr. Bunner had been or was about to be shot in the professional building on Old School Road. *Had been or was about to be*—nuts, right? But it spooked the shit out of Lucci and he—"

Latovsky slammed the phone down. He threw money on the counter for the grinder and ran out into the lot. It was clear and almost hot; not a breeze stirred. The land was still flat here, only the faintest hint of hills on the horizon.

He jumped into the car, stuck the bubble light on the roof, and hit the siren and gas. The Olds bore down to the gravel surface, the wheels spun, then caught, and the Olds careened out of the lot in a burst of brute eighties Detroit horsepower.

● ●

TROOPERS STOOD GUARD AT THE SAWHORSES SET UP TO KEEP THE crowd back; more troopers blocked the entrance to the building. Their faces were grim under their wide-brimmed hats, and Latovsky couldn't raise the breath, spit, or gumption to ask what had happened.

He flashed his badge, passed the troopers on the front door, and went into the lobby. The elevator would take too long, and he wrenched open the stairwell door, raced up four flights, then had to lean against the wall, gasping for breath, before he could go on.

He straightened up, opened the hall door and saw Lucci waiting for him in front of Bunner's office. The fire door slammed and Lucci looked up at him and shook his head.

Latovsky shoved past him, yanked the door open, and started across the outer office.

"No, Dave!" Lucci grabbed his arm, but he pulled free and kept going. Lucci grabbed him again and Latovsky turned on him and raised his fist like a club.

Lucci backed away and Latovsky turned to the door. Behind the ridged glass inset, wavy shapes of men moved around the room where Bunny had listened with unfailing attention, patience, kindness to people's darkest secrets. Latovsky grabbed the knob, but the door opened before he could turn it and Lem Meers barged into him. Meers kept coming, Latovsky fell back, and Meers slammed the door, but not before Latovsky got a glimpse of a red-smeared window letting in pink sun that glittered on the fingerprint dust in the air.

"No, Dave," Meers said quietly. "You don't want to see. They shot him in the face."

Latovsky staggered.

Shot in the face.

His legs gave way; he just made it to the couch before he collapsed, with the vinyl cushions sighing under him.

Shot in the face.

The room reeled, and he jammed his head down between his legs until his forehead touched the cool vinyl. Now kiss your ass good-bye, he thought, and the world became a soft, gray, cool fog of sweet oblivion for a few seconds. Then he felt the vinyl sticking damply to his forehead and raised his head slowly.

Meers had half his butt propped against the edge of Mrs. Meeker's desk with one foot planted on the floor, the other, in a high-laced old man's black oxford, swinging free at the end of a long skinny leg.

Lem Meers had graduated from Williams (on scholarship), gotten an M.A. from John Jay and special training at Quantico; he had been to cop conferences in London, Paris, Tokyo; had hobnobbed with the brass in Albany, had dinner twice with the governor, and still dressed like a mountain man on his way to church.

He was taller than Latovsky and fifty pounds lighter; his face was long and gaunt, with deep-set dark eyes and straight black-and-gray hair combed straight back. He was ugly until you got to know him, then he was almost handsome.

"You want water or something?" he asked Latovsky gently.

Latovsky shook his head, the room started to spin again, and he stopped moving.

"I know he was your friend, Dave. I'm sorry."

Meers meant it; he never said anything he didn't mean.

Lucci was in Mrs. Meeker's typing chair. He rode it over until he was close to Latovsky, then said, "The call came in at one, Dave. Barber took it, but it was your private line, so he couldn't get the incoming number.

"The caller was female, did not ID herself. Don't know if she even gave Barber a chance to ask. She just said that Bunner had been or would be shot in his office, then hung up. Barber thought it was one of the cranks we've been getting since the killing Friday and he made a joke of it, called her one more dumb bimbo with too much time on her hands and her thumb up her—" He glanced at Meers. "Her you-know-what. But something about it hit me wrong. After all, Bunner was your friend."

Was.

"So I called his house, sure he'd be there. Then you and he'd have a laugh about it when you got back from wherever. But Bunner wasn't home. His kid answered. He'd only gotten back a few minutes ago and he said his mother said Bunner had to go to the office to see some hairpin.

"*Hairpin.* Kids really come up with 'em, don't they? Anyway, I didn't talk to her. Figured I'd just spook her over nothing. But I couldn't let it alone and after a couple of minutes I beeped you, then came here. I knew I was being a prime asshole. Knew I'd get here and find Bunner gentling down the hairpin or fucking his secretary."

Lucci ran his hand down his face, dragging flesh with it.

"He was still warm, Dave. Blood was still liquid. If I hadn't stalled by calling his house and beeping you . . . if Barber wasn't so fuckin' cop-casual about everything . . ."

"Stop that what-if shit," Meers said sharply, then he looked at Latovsky. "Rule was here, got here before I did. He said clotting time suggests Bunner was shot between twelve thirty and one. He was probably dead by the time the woman called. I sent Dillworthy and Frawley to tell Mrs. Bunner. Then Frawley's going to pick up the secretary. Mrs. . . ." Meers flipped open his notebook.

"Mrs. Meeker," Latovsky said, "Della Meeker. She doesn't have to see this."

"She does, Dave. We'll have the body out, but the file drawers were wiped clean. Looks like the killer"—Meers never used *perp*—"took a file or files, then wiped his prints off. Scorely tried to get into the computer, but couldn't. You know Mrs. Meeker?"

Latovsky nodded; Meers picked a spot on the wall over Latovsky's head to look at and said, "Want the case, Dave?"

"Cap'n!" Lucci cried.

"Yeah, yeah. It's his friend and he can't be objective. But every incompetent asshole I ever knew got that way by being objective about his work."

"I want it," Latovsky said hoarsely. "Thank you."

"Don't thank me—it's a pisser. No prints, no—"

They heard a thunk, then shifting sounds came through the door and Latovsky knew they were settling Bunner into the gray plastic body bag. A ragged *zip* followed, the door opened, and two men in black nylon jackets with CORONER on the back in white came out wheeling the bag on a gurney. Lucci pushed himself out of the way and Latovsky pulled his feet back as they passed.

Bye, Bunny, he thought.

A sob racked him and he put his hands over his face. He heard the other men come out, cross the office to the door. No one said a word. They knew Bunner had been his friend and there was none of the usual cop badinage.

The door closed; it was quiet, and Latovsky uncovered his face.

"Where was I?" Meers asked, not looking at Latovsky.

"Pisser . . . no prints."

"No prints. It stands to reason it was the hairpin Bunner came here to see. But hairpin or not, he was rational enough to wipe his prints off. Also, the slug's gone. It went through the window, leaving a small neat hole, although Rule said it was one big-mother gun. The vagaries of impact, I guess. It might've fallen in the lot, might've even had enough momentum left to lodge in a tree or the side of a passing car. If it's out there, we'll find it, unless a bystander finds it first and keeps it for a souvenir.

"One other thing, Dave. The tape recorder on Bunner's desk was also wiped clean and left open and empty. Looks like the killer took Bunner's last tape out of the machine, then wiped his prints off."

●   ●

". . . DON'T KNOW MY NAME . . . THE LIEUTENANT'S GIVEN ME HIS word . . ."

Adam stopped the tape. Ten times through it and *the lieutenant* was still his only clue. The lieutenant had brought her to Bunner to check her story, so he must know who she was and where to find her.

He was obviously involved in the Woman-in-the-Woods case; his name would be in one of the thousand or so press stories about it. Adam would get it in the library tomorrow.

He didn't know what he'd do then. A cop wouldn't react to having a gun pulled on him the way Bunner had; cops were used to guns.

But cops could be wimps too and the Python was pretty impressive. He'd know better how to proceed when he got a look at the lieutenant.

He listened to the tape again, enthralled by the sound of her voice. Her accent was "cultured," could come from anywhere north of Washington, south of Boston. Then he stopped the tape, ejected it, and chose a cassette at random from the shelf under the machine: Yo Yo Ma plays Bach sonatas for viola da gamba. It was a lovely recording and he'd miss it.

He took the cassette out, slipped in the tape of her, then closed the case and put it back with the others.

He took the Yo Yo Ma tape to the kitchen, dropped it in the garbage, then put a frozen chicken pot pie in the microwave. The phone rang and he looked at it without moving. It was probably Naomi looking for a rematch but he couldn't do it again, literally could not. He'd tell her he was exhausted, had a hard day . . . *shooting his shrink in the face.*

He grinned at the phone, then heaved himself up from the table and answered as it started its fourth ring.

"Just about to give up on you, boy," his father said.

The old man wouldn't call unless something was wrong, and Adam examined himself mentally, wondering how he'd react if something had happened to Mike or the kids. He found he was mildly curious, nothing else.

"Mike and the kids okay?" he asked.

"Fine. Or were a couple of hours ago, when I left them. That skinny bitch served the same chili for Sunday dinner she brought yesterday afternoon. Gave me the shits fresh, dread to think what it'd do after sittin' around for a day. So I told her I'd eaten and got outta there early. Went to Matt's place and he made me a coupla cheeseburgers."

Washed down with half a dozen boilermakers, Adam thought. The old man sounded half in the bag.

"Matt makes a mean cheeseburger," the old man said. Adam waited; his father hadn't called him for the first time in months (years?) to talk about cheeseburgers.

"Anyways, I et 'em, enjoyed 'em, and talked to George Amundsen. Remember George?"

"Can't say I do, Pop."

"Yeah . . . well . . . then I came on home. Wasn't here more'n a couple of seconds when that bitch Ida comes across the street and bangs on the back door with this card with a note for me."

The old man cleared his throat a couple of times, then gave a phlegmy cough, and Adam realized his father was actually upset about something.

"Yes, Pop. What about it?"

"I don't *know* what about it! It was from a cop wanting me to give him a call. A cop from up your way, son, and I got to thinking . . . and worrying, and started to wonder if maybe you'd racked up too many parking tickets or got caught in flagrantay with that lady doctor . . . heh, heh."

The laugh was forced; his father sounded scared.

Adam said easily, "Nope, Pop, no parking tickets and the lady doctor and I did our fucking indoors."

"Yeah . . . well . . . I figured that out for myself, because this particular cop is a state police lieutenant with Major Crime Squad under his name. Didn't figure they'd send a state police lieutenant from Glenvale to Sawyerville about parking tickets or nookie snatching."

Lieutenant. *The* lieutenant, Adam thought. Anything else strained credibility. But why had the lieutenant gone to Sawyerville to see his father? The microwave timer pinged, and Adam jumped at the sound.

"Anyway," the old man said, "I thought I better call you before I call him. See if . . . you know . . . if there's some kinda trouble I oughta know about."

Just a little, Pop, Adam thought. *Just the five women in the woods slit open in the moonlight. Just a spot of trouble, Pop.*

But they'd come after him in division strength if they knew, not send a lone cop 180 miles to Sawyerville.

He said, "No trouble that I know of, Pop, and I guess I'd know, wouldn't I?"

"Sure you would, and I hate asking. But it kind'a jarred me, ya know. Seeing that card with *Lieutenant* and *Major Crime Squad* and *Glenvale* on it. Guess I'll just go ahead and call, see what the jerk wants."

"I'll find out for you if you like. Save you the long distance." Adam spoke steadily, but his heart was racing and the phone was getting slick from the sweat on his hand.

"Would you, son?" The old man sounded pitifully grateful. That way he could sink back into his daze and forget about cops, his son, and everything else.

"Sure, Pop. What's the lieutenant's name?"

• •

DELLA MEEKER FLOUNDERED ON THE FLOOR. SHE WAS FIVE NINE, and weighed about 170. She had gotten down on her knees to look in the bottom file drawer and couldn't get up again. Latovsky put his hand under her heavy upper arm and heaved. She got to her feet, nodded thanks, dusted the knees of her slacks. Then she looked nervously at the blood- and matter-coated window. Sun had baked the blood to the glass and it was black where it filled cracks that shivered out from the bullet hole.

The smell was getting worse and Mrs. Meeker said faintly, "Can we get out of here?"

They went into the outer office where the air was stale but relatively odorless, and Latovsky shut Bunner's door. Mrs. Meeker staggered to the black vinyl couch and sank down. Latovsky took the typing chair and Lucci leaned against the wall with his arms folded.

"It wasn't a patient," she said. "All the files are there."

"You're sure."

"Positive. The folders are numbered, the numbers are in sequence."

"But the cabinet was wiped."

"My fault, Lieutenant. I complained about smudges on it. The cleaning people must have polished it."

"It could still be—"

"Could, I suppose. But none of our office patients are violent or even what you'd call sick. Mr. Kinski sometimes carries on about killing someone, usually his wife. But he's just old and unhappy. Been clinically depressed on and off for years. But he wouldn't hurt anyone, especially not Dr. Bunner. He once said Bunny was all that stood between him and the oubliette. Had to look up oubliette . . . it means secret dungeon.

"Bunny says Mr. Kinski uses anger to cover his sadness, because anger hurts . . . less . . ." She started to cry. Tears pooled behind her glasses; she yanked them off, pulled out a snowy man-sized handkerchief, and wiped her eyes and glasses.

The tears were infectious. Latovsky stared past her at the outer door and swallowed until he got rid of the hot lump in his throat. When she was quiet, he said, "Did you happen to ask the cleaning people to polish Dr. Bunner's tape recorder?"

"No, why?"

"Just wondered."

They were quiet a moment, then Latovsky said, "Look, Mrs. Meeker, you might be right and it wasn't a patient. But we've got to start somewhere, and maybe it's arbitrary but we're starting with male patients between twenty-five and fifty."

"Why male, Lieutenant? The officer who brought me here said a woman called about the shooting."

Frawley should keep his mouth shut.

Latovsky said, "Yes. But the killer probably didn't call the police. We figure the woman was in the building or passing by outside and heard the shot."

Lucci straightened up as if he wanted to say something, then he shook his head and subsided back against the wall.

Latovsky said, "Can you get me a list of those patients, Mrs. Meeker?"

"Sure. We've got them computerized by vitals. It'll only take a minute once the computer comes up."

She activated it, and a few minutes later Latovsky had a dot-matrix list of twenty-six names. Then Mrs. Meeker put the handkerchief over her face and they went back to the inner office. She pulled the files to match names and found a box of back issues of *American Journal of Psychiatry* in the closet. "Don't suppose anyone'll want these," she said sadly from behind the handkerchief. She dumped them out and then put the files in the box.

"What about the tapes?" she asked.

Latovsky shook his head. "They'll take too much time to listen to. We'll probably be better off with Dr. Bunner's notes, at least for now."

They went back out and Latovsky closed the door, knowing he'd probably never see this room again. By next month it would be repainted, the window would be replaced, and there'd be an ad in the local paper: *Office for rent, suitable doctor or lawyer, prestige building . . .*

Mrs. Meeker stuffed the handkerchief in her slacks pocket, took a deep breath, and looked at her neat desk. "Can I take my things now?" she asked. "I don't want to come back here if I can help it."

"Sure."

"And the plants? They'll just die if I leave them. It's not their fault."

The lump shot back into Latovsky's throat, and he swallowed with all his might. He'd made it this far and wasn't going to let a philodendron and a couple of African violets break him down. "Of course you can take them, Mrs. Meeker."

She left a little later with a shopping bag with her cardigan, coffee mug, memo pads with a happy face and her name on them, packs of extra pantyhose, and so on. Frawley carried the plants. The door closed on them and Lucci said, "The caller was not just 'in the building,' Dave."

"Oh?" Latovsky was at Mrs. Meeker's desk with the box of files. It would take a day to get them to behavioral sciences in Quantico, a week to get answers, more time to get the stultifying jargon translated. But Al Cohen was—had been—Bunner's buddy and consultant. He would know a lot of the men in those files, could interpret what Bunner had written about the ones he didn't know. And Cohen spoke English.

Latovsky turned Mrs. Meeker's Rolodex looking for Cohen's number.

"Dave, I said—"

"I heard you." He found the number and picked up the phone.

"Then pay attention. The caller said *Dr. Bunner.* She knew his name."

Latovsky put the phone down. "Then she had to be right here."

"Exactly."

"Find her. Get the agent for the building and get names of everyone on this floor."

"Done." Lucci rushed out, elated to have something to do that could be done and Latovsky called Cohen's number. He got the service and told the woman who he was and that it was urgent he find Dr. Cohen.

"You can verify my ID with the troop, ma'am," he said politely.

A few minutes later, she called back and gave him the number where he could reach Cohen. It was Bunner's.

● ●

"MARY, IT'S DAVE."

Her eyes rolled open, looked out blearily at him, then closed again. She was wearing the same slacks and blouse she'd had on when he'd seen her this morning, but her face had aged thirty years. Cohen had given her a giant jolt of something and she was riding it to limbo. He wasn't sure she even knew who he was.

He sat down on the bed next to her. The mattress tilted with his weight and her eyes opened halfway again, then closed.

"Mary, did you talk to the man who called?"

"Sounded like a nut," she mumbled. "I'm a shrink's wife, I know a nut when I hear one."

"Did you recognize his voice?"

"Uh-uh. It was muffled and garbled, like he had marbles in his mouth."

"Bunny didn't know him either?"

"Uh-uh. But the nut said he'd kill himself and Bunny believed him. Bunny believes everyone. It'll be the death of him . . . it's been the death of him. He believed him and he went . . . he went . . . he went . . ."

Her voice trailed away, tears leaked out of her closed eyes, and she turned away from him, hunching over so her shoulder hid her face. "Leave me alone, Dave, leave me alone."

He went to the door and looked back. Mary Bunner was a tall, strong-bodied woman, but she looked shrunken in the big bed. On the dresser, he saw the cuff links and studs Bunner had worn last night, and a gold pocket watch on a chain with a frat key on it. But he'd never been in this room before, never seen Bunner with the things on the dresser, and they didn't mean anything to him.

Downstairs would be harder, especially the kitchen, where he and Bunner had drunk beer and coffee, coffee and beer, and eaten almost twenty years' worth of sandwiches and snacks.

But even the kitchen was strange after the remodeling.

Al Cohen sat at the table nursing a tumbler of brandy. Ada, his wife, was at the stove, lifting pieces of boiled chicken out of a gigantic pot with tears running down her face.

Pete, Bunner's younger son, sat next to Al. The veins in his eyes had broken from crying and they looked like they were full of blood. Al had told Latovsky he'd tried to give the kid something, but he wouldn't take it, said he had to be compos mentis to help his mother, a bit of unnecessary, endearing, adolescent gallantry. Across from him was Arnie, the Cohens' son and Pete's best friend. The kid looked totally lost as if this were his first death, the first disaster Mom and Dad couldn't fix.

Ada sobbed, "I'll make chicken salad and I've made chopped herring and some kreplach . . . oh God . . . it all sounds so alien. So . . . Jewish."

"Chicken salad's not Jewish," Cohen said, "and Swedes eat chopped herring, don't they, Dave?"

"I don't know. I'm Polish. I need to talk to you, Al."

"So pull up a bottle and talk."

"Alone."

Al sighed, took a deep swig from the glass, and stood up. He took a couple of steps, then went back for the glass and carried it carefully to the kitchen door.

"Did you call about the cold cuts?" Ada asked.

"For the ninety-fifth time, Ada, I called about the cold cuts."

They went down the wide carpeted hall lined with the hunting prints Bunner had liked to the den where Latovsky and Bunner had watched about a thousand games together. Bunner would lie on the couch, head on the needlepoint pillow, feet pushing against the far arm. The wing-chair was Latovsky's.

The box of files sat on the coffee table.

Cohen was saying, "Mary's folks are flying in from Phoenix to-night. Terry Junior'll be home in a couple of hours."

He was at Yale and Bunner had been very proud of him.

Then Cohen saw the box. "What's that?"

Latovsky told him and explained what he wanted.

"That's nuts, Dave. I don't really *know* those men, not to men-tion it's a breach of confidentiality without their consent that could get my ass sued off."

"Do you care?" Latovsky asked.

Cohen hesitated, then shook his head and started to cry. He was a big, swarthy, coarse-featured man with acne scars and startlingly light blue eyes, and seeing him cry was terrible. Latovsky turned away and went to the window overlooking the back lawn where shadows of the trees crept across the grass. It was getting late. Bunner had been dead about five hours.

Latovsky waited until Cohen was quiet, then he turned back. "I wouldn't do this to you, Al, but time's the problem, because our chances of getting him go down every hour. I could send it to the feds, ask them to rush and maybe they would, but you know what I'll get back."

"Yeah," Cohen said hoarsely. "Jargon that makes two plus two sound like theoretical physics." He pulled one of the folders out of the box, opened it, and said, "Yeah, okay, Dave."

"Thank you."

Cohen looked up at him; the tears had stuck his dark lashes together, giving his eyes a starry look.

"I'll do it, Dave, but don't get your hopes up. You're asking me to read another physician's files and intuit a potential sociopath who could shoot his doctor in the face and stay cool enough to cover his tracks. You need a psychic, not a shrink."

And Latovsky finally thought of Eve, then of the tape recorder the killer had touched when he took a tape and wiped his prints off.

● ●

IT LOOKED LIKE AN EASY RUN ON THE MAP: NORTHWAY TO THRU-way, Thruway to the Mass Pike, then south on 7.

With Bunner's little recorder on the seat next to him, Latovsky pulled into an Exxon station at the foot of the on-ramp to the Northway. Last night's rain had brought the flies out and clouds of them massed around the station's vapor lights. The gas jockey burst out of the office and dashed through them to the Olds.

Latovsky wound down the window. "Fill it, super," he said, then wound the window back up before too many flies got in.

The jockey jammed the nozzle into the tank and raced back to the office. Latovsky looked at the map again.

It would take four hours, give or take, and that would put him in Bridgeton at midnight or later.

He was going to try to use her again; he didn't want to have to wake her up to do it. Bridgeton was a tiny empty circle on the map, too small to have any place to stay except maybe one of those loathsome yuppified country inns with dirty hooked rugs. He wanted a plastic motel with clean, thick towels, cable TV, and vending machines. Torrington looked big enough to have one.

The gas nozzle popped and the jockey raced back. "Twenty even," he said and spit out a fly. Latovsky shoved the money at him, rewound the window, and started the car. Then he shut it off and sat still with the flies bombarding the windshield.

He couldn't just disappear for a night without a word. He tried the cellular phone, but the static was so thick from the flies or mountains or the general cussedness of things, it sounded like a forest fire. He hung up, shoved the door open and ran for it, waving his hands madly around his head: He leaped through the office door, slammed it after him and the gas jockey looked up at him. "What the fuck do they want?" he asked, meaning the flies.

"Blood," Latovsky said. "You got a phone I can use?"

● ●

RILEY HAD BEEN WAITING FOR LATOVSKY SINCE 10:00 A.M. HE had left the squad room at 1:15 to wolf down a ham sandwich at Rose's, then rushed back, sure Latovsky would be there by then.

But his office was still dark; the bullpen had all but emptied out. Barber sat morose and alone, fielding what looked like a sudden burst of calls.

"What gives?"

Barber put his hand over the mouthpiece. "Press, press, and more press, Riley. Hate the fuckers . . . present company mostly excepted. A guy got himself shot on Old School, in the professional building."

● ●

THE "NEW" PROFESSIONAL BUILDING WAS A SPRAWLING MASS OF stained cement that already looked shabbier than buildings a hundred years older. The lot was mobbed; cruisers blocked the drive, sawhorses were set up to keep back bystanders, and yellow crime-scene tape was looped across the front of the building.

Riley left his car out on the road and walked back, joining the crowd by entering the lot through the patch of trees at one end of it.

"What happened?" he asked a pudgy-faced woman about fifty wearing a kerchief over hair rollers.

"Guy got shot in the head, I heard." She shivered and jiggled all over, but didn't seem ghoulish or disrespectful, just honestly upset and monumentally curious.

"What guy?"

"One of the doctors, I heard. They say one of those dopers looking for drugs did it."

The Channel 6 van was there. Two Minicams waited at the edge of the crowd with their anchorman, who combed his hair like Dan Rather.

Jergens had sent Trennant to cover for the *Register.* He was at the far end of the lot, close to the tape across the front of the building, and Latovsky's Olds was parked next to some cruisers. Riley settled down to wait.

Nothing happened for a long time, then coroner's men in slick black jackets came out wheeling the stiff. From here, in the late sun, the body bag looked horribly featureless, with a smooth hump for feet, another for the head.

A hush fell on the crowd as they carried the stretcher to the gray van. Even the troopers were distracted, and one of the Minicam men slipped around a sawhorse and came at the stretcher with the camera covering his face like a mask.

He sidled along with the men, camera trained on the gray plastic. "Don't guess you'd unzip," Riley heard him say. "Heard he got it in the face."

"Fuck yourself, ghoul," said one of the bearers.

Unfazed, he kept the Minicam going until one of the troopers forced him back behind the cordon.

The coroner's men shut the back of the van and it eased its way silently down the drive, looking ghostly in the late afternoon light.

Next came four members of the squad in a lump. They broke up and went to their cars, and a few minutes later Lem Meers appeared. He spoke to one of the troopers at the door, then disappeared in the crowd, probably heading for the new silver Merk Dave said he was so proud of.

A plain car came up the drive at five and disgorged another squad man, who came around the other side and helped out a heavyset woman in rust-colored slacks and a yellow blouse. They went inside and came back forty minutes later; the woman had a shopping bag, the squad man—Frawley, it was—carried some plants.

No Latovsky.

Riley was close to the trees. The sun was behind him, a cool shadow fell across his back, and he heard flies whine in the trees. It was getting late; Barb expected him home hours ago.

He'd taken her Camry because it was anonymous and more reliable than his ancient Ford, but there was no phone in it.

He looked at the front of the building.

The glass door to the lobby was black, but lights were on in a set of windows on the fourth floor; the office of the dead doctor, Riley thought.

Latovsky's Olds looked rusted in place, as if it had been there since the last ice age and would stay until the next. He risked leaving for the couple of minutes it took to walk down to the Blue Pantry convenience store at the corner of Old School and call home.

"Don't worry," Barb said, "we've got steak and asparagus. I won't even start cooking until you pull into the driveway."

Steak and asparagus, he thought as he walked back to the lot, and his mouth watered. All he'd had today was a dried-up ham sandwich, a stale vending-machine Milky Way, and what passed in the squad room for coffee. Someday they'd wise up and wash the pot, he thought.

He went back through the trees, waving flies away, then broke out into the lot again.

The crowd had thinned, the troopers were moving the sawhorses, and the Olds was gone.

"Fuck!" he cried, and the woman in the kerchief glared at him. He raced back through the trees, slapping at the flies, taking some satisfaction in killing as many as he could.

• •

DILLWORTHY HAD REPLACED BARBER ON THE PHONE; LATOVSKY'S office was still dark. Meers was there, so were the other men, and the phones were going nuts. Trennant stuck his head in and saw Riley.

"You on this, too?" he asked.

Riley was a star of sorts—a big fish in a minuscule pond. Some of the others resented him, but Trennant was in his late fifties, waiting out his pension. He wasn't the kind to get into the who's-on-top crap anyway and he and Riley were friends.

"No. I'm waiting to ask Latovsky about the Woman-in-the-Woods on Friday."

"Yeah, they're killing each other like flies in this town all of a sudden. See you." He ducked out, then stuck his head back. "Doctor's name was Bunner, by the way. Meers is supposed to give us the rest in a few minutes. You should come down for it, get a laugh anyway."

Then he was gone, and Riley sat on the straight-backed wooden chair that must have been in situ since the thirties. His back ached, his stomach was sour and jittery from the coffee, and his eyes burned. He closed them, meaning just to ease them for a moment, and dozed. He didn't know for how long, but the bullpen was almost empty when his head snapped up and he opened his grainy-lidded eyes again.

"Feel better?" Dillworthy asked.

It was almost eight; Barb was still waiting with her steak and asparagus.

"Dave back?" Riley said.

Dillworthy adjusted himself in his underwear. "Not yet, Jim. Whyn't you go home? The others are gone."

He meant the press, who must have gone to the doctor's house to trample the lawn and spring flowers and wait for some hapless family member so they could stick a mike in their faces and ask how they felt about what happened to their father, son, brother.

Riley hated that shit.

"I'll wait a little longer," he said.

His head started nodding again, but he didn't actually fall asleep.

Trennant would get page one with the murdered doctor, but a run-of-the-mill dopehead hit would be back with the seed company ads by Thursday, and forgotten by all but the doctor's friends and family by the weekend.

But Woman-in-the-Woods rang everyone's chimes and kept ringing them; women in the Park stopped going out alone, business at singles bars was in the toilet. Woman-in-the-Woods hit that chord, that cortical horror-reflex, like Jeffrey Dahmer and John Wayne Gacey, and fascination would not flag until the case was solved or the killings stopped. And it was *his* story.

Lousy name, Woman-in-the-Woods. Too many words, too many vowels. He should come up with something better.

The women had all been killed on Fridays. Maybe *Man Friday?* But that was stinko, too. Besides, he'd no sooner go with it, full head, and the bastard would do one on Saturday.

His head nodded, then snapped up, then nodded, and Dillworthy laughed. "Your head's gonna fall off, Jimmy."

All on Fridays, he thought stuporously. Best night of the week. Poor broads got dressed up for cruising, used hairspray, cologne, extra eye shadow, then went out looking for sex, love, a little companionship, and wound up slit open and dying in a pine grove under a full moon.

Full moon.

Even the man who is pure of heart and says his prayers by night may become a wolf when the Wolfbane blooms and the moon shines clear and bright.

He was a movie buff, had a couple of hundred tapes of old black-and-whites, and he suddenly heard Maria Ouspenskaya's old cracked voice with its pushcart-peddler accent.

Eeffen de man who iss pure of heart . . .

The Wolfman.

That was more like it; that would raise goosebumps.

Then Dillworthy said, "Dave," and Riley came out of his fog.

Dillworthy was on the phone. He mumbled into it, scribbled on his pad, then mumbled some more and hung up.

He stood and hitched up his trousers. "Go on home, Jim," he said kindly. "Dave's not coming back."

As Dillworthy left the squad room, Riley bent forward to see out the door and watched him go into the can.

He looked around. The room was practically empty; no one was looking his way.

He stood up and went past Dillworthy's desk as if he were heading for the water cooler. He paused and looked down, reading upside down as he'd schooled himself to do for years: *Dave, AM. Tilden House, Bridgeton CT*, and a 203 phone number.

8

LATOVSKY SAW STONE PILLARS WITH TILDEN HOUSE on a bronze plaque and turned in. He expected a condo development, a nice one from the lay of the land, with two- or three-story units, plenty of grass, plenty of parking, a clubhouse, and maybe a swimming pool, tennis court, even a nine-hole golf course. But almost a quarter of a mile in from the road, he was still driving through woods and he started to wonder if this was the right place after all.

Then he took a curve around a fine old maple, saw what must be Tilden House, and stopped the Olds.

It was a mansion, about twenty thousand or so square feet of stone and frame, with slate roofs and too many gables to count. He was shocked, then appalled by it, and then he started to get angry, although he didn't know why. Maybe because the place intimidated him, a feeling he loathed. Or maybe because if it were hers, she was rich. Not Bunner or Lydia Rodney rich, but *rich*.

He drove around the curve and down through acres of perfect lawn and pulled up at the front.

He got out, took the little tape recorder off

the passenger seat, and climbed wide stone steps to a large, simple door. It might not be *her* house; she could be the governess or nanny, or she and her husband could rent a cute little two-bedroom above the garage.

He rang the bell, waited a second, then rang again too fast. He would wait longer before he rang the third time.

Then the door opened and he faced a man wearing a gray cotton jacket, white shirt, black slacks, and black tie, and realized he was being greeted by a butler for the first time in his life.

The man was almost as tall as Latovsky and about half again as wide, all of it solid. His thighs filled his pant legs, his neck bulged over an eighteen-inch collar.

He looked at Latovsky, then past him at the shabby Olds, and said, "Good. You've brought the TV. Miss Eve will be relieved."

Miss Eve: This *was* her house, this brick shit-house on legs was her servant. Latovsky made a low snarling noise, ripped his ID case out of his pocket, and flipped it open. The badge caught the light, looked like a hunk of gold in the sun, and the man bent and looked at it, then at the ID card with Latovsky's picture on it.

"I see," he said quietly. "I believe we spoke on the phone last night. Please come in, Lieutenant."

He let Latovsky into a marble-floored foyer bigger than his house, with a gigantic crystal chandelier and a staircase wider than his living room curving up one side of it.

"I have to see Mrs. Klein," he said tightly.

"Of course. Please come this way."

The man led him across the foyer to a set of double doors. He pulled one and both slid silently into the wall. "Please wait here."

Latovsky stepped into a room about fifty by fifty, with French doors at one end, walls of bookcases, and carpet patterned in gold and a green he'd seen only on holly leaves.

"She'll be right with you," the man said, and slid the doors closed, leaving Latovsky alone. *How do you know I won't steal the fuckin' ashtrays?* he thought.

Over a mantel of the same marble as the foyer floor was a painting of a woman. He tucked the recorder under his arm, stepped a little gingerly onto the carpet, and went up to it.

She looked like Eve, but was much, much prettier; beautiful in fact. She was dressed in a gown with dropped shoulders and the flowing cut of the thirties and was sitting on a stone bench in a garden.

The background was muted, romanticized, with the foliage behind her brushed softly, as if the artist wanted to compensate for the stark, almost harsh way he'd painted the subject. Her face leaped out of the canvas, her eyes were wide and dark, with the same green undercast he'd seen in Eve's. She didn't look like a woman having her portrait painted; she looked unhappy, almost frightened.

Of what, he wondered. *What could scare someone with the dough to live like this?*

Stepping out of a car, grabbing a swing chain, and seeing a woman slit open and bleeding to death miles away, he thought.

The doors slid again, and he whirled around to see Eve, but another woman came into the room.

She was much older than Eve, but looked like her and like the woman in the portrait. Her hair was dark, streaked with gray and done up in a rat's nest of a bun at the nape of her neck. Her sweater was faded, with pulls in the yarn, her slacks were baggy at the knees, and her loafers were runover. She looked like a cleaning lady or a destitute cousin who'd been kept on out of charity. Then she held out her hand and a gigantic diamond flashed at him.

"How do you do," she said coolly. "I'm Frances Tilden, Mrs. Klein's aunt."

Tilden: mistress of this vast mansion.

He looked into her dark, cold, totally disinterested eyes and suddenly knew she dressed this way because she didn't give a rat's ass what he thought of her clothes, her hair, or anything about her. To her, he was another servant, and she expected him to clear the table, pour the wine, or whatever his job was and get out of her face.

His anger boiled into rage it took all his willpower to control. He looked at the hand with the diamond flashing at him and didn't take it. She dropped it to her side without even raising her eyebrows; she didn't give a rat's ass if he shook hands with her, either.

"I asked to see Mrs. Klein." His throat was so tight talking hurt.

"That's impossible—my niece is resting."

"I'll wait."

"Not possible either. I'm afraid you've made the trip for nothing. I'd offer you some refreshment, but I'm sure you want to get back on the road and not waste any more time. I'll have Simms see you out."

Simms must be the bouncer-butler, who outweighed him by fifty pounds.

She went to a phone on a table that looked like it had been

lovingly polished every week for two hundred years. She was going to throw him out and there was nothing he could do to stop her short of pulling his gun on her. He had no warrant, and no judge was going to issue one for a "psychic" who'd "seen" a couple of murders.

He stood helplessly clutching Bunny's recorder as she picked up the phone and punched a button on it. She looked at him without seeing him and said, "You're from Glenvale, I understand. We used to pass through it on the way to our camp on Placid. It was just a small town in those days . . ." Then, into the phone, "Larry, the lieutenant's ready to leave."

She put the phone down.

"It was very pretty then, but that's over forty years ago, before the Northway was built. I'm sure I wouldn't recognize it."

Chitchat that probably passed for courtesy with people like this.

The doors, which must be on platinum bearings, started that smooth, almost soundless sliding again, and he braced himself for Simms to appear to "see him out."

It was Eve.

"Auntie, my hairdryer blew—"

She saw Latovsky and stopped. Her hair was wet, she had on a faded blue terry-cloth robe that his ex-wife would've given to a thrift shop years ago.

"I told the lieutenant you were resting, which is exactly what you should be doing," the aunt said.

She had that right, he thought, because Eve looked terrible. Saturday's sallowness had turned to pallor, and the shadows under her eyes looked like berry stains. If she'd slept at all last night, her dreams had been lousy.

Quickly, he said, "I know you were the one who called, Eve. I know you tried to help, but the M.E. said it was already too late— nothing could've saved him."

"You can use my hairdryer." The aunt raised her voice and Latovsky raised his. "But I've got his recorder . . . the killer . . ."

"It should be in my vanity." The aunt's voice was even louder.

Latovsky overrode her. "The killer *touched* it to take the tape Bunner made of him."

"If not, ask Laura—"

"You can help!" Latovsky yelled, and the aunt rounded on him.

"No she can't. It never helps."

"Sometimes it does," Eve said mildly. "Look how happy Meg is."

"And how miserable you are." The aunt was right again, because

Eve looked miserable and he had the feeling their verbal duel was battering her. She went to one of the chairs, sat down, and looked from one to the other.

"Eve, I'm sorry," Latovsky said. "I'd leave you alone, but a man's been killed. You can help find the killer."

"Oh, and what about the next killer and the next?" the aunt asked. "And what happens when the press finds out, and the next lieutenant thinks *a man's been killed, she can help.*"

He didn't have an answer and they looked at Eve. It was up to her and Latovsky realized he was holding his breath.

She brushed the wet hair away from her face and looked from one to the other, but her eyes lingered on Latovsky, then went to the recorder, and she said, "I'll dry my hair later, Auntie."

The aunt's shoulders sagged, but her expression didn't change and she went to the door without a word. Magnanimous in victory, Latovsky said, "I won't keep her long, Ms. Tilden."

"It's *Miss* Tilden. And you'll keep her as long as she can be any use to you, no matter how sad, sick, or frightened it makes her." She went out, slid the doors closed behind her, and he was finally alone with Eve, finally going to hear what she'd seen in Bunner's office. His heart speeded up, his legs were a little shaky, and he sat down in a huge chair across from her.

But two minutes later she was finished. She'd seen the killer's back in a beige windbreaker, heard the shot, seen Bunner's face disintegrate, and most of the back of his head hit the window. Latovsky sat with his head tilted, waiting for the rest, then realized she was done. He jumped out of the chair and stalked to the mantel.

"That's it?" He looked up at the painted woman, whose sad, frightened eyes looked out at the room.

"That's all?" He turned around. "A poplin jacket and a head of light brown hair?"

That's what he'd driven two hundred miles, shot two days and put up with Frances Tilden's snot to hear.

He came back and stood over her. "C'mon, Eve, there's got to be more than a jacket and brown hair—" Then he stopped because there *had* been more. She'd said thick, straight, crisp light brown hair. A woman's description and the exact words she'd used on Friday to describe the killer in the woods. He backed away until he felt the chair behind him, then sat down hard and put the recorder on his lap. It started to slide and he put it on the table. It would probably smudge the surface, but someone would polish it.

"Eve? Was it the same man? Is that it?"

"I could be wrong."

And pigs could fly, he thought. "If you're wrong, I'll chase my tail," he said. "But I'm doing that anyway. Jesus—talk to me. Was it *him*?"

"Yes."

"The killer in the woods."

"Yes."

"Why?" he cried, more to himself than her. "Bunner had nothing to do with the case except as my sounding board. And I didn't tell him enough to get him killed, I didn't *know* enough. So why . . . ?"

"I don't know."

"Was he Bunner's patient?"

We've got to start somewhere, he'd told Mrs. Meeker, *so we'll start with the patients.*

"I don't know."

"But what if he was? What if he was a patient *and* the killer in the woods?"

"What if he was?" she asked.

"I don't know." He got up, then sat down again. He wanted to get closer to her, but couldn't without kneeling on the floor in front of her.

He threw himself back in the chair and ran his hand through his hair. "Okay, what if he *was* a patient. I don't know how good a shrink Bunner was. I *do* know he was a world-class listener. I found that out when I went to him when my marriage fell apart and I had to talk to someone. He was my best friend, but I still meant to keep it low-key—vanilla—you know—'We don't communicate anymore, don't share the same values, blah, blah, blah.' The meaningless crap you get on morning talk shows."

"And self-help books about how to save your marriage," she said softly, and they grinned at each other.

He went on, "That's what I *meant* to say. But I looked into those clear, kind, attentive eyes of Bunner's and all of a sudden, all this *stuff* came out." *I can't stand her anymore. Can't stand the look, sound, feel of her. I can't get it up, Bunny, no matter what she does to me, and she does it all, I'll give her that. But it's no use, and if I stay with her I'll never make love to a woman again, except as an adulterer.*

"I told him things I never said to anyone before, even to myself, and maybe that's what happened to the killer. Maybe the burden got too heavy and he had to talk to someone. Oh, not to confess, just to relieve himself a little, and he went to Bunner and opened his mouth to say something low-key, such as, 'I have these impulses that frighten me, that might be dangerous' and out came, 'Help me, Bunny. I killed five women.' "

"Then . . ." Eve asked breathlessly.

"Then he pulled his trusty Magnum—" He stopped and shook his head. "Won't wash."

"Why?"

"Because he didn't just happen to be carrying around a piece that size. Besides, he called Bunner first and got him down there. He'd planned it."

"Maybe the killing wasn't impulse but the confession was. Maybe he'd made it before."

"When? I saw Bunner Saturday morning, and he said if he put patient confidentiality over the lives of five women, *he'd* be the nut. He'd've told me then, if he knew. He'd've told me later Saturday when we both saw him, so when . . ."

"At the dance," Eve said softly, and the hair on the back of his neck prickled.

"You saw . . ."

"Him and the killer at the same table."

"And Bunner was plastered."

"Maybe."

Maybe the killer had been too, Latovsky thought. And he sat down with Bunner at a country club dance and confessed to five murders. Then what? Then Bunner got more plastered because he couldn't face what he'd just heard, and he couldn't tell anyone because the killer was his patient, but he had to tell because lives were at stake, so he'd tried to get drunk enough to repress it. But the killer didn't repress anything. What he'd said in a drunken moment ate at him all night and by the time the sun came up he knew what he had to do, and he called Bunny . . .

Latovsky picked up the recorder. "I need a description, Eve. He was Bunner's patient and he went to that dance. With a description, I've got him." He slid forward in the chair until he was on the verge of falling off and held out the recorder to her.

"Will you?" he asked softly, in a voice he'd use on a woman he wanted to lay. "Will you?"

She stared at it, and he saw that look of quiet confidence he'd seen on Friday steal into her eyes and he knew she would. Maybe she hated it for ruining her marriage—maybe it would ruin her life and she knew it—but she wanted to do it anyway, the way Horowitz wanted to play the piano.

He held it out as far as he could reach and she took it from him.

He couldn't stand being this far away from her any longer and slid out of the chair and crouched on his heels in front of her.

"What I said before is still true," she told him.

"Yeah . . . you might not see anything, you might see anyone who ever touched it, including the Jap who made it."

● ●

SHE CLOSED HER EYES. SHE HADN'T DONE THAT BEFORE AND HE wondered why she did now. Then motor noise intruded and he looked up, annoyed, afraid it would distract her. A riding mower with a man in dungarees passed the French doors to the terrace and disappeared. The noise faded, and she said quietly, "Oh shit . . ." and then, "Scars . . ."

Scars? Was she back with Ken Nevins? He'd been a patient, he could've touched the recorder . . . could've killed Bunner and the women in the woods?

No—Ken's hair was thin and pale blonde, not thick and light brown.

She didn't say anything else, but her eyelids started to flutter, her mouth opened so he could see the underside of her tongue and her color went from pale to gray. It looked like shock; he'd seen plenty of it in his highway days when they chopped people out of wrecks, and he knew it could kill.

"Eve." He spoke softly, afraid to jar her. She didn't react and he touched the back of her hand. It was cold and damp. "Eve." He raised his voice a little. "Eve, it's okay . . . let it go, whatever it is. You're safe . . . you're home safe . . . it's not real."

It wasn't. She wasn't "there," wherever that was. She was an incorporeal observer to something that had happened or would happen; nothing she saw could hurt her, but it was scaring her anyway. Her color was ghastly, her eyelids fluttered like moth wings, and he didn't know what to do. He took hold of her icy hand but she wrenched it away from him and, with her eyes still closed, she grabbed the little recorder in both hands, raised it over her head like a basketball, and pitched it straight at him. He ducked and it flew past him, hit the lamp on the table behind him, and fell to the floor with a crack. The lamp teetered, then fell, and the crystal base shattered.

The doors slammed into the walls and Frances Tilden and her butler came in. They must've been right outside listening and heard the lamp fall.

Simms rushed across the room. Eve's head swung back, her eyes opened and looked blindly at the ceiling. Then her body started to topple forward out of the chair and Latovsky reached for her.

"Don't touch her," the aunt snapped, and Simms got between him and Eve and eased her back in the chair.

"I'll take it from here, Lieutenant," he said pleasantly.

● ●

SIMMS CUPPED HER HEAD WITH HIS HAND AND TILTED THE GLASS to her lips. Some brandy went into her mouth, more ran down her chin, but Latovsky saw her throat work as she swallowed. Simms fed her a little more and her color went from green to something approximating flesh. She opened her eyes and looked at Simms, then at Latovsky.

"I saw him," she choked, "this time I saw him."

She tried to take the glass from Simms, but he held it away. "Not yet," he said. "Be patient." He fed her more in tiny sips, while the aunt paced behind the couch, twisting her hands together so the diamond sent dots of the prism across the room.

"I think we should call Dr. Rubin."

"No," Eve croaked, "no."

She reached for the glass again, and Simms let her have it. She took a big gulp and choked, then another and it went down all right. She looked better, at least as well as she had when she'd walked into the room before.

Three more swallows and she'd finished the glass. Simms brought the smoked-glass bottle on which Latovsky saw the word Napoleon and refilled the glass. At this rate, she'd be plastered, Latovsky thought.

She drank, then looked at him again and said, "This time I saw him, I really saw him, Dave."

● ●

THE GATES WERE OPEN AND RILEY NOTICED THE ALARM PANEL ON one of the pillars was unlit; it must be unarmed during the day. He turned in, went up the drive to the curve around the maple, saw the house with Latovsky's car parked in front of it and stopped the Camry.

He wasn't shocked by the size of the place; he'd known what to expect from the stone pillars, plaque, wrought-iron gates, and other mansions that he'd gotten glimpses of nearby.

Latovsky must have had a stupendously good reason to come here the day after the doctor's murder and three days after Abigail Reese's. Someone in that house knew something crucial about one of the cases.

But Latovsky was not going to be happy to see him and people who lived in houses like this didn't talk to the press. Ringing the bell and asking for Lieutenant Latovsky or for an interview with the lady or gentleman of the house wasn't going to work.

"When in doubt, find a bartender," Trennant had told him a long time ago. "People tell their bartender more than they tell their priest, and bartenders talk. 'Specially if it's a man, because men gossip more than women. One of those facts of life no one likes to face."

A bartender.

It was eleven Monday morning, but even here, in this rich, lovely, isolated corner of southern New England, there'd be a bar open. He backed and filled and turned around quickly to get away before anyone looked out one of the hundred or so windows on this side and saw him.

● ●

"HE'S TALL . . . BUT I TOLD YOU THAT BEFORE," EVE SAID. HER voice was thick from the brandy. "Maybe six feet, but I think a little less. Hair's light brown, etcetera"—she grinned a little—"and he's got regular features, straight nose, longish face, nice mouth. He'd be handsome, except for his eyes."

"What about his eyes?"

"Light brown, too. Same color as his hair." She took another deep swallow of the brandy. "And they're . . . empty. Never saw eyes that—empty . . . dead . . . glassy. Like a doll's eyes." She shivered, and the aunt said, "I think we should call—"

"Doll's eyes," Eve murmured, and finished the brandy. Simms poured again.

"Go on," Latovsky said.

She looked at him blearily. "That's it."

"Can you still see him? I mean in your mind's eye?"

She nodded.

"Good. I can have an artist here in a few hours."

"No. No artist."

"But how else . . . ?"

"No artist, no nothing," she said. "It's over."

"What do you mean?"

"I mean I can't tell you any more, and I'm not going to describe him to an artist or anyone else, Dave. I also mean—I'm sorry—but I mean you have to leave here now and not come back or call or . . ."—another swallow of brandy—"or anything else," she said.

"Why!"

"Because you were wrong, It wasn't the tape of himself the killer took, it was the tape of me Bunner made on Saturday. And the killer took it because he's looking for me. *Hunting* for me . . . and I just saw him find me."

● ●

THE SUN WAS HIGH WHEN LATOVSKY LEFT THE HOUSE, AND IT was hot. Simms closed the door on both of them and said, "Let's take a walk, Lieutenant."

"Why?"

"Because we've got to talk and it's too hot to sit in the car. Leave the little recorder so you don't have to carry it."

Obediently, Latovsky opened the Olds's door and put the recorder on the seat. The crack it had gotten when it hit the floor had widened and the buttons were loose. It was beyond repair, but it was old; Bunner should've gotten a new one long ago. *Too late now*, he thought, and tears stung his eyes. He bowed his head over the recorder to hide his face from Simms.

"I broke his recorder," she'd cried when she'd seen it. "I didn't mean to—I'm sorry."

That was the last thing she'd said to him or probably ever would, because right before that she'd told him to get out. "You're the only link between me and the killer. If he finds me it'll be because of you."

"What about Lucci?" Latovsky had croaked.

"He only knows my last name, not who or where I am . . . unless you told him. Did you?" She looked terrified.

"No."

"Then it's you. If he finds me it'll be because of you. And he *will* find me unless you do what I ask."

"But . . ."

"No buts, Dave. You didn't see those eyes, I did."

"Eyes," he'd said tonelessly. Dead, glassy doll's eyes.

"I saw them in a mirror," she had said, very thickly now as she worked on the fourth brandy, "a compact or rearview mirror. He was behind me, looking at me in it . . . he'd caught me." She shivered all over and drained the glass. "So you'll go, please. And swear . . . swear you won't come back or call . . . or anything. Please—swear."

He'd done it, forcing words out through lips that felt like slabs of liver. Then she had nodded, mumbled about being sorry again, and sagged back in the chair. He'd gone to pick up the recorder, getting a little dizzy when he'd straightened up too quickly. That was when she had seen it and sobbed, "I broke his recorder . . . I didn't mean . . ."

"Lieutenant?" Simms called.

"Coming." But he waited a little longer, because he wasn't ready to face Simms yet. He'd lost Bunner yesterday, her today. It was time to crawl into a back booth at The Loft and get plastered.

Simms waited without calling again, and Latovsky finally straightened up and slammed the car door.

• •

THEY WALKED AROUND THE HOUSE, PAST A COURTYARD WITH brick paving and a six-car garage and out across the acres of Tilden land. There wasn't another house in sight and Latovsky muttered, "Big place."

"Six hundred acres, Lieutenant. And in case you ever wonder, which you might someday, land around here goes for about eighty thou an acre. A developer from Hartford once offered them twenty million for a piece of it and they turned him down. Can you imagine turning down twenty million?"

"No."

"Me either. But they're rich, Lieutenant. Can't say to the penny how rich, but I know old man Tilden left his daughters in the neighborhood of a hundred million each thirty years ago. It's doubled . . . maybe trebled by now. Eve's got her mother's portion; she'll have her aunt's too someday."

Four hundred million, give or take, Latovsky thought, and smothered a giggle he knew would come out sounding screechy and nuts.

They came to a stand of gnarled, ancient-looking fruit trees in bloom with benches under them.

"Let's sit," Simms said.

They faced each other, knees almost touching. Petals blew around like pink snow, caught in the men's hair and clothes and perfumed the air.

"The old cherry orchard," Simms explained. "Most of the trees are past bearing in spite of the blossoms, but we still get enough for a few pies and jars of jam. It's always a little cooler here—must be an underground spring or something."

"We doing the tour?"

"No need to get snotty, Lieutenant. We've got to talk and this is a pleasant place to do it."

"Talk about what?"

"Whoever Eve saw in that 'mirror.' I gather he took a tape with Eve's voice on it."

"Yes."

"Saying what?"

"That she could . . . *see* . . . things."

"That no one else could."

Latovsky nodded.

"Okay, what about *him?*"

"I don't know about him or I'd get him and she'd never have to worry."

"Get him? For stealing a tape?"

Latovsky gave a small, cruel grin. "For killing six people, Mr. Simms."

Simms jerked back, rocking the bench on its wrought-iron legs. "Holy shit."

"Yeah. One of the six was my best friend. That was his recorder . . . he made the tape."

"Tell me," Simms said softly.

"What for?"

"Because you're outta here in a couple of minutes and I'm all that stands between him and her. Tell me."

Latovsky said, "Five were women he slit open in the woods and watched die by moonlight."

"Jesus."

"The sixth was my friend; he shot him in the face with a Magnum or some comparable piece. And that's about all I know except what you've already heard—that he has light brown hair and light brown eyes; cold, dead, empty doll's eyes." Latovsky laughed mirthlessly.

"The bartender where the killer picked up the last woman looks like a white Mike Tyson and has a snake tattooed on his forearm. I can imagine asking him if he remembers some fucker with 'doll's eyes.' "

"Six . . ."

"That we know of. Could be more we haven't found and never will."

"We can't let him anywhere near her."

"No."

"You've got to keep your word, Latovsky."

"I gave it, I'll keep it," Latovsky said tightly.

"Sure, sure. A man of honor. Only time's got this way of eating away at 'honor,' until the day comes, maybe only a couple of weeks from now, when you remember how useful she could be and forget all that honor bullshit. Especially if this bastard makes it seven people . . . or eight. Then I can see you telling yourself that a vow made under duress in a rich lady's drawing room means zip compared to saving a life. That's not such an outlandish scenario, is it?"

Latovsky didn't answer. Simms brushed some of the petals out of his close-cropped gray-and-brown hair and went on. "Two reasons you can't let that happen, Lieutenant. One, if you ever come through those gates uninvited . . . if you call or write or send her a singing telegram . . . I'll break you in two."

Fuck this, Latovsky thought and tensed to show Simms-the-butler a thing or two. He sat up rigidly and gave the other man the *look* that had terrified a few killers and rapists and a lot more lesser perps, but Simms just looked back mildly. The forearms leaning on his thighs were the size of wet-cured hams, and his neck looked like a tree trunk. He could do exactly what he'd said without winding himself. Latovsky sagged back on the bench and looked down at the petals littering the ground around his feet. "And the second reason?" he mumbled.

"Good on ya, Lieutenant," Simms said, "good on ya! I was afraid we'd have to go through a lot of macho shit about who can do what to who. Maybe even have to have a little demonstration." Simms stuck his hand out. "I'm Larry Simms by the way. Simms in public, Larry in private. Please call me Larry."

They shook, and Simms sat back and looked past Latovsky at the behemoth of a house about five acres away.

"Reason two's a lot more complicated," he said. "See, Eve really can do what she says. Oh, I know you *think* you believe it, or you wouldn't be here. But I'm sure there's a whole list of reservations in the back of your mind and some of them probably apply. For instance, she can't necessarily see what she wants to when she wants to, or tells herself she can't. She also says she can't get names and I guess she can't. But in one regard, she is infallible and that is, if she does see it, it will happen—just like her mother."

"Her mother!"

"Yeah. Ellen Dodd Tilden Leigh. These people give themselves a lot of last names, don't they? Ellen had *it*—that's the best I can come up with as a name for the fucker. I tried out *psychic power*—only to myself, of course—and that sounded like something at the other end of a nine hundred number.

"Ellen Leigh had *it*, as did *her* mother, the lady in the picture in the drawing room. It did her in, by the way; she came down late one night, locked herself in the garage, stuffed blankets in the cracks, and started a couple of the cars. Gorgeous woman from the portrait and all accounts. Famously gorgeous in these parts, for all the good it did her.

"After that it was her daughter Ellen's turn. Don't know how it passes from one to the other, or why it skipped Frances. Guess you'd need a Nobel laureate geneticist to figure it out . . . or maybe it's just one of those family proclivities like making a lot of dough. In any case it went from Olivia to Ellen and Ellen tried to pretend it hadn't and she was just a nice, normal, pretty rich girl. For a while, it looked like she'd pull it off. She went to dances, had beaus, and came out the way girls did in those days. She got married, then she had Eve, and it all fell apart because she couldn't touch her own daughter for fear of what she'd *see*. Imagine, Dave. Imagine hugging your little girl when she's six and seeing her with a brain tumor at twelve; imagine what the next six years would be like for both of you."

Latovsky felt his imagination slip in that direction and pulled it back because he didn't want to know what that would be like.

Simms went on. "Got to where Ellen couldn't touch her husband either, and that poor bastard, T. William Leigh, his name was—still is, for all I know—took it as long as he could, then lit out, and Ellen took to her rooms, as they say in novels."

Latovsky looked out beyond the trees and softly blowing petals at the mammoth house, wondering which of the hundreds of windows had been Ellen Leigh's.

"And that left Franny and me to raise the kid," Simms said.

"You?"

"Me. See, Franny and I have an understanding." He saw the look on Latovsky's face and laughed heartily. "That's right, Lieutenant, that's what I mean, and stop looking like I just showed you my dick. Franny's not the first rich girl to get it on with the butler . . . except I was houseman in those days. But with us it lasted. We took one look at each other when the old man hired me thirty-five years ago, fresh from the war in Korea, and that was it for both of us. Franny's not the snob she looks like. She's not a snob at all and the fact is she'd've married me then . . . or now, I guess. But then she'd have one more last name and I'd be the stud from town who married a Tilden. Didn't set well with me at twenty-three, doesn't set any better at fifty-seven, and this way's been okay. Good, in fact—in fact, it's been wonderful. We've got Eve and each other, there'll be the baby . . ."

"Baby!"

"Guess Evie didn't mention it—not even to Sam probably. She says she's not sure and she just doesn't seem to want to find out, but Mrs. Knapp says you can tell from the rings under her eyes, and Laura, the upstairs maid, says you can set your watch for seven A.M. by the sound of retching from Evie's bathroom. And that brings me back, in a roundabout way and with a lot more talk than necessary, to reason two: Polly Bogen, who was upstairs maid before Laura. To Polly's son, Tom, to be exact."

"What about him."

"He was about sixteen back when I'm talking about: tall, handsome, bright, and the only child. The fuel that made his folks' motor go, as you can imagine. Well, one day, Ellen 'saw' him. Don't know how, since she avoided touching folks about the way you'd avoid kissing a cobra. But somehow she touched Polly or something Polly touched, and their boy appeared to her. Not as the tall, straight, handsome youth he was, but as a husked-out shell curled up like a shrimp in a hospital bed and hooked up to all the devices. His hands were claws, the way they get after years in a coma, and she knew he'd been that way a long time and would stay that way. Most of all she knew how he *got* that way, and she told Polly.

"I'm sure it tore itself out of her, because for Ellen seeing and saying what she'd seen were like a weekend in the ninth circle of hell. But the boy's life was at stake."

"What'd she tell her?"

"That's there'd be a storm Halloween night, two days from when I'm talking about. It'd be one of those fall squalls that blow down wet leaves and stick them to the road, and Tom Junior would be in a car with his buddies. They'd be drunk, the leaves would be slippery . . . you get the drift."

Latovsky nodded.

"Anyway, Ellen told Polly and Polly told us servants. She tried not to believe it, tried to laugh at it, but wound up crying because she knew what Ellen could do, we all did. And finally, Polly told her husband, Tom Bogen, Senior.

"Don't know to this day how Tom felt about second sight in general or the Dodd-Tilden 'gift' in particular, but I guess he figured he'd rather be a superstitious asshole than risk his son. Polly also told the folks of the other kids who were supposed to go out with Tom Junior that night. But they called it unGodly nonsense, said the Tilden women were a bunch of neurotic rich bitches looking for attention or words to that effect.

"The night came. Tom Senior and Polly knew better than to try talking a sixteen-year-old out of a prowl he'd been looking forward to for weeks, so they waited until he was upstairs getting rigged for the night's parties. Probably in torn jeans and a black plastic jacket with an ad on the back for a pizza parlor in Detroit—just like kids nowadays—and they locked him in.

"Polly said it was horrible. It was an attic room, he couldn't get out the window without breaking his neck, and had the sense not to try, even at sixteen, but he pounded on the door until his knuckles split and screamed names at them Polly said she'd never even heard before.

"The other boys came by to pick him up and Tom Senior went down and told them Tom Junior was under the weather and couldn't go with them. But they must've heard the real story from their folks and they hung around, yelling and hooting, honking the horn and taunting the poor kid until he started throwing himself bodily against the door, and Polly said she was terrified he'd break the lock or some bones. But it was an old house, the door held firm, and all he broke was his collarbone, but even that didn't slow him up.

"And all the time, it was a clear and mild night, Lieutenant. A perfect Halloween Eve with a hunter's moon and not a cloud in the sky. It started about ten, with a little wind and a few drops of rain on the roof, and Polly said she wept with relief when she heard it. The wind picked up, the rain turned to a squall that flooded basements, blew the power out all over town . . . and blew down the last of the leaves and stuck them to the pavement.

"The other kids went to the parties. They drank and smoked weed, then took to the road. The kid driving, secure in that sense of immortality only the young have, put the pedal to the mat, missed a curve at seventy, and plowed into another car full of hooched-up kids on grass also doing seventy. Five were killed outright, one was crippled for life, one came out the squash Tom Bogen Junior would have been, and one walked away with a few cuts. Luck of the toss, luck of the toss, Lieutenant."

"And Tom Bogen Junior?"

"Got a wife and a couple of kids, a degree from UConn, and an investment firm for the writers and movie actors in the Berkshires. But *he'd*'ve been the squash if Ellen hadn't told Polly and Polly hadn't listened. If Ellen saw it, it would happen if nothing had changed. If Eve saw it, it will happen if nothing changes. In this case, *you,* Dave.

"I know you probably see yourself as a nice, average guy except for carrying a gun; probably have a wife and a couple of kids and a raised ranch. Bet you play poker once a month, bowl, fish, root for the Mets—whatever. But in this instant you are *nemesis,* and if you don't go now, and stay gone, he will find her. Then whaddaya suppose this killer of six will do to a psychic who might see his face in a vision?"

"Kill her."

"That's what I figure, too," Simms said.

• •

THE KID IN THE GAS STATION HAD CLEAN, SHINING BLOND HAIR, pink cheeks, clear swimming-pool-blue eyes, and a Yale T-shirt. He filled Riley's tank, took the money, then told him there was only one bar in Bridgeton, a roadhouse called Burt's. He gave him clear directions and refused to take the buck tip Riley offered. He even waved when Riley pulled out. The rich *are* different, Riley thought, thinking of the rude and crude, dirty, pizza-faced kids who pumped gas upstate. Rednecks in training.

He followed the directions and found himself on the main street of a one-stoplight town that looked like a Christmas card without the snow. The street was lined with shops showing the golf and tennis clothes he saw in *Town & Country* in his dentist's office. And cars, the collective cost of which would top the gross national product of a few countries.

The street ended at a magnificent eighteenth-century steepled New England church. He turned left as the kid told him to, and five minutes later came to Burt's, which was a converted Colonial. He pulled into the lot and parked between a Rolls Corniche and a 735I BMW and across from two horse vans and a Mercedes station wagon. *Ah, America,* he thought. Show the leader of any third-world country this parking lot, then drive him down the main street of Bridgeton, Connecticut, and he'd go home with a leaden lump of hate and envy in his heart.

The Rolls was unlocked; Riley left the Camry unlocked and went inside.

It was very dim after the sunlight and it took a moment for his eyes to adjust. There were a few people at the bar and a few more in the back at booths, having an early lunch. He slid up on a bar stool, away from the other people—two men in golf shirts and tweed jackets and a woman who looked pretty run down for these parts—and examined the bartender, who was making a gimlet. He had a paunch and a heavy-featured face with sagging jowls and was thirty years too old to be moonlighting from college. He must be Burt.

Riley ordered a house draft. The bartender drew it, and a waitress came through swinging kitchen doors carrying a couple of thick, juicy-looking burgers on Kaiser rolls with fries, sliced tomato, and a whole dill pickle. She was in her late twenties, early thirties, wearing neatly pressed slacks and a crisp blouse under a beige apron.

She would know what went on locally, maybe not as much as ol' Burt, who set a beer with a perfect head in front of Riley on a cardboard coaster, but she looked a lot less taciturn than the bartender, who hadn't said a word since Riley had walked in, even to ask Riley for payment.

"How much?" Riley asked.

"Four."

Steep for a beer, but this was rich man's country. Riley left five, got a short nod of thanks, then sipped the beer (one of those imported brands he'd never find on draft in Glenvale) and watched the waitress. She finished serving the hamburgers and slid into an empty booth with a newspaper and something on the rocks waiting on the table.

Riley drank half the beer, giving himself time to savor it, then took it and the coaster to her booth.

"Hi. My name's Jim Riley."

"Mary Owen," she said with a surprised smile. Her customers probably didn't bother to introduce themselves. "What can I get you?"

"Nothing. I just wanted to talk to you, if you've got time."

Her smile faded and he laughed. "This is not a pickup, Mary. I'm a reporter for a paper in Albany."

He put the beer and coaster down on the table, took out his press card, and put it down in front of her. He gave her time to look at it, then slid into the booth across from her.

"I want to ask you about some people you might know."

"What people?" She sounded suspicious but couldn't take her eyes off the press card. Maybe she had never seen one before.

"Tilden."

She looked up wide-eyed, and he knew she knew them or about them and thought whatever she knew was fascinating.

But she wasn't the snitch type; there was something settled and neat about her that made him think this was her town; that she'd lived here all her life, as had her parents and their parents, even unto the Colonial Wars. She'd shut up like a bank vault at five if he offered her money, but she would have a sense of duty.

He said, "I was just out at the house but I couldn't get up the nerve to ring the bell."

"Oh? They're just regular people . . . well, maybe regular's a little . . ."

"Exaggerated?"

She smiled and seemed to relax a little. She sipped from the glass and he smelled scotch.

"What'd you want with them?" she asked.

He cleared his throat and looked reluctant. "This just between us?"

"Sure. If you say so."

"I have reason to believe . . . gosh, that sounds so stilted, but it's true—I have reason to believe that someone in that house, maybe one of the Tildens themselves, knows something the police and public should know."

"Such as?"

He took time to think and drink more beer before he answered. He had to be careful here; she wouldn't know or care about Terence Bunner, but the Woman-in-the-Woods case—the Wolfman as of yesterday—was on the wires.

He took the plunge. "Such as the Woman-in-the-Woods killer."

Her eyes widened more and he went on softly, rushing a little to get it out in case she was about to tell him to take a flying fuck. "I call him the Wolfman now, because he kills under the full moon. Remember the old movie?"

She was too young, but it was on tape. She nodded and shivered and he pushed a little. "Killers like him, like the Wolfman, never quit, Mary. They go on and on until they die or get caught. They're almost always caught but it takes years sometimes and a lot of people die because the cops are hobbled by all sorts of crap like probable cause and Miranda. But *we're* not. The press can go places and ask questions cops can't, and I think someone in that house knows something about the Wolfman the cops should."

"You mean Eve?" she said breathlessly.

"Do I?"

She nodded and he knew he had her and waved at the bartender for another round.

9

"SCARED?" ADAM ASKED GENTLY.
Ellen Baines nodded.

Any minute orderlies would come and take her to four, where Shelley Stern would perform a simple hysterectomy for stage-one, grade-one cervical cancer.

But the orderlies might be late, she might have to wait half an hour before the anesthesiologist got to her. No reason to let her suffer.

He prepared a pre-op jolt of Librium, slipped the needle in and out, then rubbed the injection site.

"God, you're good at that," she said.

He'd practiced on a grapefruit before he'd ever given his first shot, then on himself with B_{12}. He hated doing anything half-assed.

"I'm going to miss spring," she said. She wasn't whining; she never whined.

He pulled over the visitor's chair and sat next to the bed. "It's not spring, El, it's fly season. They'll be gone by the time you get out, then it *will* be spring and you can plant your garden."

"Already planted it," she said thickly. "Peas anyway. Hope they don't rot."

"They won't," Adam said gently.

She tried to nod, her hands slid to her sides, she closed her eyes and drifted. Adam drifted too, thinking about David Latovsky. He'd have a gun he knew how to use, but wouldn't be expecting the nice young doctor from Glenvale General to pull a Python on him. Maybe he'd fall apart the way Bunner had. Bunner would have told Adam her name or anything else he knew, but the lieutenant could be made of sterner stuff.

Adam didn't know what he'd do then.

The main thing was not to kill the lieutenant before he got what he wanted out of him. The second main thing was not to shoot him in the face the way he had Bunner. That had been horrible.

The orderlies arrived and Adam got out of their way. They stood on either side of the bed, and one, with *Ben* on his name tag, bent over Ellen. "Mizz Baines? Think you can give us a little help here?"

Her eyes opened. She stared blearily at them and tried to nod. "Just kind of shift with us, okay?"

"Okay," she whispered. They wrapped the sheet around her, then Ben said, "Now," and they shifted her quickly and expertly onto the gurney.

"Thank you," she said as if they'd just done her a huge favor. Ben grinned at her and she smiled dreamily at him and closed her eyes.

They wheeled her out into the hall and Adam followed. Ellsworth Harris, chief of staff, was coming down the hall and stopped.

"Whatcha got, Adam?" he asked.

"Early uterine carcinoma for Stern."

"Mmmmmm."

The elevator door opened, sending a shaft of white light across the floor in front of the nurses' station.

"Terrible thing about Bunner," Harris said.

"Terrible," Adam echoed. The orderly, Ben, gave Adam a thumbs up, meaning he'd wait with her until they were ready, not just leave her in the hall. Nice of him. They wheeled the gurney in, the doors closed, and Adam thought, *Good luck, Ellen . . . good luck.*

"You going to the funeral?" Harris asked.

"Sure."

It would be his first chance to get a look at the lieutenant.

● ●

ADAM STOOD AT THE HEAD OF THE MAIN AISLE OF KRANE'S Funeral Parlor's Rose Room. The carpet was rose, the wallpaper had roses on it, the vinyl seats of the wooden folding chairs were pink. The funeral was scheduled for 1:00, and it was only 12:30, but the room was crowded. Ken Nevins sat in the back row with his homely wife with the luminous gray eyes next to him. Adam remembered her from that blood-soaked night in the ER when Ken had slashed his arms to the bone.

She looked worried; Ken looked devastated. He'd lost his doctor and friend, the most competent partisan he'd probably ever have. But he knew the secret, could tell the next doctor, and the repetition would begin. *It wasn't your fault, you were only seven. It wasn't your fault, you tried to save her. It wasn't your fault, no one could have done more . . .*

It wasn't your fault would become Ken's mantra and maybe by this time next year he'd start to believe it, thanks to *her*.

Adam watched Ken a moment, then looked around for a likely police lieutenant. Silly to think he could spot him just by looking, and he'd probably wind up asking El Harris, who knew everyone in town, but he looked anyway. No one in the line in front waiting to pay their respects to the family looked right. He went along the back, then down a side aisle, and spotted a dark man talking to a tall blond Adam recognized from news photos as Rich Kramer, chief of the Glenvale police. The other man was short and skinny, his cheap suit puckered at the seams, and there was a bulge at his belt line that could be a gun. He looked like a cop, was talking to another cop, and Adam hoped he was the one, because he didn't look very prepossessing.

Adam went down the main aisle to the end of the condolers' line.

The coffin was covered with white roses, lilies, and little waxy things Adam didn't know the name for. It was closed because no embalmer's art could repair what the Python had done to Bunner's face. It had been, hands down, the most repulsive thing Adam had ever seen, and that included a pelvic exenteration he'd been roped into watching at Boston General. He had expected a small neat hole in the forehead and a mess in the back, but gases in the slug must have expanded under the skin; Bunner's face had disintegrated before his eyes like burning film, and the back of his head had blown out and hit the windowpane with a hard, moist smack, like wet clay slapped on a potter's wheel.

Adam had thought it was over and he was looking at the worst of it, then one of Bunner's eyes had given a sudden twist and popped out on the end of a quivering stalk.

Adam got in line and looked down the row to where Mary Bunner and her sons sat. At last Christmas's staff party, she'd been big, pretty, and much younger-looking than the forty-something she must be. Now she looked like a crackle-glazed figurine of a woman of seventy. Her face had fallen in and her blond hair, which had been shining with health, hung lankly under a black straw hat with a veil. The veil had come down and hung in a slant across her forehead, giving her a rakish look she'd never intended. But no one told her so she could tuck it back up.

Adam's turn came and he stood before her, aware of Bunner's flower-covered coffin behind him; it'd probably be years before Mary Bunner could stand the smell of flowers.

He didn't take her hand or touch her because she must be sick of people kissing, clutching, and crying over her, then going home to their intact families when it was over.

He introduced himself and said how sorry he was. He tried to look into her eyes to see if he'd respond to her misery, but the crooked veil distracted him, and the hoarse whisper of her voice when she thanked him for coming sounded distant as he stared at the black dotted veil.

The kids looked as dazed as their mother. They wouldn't care who he was or what he had to say, and he bypassed them and stopped at an elderly couple, whose skin looked like hide from too much sun. Probably on a golf course in Arizona or Florida. He knew Bunner's folks were dead; these must be his in-laws. Adam made his short, neutral speech, then shook their liver-spotted hands and passed on to the side aisle.

The short, dark, lieutenant-candidate was in the condolers' line and Adam sidled into the second row behind Mary and took a seat directly in back of her. By leaning forward as if the chair bothered his back he could hear what people said to her.

The short dark one's turn came, and he made a short, very stiff little speech that didn't sound like it came from a family friend. But maybe he'd been one of those childhood buddies who hadn't fit in with Bunner's adult life and they got together only sporadically, just the two of them. The possible lieutenant finished speaking, moved on a couple of paces, then came back.

"I'm sorry, Mrs. Bunner, but I gotta say this."

Her hat tilted back as she raised her head.

"We're gonna get this guy," he said. "We've got leads and we're gonna get him."

That was crap, Adam thought. They had zilch. His luck had been phenomenal; he'd even found the spent slug in the parking lot, had actually stepped on it as he unlocked the LTD. It was now buried in a patch of soft earth on the state land across from his house and he doubted he could find it himself.

"I swear, we're gonna get him," the small dark man said.

Mary Bunner's voice sounded like an old hinge. "I'm sure you will, Sergeant . . . and thank you."

Sergeant, not lieutenant. He'd picked the wrong man and would have to find an innocent sounding reason to ask El Harris who the lieutenant was.

The line petered out; loudspeakers close to the ceiling crackled softly and "Sheep May Safely Graze" came through them. A nice selection.

He'd tell Harris that he'd read about the lieutenant in the papers and wondered if cops came to victims' funerals. But that was too convoluted.

A man in a dark gray suit and a shirt so starched it looked like cardboard moved away the door stops with the toe of his shiny black shoe, and the doors started to swing shut.

He'd tell Harris that Bunner had mentioned David Latovsky and Adam wondered who he was. That was better.

The doors met, then swung in again, and a huge man came in with a girl about twelve. He said something to the man in gray, then took the girl's hand and went down the main aisle to the front. He took the empty seat next to Mary, and the boys made room for the girl between them and their grandparents. Mary raised her head to look up at the man, who must be six four or better, and she started to cry for the first time since Adam had come in.

The man tucked the sagging veil behind the hat brim, and Mary sobbed. "We're at his funeral. Oh, Dave, I can't believe we're at his funeral."

Dave, as in David Latovsky.

● ●

"IN THE SURE AND CERTAIN HOPE . . ."
Adam watched Latovsky from across the pit they'd dug for Bun-

ner. They'd put up an awning in case of rain, but the sky was clear blue, with little puffs of clouds, and enough wind to bend the heads of the daffodils around the grounds and keep the flies away.

The coffin sat in slats over the grave. Two men wearing greens came forward and slid the slats away as the pallbearers, Latovsky among them, grasped the straps on the coffin and started easing it into the ground.

The flowers on top trembled as they were lowered out of the sun forever and Adam actually felt a stab of pity for them. Felt more for a spray of cut flowers than he ever had for any human being.

The coffin touched bottom, the straps slacked, then the minister dug a silver trowel in a heap of dirt and passed it to Mary.

It made the rounds, but when it got to Latovsky he shook his head.

Either he wasn't religious or couldn't bear to throw dirt on his friend's grave.

Then it was over.

People started walking across the grass to the path down to the road. The women's heels sank into the soft earth; the men took their arms. A crowd collected around Mary for a last word or hug. Latovsky towered over them, his face grim in the sunshine.

Suddenly there was a flurry in the crowd . . . a wail of "Nooooooo. . . ." And Mary Bunner burst past the others and raced for the grave. Her hat blew off and cartwheeled across the grass, the soft dirt grabbed her heels, and she flailed her arms to keep her balance. She got to the edge of the grave, hesitated, then tensed, and Adam knew she was going to pitch herself into it. He leaped forward to stop her, but Latovsky beat him to it. He grabbed her shoulders from behind and hauled her back and she turned on him, fighting to get away. He held on to her, mashing her body against his so she was immobile. The minister ran back with his stole streaming out behind him, and the two boys joined them. Mary struggled fiercely; she was a big woman, not fat, but hefty and probably weighed almost as much as Adam. But Latovsky subdued her gently, easily, keeping his head bent back so she couldn't scratch his face.

The minister said something. She screamed, "I can't . . ." He said something else, the younger boy sobbed brokenly, and she finally stopped fighting and sagged against Latovsky.

He turned her sideways, put his arm around her waist to support her, and started walking her across the grass to the path.

She went docilely, her bare head bent.

They'd forgotten the hat, which was caught in a clump of daffodils, and Adam took a few steps toward it, but one of the boys ran back to get it. Mary's legs were wobbling; she was losing control of her muscles the way Ellen Baines had a few minutes into the Librium shot. By now Ellen's uterus and its attachments were frozen and microtomed and Lil Toomey was doing the final tumor-staging and grading. Vanderveer had done the initial pathology, but he was here.

Mary's legs gave way completely and Latovsky swept her up in his arms. She must be a hundred and fifty pounds of dead weight, but he carried her easily, with her head tucked against his chest, her legs bent over his arm.

The limousine chauffeur leaped out and opened the door, and Latovsky eased her into the back as if she were a piece of fragile china.

"Jesus," Harris said from next to Adam, "bet Dave works out lifting refrigerators."

"You know him?"

"Met a few times at Bunner's."

"What's he like?" Adam asked, watching the scene at the limousine. The boys and older couple got in back with Mary. Latovsky and the girl, whose hair was the exact color of Latovsky's, stood aside. The doors closed, the limousine hummed away, and Latovsky and the girl crossed the road to a beat-up Olds.

The girl must be his daughter, and Adam wondered where the wife was.

"Nice enough in a gruff man's-man way," Harris was saying. "God knows he's strong. Going to the party?"

"The what?"

"Don't know what else you'd call it. It's not a wake since he's in the ground. Don't know if Episcopalians have wakes, being Congregational myself. So I guess it's a party . . . at Bunner's house."

• •

THE HOUSE WAS PACKED WHEN ADAM GOT THERE. Air-conditioning fought the heat of the crowd and the afternoon sun streaming through the windows and lost. Adam kept an eye on Latovsky, which was easy since he was the tallest one there.

He followed him across the foyer to the dining room, which was set up with tables of salads and cold meats, and Latovsky got something fizzy to drink from Al Cohen, who was tending bar. Adam got a glass of white wine and started to follow the lieutenant into the hall, but Vanderveer stopped Adam at the door.

"Anything on Baines yet?" he asked.

"Not yet." Adam tried to get around him, but Vanderveer blocked the way.

"I'm sure it'll be okay. I'm sure the grading's right," Vanderveer didn't sound sure.

"I'll let you know."

"She'll be fine."

"I hope so."

Vanderveer pulled the handkerchief out of his breast pocket and mopped his streaming face. "Hot as shit in here," he said. "Well, you'll let me know."

"Soon as I do," Adam said. Vanderveer finally got out of his way, but Latovsky had disappeared.

He wasn't in the living room and Adam went down a wide carpeted hall to a space-module kitchen with women refilling platters, and Ada Cohen, whom he'd met at several hospital functions, sitting at a stark white plastic table, crying. Latovsky wasn't there.

Down another hall he came to a back staircase; Mary must be upstairs in drug limbo.

Then he came to a large den–family room that was almost as crowded as the living room, but open sliding glass doors in one wall kept it cooler.

Latovsky wasn't there either.

He went down another hall back to the front of the house and the living room and there he was, standing at the mantel with some people around him. Naomi was a few feet away with a bunch from the hospital and when she waggled her fingers at Adam to come over, he went and maneuvered himself to face Latovsky.

Latovsky didn't say much; he smiled a few times, but that only accentuated the sorrow in his eyes, and once he laughed, a sound that made Adam's flesh creep, although it was deep and pleasant. Suddenly the word *formidable* came to Adam and he knew David Latovsky wouldn't shiver or shake at the sight of the Python or fall apart at the kneecapping threat even if Adam got it out with a straight face.

The Colt would blow as big a hole in the lieutenant as it had in Bunner, but that wouldn't get Adam any closer to *her* and this man wouldn't tell him anything he didn't want to no matter what Adam threatened him with. Worse, Latovsky was big enough, strong—*for-*

midable—enough to get the Colt away from Adam and blow a hole in *him*.

David Latovsky wasn't just a dead end, he was dangerous, and Adam would be a horrendous fool to take him on with a Python, or anything else he could come up with.

Better safe than sorry, his mother would say and she'd be right again. He'd have to find another way to find *her*.

"Doctor Fuller?" Ada Cohen called from the living room doorway, "Is Adam Fuller here?"

The room hushed a little and Adam called back, "Here," and threaded his way through the crowd to the door.

"Phone," Ada said. "You can take it there." She nodded at a phone off the hook on the foyer table. "It'll be quieter than in the kitchen."

He thanked her and glanced back into the room.

Latovsky was watching him.

• •

LIL TOOMEY WAS ON THE PHONE.

"Baines's done," she told Adam, "and I got bad news and good news. Which do you want first?"

"Just say it, Lil."

"Okay. Vanderveer had his head up his ass on the grading. We've got a mitotic, highly invasive tumor and I'm regrading it three."

"Shit."

He'd told Ellen it was okay, that she'd go home to her garden in ten days. Vanderveer had made a liar out of him.

"That's the bad news," Lil said.

Adam felt someone behind him and turned. Latovsky was in the living room doorway, watching him over the rim of his glass with his eyes slitted against the carbonation. Adam's heart gave a thud, sweat popped out on his hand holding the receiver, and he turned away, cupping the mouthpiece.

"The good news?" he asked.

"No sign of local spread," Lil said. "You worked fast and Stern probably got it all. But you'll have to check."

That *was* good. He'd set up a consult with Sykes tonight, see what came next. Lymphangiogram probably, and that meant Ellen would have to go to Albany.

Even if it was negative, Sykes would recommend chemotherapy

and Ellen was in for a few long, miserable months. She'd miss spring after all.

He heard Latovsky move closer and sweat ran up his arm from the phone.

"I'll get there as soon as I can, Lil," he said.

"Don't rush. No one's going to tell her for you. Sorry, Adam, I hate shit like this."

"Me too." Poor Ellen. He had to tell her so she'd understand that it was serious, but hopeful.

"See ya," Lil said.

They hung up and he turned and almost barged into Latovsky. Adam backed up and hit the side of the staircase. He was trapped between it and the massive cop and more sweat ran down his face. Latovsky would notice, but everyone was sweating, including Latovsky.

"Fuller," Latovsky said slowly. "Any relation to Donald Fuller of Sawyerville?"

"He's my father. I'm Adam Fuller."

"Dave Latovsky." They shook; Latovsky's huge hand was cold and damp from the glass.

"Small world," Latovsky said. "I went to Sawyerville on Sunday to see your father but he wasn't home. I left a note for him to call me, but so far . . ." Latovsky shrugged.

Adam managed a smile that felt pretty steady. "He's not the best-organized man, to put it mildly, but he'll get around to it . . . ah, actually he won't, though. He asked me to find out what it was all about, seeing as I'm in Glenvale and he hates making long-distance calls."

"That right?" Latovsky's eyes bored into his.

"Yes. What did you want to see him about?"

Latovsky seemed to find Adam's eyes fascinating, and more sweat trickled down Adam's face.

"About a summer house your family rented on Raven Lake in nineteen sixty," Latovsky said.

Raven Lake.

"Oh? What about it?"

"It figures in a case I'm working on."

Woman-in-the-Woods.

"I see. Well, I guess you'll have to talk to him after all. I was only a kid then, don't remember anything about it."

"I see."

"Uh . . . that was the hospital. A patient of mine is much sicker than I thought . . . or led her to think . . . and I have to go to her."

"A patient—you a patient of Bunner's, by any chance?"

"Not anymore," Adam said, then realized how cold that sounded and tried to look sad.

"But you were?" Latovsky asked.

"Yes."

"Emotional problems?"

Snide fucking question, Adam thought, and snapped. "I didn't go to a hundred-buck-an-hour shrink for a skin rash, Mr. Latovsky."

"It's Lieutenant Latovsky."

"Oh. Well, as I said . . ."

"Yes, your patient." But Latovsky still blocked the way; his eyes drilled into Adam's, then flickered as if he finally remembered where he'd seen Adam before, and he stepped back.

● ●

THROUGH A WINDOW, LATOVSKY WATCHED FULLER BACK HIS Ford out, then down the drive. Latovsky pulled out his notebook, wrote down the tag number, then watched Fuller make a screeching U-turn and speed away to the patient . . . or away from Latovsky. He looked out at the full driveway and empty street and thought, *Dead, cold, empty eyes . . . doll's eyes.*

Unless he was drunk, and he wasn't, he had just seen them in Adam Fuller's face.

● ●

ADAM LET HIMSELF INTO THE HOUSE AND WENT RIGHT TO THE grate. He tried to pry it up with his bare fingers, but couldn't, and had to get the screwdriver out of the tool drawer in the kitchen. He slipped it under the rim and saw blood on the handle where he'd torn his skin trying to do it barehanded; *haste makes waste,* his mother would say. The handle was slippery and he had to go back for paper towels to hold it with. He got the grate up, reached into the vent, which was cool since it was too warm for the heat to come on, and grabbed the scalpel. He took time to wipe the handle of the screwdriver and put it away, then more time to cushion the blade of the scalpel with more paper towels so it wouldn't slice a hole in his pocket, and he finally left the house.

This was the moment when he was most vulnerable, because if

Latovsky and a cruiser full of cops screamed into the street with a warrant, they'd find the scalpel that had killed five women, and, in the glove compartment, the Python he'd used on Bunner.

But that was pretty paranoid; no way on earth Latovsky could have gotten a warrant in the twenty minutes that had elapsed since Adam left Bunner's, no matter what he suspected.

He wanted to run to the car anyway, but made himself walk sedately in case one of his neighbors looked out their window and wondered why the nice young doctor at number 48 was in such a rush.

He got into the car, his jacket swinging from the weight of the scalpel, and drove away.

The street was empty.

● ●

"FULLER," LATOVSKY SAID, "ADAM FULLER."

"Yeah, I got to it." Cohen took a deep swig out of his glass. He was already half fried, the glass was full again, and it looked like he was getting seriously drunk. Latovsky wouldn't mind joining him.

"I got to the M's" Cohen said. "What about Fuller?"

"You tell me."

The dining room had cooled as the crowd thinned and Bunny's last party ended. The thought choked Latovsky and he had to turn away from Cohen.

"Yeah," Cohen said softly, "it just comes out of nowhere and bites you in the ass, doesn't it?"

"Fuller," Latovsky said hoarsely.

"Okay, Adam Paul Fuller. I have a photographic memory you know." Cohen giggled drunkenly. "Actually I don't, no one does. But I remember him because his problem's interesting even if it is pretty common."

"What problem."

"A little background first. Adam Paul Fuller, M.D., Dartmouth—on a full scholarship by the way. Gotta be smart to do that, Dave; then intern at Boston General, internal medicine residency and certification, also Boston General. Came to Glenvale two years ago because we're small but choice, believe it or not, a respected teaching hospital in hillbilly heaven."

"C'mon, Al. Stay with it."

"Yeah. He's well thought of, if not particularly well liked—but not disliked either. He's unmarried, has no steady girlfriends. He'll rise in the ranks, maybe head the department someday if he hangs around, which he probably won't since the good ones don't . . . except for the likes of me and Bunny. Only me now, Bunny's not hanging around anymore."

Cohen coughed hard and took a huge swallow.

"He sounds okay," Latovsky said.

"Does, doesn't he?"

"Then why'd he see Bunny?"

"Because he wasn't okay. Because his life sucked. Because they teach you to win in med school, and you never do because everyone dies. And some die when they shouldn't, and some of them are your patients and it cuts your heart out. Hard to swallow helplessness in our Mr. Fixit world, and Fuller couldn't swallow it so he did what lots of young doctors do—he shut down."

"I don't get you."

"He stopped feeling. It's not uncommon and it's a good defense for a while. But then the day comes when you want to love a woman . . . a kid . . . a dog. To feel *something,* and you've forgotten how and are half afraid to remember because there're all those poor, sad, sick folks waiting to make a monkey out of you by dying, so you stay cold, empty, disaffected, and impotent—"

"Impotent! Is Fuller impotent?" The killer was not.

"I meant figuratively, Dave. Fuller did report one instance when he couldn't get it up with some bimbo he actively didn't like. Couldn't do the cold-hearted fucking all macho types are supposed to do. Good for him, I say; got enough cold-hearted fucking in this world. Whyn't you pour yourself a drink, pull up a chair, and we'll talk about cold-hearted fucking and how it's gonna kill half the population of the planet with AIDS."

"Another time, Al. Stay with Fuller."

"Not much more to stay with. Except for that one time, he seems to be a young man with average appetites and the ability to satisfy them, except for this one kink."

"What kink?"

"What we've been talking about. The poor schmuck doesn't *feel* anything. He has urges, they start to keep him up at night, then he goes to a bar, finds a woman, and fucks her. But he doesn't feel anything for her, so he throws away her number, goes home, and forgets until the urge comes back. But he can't call the last one because he probably doesn't even remember her name by then, so he gets another one, doesn't feel anything, and so on. It's a round robin of emotional anesthesia that feeds on itself until life in general and sex in particular are about as exciting and joyous as brushing your teeth. So he went to Bunny."

"And?"

"And it was slow going, but Bunny thought they were making progress."

Some progress. If Latovsky was right, Adam Fuller had lured five women into the woods, sliced them open from pubis to rib cage, then shot his doctor in the face. Adam Fuller was doing great.

"Why pick on him?" Cohen asked.

Latovsky couldn't tell him about a psychic seeing a killer with "doll's eyes" so he shrugged and said, "Met him here, and he said he was Bunny's patient, so I got curious."

● ●

IT WAS PITCH DARK IN O.R. 4 AND ADAM HAD TO FEEL ALONG the wall for the switch. He found it and light flooded the operating room, hitting the autoclave against the wall.

Adam pressed the old-fashioned foot pedal, the lid swung open, and steam billowed out. He stripped the paper towels off the scalpel and put the gleaming steel instrument on the tray with others beaded with steam. Half an hour in there and they'd need an electron microscope to find a trace of blood or tissue on it and backcountry cops didn't have electron microscopes.

He raised his foot, the lid closed, cutting off the hypnotic shine of the instruments in a final puff of steam.

It was over.

He couldn't risk taking another woman into the woods, but it hadn't worked with five, it wouldn't with ten, and he didn't enjoy the killing. It had never been about killing, as he'd tried to explain to Bunner. But poor Bunny had been too terrified to listen.

He had one last thing to do; find *her,* and thanks to Latovsky, he finally knew where to look.

Raven Lake.

She had seen Abby die across the lake (he'd gotten that at the dance from Bunner) and called the cops. Latovsky showed up, she somehow convinced him she'd seen a murder across that half a mile of black water, and Latovsky had taken her to Bunner for confirmation. Her seeing Ken's scars *was* confirmation, Adam thought, and she'd left

Bunner in turmoil and gone back to the house on Raven Lake that Adam's old man had rented for the summer of '60 *because she lived there.*

When he found it, he'd find her.

He'd use the Colt one last time, then drop it in one of the twenty or so lakes between Raven Lake and Glenvale. It would sink into the bottom slime and stay there until the lake dried up at the end of some future ice age, and Lieutenant Latovsky could shove his suspicions up his ass.

He wanted to enjoy the huge cop's imminent defeat, but that was no more possible than pitying the women. *All he got for all his trouble was a hatful of rain.*

He should get that line out of his head, because it smacked of self-pity and he didn't pity himself any more than he had Abby or Bunner.

He turned out the lights, left the O.R., and went down the dim, deserted corridor to the elevators. Ellen would be awake by now, but not aware enough to take in what he had to tell her. And he wanted to be sure she understood that the final diagnosis warranted the misery they'd put her through, but was not a death sentence. Far from it and with any luck she'd have her garden this time next year. "Next year," he whispered to himself as he pushed the DOWN button. "Next year, Ellen."

●   ●

"GO ON." LEM MEERS PUT A LABATT'S IN FRONT OF LATOVSKY and took one for himself. He sat across from Latovsky at the kitchen table with his storklike legs stretched to the side. Joan Meers was in the den watching the news, and the dinner dishes were done even though it was just six. The Meerses were mountain people and they ate at five and went to bed at nine. "If it ain't happened by nine, t'ain't gonna by nine thirty," Meers liked to twang. The twang was an artifact he reverted to to remind himself and everyone else where he came from.

"It was just a feeling," Latovsky said, "but it was strong, Lem. Overwhelming. A real case of that good cop instinct you told me never to ignore."

"And it told you?"

"He killed Bunner."

"This guy at the funeral."

Latovsky nodded, and Meers was quiet for a moment. He made the Olympic ring sign on the plastic table cover with the beer bottle, looked at it, then up at Latovsky. "Tell me about him," he said quietly.

Latovsky did, and Meers looked gaunter than ever and very unhappy by the time Latovsky finished.

"Dave, we can't do this. You're talking about a physician, a pillar of the community who's got the dough and smarts to sue us into the next century."

"That's why I'm asking instead of just doing it."

"And that's why I've got to say no. I can't go to Linney with 'cop instinct' on an M.D. at Glenvale General." Roger Linney was county prosecutor.

"I don't want you to go to Linney. Just tell me I can go after Fuller on the sly."

"Not on the sly or any other way unless you got something that can stretch to probable cause. Do you?"

"No . . ." Latovsky looked down at the table.

"Then Adam Fuller gets treated exactly like the others on Bunner's patient list until you do. How many, by the way?"

"Twenty-six."

"Shit."

"Yeah. It'll take weeks."

They were quiet. Meers studied the rings on the table cover, Latovsky swigged the beer, then asked, "What if Cohen says Fuller's the likeliest?"

"Then we're over the hump of *reasonable* if not probable cause and can claim good will. Will he say it?"

"Probably not," Latovsky mumbled.

"Then Fuller's just one of twenty-six until you *do* get something and if you spend an extra second on him without justification that sounds vaguely legally plausible, you'll queer the whole case. You got such a justification?"

A psychic told me, Latovsky thought.

Lem Meers was smart and imaginative, incorruptible and fair; he was the best boss on the troop, the force, maybe in the world, but Latovsky couldn't expect him to pop for a psychic from Connecticut and he shook his head.

"What about motive?" Meers asked. "Or you think he's just a nut who had to kill someone and Bunner won the toss."

"I don't think he's a nut, Lem . . ." Latovsky took a long, shaky breath and said, "I think he confessed to Bunner, then panicked when he realized what he'd done, and killed him."

"Confessed what?"

Another long, even shakier breath, and Latovsky said, "Killing the women in the woods."

Shock flashed through Meers's eyes. It took him a moment to regain his normal imperturbability, then he asked gently, "More cop instinct, Dave?"

"Yes, and I know exactly how it sounds, so don't bother telling me."

Meers gazed at the man he'd known for twenty years. Dave Latovsky was the best he had, the best there was short of the Bureau, and maybe even better than their best. In another time and place, with more to do than clean up the debris of human greed, lust, stupidity, and bad temper, Latovsky would have been a legend. But this was here and now and Dave's personal life was a wreck. He lived alone on a backwoods lake, fished alone, spent two weekends a month with his beloved daughter, one day a month with his beloved mother, and a few nights in between with his girlfriend, who was not beloved. His best friend had been shot in the face on Sunday, planted today, and it wasn't such a stretch to see how Dave could mistake loneliness, anguish, and thirst for vengeance for good cop instinct.

Maybe Meers had made a mistake giving Latovsky the Bunner case after all, and he looked hard for a trace of murkiness in his old friend's eyes.

But they were as cold and clear as ever, icily perceptive eyes that saw everything they looked at, whether they wanted to or not. An admirable trait in a cop, not so great in a husband or lover, Meers thought. For instance, Allison hadn't been a bad woman. She'd had her petty, bitchy moments just like most people, maybe a few more than average, but she was also gorgeous, with eyes like a Byzantine mosaic and tits like footballs. She was a good housekeeper, a conscientious mother, and she'd been mad about Latovsky. Another man would've discounted her lapses or never seen them. But Latovsky had turned the icy white light of those eyes and the mind behind them on his wife's behavior, had seen every small mean thing she'd ever done for exactly what it was—small and mean—and couldn't not see, forget or forgive.

Now that brutal clarity had turned itself on a down-home doctor—a healer, a white hat—and seen a killer. Dave believed it to his core or he'd never hang his ass out to dry like this. And because he believed it and because he was Dave (and there was nothing wrong with his mind, even if his emotions were as husked out as a long-dead beetle), Meers had to believe it a little, too.

● ●

LATOVSKY DIDN'T HAVE MEERS'S PERMISSION TO GO AFTER FULLER when he left Meers's house, but didn't have his interdict either; a very important point and they both knew it. Meers had called a buddy of his at Quantico, gotten access to the big computer without forms and faxes, and found nothing on Fuller, but Latovsky hadn't expected him to: Adam Fuller was a choirboy . . . with a glitch.

It was starting to get dark, the town was shut down, and from now until seven tomorrow morning there'd be plenty of parking places on Main Street. Rose's was closed, the lights glowed invitingly through the windows of The Loft, and Latovsky thought of stopping for dinner and a drink—or five drinks—but he kept going, trying to figure out what to do next.

Sleep, he thought. Go home, put a frozen pizza or chicken pie in the microwave, try to relax in front of the tube for an hour or so, then sleep and wake up clearheaded.

He was through town, at the far end of Main Street where buildings petered out and the in-town two families started, when he realized he was kidding himself.

This was the day of Bunny's funeral and Latovsky knew who killed him. He could not go home and pretend it was a day like any other and he hit the brake and pulled into the IGA parking lot. A few late shoppers were trundling carts to their cars, the vapor lights were on and the first flies of the evening massed around them.

He stopped the car and picked up the phone. The station was only three miles away; the phone worked and he got Barber.

"I need an address for Adam P. Fuller."

"D'ja try the phone book?" Barber asked. He really meant it, and Latovsky said, "God, what a brilliant idea; I might even do it if I had one."

"Sorry," Barber mumbled, and put Latovsky on hold. A couple of minutes of dead air and Barber came back with an address on Rusty Pond, about ten minutes from the IGA. Latovsky fished for his pen to write it down, then realized *48 Rusty Pond Road* had burned into his brain the second he'd heard it and would probably stay there long after he'd forgotten his current address or his mother's. Only Eve's would stay with him longer—Tilden House, Old Warren Road, Bridgeton—and the picture of her that went with it, with her greeny brown eyes sparkling with half-drunken tears when she'd seen Bunner's busted tape recorder.

He put the Olds in gear, drove out of the lot exit, and turned left, away from his house. As he fed the Olds gas, the ridiculous phrase *The hunt is up* went through his head and his heart beat a little faster.

●   ●

RUSTY POND WAS A CUL DE SAC WITH STATE LAND ON ONE SIDE and a block of builders' Colonials on the other that probably had pink tile bathrooms and pistachio green toilets, tubs, and sinks. Some building conglomerate must've made a killing on closeouts of pink tile and pistachio green bathroom fixtures in the fifties, Latovsky thought.

The houses were small and neat and Fuller's was the neatest, with a crew-cut front lawn and shrubs trimmed to wooden perfection.

Latovsky went to the end of the street, turned around and parked in the lay-by the state had cut for hikers and fishermen. He waited until the sky went from dove gray to gunmetal, then sprayed himself with Cutter's bug-off and walked back along the road to number 48.

The house was dark but Fuller could have returned from the hospital and be eating his solitary supper in the back. Latovsky knew from Cohen, who knew from Bunner's file, that Adam Fuller lived alone.

He went along a side path between Fuller's land and a hedge that bordered the lot next door to Fuller's garage. He looked in the side-door window and saw his reflection, backed by the sky; cupping his hands around his face, he looked again and still saw nothing. The door was unlocked; he opened it and shone his penlight around an empty, immaculate garage that didn't even have an oil stain on the concrete floor.

He closed the door and went along the path to the back yard.

"Don't shit on the Constitution any more than you have to," Meers had pleaded with him. But he was already doing it and whatever he found—such as an oil drum in which Fuller had burned clothes stiff with Abigail Reese's blood or a soft patch in the earth where he'd buried the "big-mother" gun he'd used on Bunner—would be tainted fruit of the tainted tree: *toxic* fruit.

He could claim that he just happened to be next door, looked over and saw . . . whatever he saw. But even that meager fiction went to hell when he got past the house to the back yard because it was ringed with evergreens so thickly planted you couldn't see a bonfire from the next yard.

There wasn't anything to see anyway; a back porch, dark windows, a hose wrapped around a caddy and attached to a spigot in the side of the house. Not even a barbecue or outdoor table; Adam P. Fuller, M.D. and serial killer, didn't do much outdoor entertaining.

Latovsky flashed the penlight across the back porch and got a gleam of glass in the back door. He went up the wooden steps to a decklike porch and looked through the glass into a kitchen lit from the hall. It was the dim, solitary light people leave on so they don't come back to a dark house and it showed a room of regimental neatness: no orange juice or milk carton had been left out, no coffee pot waited to be washed later, no box of cereal sat on the counter or dishes to be rinsed for the washer. The kitchen was perfect—like Latovsky's kitchen.

The table was covered with a flowered plastic cloth, like Meers's and Latovsky's and probably most of the kitchen tables in town. Levy's variety store in Glenvale center must do the bulk of its business in flowered plastic tablecloths.

The table was clear, the counters bare except for a set of ceramic canisters and an old-fashioned cookie jar in the shape of a puffed-cheeked face with a three-cornered hat for the lid. Odd for a man living alone to have a cookie jar; maybe Fuller was a fag who screwed the women to show he wasn't, then realized anew that he was and killed in a convulsion of self-loathing.

Shit-think. You didn't have to be a fag to have a cookie jar.

He turned away. There was a recycling setup on the porch with separate bins for glass, cans, paper, and plastic, and next to them a large, high-impact-plastic garbage container.

Latovsky raised the cover, and smells of spoiling food, coffee grounds, and moldering citrus rinds wafted out.

He didn't want to, but there was nothing left to do except cut dolls out of the papers waiting for the recyclers. He pushed up his jacket sleeves, unbuttoned the cuffs of the good dress shirt he'd put on for Bunner's funeral (that seemed half a century ago), rolled up the sleeves, and dug in.

He felt soft this, slippery that, found cartons from lots of frozen dinners, especially Swanson's chicken pot pies, which Latovsky also favored.

Fuller made fresh morning coffee, as Latovsky did, and squeezed fresh orange juice, which Latovsky didn't. Then he touched something small, hard, and sharp-edged that didn't feel like the rest of the muck, and he made himself grasp it and pull it out.

He shone the penlight on it and saw smeared thick yellow ooze that he recognized as chicken pot pie gravy. He carried it down the steps to the edge of the lawn, wiped it clean on the grass, and shone the penlight on a tape cassette of Bach sonatas played by Yo Yo Ma.

Fuller had good taste in music, or maybe not, since he'd thrown this away. Maybe he'd grabbed it in a rush in a discount mart thinking it was 2 Live Crew or some other bunch of morons, and he'd put it on, expecting mindless cacophony, and gotten Bach, then pitched it out in a rage . . . but kept the case?

Why?

To hide the tape he'd taken from Bunner's machine.

The answer came without thought or fanfare. One minute he didn't have it, the next he did, and he knew Eve had been right about the doll's eyes as she had about everything else.

He jammed the cassette into the pocket of his good suit, gravy and all, and pounded back up the wooden steps, shaking the whole porch structure.

No more Mr. Nice Guy, he thought crazily and turned the knob. The door was locked, of course, but the lock didn't look like much and he took out his Swiss army knife, which had an awl kind of thing he'd never used before. He pried it up and thought, *Tainted fruit, nothing.* He was about to break and enter and commit criminal trespass, and Linney was too much of a hard-ass to let it go. He could wind up in the slammer, and even if he got clear, the tape would be inadmissible. But Meers had friends among the brass; he'd figure out some way if Latovsky presented him with hard evidence that Fuller had shot Bunner. He let all this flash through his mind for a nanosecond, then thought, *fuck it,* jammed the awl into the lock—and heard tires crunch on gravel. He froze as the garage door ratcheted open and a car pulled in.

Latovsky pulled the awl out of the lock and crouched on the deck.

The engine stopped, the car door slammed, followed by the click of leather heels (dress shoes for the funeral) on the garage floor. The door into the house opened, then closed, lights came on inside, made slanting rectangles on the porch and Latovsky was trapped. He was six four and weighed 230; if he tried to slip down the slat steps like a wood nymph and disappear into the ground fog, Fuller would hear him, throw open the door, and it would all be for nothing. Fuller was a fiend, not a fool; he'd know what he had that could hang him and he'd destroy the tape.

Latovsky stayed in the crouch, listening to Fuller on the other side of the wall. Water ran, but not loudly enough to drown out other noises, then the furnace throbbed as it fired up. It was getting cold; Latovsky's hands were damp from the garbage and freezing as the goo on them stiffened. Flies whined around his head, attracted by the smell, but the Cutter's kept them at bay. His spine felt fused; he thought it would pop like gunshots if he straightened it. He couldn't stay like this much longer: another minute or two at most and he'd have to move.

Then he heard the click of leather soles crossing the kitchen. They faded away, and the opening chords of Beethoven's Fifth crashed through the house. Under its cover, Latovsky eased himself down the stairs and scuttled around the side of the house to the road.

● ●

ADAM HUNG UP HIS JACKET, PULLED DOWN HIS TIE, THEN WENT back into the den and sank into his easy chair. For once, he was too lazy to untie his shoes properly, and he pushed them off with his feet, scuffing the heel of one. His mother would not approve.

He gave himself five minutes of listening to music, then hauled himself to his feet and headed for the kitchen. He couldn't remember ever being this tired; partly the strain of waiting for Latovsky to ring the bell with a warrant, he thought, and partly the wait to give Ellen Baines the rotten news he had for her. He'd tried, but her eyes had opened slowly, looked blearily at him, then past him, then closed again.

He'd tell her tomorrow.

He picked up the phone, punched in the number in Sawyerville, and his father answered on the second ring, sounding more or less sober.

"It's Adam, Pop."

"Recognized your voice," his father said drily.

"I spoke to that lieutenant, the one who left the card?"

"Remember that too."

"Yeah, well, he said all he wanted was to know if we were the Fullers who rented a cottage on Raven Lake for the summer of nineteen sixty."

Silence at the other end.

"Were we, Pop?"

"What's he want to know a thing like that for?"

"Something about a case he's working on. Were we, Pop?"

"Jesus, I almost forgot, it was so long ago. Yeah, we were, boy. Best summer we ever had, too. You'n Mikey were in that lake or on it in a little skiff that came with the house all day every day. Unless you were on the swing. You were mad about that swing."

Swing. He saw the sky moving in jagged patches through a jigsaw of leaves. *Swing . . .*

He tried to hold on to the vision, expand it to see the house and lake . . . and maybe his five-year-old self and twelve-year-old Mikey. But the picture faded until it was only words: *jagged patches of sky through leaves.*

"Where was it, Pop?"

"Raven Lake, just like we been talking about." A hint of impatience.

"Where on Raven Lake?"

"Don't remember anymore—it's been thirty years."

The old fart had to remember. Adam had seen lights from twenty or thirty houses around the lake from Frank's parking lot and there'd be more that were shut up until the flies were gone. He had to have the address.

"Try, Pop."

"I could try till my balls turned to brass, boy. I can't and that's—" He stopped, then said excitedly, "Hold on now, just hold on a damn minute here. Bet it's in your ma's files. Woman kept every piece of paper ever crossed her hand, all neatly labeled and filed. You remember her files, son?"

Adam did: a series of large brown cardboard accordion envelopes with elastic around them. He'd looked in them years ago in case his father or brother (slipshod men) had missed important papers. The cardboard was faded and grainy, the elastic had lost its snap, but her neat backslanted printing was still clear and black against the ivory-colored index tabs and, halfway into the first accordion, he'd started feeling uneasy. The feeling reminded him of when he played Joseph in the grammar school Christmas pageant, a feeling that he'd swallowed something alive and it was trying to bat its way out of his gut. Only handling something *she'd* handled was much worse than the Christmas pageant jitters; it actually made him sick to his stomach and he'd given up less than three quarters through the first of about twenty accordions.

Everything that had been hers had the same effect on him, except the old cookie jar. It was in the shape of a head with puffed red cheeks that were supposed to look cheery, but he'd always imagined a sad look in the eyes, and globs of glaze around the lids made them appear to be brimming with tears. It was the only thing he'd taken from the house in Sawyerville, her only possession that didn't give him the whim-whams.

He couldn't remember her face, which was another oddity. There were photos of her around the house wearing one of her endless collection of flowered dresses and he'd looked at them, tried to fix the face in his mind. But it was gone the second he looked away, leaving him with an image of a flowered dress and a smear where the head should be.

His father came back on. "Got it, son," he said happily. "She kept the lease. Kept a lease on a summer house we rented in 1960. Whatta woman! She should've been CEO for some big corporation or something."

"The address, Pop?"

"Lease is between me'n Alan Rodney of Glenvale. It's for July and August nineteen sixty for five hundred bucks. Can you believe it? Five hundred bucks for a season in a house right on the lake; close enough to spit in it from the back porch. Bet it goes for five thousand nowadays."

"The address, Pop?"

"Three hundred Lakeshore, Raven Lake."

10

THE WIND HAD SHIFTED BY MORNING, AND IT was cold and starting to drizzle from sky the color of a cataract when Adam pulled past 300 Lakeshore and parked on the road shoulder.

He couldn't march up the driveway to the front of the house. She might know why he was there if she saw him, and call for help. He wanted to get into the house without her knowing, if he could, but that meant getting a look at the place first.

The best way was through the woods.

He sprayed on bug-off, got out of the car, and went into the trees. It was easy going at first, then the trees and underbrush thickened, twigs lashed him and caught at his clothes, and decades worth of dead leaves underfoot had gotten slippery in the drizzle. He should have seen the lake by now and started to worry that he'd gone wrong and was paralleling the lake instead of heading toward it. He'd have to go back to the road (if he could find it) and start over, staying closer to the drive. Then he saw a flash of inky water and got his bearings. He veered right, and a few yards more slogging brought him to the clearing and the house.

The house was small and pretty, with a patch of lawn in front and evergreen shrubs along the front porch. But the windows were dark, there was no car in the turnaround, and no garage. You had to have a car out here, so she must have driven into town.

He could've passed her car in the Grand Union lot in Raven Lake, or maybe she worked in an office in town or at the little stone bank on the main drag. He didn't know if she had a job, was old or young, single or married, pretty or plain. He didn't know anything about her except that she could *see* what no one else could, and she was dangerous.

Not just dangerous, he thought, and an idea flashed through his head. It came and went before he could catch it, and he told himself it probably didn't matter anyway. But it did, something in the back of his mind insisted, it mattered a lot.

He tried to recapture it and couldn't.

If it was important, it would come back to him sooner or later, and he stepped out of the shelter of trees into the clearing.

He didn't remember the house, or the swing his father said he'd loved. *Wrong, Pop,* he thought. He'd never loved anything. But he'd played on it, must've yelled, "Higher, Daddy, push me higher," the way kids do. Or more likely, "Higher, Mikey," since his old man would have been in Sawyerville during the week and sitting on the porch here getting shit-faced on weekends.

And where was his mother all that time?

Inside, he thought. Ironing, baking, cooking, and cleaning. He tried to see her doing it, but only got the usual image of her flowered dress, broad shoulders, and strong pillar of a neck rising to the stocking-mask blur where her face should be.

He passed the swing and went up the porch steps to the front door.

It was locked, but the lock was old; he could get in and be waiting when she got back. He slid his Amoco card out of his wallet, jammed it into the door slot, and pushed. The latch resisted a second, then gave way and snapped back. He froze and listened in case the signs were wrong and she was there after all. He didn't hear anything except the honk of a lone outrider goose leading the way north for the summer, and he opened the door and entered the house on Raven Lake for the first time in thirty-three years.

● ●

THERE WAS A SMALL ENTRY WITH A HOOKED RUG ON THE FLOOR, and to the right a large sitting room with a stone fireplace, more hooked rugs, and large pieces of furniture covered with dust sheets.

The dust sheets took a second to register, then Adam leaned against the door frame, a little surprised at how disappointed he was. You didn't cover your furniture with dust sheets to go shopping in town; you did it when you were going away for a long time . . . or when your last tenant had left, and your next one hadn't arrived yet. Either way, she was gone. His search wasn't over, after all. It had just started, and he didn't know what to do.

Go back, he thought. It was a little after ten; if he left now, he'd be back in Glenvale to talk to Ellen Baines before they brought her lunch.

But he was here; there might be a clue in the house to who she was or where she'd gone. He was also curious if anything about the place would bring back that "best summer ever."

He pushed himself away from the wall and crossed the sitting room to a rolltop desk in the corner. He avoided the waxed floor that he might leave footprints on and pulled on the gloves he'd brought before he rolled up the top. The drawers were empty but, crumpled in the back of a cubbyhole, he found a 1988 bill from Adirondack Oil marked paid, and a receipt from Raven Lake Ski and Sport dated eleven days ago. It was for $250.00 and made out to S. Klein.

She could be S. Klein or it could be her husband's name. Someone at Raven Lake Ski and Sport might remember S. Klein spending $250 on item 406 in burgundy. He slipped the receipt in his pocket and went on with the search.

Nothing else at all in the sitting room: The drawers in the tables were empty, the hearth had been swept clean. Nothing in the linen closet or hall closet either, except bent wire hangers.

The first bedroom he came to brought on a sinking sense of recall much stronger than he'd had in Frank's parking lot six days ago.

He didn't *remember* the room, but he knew it had been Mikey's and his and there'd been bunk beds in place of the neatly made twins with an Adirondack table between them.

He searched the room and only found more twisted hangers casting strange spidery shadows on the closet wall. Then he went on to a hall bathroom that smelled of a new plastic shower curtain they'd put up for the tenants who'd arrive in a van with kids, toys, videos, and the wife's favorite skillet. The bathroom was spotless. The pebbled window high in the wall was painted shut; the lights and a vent fan came on when he flicked the switch.

They'd left the electricity on.

He didn't know why that seemed important to him, but it did.

The next room was much larger, with a king-sized bed covered with candlewick as blindingly white as the spread in his folks' room had been before his mother died. The sight of it brought on the shivers and low-grade nausea he'd felt in the master bedroom in Sawyerville and he had to force himself to go in and search. He found a bottle of aspirin in an old-fashioned tin medicine cabinet, more hangers, and a lone, lint-covered man's sock in the back of a bureau drawer.

The next room was neutral, a den with built-in book shelves, with a few tattered copies of Reader's Digest condensed novels, an ancient cribbage board, and a phone and phone book.

He opened the phone book and ran his finger down the K's without much hope. No Klein, S. or otherwise, and he put the book back and went out into the hall.

It was a small house. There was nothing left to look at except a room behind a swinging door with a brass handplate that must be the kitchen. He pushed open the door to an old-fashioned room as spare and spotless as the O.R.s at Glenvale General. The counters and sink, cabinets and walls were white; the floor was green-streaked white linoleum and there was a white porcelain table with rust-colored nicks around the edge, one of those solid old tables that had probably been there for a half a century. Across the room was a black rotary-dial wall phone with a pad under it. The pad looked blank from here, but if he ran a pencil lightly across it the way they did in spy movies, her last message might appear with a better clue than the receipt. It was a long shot, but worth trying. He started to enter the kitchen and couldn't get his foot to cross the threshold.

He couldn't believe that had happened and he tried again by sliding his foot up the doorsill to the middle, and there it froze solid no matter how hard he tried to push it across.

He tried again, then again, but some connection between his brain and lower limbs seemed to have snapped, and he couldn't perform the simple task of getting his foot to cross the threshold of the nice, old-fashioned kitchen.

It was absurd. There was nothing more automatic than putting one foot in front of the other except for breathing and blinking. You could always do it, unless you'd had some central-nervous-system injury.

He took another tack and raised one foot straight up in the air like a stork, then tried to swing it over the sill. It got halfway and stopped as if an invisible wall or forcefield filled the doorway. He tried the other foot with the same result. Then he decided to jump across.

He tensed, his muscles tightened the way they should, but his body wouldn't move.

He was covered with sweat by now; it ran down his face and back, his shirt clung to him, the Python he'd meant to use on her felt like a block of wet ice in his belt. He slackened his body, trying to fool whatever it was into thinking he'd given up, then he tensed quickly to jump and couldn't.

He sagged against the door jamb and looked at the room, trying to see what about it was doing this to him. He saw plain cabinets with glass knobs, old drawers with painted cup-pulls, then his eyes came to the sturdy porcelain table and his mother's voice chanted, "Dirty, dirty, dirty."

That was madder than not being able to enter the room. His mother had been dead over thirty years, he wasn't hearing her voice . . . but he was. It was slow, sly, insinuating, in the sing-song rhythm of *we know where you're going* like a nasty kid. It came at him, closed around him, and he backed out of the doorway, then looked up and saw a largeish, lumpy mass in the ceiling covered with layers of white enamel. It had been painted over so many times the details were lost, but he knew it was a pulley, and what felt like a solid wall of burning vomit filled his throat.

He was going to puke all over the clean waxed floor, and the thought horrified him.

Horrified him!

He'd sliced open five women and shot Bunny in the face with equanimity, and throwing up on a clean floor horrified him! He'd have laughed until he cried if he weren't so sick.

He clapped his hand over his mouth to keep it back and looked wildly around. He'd never make it to one of the bathrooms, racing across the kitchen to the sink was obviously out of the question, and he ran for the front door.

He tore it open, lunged across the porch, and hung over the rail, vomiting wildly until his middle felt as if it had collapsed against his spine and nothing came up but long strands of clear bile. The door was open behind him and the ghost of her voice came down the hall and out into the damp, cold air. "Dirty, dirty, dirty."

● ●

ADAM HUDDLED AGAINST THE PORCH RAILING WITH THE COLT digging into his side and his mouth sour and slimy. At least he'd done it on the grass and a good rain would get rid of it.

He pulled the Colt out of his belt and laid it on the porch floor, then looked back through the open door at the hall to the kitchen. "What happened?" he mumbled. "What the fuck happened?"

You know, Sport, Bunner would say, *It's down there . . . dig for it.*

He did.

"Dirty, dirty, dirty," his mother had chanted, so something had been dirty, obviously the kitchen. They'd arrived here that long-ago summer and found a dirty kitchen, worst kind of dirt too, grease from food she'd never cooked, old food she'd never bought moldering in a filthy refrigerator. No cleaning crews in those days, she'd had to do it herself, and she'd been furious and screamed at him and . . .

Horseshit.

That kitchen could have been filthier than an outhouse in Calcutta with the floor and walls covered with inches of grease with hair thick as a pelt stuck in it. She could've screamed and ranted, crowned him with a frying pan, and it still didn't explain the sick mindless dread that had attacked him like a rabid wolf.

Something else had happened in that room, something *seminal.*

Good word . . . *seminal* . . . spectacular word, like genesis . . . *in the beginning.*

In the beginning was the kitchen, the porcelain table, the pulley, and most of all, the scars. They were the key piece in a jigsaw he'd been trying to put together ever since he could remember and that was ever since his mother died, because everything before that night when the troopers came . . .

"Mr. Fuller, I think you better sit down," said the big blond one with white lashes and eyes like washed sapphires.

They'd all sat, except Adam. He didn't remember not sitting because his sentient life began when the big blond said, "She is dead, sir. I'm sorry . . . that intersection out on six by the dairy . . . should be a stoplight there. Guess there will be after this. Mr. Fuller, I think you better sit down."

And Adam came to like Snow White coughing up the chunk of poisoned apple and found himself at the living room window looking out on Barracks Lane at the troopers' cruiser. It was lit up like a spaceship on wheels with radio static coming out in bursts. It was a spectacular sight and he hoped Tommy Van Damm across the street could see it parked in front of his house.

"It was instantaneous," the trooper was saying over Mike's sobbing. "She didn't know what hit her."

Everything before that night was a soft, gray, impenetrable haze. He had come to at the word, *dead*, at the age of nine, with a belly full of scars he didn't know how he'd gotten and emotions that ran the gamut from fear to fear. Until he'd looked up at that pulley and felt sheer, devouring, murderous horror. So the pulley was one more piece he couldn't fit . . . *but she could.*

The thought didn't hit him, his mind didn't light up and play "The Star-Spangled Banner." It was just *there,* leaving him wondering why it had taken him so long to think of it. He'd started to when he'd gotten his first look at the house and thought *not just dangerous,* but it flashed past too fast for him even to find words for. He had the words now—*she could.* She'd done it for Ken Nevins, she'd do it for Adam. It was important for the electricity to be on because they might need light when he found her, brought her here, made her stand under the pulley and tell him the seminal event (his version of genesis) that had taken place in the kitchen. Then he'd kill her.

● ●

"S. KLEIN," SAID THE WOMAN BEHIND THE COUNTER OF RAVEN Lake Ski and Sport. It must have just opened recently for the season and some of the shelves were empty, waiting for deliveries.

"It was just eleven days ago," Adam said.

"I can see the date," she said coolly.

Easy, he thought. *Don't annoy her, don't arouse her suspicion.*

She said, "I just don't remember. I probably didn't wait on them and I don't know who did. Maybe one of the part-time girls."

"The customer rented the house at three hundred Lakeshore."

"I'm sorry. We don't ask for addresses unless we're going to deliver. But whoever this was took it with him and paid cash."

"Him?"

"Probably. The item's a man's sweater. But women sometimes buy men's sizes in cashmere because it runs smaller." She frowned, then said, "Why don't you call Mrs. Rodney? She owns three hundred Lakeshore. Her son comes up here to fish, even in winter. They build a shack on the lake and cut a hole in the ice. Some men are insane about fishing."

"Where can I find Mrs. Rodney?"

"Glens Falls . . . maybe Glenvale. Just a second. Nan," she called to the back.

"Naaan . . ."

"Yeah?" a woman's voice answered.

"Where do the Rodneys live?"

A woman appeared in a curtained doorway holding a bunch of blouses she must have just unpacked and said, "Glenvale."

● ●

ADAM SAW THE BLUE ESCORT AGAIN ON THE SOUTH RAMP TO THE Northway. He thought he'd seen it behind him on 128 before, on Main Street when he'd parked in front of Raven Lake Ski and Sport . . . and there it was again.

He pulled into the center lane and pegged himself at fifty-five. Wouldn't do to get pulled over with the Python in the glove compartment. The Escort also shifted lanes, staying a few cars back. Adam stayed at fifty-five in the travel lane until they approached the Warrensburg exit, then he swerved into the slow lane and dropped to forty.

The other car slowed fast, a horn honked, brakes squealed, and it pulled into the slow lane and let the distance open up again.

It couldn't be Latovsky, he wouldn't be this inept.

Adam speeded up a little; so did the Escort, and an hour later Adam took the first Glenvale exit. He didn't see the Escort on the ramp or on Cannon Road and he dropped back to forty through the outskirts of town, along King George to Rusty Pond.

No Escort.

A few yards from his street, he floored it and the big Ford leaped forward as the needle swung to seventy. He tromped the brake, screeched into Rusty Pond, then floored it again, screamed into his driveway, and came to a shuddering stop a few inches from the garage door.

He killed the motor, slumped in the seat so his head was invisible through the rear window, then angled the rearview mirror to reflect the street. A minute passed, part of another . . . and the little blue Escort tooled by heading for the turnaround at the end of the cul de sac.

Adam was shaking and sweating and had an almost overwhelming urge to urinate but he made himself stay where he was, trying with all his might not to wet his pants.

A minute later, the little car made the turnaround and tooled back to King George.

They were following him.

● ●

"Then?" Latovsky asked Dillworthy.

"Then, he pulled over to the side of the road just past three hundred, and went through the woods to . . . someplace."

"Someplace?"

"He'd've made me in the woods if I followed."

Bullshit, Latovsky screamed inwardly. That house was ringed with trees and Dillworthy could've followed without getting made if he'd been a little careful. But it was cold and damp, the woods were buggy, and he knew Dillworthy had stayed in the car, cycling the heater on and off and reading the sports section.

In the supersoft voice the men had learned to fear, Latovsky said, "Did it occur to you there was a house up there and the doctor did not have a key . . . but might have gone in anyway, and we'd have him for B and E and get a warrant to search his house to see what else he'd stolen?"

"Stolen! He's a doctor, for Christ's sake, he didn't steal—"

"Oh, shit!" Latovsky clutched the sides of his head. "You stupid, lazy, shit-kicking rube. We had a chance for a warrant and you blew it."

"Don't talk to me like that," Dillworthy said quietly. "It never occurred to me a doctor'd break into some crum-bum summer house. And you never said he might. Maybe I'd've thought of it on my own fifteen years ago, but that was then, this is now—and this is Glenvale, not Boston. Most of us haven't done anything since the academy but break up bar fights and pick up the pieces after some son of a bitch takes a baseball bat to his old lady. You want a bunch of supersleuths, Latovsky? Call the Feds, call the fuckin' marines, but don't expect me or anyone else to turn into Sherlock Holmes because you got a bug up your ass. We'll try because you got a lotta currency with us, but you're gonna spend it real fast if you start calling us names."

Dillworthy ran out of breath, then stared at the wall behind Latovsky. Latovsky waited a moment, then ran his hand down his face and said quietly, "You're right, Dill, and I am truly sorry."

Dillworthy blushed and stammered, "Yeah . . . well . . ."

Latovsky's apologies were like snow in June: rare but not unheard of. They were also heartfelt.

"Where'd you leave him?" Latovsky asked.

"In his driveway. I didn't know that street's a cul de sac and I bumbled in, then had to bumble back out again, passing him twice."

Latovsky *had* known and hadn't told his men. He was as bad as they were, one more rube who couldn't find dogshit on his shoe.

"So he went home," Latovsky said.

"Now who's being dumb? He was in the car, lying in wait to watch me blow whatever cover I had left."

"Then?"

"Then I finally got my brains outta my anus and I pulled around on King George into another driveway. This time, *I* lay in wait and sure enough out he comes a few minutes later and heads for the hospital."

"Then?"

"Then I tagged him there and called Frawley from the lot to take over. I came here when Frawley showed up."

"And Fuller?"

"Still there. Frawley called a few minutes ago to say he was in the doctors' lounge using the phone."

● ●

THEY HAD FOLLOWED HIM, THEY COULD HAVE TAPPED THE PHONES in his house and office, and Adam used the pay phone in the lounge. He was in the booth a while, his hand and ear were damp, and he was glad to push open the door and come out into the empty lounge.

He'd made two calls, first to the law firm that had handled the closing on his house. He had been transferred to a John Farber, who had listened, then said excitedly that it was an interesting case. The squad was the state; the state had deep pockets, and Farber probably had six-digit figures dancing in his head. "Although I doubt it'll get very far," Farber had said a little regretfully. "Unless they've really got something on you, which I gather they haven't."

"Nothing," Adam said with perfect confidence. "Nothing at all."

"Then they'll come off it. I guess that's what you want?"

An upswing in the tone, and Adam had thought John Farber was hoping it wouldn't be that simple.

"That's what I want," Adam had said firmly.

"Well, as I said, unless they got something, a phone call and a follow-up letter'll do it. Cops cover their asses these days."

It had been a very satisfactory conversation and Adam was sure he was free of Latovsky.

The best defense is a good offense, his mother used to say.

Then he'd called Mrs. Alan Rodney, owner of the house on Raven Lake, and that was much less satisfactory. She didn't know the last tenant's name offhand, would have to look it up, she'd told him. He'd said he'd call back and she'd said to give her half an hour.

Half an hour was too short to get involved in something else, too long to sit staring at the wall or the page of a magazine. He went to the fountain and drank to get rid of the tinny taste in his mouth, then went downstairs to see if Davis had the results of Ellen Baines's lymph-angiogram.

Davis stuck the floppy film on the light box and smiled hugely. "Real pretty," he told Adam. "Lady's clean as a whistle. Good news."

Fabulous news, and Adam wanted to run up and tell her. But he needed more time to explain to her what was going to happen next. Sykes wanted to do prophylactic chemotherapy and Adam agreed; *better safe than sorry,* his mother would say. God, what a banal woman she must have been. A perfect match for the old man.

The drugs would make Ellen sick, but there were good antiemetics these days. She'd also probably lose her hair and that bothered some women more than the constant nausea and fear of death, but he'd found a beauty shop right here in Glenvale that sold human hair wigs at a decent price.

● ●

"WHAT?" LATOVSKY SNARLED INTO THE PHONE.

"It's Lydia Rodney, Lieutenant. I do hope this isn't a bad time."

"No, of course not, ma'am." He softened his tone. "I'm sorry."

"I just had a very odd call that I thought you'd want to know about. From Raven Lake, from a little dry-goods store there. It seems someone charged a couple of hundred dollars, signed for it, then didn't pay the bill. Whoever it was left the address of our house on the lake, but when the store called, there was no answer, naturally. Now they say they can't read the signature and would I give them the name and permanent address of my last tenant. I can understand the signature being illegible. I'm afraid penmanship's gone the way of sloe gin."

"You told . . ." Latovsky choked.

"I did no such thing, Lieutenant." She sounded insulted. "I told them I'd have to get back to them. But they said it was long distance, and since I was doing them the favor, they'd call me. Very odd, as I said. I know Nan Linz, the owner, and I can't imagine her letting someone take two hundred dollars' worth of merchandise with nothing but a signature or worrying about my phone bill. I remembered you were interested in the house, and surmised you might be interested in this."

"Good, Mrs. Rodney, good and bless you," he said weakly. "Now tell me about the caller."

"Nothing to tell, really. He sounded perfectly ordinary."

"*He*."

"Definitely."

Fuller.

Latovsky made his mind move as fast as it could and Mrs. Rodney had the sense not to keep saying, "Hello, hello . . . anyone there?" She just kept quiet and let him think.

Fuller was hunting for Eve. He'd found the house and something in it. Whatever it was hadn't led to Eve yet or he wouldn't have bothered with the store or Mrs. Rodney. But he'd found the old lady and would know she knew the name and address. If she refused to tell him, he'd wait until she and her maid were out, then he'd break in, pry open the pretty little antique desk in the sitting room or a mission oak file cabinet in another room, and there would be the last lease on 300 Lakeshore, signed by S. Klein of Bridgeton, Connecticut.

Or Fuller wouldn't wait until the old lady was out, but would break in in the dead of night because two more murders wouldn't bother him.

"Mrs. Rodney?"

"I'm still here, Lieutenant."

"On no account give him that name."

"I won't."

"There's more, Mrs. Rodney. You'll have to lie to him."

She didn't say anything.

"I want you to tell him you don't know the name—don't remember or never did know it. I want you to tell him you can't get it either, because you burned all the papers connected with the house by mistake. Then, Mrs. Rodney, I want you *to* burn them."

"What an odd request."

"You'll do it?"

"You think I'm in some kind of danger, don't you?"

He didn't answer.

"It's hard to see what could constitute danger at my age, but I'll do exactly as you ask."

●　●

ADAM'S FACE FELT AS IF HE'D BEEN IN THE SUN TOO LONG AND HIS heart thudded against his ribs. Maybe it was just anticipation of getting his own way, but that seemed too mild for what was going on inside him.

He deposited the quarter, dialed, and the phone started to ring. He imagined the old lady (she'd sounded ancient) crossing a room and, rustling in her gnarled hand that couldn't keep itself still, was a sheet of paper—a lease, a list, a rental record—with the name he'd been waiting for for what seemed like his whole life.

Her legs were thin, shot with bulging black veins, and the trip to the ringing phone was slow and difficult. She was almost there, he thought . . . three rings . . . four. *Come on, old lady.* He drummed his fingers on the shelf under the phone. "Come on!"

Then she answered and, with a few words that he couldn't believe he was hearing, she demolished everything.

All he got for all his trouble was a hatful of rain. All he got for all his trouble . . .

"I'm so sorry," she dithered. "It was a dreadful mistake, but the leases are ash and there's nothing I can do about it."

"But surely, surely—" It took all his control not to shout at her (and he was amazed that he wanted to). "Surely you remember who was living in your house last week."

"Surely, surely, I should," she said, "but I seem to forget everything these days. Why, just last week . . ."

She launched into a long, rambling, Alzheimer's-sounding tale, got lost in the middle of it and petered out in midsentence.

"Is there someone else who'd know?" he asked. He'd gotten some control back, his voice sounded all right. "It was a very expensive item . . . cashmere, you know."

"Cashmere! I saw a cashmere sweater at Rosner's, right in Glenvale. Right on Main Street, and they wanted three hundred dollars for it. Imagine! And this is *Glenvale*, not Monte Carlo. I think it was three hundred dollars . . . I think it was cashmere."

"Maybe a member of your family . . ." he said desperately.

"My family? What about my family?"

"Would one of them know?"

"Know what?"

"Who rented the house." His voice was scaling out of control again. He wrenched it back with an effort, concentrated on keeping it steady.

"Of course not. It's *my* house, left to me by my dear father. It's *my* responsibility, not theirs." She trailed away again and nothing came over the line but the ragged sound of her breath, which probably smelled of dentures. Poor, sad, silly old thing, who probably wouldn't remember her children's names or her own this time next year (if she lived that long), had burned some papers and with them his chance of finding *her*.

He hung up without saying good-bye and called the store in Raven Lake.

"You again," the woman said when he told her who it was. He must not have made a very good impression.

She said, "Yes, I asked Lorraine. And she remembers him because she said he was good-looking. *Him*, not her. Definitely a him. And she doesn't know anything else about him. Now, if you'll excuse me," and she hung up.

● ●

"AND THE LEASES?" LATOVSKY ASKED.

"Now snapping merrily away on the hearth," Mrs. Rodney said happily. "I only wish it had been harder to sound so fuddled."

Nothing fuddled about her, Latovsky thought.

Maybe he'd ask if he could come to tea when this was over, bring his mother, who'd make some of those little crustless sandwiches he could eat about eighty of. Suddenly, he felt good and found himself smiling into the phone.

"Have I now circumvented the danger to myself?" she asked.

"I think so, but I still want you to lock up carefully at night, Mrs. Rodney. I'm very serious about that. And I'm going to have a Glenvale police cruiser drive by every hour after dark for the next few weeks; it'll attract less attention than a state car."

"Do tell the officers to stop in for something hot to drink. Any time before ten . . . or even after. The old don't need much sleep, you know. That's one of those old wives' tales that turn out to be gospel."

They hung up. He took out the list of tenants she'd made on her thick cream-colored stationery and the Xerox copy he'd made of it and tore them to confetti, then dropped them in his wastecan, watched them drift into it, and felt even better. He'd foreseen something even Eve hadn't and had broken the last link between her and the killer in the woods, a link only he could break, and he felt good for the first time in days.

In the middle of his moment of self-congratulation, Meers called and told him to come to his office.

● ●

"Jig's up," Meers said.

"What jig's that?"

"The Adam Fuller jig, Dave. Just had a call from an attorney, name of John Farber, of Macready, Ruskin, Farber, and so on, to tell us that Dr. Adam P. Fuller is getting ready to sue the squad for harassment unless such harassment ceases at once."

"He's bluffing!" Latovsky choked.

"About which, Dave? Making the tail on him or suing us because of it."

"Oh, he made the tail. We couldn't follow a blind deaf mute without getting made. But he ain't gonna sue, Lem. Killers don't sue cops."

"You willing to bet a coupl'a hundred thousand bucks on that?"

Latovsky didn't answer.

"I'm not," Meers said, rolling an unlit cigarette over and over in his fingers. He'd been trying to quit for years, did so on and off, and his face would lose some of that cadaverous look for a few months. Then he'd go back and his cheeks sank in again.

Latovsky wanted to reach out and snatch the cigarette away from him, but the truth was, he wanted one too, even though he'd quit years ago.

He watched helplessly as his boss stuck the Marlboro in his mouth, pulled out his ancient Zippo, and lit up.

He inhaled like a man drinking water after five days in the desert, then he looked at Latovsky.

"You're off Fuller and he's back to what he was day before yesterday, one of twenty-six patients between twenty-five and fifty years old. And do me a favor, Dave—don't argue with me."

He asked this last very gently.

"Okay, Lem, but smoke this with that toxic crap. While I'm observing the legal niceties and going after twenty-six instead of one, another woman could find herself slit open and drying out in the moonlight. Then what, Lem?"

"Then we lose a lot of sleep," Meers said, looking fondly at the glowing end of the cigarette. "That's part of what we get paid to do. I think it stinks, I think the legal system sucks, I think all the things you know I've thought for twenty years. But I've got forty cents in the squad budget and that's not as much of an exaggeration as you think. If Fuller sues us—we're finished. And I can't, *can't* risk the whole squad, which we've both worked our asses off for, because you got a 'feeling' at your best friend's funeral.

"Go after Fuller, Dave, go after the other twenty-five. Do the miserable old cop work. Something will shake out that Linney can take to a judge and if it doesn't, it probably wasn't Fuller anyway.

"In the meantime . . ." Meers drew in smoke, his eyes got a little dreamy, and Latovsky thought he was actually getting high on it. "In the meantime," Meers said, "I want you to take the weekend off. Take the kid fishing and come back rested and with a clear mind. That's an order, Lieutenant."

● ●

"Congratulations, Eve," Joe Rubin said.

He came around his desk, flopped into the big leather chair, and beamed at her.

"You're sure?" she said faintly.

"Positive, and you're farther along than you think: into the fourth month, I figure, so you'll be as big as a house through summer, something most women try to avoid. But I gather this wasn't planned."

Eve didn't say anything.

He looked at her with the intent kindness she was used to from him. He must be pushing seventy; his cheeks and temples had gotten a little sunken and his jowls were loose, but his eyes were bright, his hair still thick and iron gray.

"Eve? Fran told me Sam was gone."

"It's Sam's baby, if that's what—"

He held up his hand. "It's not. I just wanted to know if he or someone's waiting for the news."

"He's back," she said evasively.

"Well, now. Well . . . that's good news, Evie. Maybe this time . . ."

No, not this time, Eve thought. *Not ever.* They were trying, you could feel the trying in everything they said to each other, in every tentative touch between them. No, dear Doctor Joe, not ever.

She slumped in the chair.

"Hey, I've got a little something for occasions like this," he said heartily. He stood up and went to a cabinet against the wall. She stood too and wandered to the window around the corner from his desk. It looked out on Elm, which had been lined with the trees until the Dutch disease killed them. Now they had Chinese elms that were supposed to be resistant and would probably look pretty good in a hundred years or so.

The houses across the street were eighteenth century. Some had been converted to offices, one housed the town library, a few were still private homes, with gracious lawns that looked in need of the season's first mowing. The grass was tender green, the leaves were fresh, not dusty looking the way they'd get in July, when it was hot . . . and she'd be "big as a house."

A baby . . .

She'd ask him when a sonogram could tell if it was a girl or boy; she knew about sonograms from Meg. She also wanted to know if she should have amniocentesis to rule out birth defects, because she was thirty-one, past the optimum child-bearing age.

Sun glanced off a window of one of the houses across Elm and back into her eyes. She blinked and saw a street covered with tanbark and heard the clop of horses' hooves. A woman stood across the way under a huge old spreading elm, the likes of which had not been seen in Bridgeton since the 1960s. She wore a hoop skirt, tightly laced bodice, and had a tiny waist. Her dark hair, the exact color of Eve's, was pinned in a crown of smooth braids, and Eve knew her eyes (although she was too far away to see the color) were brown with a greenish undercast that made them look olive drab in sunlight.

The woman looked up at the window and her mouth moved. Eve strained to hear, pushing her forehead against the window pane but the voice was too faint. The woman spoke again, moving her lips very deliberately, and Eve read, "Watch out."

Eve gasped, jerked her head sideways, and banged it against the window frame.

"Eve!" Joe Rubin cried. He was holding a Dixie cup in one hand and a bottle of Glenfiddich in the other.

She staggered; he slammed the cup and bottle on the desk, ran to her, and helped her back in the chair.

She sank into it, put her head against his shoulder, and smelled his piney aftershave and the starch in his white coat.

"Evie . . ."

"It's okay," she said. "It really is. I just . . . I guess I'm a little shocked."

Joe picked up the Dixie cup and handed it to her. Everyone was feeding her liquor lately; if they kept it up she'd be an alkie before her seventh month.

"And why're you shocked?" Joe asked gently. "What'd you think would happen if you screwed without protection?"

"I guess I didn't think."

"Eve, you're not going . . ."

"To have an abortion? Not if everything's okay."

But maybe everything wasn't okay, maybe that's what the woman in the vision (a great-great-great grandmother, a long-gone Tilden matriarch and victim of "the thing") had meant by *watch out*. She gulped the scotch, which was smokey and smooth and went down like liquid silk. "That's your last drink," Joe Rubin said. "Except for a glass of something at Sunday dinner—one glass, once a week. I'll give you some vitamins, and take Tylenol if you get a headache. You shouldn't swallow a lot of crap when you're pregnant. How's your tolerance for iron?"

It was after three when she left the office. The street was just a street with asphalt, not tanbark, and the elms were the struggling scraggly ones she was used to. The sun glinted off the chrome on the cars at the curb and she wondered if small towns in Germany had as many Mercedes and Beamers as they had in Bridgeton.

She looked across at the spot where she'd seen the woman under the fine old long-dead elm trees and thought, "Watch out for what, Granny?"

A man passing gave her a startled look and she realized she'd said it out loud.

● ●

AT THAT MOMENT, MAX JERGENS TURNED OVER THE LAST PAGE OF Riley's piece and looked up at him. It was hot for early May; sun coming though the dirty window bleached the dingy gray walls to a soft, almost pretty color.

"Wolfman," Jergens said almost reverently. "Jesus, that's good, Jimmy. That's terrific. The Wolfman . . . how'd you ever think of it?"

"It's an old movie," Riley said, then imitated Maria Ouspenskaya's crackling old voice. " 'Eeffen de man who iss pure in heart and saysss hiss prayers by night, may become a volf ven de Volfbane bloomz . . .' "

"What the fuck's volfbane?"

"It's wolfsbane, actually, a member of the aconitum family. I looked it up."

"Oh. Well, can it, most people won't know what you're talking about."

Riley shrugged and Jergens said, "The rest's good, only . . . only . . ." He looked down at his hand curled on top of the computer paper. "Only . . ."

"Only what?"

Jergens hated saying anything unpleasant, one of the reasons the *Register* was the vanilla rag it was, Riley thought.

"Only it's . . . well . . . it's fluff, Jimmy."

"Yeah, but it's *fun* fluff for a change. It's May, and we've already printed sixteen recipes for rhubarb pie, with and without strawberries; twenty-five descriptions of spring-fling dances and coming-out parties; and fifty pieces on garden shows. At least this is good down-and-dirty fluff."

"Yeah, it's got it all, doesn't it?" Jergens turned the pages over, title up: *The Cop, the Clairvoyant, and the Wolfman.* "Everyone loves murder and creepy-crawlies and dumb cops."

"He's not a dumb cop."

"No? He consults a psychic in the middle of a serial murder investigation? What would you call him?"

"Desperate."

"And what's this desperate cop's name, Jimbo? And the psychic's?"

"And the Wolfman's?"

"Don't get nasty. How do we do a story like this without names?"

"The woman's rich. I mean a few hundred million worth of rich, with probably forty lawyers on retainer. I use her name and you might as well lock the front door for good. The cop . . . the cop . . ."

"C'mon."

"The cop's a good cop; what he did was dumb and I expected better of him, but he's still a good cop and I don't want to hurt him."

"It better not be Lem Meers. I know he comes off like a retarded Abe Lincoln but he's the last man on earth you want to fuck with. And that Polack who shills for him is the second last—" Jergens stopped, then laughed. "Fair-skinned Irishmen can't hide shit, Jimmy; you look like a stoplight. It's him, isn't it? The Polack."

"I'm not saying, and if naming whoever is the only way this sees light . . ."

He reached for the stack of papers. Jergens slammed his hand down on it and passed Riley's death sentence by saying, "Leave us not be hasty—you don't want names, we don't print names."

"I<small>T'LL BE BAD, WON'T IT?</small>" E<small>LLEN</small> B<small>AINES ASKED</small> Adam. She meant the chemotherapy and he knew she was praying for him to say, "Not bad at all, piece of cake." But it would be bad, possibly horrible, depending on her reaction to the drugs, and he wanted her to be ready for it. Not terrified, but ready. So he told her, quietly and precisely so she'd know what to expect. It sounded as bad as it would probably be, but she didn't moan or whine, didn't interject any *Oh Gods* or *why me's* or other crap most patients came up with. She just listened in silence, her head tilted a little to the side, and when he'd finished she asked the only question worth asking, at least to his mind.

"Is it worth it?"

"Yes."

"Really worth it, Adam?"

He didn't let his patients call him *Doctor* when he called them by their first names. If they wanted formality, he was Dr. Fuller, they were Mr., Miss, or Mrs. So-and-So, otherwise they called him Adam.

He said, "Let me put it this way, Ellen. I believe you will be trading a few miserable months for years of a normal, healthy life."

"Years!" She sounded startled, and he smiled and took her hand, which was swollen and discolored from the IV.

"Years. Of course, you can walk out of here and get hit by a truck . . ."

Then she asked the question she'd have had to be a bald male not to ask. "Will I lose my hair? I've heard people lose their hair."

They'd start the drug as soon as she'd recovered sufficiently from the surgery—two, maybe three weeks, he figured. In the meantime, he'd send her home to her husband; she'd see her kids and grandchildren and work in her garden.

Before he let go of her hand, on an impulse that didn't come from any emotion he was aware of, he raised it briefly to his lips, then left her and went down to the cafeteria for lunch.

He got a boiled-looking hamburger from the steam table, added some limp cole slaw and a diet Coke, and looked for a table. The place was packed, but three interns were piling their dishes on the trays for the conveyor belt into the kitchen and he went to their table.

"You done?" he asked, resting his tray on the back of a chair.

"Yes, sir. Be out of here in a second," one said.

The *sir* made him feel old. He didn't know these three yet. It was spring, Glenvale was small but respected, and new interns were showing up every day. They finished and carried their dishes away, leaving a newspaper on the table.

"Hey, your paper," he called after them.

"Keep it," called a tall one with a wave of shining blond hair across his forehead. The women were going to love him, Adam thought.

He sat down, neatly arranged his plate, soda can, utensils, and scrap of paper napkin. Then he opened the paper, leafed through it back to front, and took a bite of hamburger that tasted better than it looked. The Red Sox were going nowhere as usual; the Mets were up there, but would probably be in the toilet by the middle of the season to his old man's chagrin. He passed wedding announcements, recipes, ads for supermarket specials, and preseason bathing suit sales, saw the word *Clairvoyant* and stopped. It was a word that he'd never thought of in connection with *her*, but he liked it better than *psychic*, which reminded him of an overmade-up con-lady with hoop earrings and a storefront with Madame So-and-So, Reader and Adviser, in chipped gilt on the window.

Then he took in the whole headline, *The Cop, the Clairvoyant, and the Wolfman*, and started to read. Two lines into it, he knew

Latovsky was the cop, he was the Wolfman, and *she* was the clair-voyant. He read it over and over, hoping for information that had escaped him last time through. Lunch hour ended, the cafeteria cleared out, and his beeper went off. He silenced it and kept reading while whitish flecks of grease congealed on the hamburger.

At last, like a kid saving the frosting until the cake is gone—the best for last—Adam looked at the byline.

• •

"Hiya, Dave." Riley tried to sound casual but his voice was tight because he knew Latovsky would be pissed off about the piece. He did not expect the rigid, pallid mask of utter rage he saw when Latovsky closed the door carefully, then turned to face him.

"Dave . . ." Riley's voice shook.

Latovsky drew his ashen lips back from his teeth, raised the rolled-up copy of the *Register* in his hand, and pitched it at Riley. Riley's hand flew up and deflected it. It fell on the desk and unrolled as Latovsky advanced on him.

Riley gave a loud, wordless yell for help, but it was lunch hour; the few left in the bullpen were hunched over terminals and the ceiling was acoustic tile, put up to muffle the clack of typewriters years ago.

The huge man coming at him like a moving wall could pound his head to mush, and no one would hear. Riley shoved his chair back, but the wall stopped it and he was trapped.

"Dave . . . c'mon . . ." he quavered.

Latovsky reached across the desk and grabbed a handful of Riley's shirt; he hauled him out of the chair, Riley's pelvis smacked the desk edge, and he yelped in pain. Latovsky drew back a fist the size of a baseball mitt, and Riley could already feel the dull, deafening, bone-crushing thud it would make when it smashed into his face.

"Dave . . . David . . . don't hit me." He tried not to whimper.

"Hit you!" Latovsky rasped. "I'm going to string your guts on the walls."

The fist started to move and Riley shrieked, "Stop or I'll print the names!"

"Names . . ." Latovsky hissed. The fist wavered.

"Names, you crazy prick. Her name, your name . . . and then I'll sue your ass to perdition. You'll be lucky to punch a clock in a toxic waste dump."

"Names . . ." Latovsky sounded confused.

"Names, you maniac!"

Latovsky let him go as suddenly as he'd grabbed him. Riley was off-balance and he started to fall forward across the desk, with his feet slipping on the floor tile, his face aimed straight at the spindle for telephone messages. He threw himself backward with all his might, his feet caught on the tile, and he fell into his chair. It teetered, he flung himself forward, wrenching his back, and the chair righted itself with a crash that shook the office. No one came in to see what the commotion was.

"Names." Latovsky backed away from the desk. "What about names?"

Riley grabbed the rolled-up paper and pitched it back at Latovsky. Latovsky caught it in midair, then backed up until he felt the visitors' chair behind him and sank into it. He unrolled the paper and Riley watched his eyes race down the page.

"No names." Latovsky choked. "I thought . . ."

"Bullshit! You saw it, jumped in the car, stuck the bubble on the roof, and raced here ninety miles an hour, working yourself into a frenzy. *Think* is exactly what you didn't do."

"But you know . . ."

"Of course. She's Eve Tilden Leigh Klein. Sounds like a joke, doesn't it? And she lives in Bridgeton, Connecticut."

"How?"

"From a waitress at a roadhouse there."

"A waitress."

"That's right, Latovsky. A waitress."

Riley's voice still shook wildly and sweat was pouring off of him. He was a physical coward and always had been: a pantywaist who'd been the butt of every bully in the schoolyard. But Dave Latovsky had never been one of those bullies in spite of his immense size (six one at thirteen) and legendary temper . . . and suddenly Riley remembered Bunner from those days. He'd remembered the name; now he put a face to it. First a boy's, then a man's, and then he remembered that Latovsky and Bunner had been best buddies and shame at his callousness about Bunner's winding up on page eight by Thursday brought tears to his eyes. He stared at the desk top, blinking until they were gone. Then he looked up; Latovsky held the paper loosely in one hand, his eyes were half closed, he looked on the verge of dozing.

"Dave, I'm sorry. Dave . . . talk to me . . ."

"You followed me," Latovsky mumbled.

"No. You called in, Dillworthy wrote down where you'd be, then went to the can, and I read it on his pad.".

Latovsky let go of the paper and it slid off his thigh and fell to the floor. "What a bunch of shit-kicking hillbillies we are," he groaned. The rage was gone; he looked exhausted, his huge body sagged in the chair.

"No, you're not: I got lucky and hit paydirt. If you can call crap like that"—Riley nodded at the paper on the floor—"paydirt. The main thing is there're no names, no harm done, except to you and me if we keep at each other like this."

Latovsky looked past him without saying anything.

"Dave, can we do a little damage control here?" Riley tried not to sound like a terrified adolescent.

"Such as?"

"Such as talking this out over a beer and some food."

Impossible to stay mad on a full belly, Riley's father used to say.

Latovsky didn't answer.

"C'mon, Dave."

"A waitress," Latovsky said wonderingly. "Things you can't figure. A waitress."

● ●

RILEY AND LATOVSKY ORDERED CORNED BEEF, WHICH WAS PERfectly sliced by a black man with bulging biceps and piled on sour rye.

The place was crowded, but they got one of the high-backed wooden booths after waiting a few minutes and slid into the hard seats covered with thin, worn vinyl pads.

They were both upset by the scene in the office, and they ate and drank off the first mugs of icy draft in silence. A busboy cleared the plates and the waitress brought them fresh mugs. Latovsky took a deep sip and said, "Okay, Riley. Talk to me."

He no longer looked furious or exhausted; his eyes were cold and watchful.

"Not much to talk about," Riley said. "I found the waitress in the local roadhouse—the only bar in town—and got her to talk by telling her she might help catch the Wolfman. What do you think of the moniker, by the way?"

Latovsky shrugged.

"It's from the old movie," Riley said. "You remember it?"

"Sure. Saw it on about its twelfth go-round when I was a kid."
Latovsky looked off into space. "I remember the end where they kill
him and he turns back into a man . . . Lawrence Talbot. Crazy the
things that come back to you. I remember he turns back into a man
and it hits you he never meant it, that he was a . . . victim of
circumstance . . . and then it was sadder than it was scary." He
focused on Riley again. "Okay, you went to Bridgeton, found a waitress in a roadhouse, fed her hooch, and she fed you a malicious fable
about a local psychic and you believed her."

"*She* believed it. I didn't."

"But you printed it."

"If we only printed what we believed, all newspapers would be half
a paragraph long. And the waitress wasn't drunk or malicious, she liked
Eve Klein, as much as you can like anyone you think can touch you and
tell you you're going to get hit by a car on April fourth, nineteen ninety-
seven. She was certainly in awe of her and wanted to talk about her . . .
about the whole family. Said lots of them had 'the gift,' generations of
them going back to land grants, or so the legend goes. Seems one male
Tilden was even hung as a witch in sixteen something. In recent times,
it drove the grandmother to suicide and the mother to locking herself
up in that palace for twenty years. No one knows how it'll end for the
daughter, of course. So far, she's found a set of emeralds that disappeared in the sixties and saved the waitress's mother's life."

"How?" Latovsky leaned his arms on the table, all his attention
on Riley, and Riley thought, *He cares—he believes this horse hockey and
cares.*

He said, "Seems the waitress was serving the Seer and her best
buddy one day and the Seer stopped in the middle of whatever she was
saying, looked up at the waitress, and, in a sort of please-pass-the-
catsup tone, says, 'Your mother's on the kitchen floor and can't move.'
You know, *Lady bug, lady bug, fly away home.* The waitress went nuts
as I gather anyone in that town of Gullible Gulch would, and she
called the medics and raced home. Seems the old lady had a stroke and
took a header, or took a header and had a stroke. Either way, they
treated it before it turned her brain to cottage cheese, and the waitress
thanks the Seer. I heard this ninety-three-octane bullshit and knew
why you'd gone to Tilden House. Shocked the shit out of me," he said
quietly.

"Expected better of me, did you?" Latovsky asked.

"Sort of."

"Sorry to disappoint you, Riley." Latovsky didn't sound sorry. "Who else have you told about her?"

"No one."

"Barb?"

"No one."

Latovsky moved the mug around the table and looked at the whorls of moisture. "You know, we had a kind of pact, Jim. We never said it, but we both knew it. I never lied to you, you never went behind my back. Now you've broken it." He looked up at Riley. "And I figure you owe me one. What do you figure?"

"Depends," Riley said miserably.

"On the debt?"

Riley nodded.

"Your word never to tell anyone who or where she is."

Riley smiled in relief. "Easy, Dave. I never would anyway."

"I need your word on it, Jim."

"You've got it."

"Your *spoken* word," Latovsky said softly. Riley wanted to come up with a fast, on-target line about how if he said it, he'd do it, à la Spenser, the honor-bound detective on late-night reruns. But he couldn't think of one, wouldn't use it if he could, because Latovsky's friendship meant too much to him. Maybe because Latovsky would be squad captain when Meers retired in '97. But maybe even more because Latovsky had never been one of the overgrown creeps who'd gotten an immense kick out of smashing little sissy-fairy Jimmy Riley in the face to see him blubber.

"Sure, Dave. On my mother's grave if that'll make you happy."

"Your mother's not dead, Riley."

"No."

"Then on your mother's life," Latovsky said, and Riley felt his skin prickle. He thought of boys pricking their fingers to sign in blood on three-hole, college-ruled looseleaf paper and almost laughed. But it wasn't funny. Latovsky wanted to protect the woman from Connecticut whom he believed had the gift of gifts and, with a solemnity that surprised him, Riley raised his right hand and said, "Okay, Dave, on my mother's life, I'll never tell anyone who she is. Happy now?"

"Sure," Latovsky stuck out his hand, they shook, and Latovsky started to slide out of the booth.

"Hey, where're you going?"

Latovsky slid back. "We got more business?"

"You bet. What'd she tell you about the Wolfman?"

Latovsky laughed. "I thought you thought it was shit on toast."

"I do."

"Then what do you care what she told me?"

"I don't, but I do," Riley mumbled, and grinned shamefacedly. "Maybe I'm as gullible as you are . . . or something."

"Or something." Latovsky grinned. "Ah, Jimmy, I'd tell you, but I'm outta time. I'm supposed to pick up Jo and Jeanne's kid Matt in half an hour. Meers ordered—and I mean *ordered*—me to go fishing to clear my head. And I'm taking the kids."

● ●

As LATOVSKY HEADED UP THE NARROW AISLE TO THE DOOR OF Casey's Good Time Saloon and Restaurant, Bill Lyons, the new head of personnel for the *Register*, stared at the phone ringing on his desk. He'd only been in Albany three weeks, hated it, and longed to be back in D.C., where no one above the janitor answered their own phones. But his rotten secretary, who had Fu Manchu nails and the dedication of a gnat, was late coming back from lunch. The phone started its third ring; on the fourth, the call would cycle back to the board, where they'd take a message, and he meant to let it do just that but Madge Myers, the comptroller, happened to pass his open door and look in. She looked at the ringing phone, then at him, and the look said, *You limp-wristed D.C. slug. This is Real America where we get up at five, eat dinner at six, shovel our own snow, and answer our own damn phones.*

He gave her a crooked grin and grabbed the phone. "William Lyons," he said, and she passed by.

"Personnel?" asked a muffled, garbled voice. The caller had a rotten cold or the phone system (which belonged in the Smithsonian) was on the fritz again.

"This is personnel."

"I'm looking for Jim Riley."

"They can connect you directly." Lyons reached for the hold button, trying to remember how to transfer a call.

"I don't want to talk to him," the caller said quickly.

"Oh?" A warning bell went off in Lyons's head. He never gave credit information on the phone.

"What *do* you want?"

"I'm an old buddy of his." The guy's cold was really bad, must be something going around with the change of weather. The climate was abysmal, sixty one day, twenty the next.

"We were stringers together," the caller said. "Palled around for a few years, then lost touch. You know how it is. I didn't even know where he was until this morning when I blew into town and saw that little piece of his."

"Oh?"

"Knew it was *the* Jimbo from the style. And I thought it'd be fun to surprise him, you know? Just show up at his house tonight with a bottle and kick around old times."

"I see."

"Only I don't know his address, and if I have to ask him, it won't be a surprise anymore."

"Uh-huh." Lyons would never give out a *phone* number, but an address seemed harmless enough. After all, they weren't talking about Kitty Kelly or Teddy Kennedy here. The worst that could happen was that Riley'd get some extra junk mail. And if Lyons refused to help, the guy (who was almost certainly on the up-and-up) would call Riley and tell him how the hard-ass in personnel had ruined his nice surprise. Then Lyons would make an enemy of the most respected reporter on this rag only three weeks into the job.

"Uh, what's your name?" he asked.

"Latovsky," said the caller. "Dave Latovsky. But don't tell him, okay? Like I said, it's a surprise."

No one could make up a name like Latovsky, and Lyons brought Riley's file up on his terminal.

● ●

RILEY DIDN'T LIVE IN ALBANY AS ADAM ASSUMED, BUT ON Friends Lane right here in Glenvale, ten minutes from the hospital.

He thanked the man and hung up. Then he unwound the handkerchief from around the mouthpiece and took the plastic tooth protector out of his mouth.

● ●

"BARB?" RILEY CALLED.

Her car was there, but she didn't answer. Maybe Lisa had driven today, but Barb should be home by now anyway, unless they'd sprung one of those "team" meetings on her. She loathed them, called them arrant bullshit, said they'd lick illiteracy in America in a month if they taught as much as they met.

He stripped off his jacket and hung it up, then went down the hall to the little washroom under the stairs. His back still ached from the wrench of trying to save himself and his chair from toppling over, his nerves still tingled with the memory of Latovsky's pork roast–sized fist poised to smash his face in, and as an extra added—a little icing on the cake of this truly lousy day—he was getting a sinus headache.

He pulled down his tie, unbuttoned his collar, and turned on the hot water. When it steamed, he soaked a washrag and pressed it against his aching eyes, then looked at himself in the mirror. His eyes were already swollen; the headache was going to be a doozy. He'd take some antisinus crap, eat lightly, and go to bed.

He heard a thump, turned off the water, and opened the washroom door.

"Barb?"

No answer; it must have been a squirrel on the roof or a branch hitting the house. Something was kicking up out there; the spruce trees along the Northway had thrashed in the wind and the sky was pale gray by the time he pulled into his driveway. Dave was going to have rotten weather for his fishing trip with "the kids." They'd be Latovsky's Jo and Jeanne Hinkley's little boy, whose name escaped Riley. Jeanne was pretty, funny, and bright; she had long legs, big tits, and was mad about Dave, as a lot of women had been through the years. He should marry her. Probably would as soon as he got over his letch for the Sybil from Connecticut . . .

The thought came out of nowhere and took Riley by surprise. But he knew it was true the second he had it.

Poor Dave had conceived a passion for the lady from Connecticut, who was already married and must be more than a little nuts.

Riley was sorry he hadn't gotten a look at her. He'd asked Mary Owen if she was pretty, and Mary had said, "More what you'd call 'handsome,' like they say in novels."

Whatever it was thumped again and he called, "Barb?"

Still no answer, and he squeezed out the rag, hung it up, and went down the hall to the kitchen door. She might be in the basement doing laundry, but not on Friday, he thought. They usually went out, or she'd cook something a little special to celebrate the start of the weekend.

He pushed open the door and saw her.

She was tied to a kitchen chair with clothesline, with a dishtowel around her mouth as a gag. Her eyes rolled above the brightly colored cloth, fixed on him, and he froze.

"Barb . . ."

She jerked her head forward and squealed under the cloth, trying to tell him something. But he was too stunned to get the message or do anything but leap forward to tear the gag out of her mouth. Then he saw movement out of the corner of his eye, turned and saw a man in black with a black knit ski mask like a commando in a forties B movie.

The commando had a gun trained on him, a big one with a chrome body and Bakelite insets in the handle that Riley knew, as any crime reporter (or movie buff) would, was a Colt Python.

The commando gestured with it and said quietly, "Inside."

Riley clutched the door, afraid he'd fall to his knees if he let go.

"I said inside." The man jerked the gun, and Riley let go and took a staggering step into the room. His legs felt like mush but held him up. He realized, too late, that Barb's head-jerking had been a message for him to run while there was still the ghost of a chance of getting away. He might have made it; could have leaped back, yanked the door shut, and could be racing across the lawn to the Edelmans next door to call the cops.

He'd blown it.

But it didn't have to be the disaster it looked like, didn't have to be a disaster at all, and his mind started to work in spite of the panic blowing hotly in his chest like a breath of hell. They were being robbed; it was simple and happened all the time to all sorts of people. Some South Albany crack-head had decided to come north and try his luck in Glenvale and the moron had picked their house.

Really dumb because they had zilch. The TV, the VCR, Riley's collection of movies that were worthless to anyone but him. His PC, a good IBM clone, but the insurance would cover that. The only real loss would be his grandpa's old gold watch, but it was rolled in a sock in his dresser drawer and anyone dumb enough to choose to rob the Rileys instead of one of the families on Greener, or another rich street, might miss it. *Would* miss it, Riley concluded. The watch was safe, and Riley was suddenly calmer. Much calmer now that he knew what was going on. His legs stiffened, his facial muscles relaxed; his eyes moved almost easily from the enormous gun to the mask's eyeholes, like pits in the knit.

"Take what the fuck you want and get the fuck outta here," he said. His voice was steady (Latovsky would be proud of him) and saying *fuck* seemed to help for some reason.

The mask's mouth slit writhed and the commando said quietly, "What the fuck I want is her name, Mr. Riley."

The panic started to come back, and with it a dizzying sense of disorientation, because he didn't know what the commando was talking about. He forced the panic back down, swallowed a glob of burning spit, and asked, still pretty steadily, "Whose name?"

The mouth slit spread as if the commando smiled and he said, "Isn't that just remarkable. You have something so deeply embedded in your mind, you're sure everyone will automatically know what you mean. But of course they won't."

The voice was low-pitched and well modulated, the accent educated. *Embedded* was not a South Albany crack-head's word, and the panic started blowing up again.

The commando said, "I mean the woman in your article, Mr. Riley. The Clairvoyant."

Her. The Sybil from Exurbia whom he'd just sworn on his mother's life never to name. But Latovsky didn't expect him to get his head blown off to keep the oath. He didn't expect it of himself.

He tried once anyway. Feebly, but he did try.

"I don't know her name," he said.

The commando took a couple of long strides across the kitchen and crouched down next to Barb. He put the gun against the side of her knee, digging it into the folds of her corduroy skirt.

"Try again, Mr. Riley," he said almost pleasantly. "Who is she?"

He looked up at Riley, the overhead light pierced the eyeholes of the mask and Riley saw eyes as expressionless as marbles, except for what looked like mild curiosity, maybe about how long this was going to take.

The panic blasted through Riley's meager defenses and his mind went blank. He could barely have told this glassy-eyed son of a bitch his own name, his best friend's . . . not his address or phone number, and not the name of a woman he'd never heard of before Monday.

The commando cocked the gun and Riley tried to remember. Tried so hard he actually grunted, but nothing came through the white haze of panic that practically blinded him and smeared all his thought . . . except for a stubborn picture of the mean little sign on Route 7. It said CONNECTICUT, with no WELCOME TO or state flower or bird or anything but some lines about gun laws.

"One more time, Mr. Riley," the commando said. "Who is she?"

"Connecticut . . ." Riley gasped.

"Not good enough," the commando said almost regretfully and pulled the trigger. The blast was muffled by the skirt and Barb's leg, but it shook the room, and a mist of blood, pulverized flesh, and bone filled the air and settled almost lazily against the walls and cabinets, like the back puff from an oil burner. Riley and Barb screamed. Riley's scream sank to a sick screech and stopped, but Barb went on until the sound sang in his teeth like biting on foil. Then it cut off and she slumped forward, held in the chair by the clothesline. Her head sagged forward, the smoke cleared around her, and Riley saw shards of bone, shredded flesh, and tendon where her lower leg had been.

The commando put the gun to her lolling head and looked out of the holes in the mask at Riley.

"Again, Mr. Riley. Who is she?"

Horror smashed through the panic, the name came to him, and he threw back his head and raged, "Eve . . . Eve . . . Tilden Leigh . . ."

● ●

"Adam? Adam, come in," Ellsworth Harris said.

Adam entered a foyer with bleached parquet floors and a modern light fixture that had glass starbursts at the end of curled brass rods. It was one of the ugliest objects he had ever seen.

"I hope I didn't interrupt your dinner," he said.

"No . . . well, yes." Harris looked at the cloth napkin in his hand. "But don't worry about that; please come in." Adam followed him into a den paneled in pickled pine with a white rug and white furniture. Only the books and the TV the Harrises had left on when they went in to their dinner had any color.

Harris sat on a huge white couch with a glass-topped table on a white enamel frame in front of it.

"Sit, Adam. Can I get you a drink?"

"Thanks, El. I don't have time."

"Well . . . sure. What's wrong?" Harris asked almost eagerly.

That was the reward for never complaining, never making trouble, Adam thought. His mother had taught him that; his mother had been no one's fool. And now, when he had done something out of the ordinary and come to Ellsworth Harris's house at dinner hour, Harris was all attention. He'd probably grant Adam whatever he asked, since he had never asked for anything before.

"It's my father," Adam said.

"Oh, dear . . . I hope . . ."

"I think it's okay," Adam said. "I talked to his doctor, and it seems he's had some kind of coronary event, a small one. Still, they'll have to do the thallium scan and maybe cardiac catheter. And then, maybe . . . well, you know, El, you're a cardiologist."

Or used to be, Adam thought: Now Ellsworth Harris was a glad-handing ass-kisser who wandered the hospital halls like a lost soul in a cave, when he wasn't administrating, whatever that entailed.

"Anyway," Adam went on, "the old guy's scared shitless. So's my brother."

"Didn't even know you had a brother, Adam."

"No reason you should," Adam said humbly. "But Mike's scared, too, and I thought it would be easier on both of them, and my sister-in-law"—Claire the scrawny, Claire the sharp-eyed bitch—"if I were there to explain what's happening as it happens."

"Of course," Harris said. "Of course."

"Bill Sillbrooke and Chris Tufts'll cover for me, and we've got the new guy . . ."

"Perkins," Harris said.

"Perkins. So I thought . . ." He looked down like a kid in the principal's office. Harris had kissed so much ass to get the new wing, the remodeled library, the MRI, he probably loved having his own nuzzled every now and then.

"Sure," Harris said quietly. The tone was unexpected, and Adam looked up. Harris was staring off into the distance, his eyes misty. *He cares,* Adam thought, totally nonplussed. *He thinks my dad's sick, and he feels sorry for me. He pities me. How, El? My God . . . how do you do it? Tell me, El; just tell me how to look like you look this second, and I'll be your slave for life.* Then Harris said, "My own dad died last year, Adam. Remember?"

Adam nodded.

"I was shocked at how much I missed him," Harris said. "Still miss him, and it still shocks me." He looked into Adam's eyes and smiled gently, with warmth, humanity, a little sorrow, feelings Adam would kill for. Had killed for.

"Take all the time you need, Adam."

12

EVE FOLDED THE EGYPTIAN COTTON PAJAMAS she'd bought Sam last Christmas. They were barely worn—he must have brought them only to please her—and she ducked her head to hide the tears in her eyes as she stuffed them into the suitcase.

"Where'll you go?" she asked. Her voice sounded okay.

"My mother's. No more tall timber, so you can find me if you need me. Only don't need me too often, Babe. This is hard enough."

She nodded and he said, "I'm sorry, Eve."

It was about the eightieth time today he'd said it, and she felt a stab of annoyance. But annoyance was easier to handle than the hot heavy pain in her chest. She could probably get rid of that by throwing herself on the bed and sobbing, but that wasn't her way, any more than it would be Frances's. Besides, under the ache of sorrow and loss was relief. He'd been right this afternoon when he'd said, "It's not going to work, Eve."

And she'd felt a burst of relief to have it out in the open, and that he'd been the one to say it.

They had been in the drawing room; Mrs.

Knapp had just cleared away the tea tray, Larry was driving Frances to some committee, and they'd had the drawing room to themselves.

Eve had twisted her hands in her lap, and Sam had leaned forward to explain himself. She'd almost told him not to bother, because it didn't feel any righter to her than it did to him. But she'd thought he needed to say his piece and she'd kept quiet.

"I was so glad to see you up there, Eve. Elated," he'd said. "I thought I was being a yutz to stay away . . . that we'd make it somehow . . . that love would conquer all and other such horseshit. I was wild to see you again, even after just the few days since Saturday. I love you, Eve, I've always loved you."

Get on with it, she'd thought. No use saying all this sad silly stuff now.

He'd gone on, "Then I rounded the curve in the drive, saw the house, and suddenly felt like a parolee going back to the slammer."

"That bad?" She'd been startled by the harshness of the image.

"That bad. Not because of you . . . never because of you. But I saw this house and realized I was coming back to fifty years of never having a private moment. Of never being able to keep any of the silly little secrets everyone keeps. I was coming back to you kissing me good night and seeing me in a weak moment flirting with the cutie at the water cooler or getting drunk at a party and sticking my hand up a stray skirt for that feel of strange flesh every man gets a yen for. I could never lie that I had a headache or a touch of flu to get out of dinner at the club or bridge at Meg and Tim's—you see what I'm saying, Eve? I'd try and fail . . . try and fail . . . and I'd wind up going nuts or eating rat poison, or blowing my head off."

Or sniffing exhaust from a '39 Continental, Eve had thought, and looked up at the portrait of Olivia Tilden.

"I just can't hack it," Sam had said.

The very words her father must've said to her mother with the 1962 equivalent of *hack.*

She had not argued or pleaded or told him about the baby to keep him; she'd said she understood, and the terrible thing was, she did. She'd walk out on it too, if she could.

Now it was almost midnight. They'd planned for him to leave late at night so there'd be no questions, no black looks from Larry, tears from Mrs. Knapp, or that awful, ultra-bland look Frances got when something made her desperately unhappy.

In the morning, Eve would tell them he was gone, then she'd get out of the house and stay out until everyone had gotten a little used to the idea that the three-day reconciliation was over.

She closed the suitcase, started to drag it off the bed, and he took it from her.

"I'm sorry, Eve."

"Don't say that again," she snapped, suppressing an urge to slap him.

He was sorry . . . she was sorry, everybody was sorry. Some crazed gene had gotten stuck in an old family of superrich fools who'd somehow pissed off the gods, and everybody was sooooo sorry. Distant sorrow, such as you'd feel for the starving children of Somalia unless they happened to do their dying on your front lawn. Very distant to everyone but her, and her poor, poor mother and grandmother . . . and the great-great-great-grandmother in the hoop skirt who'd stood under an old elm and mouthed, "Watch out."

Oh, I'll watch out, Granny, she thought as she followed Sam out of the room. She caught sight of the new TV she'd gotten for his return and almost sobbed out loud, but choked it down and thought, *If only I knew what to watch out for.*

They made their way down the stairs, only turning on lights they needed and turning them right off again, in case Frances was alone tonight, wandering her sitting room with a spell of insomnia, and happened to see the light under her door.

They got down to the entry hall and Eve pushed the switch for the chandelier. It was on a dimmer; she kept it low so they had just enough light to see by.

He put the suitcase down and they faced each other. She'd been twenty-four when she'd met him, twenty-five when they married, and for five years it'd been fine. Better than fine until her mother died and left Eve the Dodd-Tilden legacy, like a monster flea jumping off a dead dog onto a live one, she thought. Sam was the only man she'd ever "known," or maybe ever would.

The feeling of loss was almost unendurable, but her genes for hiding it were as strong as the genes for "the thing," and she looked steadily up at her about-to-be-ex-husband. He made a move to hug her, but she knew he didn't really want to because she might see something, and she stepped back. He picked up the suitcase and said, "The alarm?"

"Yes."

"Eve . . ."

"Just go, Sam. No blame."

She tried to believe that, to not hate the unknown Tilden forebear who'd done something heinous enough to bring this curse on them.

She opened the door for him and he said, "I love you, Eve. Always will." He choked on *will,* then rushed across the front terrace and down to the car he'd brought around earlier so he wouldn't have to get it out of the garage.

She closed the door, leaned her head against it, and whispered, "I'm going to have a baby." She wanted to throw it open and yell it, then he'd come back . . . do the right thing . . . the way her father must have. And a year or so down the road, he'd walk out like her father had, or eat rat poison or blow his head off.

She heard the car start, then hurried to the alarm panel in the dining room. She pressed *pause control,* then the gate control pad, and a line of yellow, high-tech–looking lights blinked across the chrome panel. He had seven minutes to get down the drive and out on the road; then, if the gates weren't closed the lights would turn red and the alarm would go off. The gates would slam shut, the private alarm company would send about forty men, not to mention the local cops, who'd be alerted automatically. It'd gone off on its own a few times before they'd gotten the kinks out of the system and it had been like the final alert for World War Three.

She watched the panel carefully; the lights blinked a few minutes later to show Sam breaking the beam as he went through the gate, then they went back to steady cat's-eye yellow and she closed the gate. The lights went out and she countermanded the *pause.*

He was gone.

She went into the kitchen, poured a glass of milk and took a couple of the pecan cookies that Mrs. Knapp had made especially for Sam. She'd see some were gone, demand to know who'd eaten them because they were for Mr. Klein. Eve would tell her he was gone and Mrs. Knapp would cry, Larry would brood, and Frances would be totally, ostentatiously nonreactive, like some rare, inert element.

And Eve would get out of the house and stay out for the rest of the day.

She forced the milk and cookies down, standing at the marbletopped counter Mrs. Knapp kneaded bread on, then she rinsed the glass and her mouth, spitting nut fragments into the sink.

Mrs. Knapp would have a seizure if she saw them and Eve cleaned the sink with detergent, then wiped it so it shone the way it had before.

She turned off the kitchen lights and went back through the butler's pantry, past the door to the breakfast room and into the huge, formal dining room they almost never used.

She was abreast of the head of the table when something made her stop and face the windows. They were long and narrow, draped in pale gray damask with inside sheers. Slowly, not knowing why, she went to them and pulled the sheers back to look out. Moonlight turned the driveway silver; the lawn was a blackish green ground-sheet ending in the black, spiky, impenetrable-looking woods.

A shiver racked her and she thought, *Something's out there.*

Sam hadn't gone through the gate after all. He'd changed his mind, was willing to give it another go, and she didn't know if she was elated or sorry . . . only the alarm was armed. It could not be Sam.

Her hands were still warm from washing out the sink; she slid them up her chilled, goosepimpled arms inside her robe sleeves and thought, *Scars.*

● ●

ADAM HAD DONE IT; HE'D FOUND THE ROAD, THE HOUSE, AND *her.* He'd also found gates fifteen feet high, with wrought-iron spikes on top that would probably impale him if he tried to get over them.

Walls along the road, even higher than the gates, enclosed the land. They were well mortared, with no toeholds for climbing that he could see in this light.

Rich, Riley had screamed at the end. "She's rich . . . no one gets to people that rich!"

Rich she was. Tilden House was a walled estate, with pillars with a red light on one of them that must be the alarm. Even if Adam got past the alarm, over the walls, and across God knew how many acres of land, he'd find a thirty-room house crawling with servants.

All he got for all his trouble . . .

"Can that," he snapped to himself.

This wasn't a magic tower, she wasn't locked up in it like a fairy princess. Sooner or later, she'd come through those gates and when she did, he'd be waiting. He'd follow her to town, to the parking lot of a shopping center, the house of a friend, and maybe the friend lived in a place as isolated as this.

Lights came through the trees; he heard a car motor and hunched down in the seat. Then the red light went out; the gates clacked and started to swing open.

He couldn't believe his luck.

He laughed a little wildly and whispered, "Up yours, Riley," then slid out of the car, closing the door quietly. He crouched behind the fender and watched over the hood of the car. The gates hit their stops, rocked back and forth, and a car that looked comically small compared to the pillars, like the circus car ten clowns pile out of, tooled through the open gates and headed up the road toward the town.

The motor of the other car faded, and Adam ran. The gates started to shut, but the road was narrow; he'd make it with time to spare, was so close now he felt the slight breeze the gates made as they swung, then saw the red light had turned yellow.

The gates were alarmed, the grounds must be too; with beams that would silently alert the cops if he broke them. The Tildens were rich, and the cops wouldn't hang around to have another cup of coffee or doughnut. They'd get here . . . and get him before he was halfway up the long drive that disappeared into the trees.

He ground to a halt and watched balefully as the gates met and latched. The little light turned red again, glowing fiercely in the dark like the eye of a tiny, ferocious animal.

•   •

VACANCY BLINKED ON AND OFF IN GREEN NEON. THE MOTEL looked immaculate, with freshly painted white units, and no cigarette butts or crumpled paper cups in the driveway. Good—Adam could never sleep in a dirty place, thanks to his mother.

The office was spotless, with gray carpeting and a long, polished pine counter. The man behind it was about sixty, with thin pale hair and nails trimmed to the quick.

"Forty, cash or credit card," he told Adam. "We eat the tax until July, then the room goes to eighty and you eat the tax." He smiled, showing teeth too perfect to be his own, and pushed the registration card across the counter. Adam gave him two twenties and signed A. Harris, Greenville, New York (he didn't know if there was such a place). He changed a digit in his license number in case Latovsky or anyone else tracked him this far after they found her body . . . if they ever did.

"Free continental breakfast," the clerk said. "Juice and coffee, Danish or doughnut, served right here." He nodded at an alcove with a trestle table with stacked cups and saucers and a shining coffee urn. Then he gave Adam the key to unit 12.

Adam shaved and showered to save time in the morning, then wrapped a towel around his waist and settled himself in front of the TV, sure he'd be too keyed up to sleep. But he woke up to a blank, softly roaring screen and a stiff neck from sleeping in the chair. It was after four, the sky was turning gray. He massaged his neck, then pulled down the bed cover to get a couple of hours' more sleep. At nine, he'd be back on Old Warren, down the road from the gates, ready when she came through them.

He was almost asleep again when it finally hit him that she could come and go a dozen times, a dozen feet from him, and he wouldn't know it, because he had no idea what she looked like.

● ●

"DO YOU HAVE THE DATE?" THE LIBRARIAN ASKED ADAM.

She was about fifty, with a very long face and hair so tightly curled it looked carved. She had on a pink sweater set that reminded him of his mother for some reason. He'd always thought of her in the flowered dresses, yet she must have worn something like this, because at the sight of it, with the cardigan held on the woman's shoulders by a brass chain, he saw his mother's broad shoulders and the blur of her face.

"I'm afraid I don't," Adam said.

"Oh dear, that could be a problem. You see, the paper's index is only computerized from nineteen eighty-seven on. You'll have to dig for anything before that, and I do mean dig. The existing indices are so sloppy as to be worse than nothing. We have a county paper, a real newspaper, and it's been on the computer since eighty-four."

"But this is much more likely to be in the town paper," Adam said. "Why don't I try from eighty-seven on."

She set him up in a windowed cubbyhole with a terminal and discs for the *Oban-Bridgeton Ledger* from 1987 to the present.

"It's really a lousy paper," she confided. "We call it the *Poop*."

He laughed dutifully and she left him alone.

Sun coming through the window glared on the screen and he shaded it with one hand and slipped in the Jan–Jun 1987 disc. He typed *Tilden, Klein, Leigh* in that order, but only *Tilden* came up on the screen. He tapped *run program* and lines of green type appeared: That spring, Frances D. Tilden hosted flower shows in Bridgeton, Oban, and Sharon; Lawrence Simms of Tilden House was marshal of the Memorial Day parade. On the next disc, Frances Tilden donated a new wing to Oban Hospital, a playing field to the town's Little League, a Lincoln limo to Meals-on-Wheels, and fifty turkeys to a shelter in Torrington for their Thanksgiving dinner. Lines of type rolled up the screen as Frances Tilden parted with thousands.

Rich, Riley had screamed. *No one gets to people like that.*

We'll see, Adam thought, and slid in the next disc.

Frances Tilden gave away more money, went to more garden shows; she attended a benefit for Public TV in Westport and another for the Knapp Museum in Oban and won a bridge tournament. No Eve Tilden, Leigh, or Klein—no Eve anything, and his hands started to sweat. He wiped them on his handkerchief, then reached for the next disc. His mouth was sour and his bowels felt hot and jittery. He should've eaten more than the freebie motel breakfast of Danish and coffee. When he finished here, he'd stop for something—it rolled up so fast he almost missed it and had to go back: *Eve Tilden Leigh to Samuel Daniel Klein, May 9, 1987.* It was a wedding announcement on page 3, section C of the *Oban-Bridgeton Ledger.* No guarantee there'd be a picture of the bride, but it was likely, given the prominence of the family.

His hands were still sweating when the librarian brought him the issue in a plastic binder and he had to wipe them again so he wouldn't leave finger marks on the newsprint as he turned the pages. It was between the local soccer scores and real estate ads in which houses seemed to start at a million. It was one column written in fulsome small-town-paper prose, and there *was* a picture. It was grainy, amateurish, taken from a distance. But the light was on her strong, clear, handsome face and he knew he'd know it anywhere.

• •

Two hours after Adam returned the May 9, 1987 *Ledger* to the librarian with thanks, Lucy Evans rang Jim and Barb Riley's doorbell. Barb had said she was going to the mall around lunchtime and Lucy wanted to go with her.

There was no answer. Barb must've gone on without her and Lucy was sorry because she didn't see much of Barb during the school year, and she'd hoped they could have lunch together and take advantage of the spring sales.

She started back down the walk, passed the open garage door, and saw Barb's car. She must've taken Jim's—only his was there too she saw a couple of steps farther on. She stopped and looked back at the house.

Maybe they'd taken a walk or gone jogging, but there weren't any nice walks around here and jogging on the narrow busy roads was a little like the old joke about playing in traffic.

They could be around back doing some spring yard work, and she went around the garage along a stone path to the yard. It was empty. She went up on the deck, crossed the slats to the kitchen door, and rang the bell. She heard it tinkle inside the house and called "Barb," then listened for water running or the rush of the washing machine, but the house was silent—too silent—and a prickling feeling ran up her arms and across the back of her neck.

"Barbara . . ." she called uncertainly, and knocked on the glass portion of the door. No one answered and the prickling sensation intensified.

She looked back at the yard, hoping Jim would appear from the ring of trees with a stack of windfalls for firewood, but he didn't and she turned back to the door.

The Rileys did not have a mudroom; the door opened right into the kitchen. The white eyelet curtains were open and Lucy looked in. Her own face loomed in the glass, with the tips of the trees around the yard behind her. She cupped her hands around her face to kill the reflection and saw a couple of piles of rags covered with dark red paint that also splashed the counter, cabinets, floor, and walls. It took a second for her to register what she was looking at, then she tried to scream but only made a hoarse gasping sound that tore her throat. She threw herself back from the door, then staggered wildly down the stairs to the grass, trying to get her voice to work.

●   ●

"THIS TIME, GET A LAWYER," MEG SAID.

Eve didn't answer.

"Evie, are you listening to me?"

"Lawyer," Eve said, and thought *scars, scars, scars.*

The word had been at her all night and day, like a dripping faucet or that Oriental water torture designed to drive you mad.

Scars, scars, scars . . .

"Eve!"

"I'm listening, Meg. I should get a lawyer."

"I mean it, Eve. You're too rich to play it half-assed."

Scars, scars.

Eve blinked against the word and the sun shining in her face. They were in the back yard of Grayson, Meg's house. Calling the ten or so acres of lawn behind the mansion the yard was a conceit of Meg's mother, who claimed she had the common touch. "Accent on common," Frances had said once in a rare display of bitchiness.

Scars, scars, scars . . .

They were drinking gin and tonic, light on the tonic, and Eve had already had one, hoping to get high enough to stop the word. Her tongue felt a little thick, her upper lip was getting numb, but the word kept at her. *Scars, scars, scars . . .*

And this time, she got a flash of that kitchen back at Raven Lake with the white bulge in the ceiling and tried to figure out where the word and picture came from. Scars could be anything, everyone had scars, especially Ken Nevins, but she knew they were someone else's. Maybe her own from scratching the chicken pox scab next to her eye, or the time she dove into the freezing bay in Maine and slashed her chin on a rock. The reason for the kitchen vision was a total mystery.

"There's money at stake," Meg said.

"Money? You think Sam's after my money?" Maybe arguing with Meg would distract her.

But Meg shook her head. "Be better if he were, then we could bitch about him and you could feel abused. This way's a dead loss."

Scars.

Meg stirred the ice in her glass with her finger and asked, "Did you tell Frances?"

"I told them all at breakfast. Mrs. Knapp burst into tears and fled to the kitchen, leaving dirty dishes all over the table. Larry looked like he'd just heard someone had died and took himself off to do something to the cars, and Frances ostentatiously did not react."

"Dear Frances," Meg said.

"It was *not* dear," Eve snapped. "Talking to her was like talking to a refrigerator door."

"What's the right reaction?" Meg asked gently.

"I don't know. Yours . . . telling me you're sorry, telling me to see a lawyer, getting me drunk."

Meg grinned. "For drunk, you need a refill."

She took Eve's glass.

"Oh, Frances invites you and Tim for dinner and bridge tonight," Eve said, leaning back in the chair.

"Great, can't let anything like the end of your marriage put a crimp in Saturday night bridge."

Eve smiled for what felt like the first time in days. "That wouldn't be the Tilden way."

Meg carried the glasses back into the house, and Eve turned her face to the sun and closed her eyes.

Scarsscarsscarsscars . . . the words ran together like a snare drum and there was that bulge in the ceiling again. Dave had said it was a pulley but it didn't look like anything except a giant carbuncle ready to burst.

Horrible image; she sat up and opened her eyes and Meg came back with two frosted glasses with lime slices stuck on the rims. She handed one to Eve, Eve reached for it, thought *scarsscarsscars*, and the glass slipped through her fingers and fell on the grass. It tipped, spilling ice and liquor, but didn't break. She slid out of the chair, picked it up, and tried to grab the ice cubes with bits of grass stuck to them.

"It's okay, Evie, the ice'll just melt, it's okay."

The little lime slice that had looked fresh and perky a second ago was torn and limp and Eve's eyes filled with tears. She bowed her head and turned away so Meg wouldn't see them, but Meg knew her too well and she slid down on her knees next to her and put her arm around her. "Eve? Oh, Evie . . . I'm so sorry . . ."

"S'okay," Eve mumbled.

"No it's not." Meg sounded angry. "It is definitely *not* okay. They're making hamburger out of you and I hate them for it. You're psychic, not incontinent; you don't fill your pants at the dinner table and I'm sick to death of them acting as if you did. It's a gift, a power that could be fun and useful . . . my God, useful."

Dave Latovsky thought it was useful too.

"My Christ, think of it, Eve! Think what you could do with it. What your mother could have done if she hadn't been so . . . morbid. She was the only woman I ever knew who could look at a field of flowers and think about funerals. And your husband—forgive me, Eve, he's a nice guy, and all that, sweet and handsome and I guess he's sexy if you like the type—but he's another one who's made you hate what you can do. He's let himself be emasculated by something that should thrill him, and between him and your mother, they've made you believe a gift is a handicap, power's a curse . . . and they make me sick! You're *psychic*; you can go places, see things no one else can . . . and that's fabulous and awesome and most of all *useful*." She stopped herself suddenly, grabbed Eve's empty glass, and said, "Sorry. But I've been wanting to say that for a long time. You can tell yourself that it's just the gin talking if you want. But I think you know better."

She hauled herself up, took the glass back into the house, and Eve watched her go, surprised by the outburst. Meg meant well; so did Dave. But they couldn't imagine what it had been like to grab a swing chain and watch a woman bleed to death, or stand in the doorway of Bunner's office and watch his face blow away and not be able to stop it. Or to see that terrified little boy on the swing go to the woman waiting to do God knows what to him and not be able to protect him. *Scarsscarsscarsscars . . .*

They didn't know the dread that ate at her since she'd touched Bunner's recorder and seen those dead eyes in the mirror . . . *scarsscarsscars . . .*

Meg came back with the fresh drink.

• •

EVE WAS LATE LEAVING MEG'S. SHE HAD TO HURRY TO SHOWER and try to sober up before Tim and Meg and the Adamses and Raskins got there at seven.

She jumped into the LeBaron. A wave of dizziness caught her and she belched and tasted gin. Dr. Rubin would be very unhappy with her. She should probably go back and ask Meg to have George drive her home. But it was Saturday and she didn't see the big Mercedes; George must be in town doing the week's shopping or waiting while Meg's mother, Lila Grayson, visited friends. Meg's mother was very disorganized and George always had more than enough to do on Saturdays without having to cart Meg's drunk friends home.

Eve waited, breathing in the soft late-afternoon air. It was cooling down, would probably go into the fifties tonight. *Perfect weather,* she thought, *fifties at night, seventies during the day . . . perfect.*

She sat up suddenly and realized she'd actually dozed; her head throbbed, and sweat from the heat of the sun coming through the windshield stuck her clothes to her, but she was almost sober.

She looked at the house and wondered if Meg was watching her and giggling. Eve waved in case she was, then put the car in gear. *Scarsscarsscarsscars . . .*

And took off down the driveway.

It was a straight run from the house, and the gates would be open during the day, but a dip hid them and she didn't see the car parked across the driveway blocking the road until she was on top of it. She stood on the brake; the LeBaron screeched and skidded and came to a shuddering stop with the front fender about an inch from one of the stone pillars, and the front bumper almost touching the other car's rear door.

She slumped against the wheel, with sweat pouring down her face and her hands shaking helplessly at the near miss. She should have asked George to take her no matter how many Saturday errands had to be run.

She raised her head, wiped the sweat out of her eyes, and looked out at the other car. It was a light blue Ford, much bigger than the LeBaron, and it looked empty. Someone had blocked the Grayson drive and blithely walked away to pick wildflowers or mushrooms or just take a goddamn nature stroll in the afternoon sun.

She honked the horn furiously, then stuck her head out the window and screamed, "Move it." *Just like a fishwife,* Frances would think but never say.

Nothing happened. No one came stumbling out of the woods, looking shame-faced at obstructing the drive out of the huge Victorian monstrosity.

"Hey," Eve shouted again, "you're blocking the road." Her voice died away; there wasn't a sound except for a light breeze rustling the tops of the trees.

She went to unbuckle her seatbelt but it wasn't on, and she opened the door and got out. The other car was so close to the pillars she had to squeeze past it to get to the road. She moved around the trunk of the Ford into deep grass and a cloud of spring flies (nothing to what they had upstate, but bad enough) flew up and batted her legs under her skirt. She plowed through the grass to the pavement, looked in the car window, and saw the keys in the ignition and a blanket over some parcels or luggage in back.

Maybe the Ford had stalled and the driver was slogging his way to town to get help. But he could have walked up to Grayson and asked to use the phone.

She looked back at the gigantic stone house with its forbidding stained glass and the huge, disproportionate veranda and understood how a stranger might feel intimidated and prefer to walk the three miles to the Shell station.

Only the car looked too new to break down . . .

SCARSSCARSSCARSSCARS . . .

It was getting louder, more insistent; her head throbbed and her vision blurred a little.

Even a new car could break down, and maybe the driver had just walked off in a fury and left the keys, hoping someone would steal it (if they could get it started) and he'd collect the insurance.

Wrong neighborhood, buddy; no one around here'd steal anything under an S-class Mercedes, she thought.

If she could start it, she'd just move it far enough to unblock the drive and no harm done, and she reached for the door handle on the driver's side. If it was locked, she'd have to go back to Grayson and call a tow to move the Ford. But the keys were in it; it must be open unless the fool had locked himself out. She touched the handle and *Scarsscarsscarsscarsscars* blasted through her head. She saw the painted-over white pulley on the car window . . . and over it Great-great-great-granny's face, with her mouth moving silently but urgently—*watch out . . . watch out . . .*

It was so vivid she jerked her hand back and looked up and down the road. It was empty and quiet. Seeding maples sent their little flyers through the air and everything looked peaceful, but something was wrong here, she had to move this obstacle and get away. She grabbed the handle and pulled, the door swung open, and she slid into the seat and turned the key. The buzzer sounded to remind her about the seat belt, the gas needle swung to full, all the other dials did what they were supposed to.

She heard something shift behind her and, with *scars* screaming through her pounding head and the bumpy white bulge of the pulley half blinding her, she looked in the rearview mirror and saw the empty, light brown doll's eyes looking back at her.

● ●

PETE ANSWERED THE PHONE. "DUSSAULT'S."

"Mr. Dussault, my name's Meers, Lemuel Meers. I work with—"

"I know who you are, Cap'n Meers. You're Dave's boss."

"Well . . . yes."

"Dave's not here, sir."

"No . . . he's fishing, right?"

"Right. Out on Chalice, and he sure had a nice day for it."

"Mr. Dussault, I know this is an imposition, but I've got to talk to him. Is there any way you can get him to call me?"

Pete fell silent. His eyes roved over the neat counter and cash register, with the pie case behind it, and, to his right, the shelves of STP and Quaker Oil. It had been a gorgeous day, with enough wind to keep the flies from settling. A perfect day for fishing a wilderness lake like Chalice, even with kids who were always more trouble than they were worth in a boat. He glanced out the front window; no one was pumping from the self-serve, no one waited for him to come out and pump for them, and he had no excuse to hang up. He knew something had happened for the captain to call Dave up here, and whatever it was would be bad because no one ever got good news from a cop. He hoped it wasn't Dave's mother . . . or his girlfriend, Jeanne. Jeanne was nice as fresh pie and about as wholesome, and her little boy was with Dave this minute along with Dave's kid. Of all the people involved with Dave Latovsky, his ex-wife was the most expendable. Pete blushed with shame at the thought and said quickly, "What happened, Cap'n Meers?"

"A murder—two murders. Friends of Dave's . . . but not best friends, you know what I mean?"

"Sure."

"But that's not why I'm calling, I mean not because they're his friends." Meers's voice had taken on a mountain lilt and Pete wondered if the captain was mocking him, then realized it was genuine. He was talking to another mountain man.

Meers said, "I mean it's not the kind of news I'd give Dave one second sooner than he had to hear it. No, Mr. Dussault, I'm calling because I need his help."

"I understand, sir. But we got a kind of problem here. Don't know if you know this area."

"No. I'm from up north of Raquette Lake."

"Ah . . . well, Chalice makes Raquette look like Central Park if you take my meaning. It's a twelve-mile Jeep ride to Chalice. Takes a couple of hours even in the Cherokee." He looked out again. Don Wallbrun was filling his rustbucket and clouds were piling up, dimming the light. There'd be rain and/or sleet by midnight.

"And it looks like some weather coming." He spoke morosely, because he already knew he was going in after Dave. A double murder wasn't the kind of thing you ignored because of a little weather.

● ●

HALF AN HOUR LATER, WITH SANDWICHES, A THERMOS, AND HIS sleeping bag in case he got stuck for the night, Pete Dussault set out for Chalice. It was a gorgeous lake, but getting there was not half the fun, and Dave was a fool for taking the kids, although he'd done it before. So had Pete when his kids were little.

The road cut off the paved two-lane at an innocent, totally misleading wood-burned sign, CHALICE LAKE, 12 MILES. It was probably the worst twelve miles in the eastern hemisphere. He doubted even the Alaskan outback had anything much hairier, and calling it a road was like calling a cream puff a doughnut because both were round.

Pete turned into it with that little flutter in his middle he always got when he took the Chalice Lake Road, as he'd probably done a thousand times in his life, because you never knew what to expect. Today—tonight rather, since the twilight faded fast as clouds thickened—it was about average. It must've been a logging trail back around the turn of the century, and once every dozen or so years, the state graded it and scattered some gravel around. You couldn't even do the first hundred yards in two-wheel drive, and he'd had to tow out a whole range of Japanese off-roaders and even a couple of Range Rovers. It was a Jeep road; nothing else could make it.

The Cherokee heaved over submerged boulders, settled into potholes so deep you drove down one side and up the other. He let the Cherokee find its own way through slick sections where springs had broken out and turned the track (better word for it than road) to pudding.

He averaged six miles an hour (which was pretty good on the Chalice Lake Road), and when he reached the "parking lot" at the lakeside, it was night. One of those dead-black starless nights when the air felt like ink and seemed to gobble up the headlight beams.

He tried the side spot, but that didn't illuminate much except Latovsky's Cherokee parked next to the boat landing.

He turned off the spot and headlights and saw the tiny, golden dot of Latovsky's campfire across the lake.

It was too far across the black water under the black sky; the lake bottom shifted with the seasons, and deadfalls from winter would be rising. He'd make it there, okay; he and Dave could make it back. But their chances of hanging up on a sandbar that hadn't been there last summer or getting hit with dead wood and turning turtle were pretty good.

Not a risk you'd take with two kids in the boats.

He'd wait for first light to bring them back: he and one kid in his dinghy, Dave and the other kid in his.

Captain Meers's poor dead folks wouldn't be any deader by morning.

● ●

EVE KNEW SHE WAS AT THE LAKE, BUT COULDN'T SEE THE WATER until the headlights hit it. A lot of people probably didn't see it at all after a few drinks and heaved over the strip of reeds to find themselves hubcap deep in water, sinking into the muck.

"Turn left," he snapped, and dug the gun deeper into her neck. The muzzle scraped her skull and the pain made her dizzy. She made the turn, and a few minutes later the Ford heaved off the pavement onto the gravel road that led past 300 Lakeshore, the pretty little cabin on the lake where her husband had taken refuge from her and *the thing.*

"You know where we're going, don't you?" the man asked softly.
"Yes."
"You were there that night."
"Yes." She didn't have to ask which night.

He dug the gun deeper and she said, "Keep that up and I'll pass out." He eased up a little but there must be one hell of a bruise in the spot by now. He'd been leaning over the back of her seat with the gun jammed into her neck for four hours, except for a moment of blessed respite when he'd given her the toll ticket and money at the Thruway exit.

She had pulled out into the big, confusing Northway interchange, one way to the mountains, the other to Utica and points west, and thought of taking the wrong road. But he'd only force her to go back or shoot her and shove her body out of the car.

She knew he was going to kill her; her only question was why he hadn't already. At first she'd thought—when she could get past the panic enough to think—that he was taking her someplace remote to hide her body. Then they'd come to the Thruway, he'd ordered her to take the north ramp, and she knew where they were going, but not why. Driving all the way to Raven Lake to hide a body was absurd.

Now they were there, abreast of number 300 Lakeshore, and he said, "Turn."

The Ford ground up the drive and the headlights swept the forlorn-looking little house. She pulled up next to the swing and stopped. "Kill the motor," he said. She did, then started to tremble, making the key chain with the little caduceus on it swing back and forth. At first, back at Meg's, she'd been too terrified to think about the caduceus; but as the trip wore on and her panic and terror turned to something low-grade and grinding, like seasickness, she found herself wondering if he was a doctor.

He sat back and the gun stopped digging into her flesh. The relief was indescribable; she felt her muscles start to slacken . . . then he hit her with the gun.

It felt like a tap. She thought he'd done it inadvertently, but it must have been much harder than she realized, or he knew exactly where to hit her, because her head snapped forward and whacked the steering wheel, and her body slid helplessly across the front seat.

The next thing she knew she was upside down, with her head, which felt swollen to the size of a soccer ball, dangling. She forced her eyes open and was hit by a burst of color. She thought it must be an effect of the blow, then realized it was the multicolored hooked rug in the foyer of the house. He was carrying her over his shoulder fireman fashion, with her head hanging like a dead chicken's and her butt jutting up. She wanted to laugh, but her head hurt too much and she was glad to pass out again.

• •

A LONG, THIN STREAK OF BLISTERING PAIN RACED UP HER ARM, and she snapped her eyes open and saw him pull a spent syringe out of her arm. He'd injected her with something that burned all the way to her shoulder and she tried to scream. A hoarse croak came out and he looked at her. The dead eyes met hers, and she thought of her volunteering days at Oban Hospital, where there'd been a Vietnam vet with a glass eye.

"It's okay, Eve," he said in a shockingly gentle voice. "It's just a harmless preanesthetic that'll put you out for a while. I'm sorry to have to do it this way, but I . . . I . . ."—he had to force the words out—"can't . . . face that . . . room at night."

He meant the kitchen and she didn't blame him.

"You'll sleep," he said, "not deeply enough to perform surgery, but that's not on the agenda."

He *was* a doctor; *doctor–serial killer, baby sitter–ax murderer,* and she giggled. He grinned at her, his eyes and teeth glittered in the lamplight, and he needed a shave. He looked like a wolf.

She closed her eyes to blot him out and drifted.

Whatever he'd shot her full of worked fast, and the pain in her head and arm stopped. She snuggled against the dust-sheeted couch and was amazingly comfortable. Cessation of pain is the only real pleasure, her mother used to say. It must've been her mother; she couldn't imagine Frances coming up with that one.

Poor Frances must be frantic. They'd found the LeBaron by now (whenever now was) and called the locals. But they were a useless bunch who bulked themselves up with enough hardware to fight a war and sauntered down Main trying to look as if their balls were too big for their thighs to meet.

Useless.

Frances knew who she had to call, and she'd do it no matter how much she disliked him. She'd call Satan to save Eve, *but soon,* Eve thought, *please, Auntie, call Dave soon.*

● ●

RAIN ON THE ROOF OF THE CHEROKEE WOKE PETE. HE LOOKED out and saw it blowing across the lake in sheets in the dawn light. It was going to be a miserable trip across and back—the kids would have to bail the whole way—but there was enough light to see by, no one would drown.

He quickly drank some coffee from the thermos, gobbled two of Bessie's sweet biscuits, then pulled on his poncho and stuck his head out and saw an arrangement of dark lumps was coming toward him through the curtain of rain. He halloooooed and Dave halloooed back.

Dave was bringing the kids in before this crap turned to sleet, as it would if the temperature dropped half a degree. Pete pulled the poncho hood up and jumped out in the rain to help beach the dinghy.

● ●

MEERS PULLED OUT A RING OF KEYS WITH A PURPLE RABBIT'S FOOT that Latovsky had seen in Riley's hands a thousand times. He looked away to get it out of his sight and saw the impatiens Barb must've just planted poking through the wet dirt. Then he didn't know where to look and kept his eyes trained on his feet on the stone stoop.

Meers broke the crime scene seal and opened the door. A draft of steamy air blew out at them and Meers said, "Jesus, we left the heat on." He crossed the foyer to an old-fashioned dial thermostat. "We were all pretty rattled," he explained, "even Rule."

He turned the dial and the furnace stopped rumbling.

"They were in the kitchen." Meers nodded down a short carpeted hall to a closed swing door. "The bodies're gone of course, but I had them leave the rest intact so you can get oriented before you see the photos.

"People next door heard shots last night, but thought it was truck backfire on the Northway, which is about a half a mile away. Then, about noon, a neighbor lady came over, saw the bodies through the window in the back door, and understandably had hysterics. It took her a while to calm down enough to make sense and by the time her husband called in, and the locals figured that they couldn't handle double murder and called us, it was almost four."

He led the way down the hall and stopped with his hand on the door. "It's a mess, Dave—I'm really sorry."

"You didn't make it, Lem."

"I know."

Meers pushed open the door and a stench of baked blood and spoiled meat rolled at them. "Shit." Meers ripped his handkerchief out of his pocket and put it over his nose and mouth. "Shouldn't be this bad," he said, his voice muffled by the cloth. "Wouldn't be if we'd turned the heat off."

Latovsky breathed through his mouth and looked past Meers into the Rileys' kitchen. One side of the room was covered with blood, with coin-sized wafers of putrid flesh glued to the surfaces.

He choked and turned his head; then he took a deep breath and rushed across the room, sidestepping a big tacky puddle around a chair set in the middle of the floor. He tore open the back door and waved it back and forth to clear the air. But it had been warm and still since the rain stopped; the sun was a silver smear behind a glaze of white cloud cover and nothing stirred except the drip of water from the porch rail and Riley's kettle barbecue.

Latovsky remembered Riley broiling steaks on it last summer.

The possessions of the dead were always sadder than the repulsive corpse, he thought. And he was hugely glad that his last memory of Riley would be the fair, red-faced man raising his hand to make a vow in Casey's bar and grill.

He left the door open and turned back into the room.

The slugs had gone through the Rileys and still had enough firepower to splinter doors of three cabinets; two on the wall, one under the sink.

"What'd he use?" he asked.

"Big-mother gun," Rule said.

Bunner's killer had used a *big-mother gun*, but there was more to it that Latovsky couldn't get hold of. He tried for a second, then gave up and opened the splintered cabinet under the sink. It contained cleaning supplies. The bullet had nicked a bottle of Dawn and it lay on its side leaking green goo. The fresh smell fought the miasma in the room, making it worse by contrast, and Latovsky was suddenly a hair from being violently sick. He pulled out his handkerchief and plastered it over his face. It had been in his pocket two days and smelled of fish and wet wool, but that was infinitely better than the reek around him.

He reached past the detergents, furniture polish, and scouring powder and touched the back wall of the cabinet, which was the outer wall of the house. He found the hole in the plasterboard, but no slug.

"He dug them out," Meers said. "All of them."

Latovsky stood up and looked around. Three shots; two for the Rileys . . .

"What was the third shot?" he asked.

"I'll tell you when we get out of here and breathe, and it better be soon."

Meers's eyes were calm above the handkerchief but his forehead was shiny greenish white and his eyebrows looked like blackbird wings against it.

Latovsky's gag reflex was also getting out of hand and he took a fast, last look around the room.

The chair surrounded by the pool of tacky blood had a blood-encrusted clothesline drooped around it and a lump of cloth stiff with blood on the seat. One side of the room was an abattoir, the other was clean; two of the shots had been fired from more or less the same angle, almost the same height, but the third, the one that hit the cabinet under the sink, was much lower and on a totally different trajectory. Yellow tape marked a body against the wall near the door and the outline of what looked like a foot at the base of the chair.

"What about the other foot?" Latovsky asked, and Meers got even greener.

"Later."

"Okay, let's get out of here."

They rushed through the door, uncovered their faces and breathed. "Jesus! . . . Let's sit down," Meers said, and they went into the Rileys' den.

It was a pleasant room, with a patterned rug and a wall of built-in shelves. The bottom shelves were taken up with a fairly new 27-inch TV, a hi-tech–looking VCR, and a compact disc player. Riley's PC sat on a desk near a window that let in the silvery, misty sunlight.

"He didn't get much," Latovsky said.

"He didn't get anything." Meers sat in a chair next to a modest brick mantel that made Latovsky think of the marble mantel at Tilden House . . . then of Eve.

"The wife had three hundred in cash in her nightie drawer, where I guess a lot of women keep emergency money. Joan does," Meers said.

Allison too, Latovsky thought. Her fuck-off fund she called it, to keep him off balance. It had never occurred to her that *he'd* do the fucking off.

"And there was an antique pocket watch in Riley's dresser," Meers went on, "a real golden oldie worth more than everything in the house. Also, the wife was wearing a gold chain and her engagement ring. Hardly the Hope diamond, but still worth something. He didn't get any of it."

"Maybe they came home early and surprised him."

"So he tied the wife to the chair? Then kneecapped her—that was the off-angle shot, by the way."

"Kneecapped!" Latovsky sat down hard on the chair across from Meers. "What the fuck for?" he asked sickly.

"That's the question, and the obvious answer is the Rileys were dealing and the killer was trying to find out where they kept the stuff."

"Shit, no!"

"He'd hardly tell you if he was . . . you're a cop."

"Lem, I never even saw Riley smoke a joint."

"What about the wife?"

"She was an English teacher at Oneida High, a neat, sweet little woman who loved to cook. She'd no more sell, snort or smoke shit than my mother would."

"I was afraid you'd say that." Meers sank back in the chair. "Then there was no stash and the kneecapping's a mystery."

"Could he have done it for fun?" Latovsky asked faintly.

"I asked Rule and he said no. Said your recreational torturer—his phrase, not mine—would draw it out, make it last; he'd use a razor or lit cigarette or a low-caliber piece if he used one at all. But this was strictly amateur hour, because the cannon he used blew half her leg off. That's what happened to her other foot, by the way—we found it wedged under a cabinet." Latovsky saw a shudder run through Meers, but he went on calmly. "Rule said she was out in maybe a minute or two and probably dead by the time he put the gun to her head. No *fun* in that."

No fun . . . that half-thought triggered by "big-mother gun" swam at Latovsky again and he tried to grab it. But he was exhausted;

a soggy doughnut in the sodden tent at five this morning was the last thing he'd eaten. He'd get past the sight and smell of the kitchen and force himself to eat, then maybe whatever it was would come to him.

● ●

HE DROVE TO JEANNE'S TO PICK UP JO, BUT SHE AND MATT HUD-dled in front of the TV in the den watching Lamb Chop (probably Matt's choice) and trying to look like orphan refugees who'd die if they were separated.

"Jeannie says I can stay," Jo said, "and Matt wants me to."

Jeannie always said she could stay, Matt always wanted her to; his chin was already trembling at the thought of losing her.

"Your mother's expecting you home," Latovsky said.

Jo made a face. She'd reached the age when her mother's expec-tations didn't mean much.

He looked helplessly at Jeanne, who stood in the archway be-tween her tiny dining room and the den. He suddenly wondered what the dining room at Tilden House was like.

"I'd like her to stay," Jeanne said. "So would Matt. Why don't you call Allison?"

She took herself off to the kitchen so she wouldn't hear his end of the conversation with his ex-wife, and he used the phone in the front hall so Jo wouldn't hear in case there was a row. But Allison was amenable and he didn't hear any of that whiney hurt in her voice. Maybe she had a date.

Their conversations were grim and short, full of guilt for him unless they fought, which didn't happen much anymore.

He hung up and went back to the den, where the kids had forgotten Lamb Chop and were watching the door to hear their fate.

"You can stay," he said, and they yelled "Yay" and hugged each other.

He went to say good-bye to Jeanne and she gave him a long, slow, open-mouthed kiss that found a weak spot in his groin and made him want to stay too . . . but there was no time.

He was still wearing fishing clothes, and he drove home and pulled off the boots that felt like fifty pounds of lead melting into his feet. Then he stripped off the itchy wool fishing pants and stood under the shower. He dressed, wolfed down a peanut butter sandwich, and left the house.

The sun was burning off the haze from the rain, and the pavement and hood of the car steamed. He drove to the station, which was stone-walled and always cold. He got a ham sandwich from the machine and some coffee, and went into his office to read the preliminary reports from Rule and Lucci.

Meers's door was closed, so he was there. Probably on the phone with a Quantico buddy, asking if they had anything on the big computer on a mutt who got his jollies kneecapping women with a Magnum.

The unmemory came back. It was stronger, but still not coherent: *No fun . . . big-mother gun. Big-mother gun* kept at him because of Bunner, but *no fun* eluded him, and he didn't know how they were connected or what Barb Riley could have known to make the killer blow her leg off when it was *no fun.*

He let the words chase each other through his head for a moment, then he gave up and called Riley's boss on the *Register.* It was Sunday afternoon, but Max Jergens was at work.

"I'm sorry to ask this, Mr. Jergens, but is there any chance the Rileys were dealing drugs?"

"Drugs!" Jergens exploded. "Shit no! Whatever put a maggot like that in your head?"

"Barbara Riley was kneecapped."

Stunned silence, then Jergens said miserably, "She taught high-school English, Lieutenant. Think someone kneecapped her to drag the figures of speech out of her? Just had to get the difference between a simile and a metaphor? What the fuck went on in there?"

"I don't know."

"Well, you fuckin' well should. You're the fuckin' cop."

"I'm sorry," Latovsky said meekly.

Another silence, then Jergens said, "I'm sorry, too, Lieutenant, you don't deserve that. I'm upset, we're all upset. Kneecapped! I don't get it."

"Neither do we, Mr. Jergens. Was Riley working on anything you'd classify as controversial?"

"Controversial enough to get him killed and his wife"—Jergens choked on the word—"kneecapped? No. The Wolfman story was his . . ."

Wolfman. The hair on Latovsky's neck stirred.

". . . and he was getting background for a piece on Leo Shine, the state senator."

"Anything there?"

"No. Shine's eighty in the shade and about as controversial as Dwight Eisenhower. Well-liked old fart, and Riley thought it'd be a good idea to write something *nice* about a politician for a change. Thought it was important. Leo Shine did not kill Jim Riley, Lieutenant. Then there was the piece on Friday about the Clairvoyant."

Clairvoyant. Big gun, no fun . . . add *Clairvoyant* and *Wolfman.*

He had it now, just needed a second to think. They hung up and the buzzer sounded a second later. Barber told him he had a call from someone at the *Register* and Latovsky grabbed it thinking it was Jergens with something to add. But another man asked, "Are you in charge of the Riley murder investigation?"

"Yes, sir. What can I do for you?"

"My name's Lyons, Lieutenant. Bill Lyons. I work at the *Register* in personnel?" He made it a question.

"Yes, sir," Latovsky said patiently.

A moment of silence, then, in a tone of true misery, Lyons said, "I think I talked to Jim Riley's killer on Friday."

And he told his story.

"His name was not Latovsky," Latovsky said softly.

"I know. I know that now. I know."

"Was there anything at all familiar about his voice?"

"No. I wouldn't know anyway because the guy sounded garbled and muffled, like he had a bad cold."

"Muffled?"

"Yeah, like he was sick or maybe . . . I guess . . . disguising his voice."

"Muffled," Latovsky whispered.

"Jesus, that's what I said."

A muffled voice had lured Bunner to his office on Sunday and shot him with a big-mother gun. The killer in the woods, according to Eve, the Wolfman who killed dispassionately, according to Rule, had *no fun* doing it or kneecapping Barb Riley. He'd tortured her for information, but the gun was too big, and she couldn't tell anyone anything after it blew half her leg off. But what did Barb Riley, English teacher, *know?* The difference between a metaphor and a simile? The meter of the *Iliad?* Jergens's cracks were getting in the way, Latovsky shoved them out of his mind and got Lyons off the phone. The intercom rang again.

"What now?" he yelled into the phone. He was yelling too much—the men would wind up hating him.

Barber said, "Woman's calling long distance. Tried to put her off, but it was like putting off the queen of England . . . very haughty lady. Name of Tilden."

Eve. It wasn't Barb who knew, it was Riley. The Wolfman tortured the wife to get the husband to talk, and Riley heard his wife's shriek of agony, saw her flesh and shattered bone explode across the kitchen—and told the Wolfman everything.

He groaned into the phone.

"That mean you won't talk to her?" Barber asked.

"No, you numb-nuts bastard," Latovsky shouted. "Put her on."

He waited with his heart pounding as clicks connected him to Eve. In a second, he had to tell her he'd sicced the six—make that eight-time—killer with the doll's eyes on her after all. Riley's doing, but Latovsky's fault, and she had to cover her ass. But she had money and people to help her. She could spend the summer in Nova Scotia, on the coast of Maine, Vancouver Island, the Riviera. Not too shabby, and in the meantime Latovsky would get him. Fuck Meers and Linney and the legal system. He'd get Adam Fuller, and she could come back to her husband, have her baby . . .

A last click (after enough of them to connect him to Ulan Bator) and Frances Tilden said, "Lieutenant—"

"Eve," he cried. "I've got to talk to Eve," and she said, "I wish you could."

● ●

THE KITCHEN EVE REMEMBERED HAD BEEN STARK WHITE, WITH white cabinets, walls, counters, curtains, and a ceiling so white you couldn't look at it without blinking, with that white-on-white bulge on it.

In reality, the linoleum was streaked with green, the counters had faded to ivory. The stove top and wall phone were black, the curtains yellow, and the nicks around the edges of the porcelain table rust brown.

"Go on." He prodded her with the gun and she took a few steps, then turned, expecting him to be right behind her. But he was still in the doorway and there was finally some expression in his eyes. It looked like fear, and sweat ran down his face and neck into the collar of his clean shirt. He'd actually had the foresight to bring a clean shirt, along with a lot of other stuff, including the syringe full of whatever he'd shot her full of last night.

They stared at each other, then he raised his foot, let it hang comically in midair a moment, then put it back down on the same side of the sill. He could not come in here for some reason, and she saw her chance. Her eyes flashed around the room and came to the back door, bolted and chained from the inside. She saw herself ripping off the chain and bolt, tearing the door open, and running for her life . . . and he'd shoot her before she even shot the bolt.

"No way out, Eve," he said quietly. "You might as well tell me."

"Tell you what?"

"What happened to me in this room."

To the terrified little boy on the swing.

Eve looked up at the bulge so quickly, her neck crackled and she got dizzy from the last of the drug hangover. It had been bad when she'd come to, but he had a coil to heat water and instant coffee with packets of sugar and creamer and paper cups. He'd given her the coffee, then let her use the toilet and shower while he stood outside, with the gun presumably trained on the closed door in case she tried to get away. No way to do that. There was a little window high in the wall, and she stood on the toilet seat in her stocking feet and tried it, but it was painted shut. She could throw something through it, but he'd hear the glass break, shoot the door open . . . then shoot her. He must have checked the window before he let her in there because he'd been very careful, very well prepared about everything. He'd even brought cellophane-wrapped Danishes drizzled with sugar frosting, the first bite of which made the inside of her mouth ache because it had been so long since she'd eaten.

The coffee, shower, food had gotten rid of the hangover until this reeling second when she looked up at that thing in the ceiling.

She leaned on the porcelain-topped table to steady herself, smelled butter cookies baking, and jerked her hands away. The smell faded, but stayed in the background.

"I can't help you," she said without looking at him. "I have no idea what happened to you."

"No . . . but you can find out. That's why you're still alive."

That's absurd, she wanted to say, but if she convinced him it *was* absurd, he'd kill her.

"Maybe I can." She drew out the words. She'd have to draw everything out, slow it down to buy time for Dave to find her.

"I can give you a clue," he said softly. He put the gun on the floor next to his foot, then he pulled up his shirt and T-shirt, exposing a chest thatched with light brown hair that thinned to a line running into his pants.

What, no blue light? she thought madly.

He unbuckled his belt, started to undo his fly, and she turned her head away. Then she heard his buckle rattle, his fly unzip, and she shut her eyes.

"Look," he said, but she kept her eyes shut.

"I said look!"

She heard him pick up the gun, and she opened her eyes and finally saw the scars.

He'd kept his pubis modestly covered, but his abdomen was bare and hundreds of scars ran every which way across it from his navel to the line of his pants. Some were pale threadlike lines, others were liverish welts that looked tender. They were cuts, not burns like the scars on Ken Nevins's hands, and these were no accident. They had been made. Someone had done this to him!

She tried to say something: *Oh God,* or *how could they,* meaning whoever had done it. But she couldn't make a sound.

"Look!" he commanded.

He didn't have to because she couldn't tear her eyes away. The baking smell suddenly intensified, and she tried to drive it away because she didn't want to see what was coming next. She thought of her mother-in-law, Greta, baking cookies in her kitchen. But even having that good, kind, wholesome woman in her mind, in this horror room with that poor scarred monster in the doorway, was obscene, and she pushed the vision of Greta away.

"Do you have to touch them?" he asked, blushing.

Her skin shriveled. "I can't . . ."

He looked down at himself. "No, I guess not. I don't see them head-on very often, tend to forget how bad they are."

He pulled his shirt down and his pants up with one hand, keeping the gun trained on her. He got the fly zipped, but couldn't manage to hook the waistband and it stayed open with his belt dangling.

He smiled wanly at her. "Show's over," he said softly. "Now . . . tell me . . ."

Cooking-butter smell filled the air, made her queasy. It was going to happen, but she didn't want it to; wanted to tell him it didn't work that way. That she might see what he wanted her to, or she might see anything about anyone who'd ever been in this room, back to the original farmer whose barn this had been. She might see him feeding his chickens, mucking out a stall. She might see any of the countless family gatherings that must've taken place in here since it became a kitchen . . . but that was crap and she knew it. She could go where she wanted, when she wanted, and she better finally admit that to herself or she'd never leave this room alive.

"Go on, Eve," he said softly, sinuously, using the same low seductive tone Dave Latovsky and Meg had used on her when they wanted her to do it. *Go on, Eve. Tell me the past and future, the way and truth. Tell me where Grandma's emeralds are and if my husband's fucking another woman. Tell me who played on that swing and what the killer looks like.*

And now, *Tell me how I got the scars.*

She knew what to do. The pulley was the heart of this room, the table was right under it, and she put her hands flat on top of it. The smell of baking butter and sugar was suffocating; she felt heat from the oven and looked at it. It had been all white, with a stainless-steel handle; now it was trimmed in black with a black Bakelite handle. She looked up and saw the unpainted pulley, with a rope through the wheel. The wheel squeaked softly as it turned, the rope pulled taut, and a woman chanted, "Dirty, dirty, dirty . . ."

● ●

LATOVSKY SAID, "MISS TILDEN, I'M GOING TO MAKE ANOTHER call with you on the phone, so just hang on. We'll be talking to a man named Berger from the FBI. Okay?"

"I just hang on?" she asked meekly.

"Yes, ma'am. It'll only take a minute."

He put her on hold and felt himself run out of breath. "Breathe out," Bunner used to tell him. "Hyperventilating comes from gasping in and forgetting to let it out."

He forced himself to exhale in a slow stream that warmed the mouthpiece, then he buzzed Barber.

"Listen to me, Larry." He never used Barber's first name, was surprised he even remembered it. "I've got a Miss Tilden on oh-three. I want you to keep her there; at the same time, I want you to get Stan Berger on oh-four, then I want you to conference the calls."

"You mean so you can all talk at once?" Barber said brightly.

"That's right, Larry. And if you lose one of them, I'm going to suspend you."

Silence at the other end.

"Do you understand me, Larry?"

"Yes, sir, I understand."

Latovsky tore through his book and found Berger's number, got Barber back, gave it to him, then hung up and waited.

It was no ordinary kidnapping; the FBI would do their stuff, but there'd be no ransom call or note. Fuller had her and she was already dead, or would be as soon as he got whatever he wanted out of her, and it wasn't money. But that was an assumption, the one thing a good cop never made, and he wanted to be a good cop this minute more than he'd ever wanted anything in his life.

"Eve . . ." He didn't mean to speak out loud and was startled by the sound of his voice. The phone beeped, he grabbed it, and Barber said, "Okay, Mr. Berger . . . ma'am . . . you can go ahead now."

Latovsky made the introductions, then let the other two do the talking. After Frances Tilden explained, Berger said they would put a wire on the phones at Tilden House and so on. This was all in case Latovsky was wrong and it was the straightforward kidnapping of an heiress after all. Latovsky waited another minute to make sure they were in sync, then he disconnected himself and went to find Lucci; he was probably about to face Adam Fuller and his "big-mother gun," and he wanted backup.

● ●

"DIRTY, DIRTY, DIRTY," THE WOMAN CHANTED IN A SLOW, SLY voice that made Eve want to clap her hands over her ears. The gray light coming through the windows brightened to streaks of yellow sun, the nicks around the edge of the table were gone, and the little boy who'd been on the swing was lying on his back on top of it. He was undressed from the waist down; his knees were tied to the pulley rope and raised, exposing his bare buttocks and thighs. He was sobbing, weak sobs that made Eve think he'd been crying for a while.

His trousers and underpants were neatly folded on a chair and the room was cleaner than clean . . . cleaner even than Mrs. Knapp insisted her kitchen be when the dailies got done with it. Smells of wax and pine oil fought the baking aroma.

"Dirty, dirty, dirty," chanted the voice. "Gotta get it clean . . . gotta dig it out."

Sun hit the boy's face and he turned his head. On the table in front of his raised pelvis was a snowy towel with a gleaming hobby knife, a vegetable knife, and a single-edged razor blade on it; also a deflated pink enema bag, a bedpan, and a blue jar of Vaseline.

The frame widened and Eve saw the woman's broad back in a silky flowered dress. She had thick dark hair with strands of gray in it pinned into a smooth solid bun. She was tall and heavy, big-boned, not fat. The boy looked like a wraith compared to her—the ghost of a child.

"Ready?" she whispered. The boy whimpered and she grabbed a hunk of thin thigh and pinched so hard it looked like her fingers met through the meager flesh. "I said, ready?"

"Yes," the boy choked.

"Good—just gotta check." Her voice was deep, almost mannish, but toneless like a recording played at the wrong speed. She went to the window, facing Eve as she did, and Eve looked into dark eyes sparkling with crazy hate. She had never seen such total screaming madness without any hint of moderation or reason in them. She wanted to scream, but no one would hear her.

The woman's middle bulged as she leaned against the sink and looked out the window.

"All clear," she caroled. "There's just us . . . just you and me, little bastard."

She advanced on the table and the boy hiccuped in terror and tried to say something, but couldn't. She picked up the enema bag, brought it back to the sink, and filled it with cold water. It ballooned, and Eve forgot and cried, "He'll never take all that—you'll kill him!"

The woman hummed to herself and squeezed in some Ivory Liquid, then she chanted, "Dirty, dirty, dirty . . . gotta clean it up inside and out . . . dirty, dirty, dirty . . ."

She turned on the boy and almost screamed, "Dirty! And cleanliness is next to godliness. So you hate dirt as much as I do, don't you, little bastard?"

The boy sobbed wildly, but managed to nod his head. She carried the enema bag back carefully without spilling a drop, then dunked the nozzle into the jar of Vaseline and stared at it, glittering in the sun.

She tore her eyes away from the greased nozzle, pushed the bedpan under him, and, with a little frown of concentration on her face, she spread his buttocks and slid in the tube. Eve tried to close her eyes, but that never worked; she turned away, but the picture turned with her and she saw the boy's eyes widen, then squeeze shut; then he screamed and water sluiced into the pan, leaving a thin foam of soap bubbles on top. Finally the screams sank to moans and stopped; his face didn't have any more color than the top of the table and Eve thought he'd passed out.

The woman eased the pan out from under him and carried it out of the room.

Sweat darkened his hair, his eyelids were thin as tissue, and a tiny blue vein pulsed in his white forehead. Eve wanted to stroke his head, push the wet hair off his forehead, to shade his eyes from the harsh ceiling light the lids looked too thin to keep out. But she couldn't see her own hand when she raised it.

The woman came back without the pan and leaned over to look at the boy's face. "No playing possum now . . ." She snapped her fingers in his face, and Eve prayed that he'd stay out and miss whatever else this unspeakable bitch had in store for him, but his eyes fluttered and opened. The woman giggled happily and picked up the hobby knife.

"Lookie, lookie, lookie, here comes cookie," she sang in that basso voice. The boy's eyes rolled, he saw the hobby knife, and he found the strength to scream again. The sound rocketed off the walls and hard surfaces of the room and the woman started, afraid someone would hear. But no one did, and she leaned over him, held the knife up so it caught the sun, and snarled, "Shut up, bastard, or I'll slit you from stem to stern. I'll slice off your dingus and shove it in your mouth. You hear me, bastard?"

He stifled himself and the woman's eyes lit up with mad anticipation as if she were about to devour her favorite comestible, then she put the knife blade against the boy's smooth belly (it was the first time, there wasn't a mark on him) and pressed a little tentatively. The boy jerked and drove the knife deeper; blood spurted out and the woman yelped, "Messy" and ran for the paper towels over the sink. She passed Eve again, and Eve begged wildly, "Please . . . please . . . please . . . oh please." But it was hopeless; this back-room horror show had been over and done for thirty years.

The woman wadded up paper towels to mop the blood and went back to a . . . *different table in a different room.* The baking smell and light ripples from the lake disappeared, the sun lost its hard-edged clarity, and the light was soft, gray, wintery.

This kitchen had cedar cabinets, beige vinyl-tile floor, counters of beige Formica with a design of pears and apples, and the pulley was gone.

She'd gotten around this by tying the boy's knees to the handles of the wall cabinets behind him, raising his bare legs and butt even higher, exposing him even more. He was older, his legs had some muscle, but he was just as scrawny. His ribs looked like vines through his shirt, his knees and ankles were lumpy knobs of bone . . . and he was covered with the scars. Some were old, healed welts, others were fresh and raw. It must have been going on for years by now, because the boy looked about eight, although it was hard to tell since he was so thin and probably undersized. His face was longer, his features more formed, and his eyes were blank and empty, exactly like the eyes of the man in the doorway in 1993.

The woman hadn't changed at all.

Except she seemed more urgent, enjoyed herself less. Maybe be-'cause he was so impossibly, almost supernaturally calm. He was also taller, harder to position; his genitals were heavier, his feet larger. He was growing up, her time was almost up, her chance to hurt him finally and forever was dwindling, and she was too crazy and stupid to see that she already had.

She picked up a big knife—*no more Exacto, no more Mrs. Nice guy,* Eve thought crazily—and she made a long shallow incision across other cuts that were still raw. The pain must have been excruciating, but the boy looked as if he were watching a boring lantern show on the ceiling. Blood ran; she mopped it up, then stood helplessly over him, not know-ing what to do next. Her dark, insane eyes brightened as if she'd thought of something delicious, and Eve tried desperately to come back. *It's 1993, the "police action" in Vietnam turned into a war we lost; we sent men to the moon; a space shuttle blew up and killed seven people, including a schoolteacher from New Hampshire. It's 1993, Bill Clinton's president. I'm pregnant, Sam's gone . . . it's 1993.* But the vision stayed firm and clear. The woman came to the counter and picked up a bottle of rubbing alcohol, soaked paper towels in it, then went back and jammed them on the running cut. His body quivered but his eyes stared emptily at the ceiling as if she'd done it to someone else.

"Acid," she screamed in frustration, "I need acid."

Then her eyes got that hot, crazy brilliance again, and she put the bloody wad of paper towels down, grabbed the shriveled organ in the boy's crotch, and singsonged, "Lookie, lookie, lookie . . . here comes cookie!" She tremblingly put the knife against the base of it and Eve knew she wanted to do this more than she'd ever wanted to do any-thing in her life. Was a hair from doing it, but knew she'd never get away with it. She never had done it because he'd made love to Abigail Reese before he'd sliced her open.

"Lookie, lookie, lookie . . . here comes cookie," she chanted, then screeched, "Look bastard, look what I'm going to do to you." He fell into her trap, raised his head, and saw where the knife was. His skin went from ivory to green and he looked scared. Just scared . . . not terrified, pleading, or pitiful as he had before; just scared, then accepting. His head fell back on the table, he closed his eyes, and waited for her to do it.

The transformation from the pretty, vulnerable, terrified little boy on the swing to the monster in the doorway was complete.

Eve whirled around to throw up in the sink of that other kitchen and saw a ceramic cookie jar shaped like a head on the counter. Mrs. Knapp had one that looked almost manically cheery, but this one appeared sad, as if it could see the boy and wept for him. Then the cookie jar disappeared, the sink she bent over changed from stainless to enamel with a modern one-armed faucet, and she was back.

● ●

"WHY," HE ASKED OVER AND OVER, *WHY, WHY, WHY* . . . LIKE a kid.

"I don't know, I never see why," Eve said.

They were in the living room. He sat on the chair Dave had sat in; she was on the dust-sheeted couch. They used to cover the furniture at home when they went to Maine for the summer and they'd sometimes come home unexpectedly and find dim rooms full of low-slung ghostly shapes, and she and Meg had spooky fun playing hide and seek under the dust sheets.

Oleee olleee ocean free . . .

She might never be free again, might not live to leave this house because she'd done what he'd wanted and taken away his only reason to keep her alive.

But he didn't look ready to shoot her; he held the gun loosely, resting on his thigh. She'd never seen a handgun this close up before, but thought the lever at the crest of the butt must be the safety, and it was down. That must be *off*.

She'd never get it away from him, no matter how loosely he held it, but she might make it to the front door before he could grip it, cock, aim, and fire at her.

"She must have had a reason," he insisted.

"She hated you."

She was much closer to the door than he was. She had to get around the end of the couch, then make it ten feet to the door. She didn't dare look back at it but she thought there was a little jog in the wall to hide her. She might make it outside, across the clearing and into the trees before he shot her. No point trying for the car, he'd never be careless enough to leave the keys in it, and life had not prepared her to hot-wire a car. She almost grinned.

"But why?" he asked.

He'd probably get off a shot, but she could make it to the trees with a bullet in her shoulder . . . only he'd aim for her back, the widest part of her. That didn't mean he'd hit her; he was a killer, not necessarily a good shot.

"What could make her want to hurt me like that?" he asked wonderingly.

"She didn't *hurt* you," Eve snapped; wrong tone to take to a killer with a gun, but she couldn't help it. "She tortured you, wanted to castrate you—would have if she'd thought she could get away with it."

"But *why?*"

That question again—the madman who thought other people had sane reasons for what they did.

"I don't know," Eve mumbled.

"What did I ever do to her?"

"Nothing. You were just a kid, you couldn't do *anything* to her." That should end the whys, she thought, shifting to get closer to the end of the couch. But he came up with a new one.

"And why'd she call me bastard? My mother never swore. If she said it, she meant literally *bastard.*"

Eve stared at him transfixed, the gun, the distance to the door, and her plan of escape forgotten.

"Why?" he insisted. "They were married when they had Mike and he's seven years older than I am. My mother and father . . ."

"Your mother! That bitch wasn't your mother!"

● ●

LATOVSKY SLIPPED THE PICK INTO THE LOCK, FEELING FOR THE slot in the works. "What's the point?" Lucci whispered tensely. "He ain't here."

"Maybe she is."

Slit open and hung out to dry in the attic, he thought. *Shot in the face in the basement.*

"Dave, we ain't got a single piece of legal paper."

"Want to leave her if we find her?"

"Don't talk like that." Lucci was whispering although no one was around. The house was dark, the garage empty. No one had answered the bell or their pounding on the front, then back door.

Latovsky felt the groove he was looking for and twisted the pick. The latch clicked back and they entered a dark kitchen (no hall light this time) and started their search of Adam Fuller's superneat house on Rusty Pond.

The basement was dry, swept, and empty; there was nothing on the first floor, and they went up to the second and looked into empty, immaculate bedrooms. They pulled down the folding stairs to the attic and Lucci went up because the stairs looked flimsy for Latovsky's weight. Lucci found the switch, a shaft of light came through the opening and fell on the hallway floor, then Lucci's head appeared at the top of the steps and Latovsky had to remind himself to breathe.

"Nothing," Lucci said. "Not a single carton, old sewing machine, or dressmaker's dummy. Ever hear of an empty attic?"

They searched Fuller's room; the bed cover was smooth, the dresser clear except for a framed picture of a large man about forty with a couple of kids. Fuller's clothes were hung with space between them so they wouldn't get crushed; clean shirts on hangers were covered in plastic from the laundry. His shoes were racked and lined up with military precision like Latovsky's shoes. He'd get rid of his shoe rack when he got home, he thought.

There was an address book in the bedtable drawer with numbers for Mike at work in Sawyerville, Bunner, the hospital, and Ellsworth Harris. Latovsky scrawled that one in his notebook.

They left the room and went back downstairs, not knowing where to look or what to look for. The silent, immaculate house mocked them, and Latovsky knew she'd never been there.

Fuller had killed her where he'd found her; Berger and company would find the body in a patch of woods in northern Connecticut.

The thought brought him to a shuddering standstill and he had to lean against the wall for support.

"All done, Dave?" Lucci said hopefully.

"Not yet." He forced himself away from the wall and took up the search again. They came to the den and Latovsky finally fixed on the tape deck and shelf of cassettes; he stopped so abruptly that Lucci ran into him.

"What now?" Lucci asked.

Latovsky went to the shelf and ran his finger along slipcases until he came to Yo Yo Ma/Bach in white letters on a black background. He shook out his handkerchief, wound it around his hand, and slid it out.

"Jesus, Dave, what now?"

Still using the handkerchief, Latovsky took out the cassette, pushed it into the front-loading player, and Lucci said, "You got an urge to listen to Bach while we're shitting all over our careers here?"

Latovsky didn't answer. The tape hissed over the heads, then Bunner's voice came through the speaker. ". . . most of the story. You were in front of a house on Raven Lake . . ."

"That's not Bach," Lucci cried. "Who is it?"

"Terence Bunner."

"Why'd Fuller make a tape . . . ?"

Then it dawned on him, and his fine sallow face got very still; he looked up at Latovsky through his thick lashes and said, "He didn't make it, did he; he took it . . . he's . . ."

"That's who he is, Mike."

"He killed Bunner."

And the women in the woods and the Rileys. But it was too much to lay on Lucci at once. Latovsky could see it getting funny and Lucci finally asking, "Think he killed Cock Robin too?"

● ●

"I'M SURE THE HOSPITAL SWITCHBOARD TOLD YOU DR. FULLER wasn't there," Ellsworth Harris said.

"They did," Latovsky said, "but he's not home either and we thought you might know where he's gone, Doctor."

They were in the Harrises' foyer under a brass-and crystal chandelier shaped like a tarantula. The Harrises wore golf clothes and Mrs. Harris hovered in the background, twisting her golf gloves and trying to keep her face politely expressionless. She should take lessons from Frances Tilden, Latovsky thought.

"I can't imagine what Adam's done to attract the attention of the state police," Harris sneered. "Run up too many traffic tickets, I imagine."

Eight murders and one kidnapping, Latovsky thought and said, "Not traffic tickets."

"I see. Well, before I discuss Dr. Fuller or his whereabouts, I think I should know what this is about."

Oh, should you . . . Latovsky felt his control slip and saw himself grab this asshole by the lime-green golf shirt with the little polo player insignia and slam him against the wall. He clenched his fists, cleared his throat a couple of times, and said pretty calmly, "Play it like that, Doctor, and I'm going to arrest you for obstruction of justice, obstruction of an officer in the performance of his duty, and maybe throw in accessory to a class-A felony."

Harris blanched. "Uh . . . maybe I better call my lawyer."

"Maybe you better tell me where Fuller is and we can do the whole lawyer dance later."

Harris looked at the huge cop; his fists were clenched and the tendons stood out in his neck like rope. His gaze shifted to the skinny sidekick who had the soft, long-lashed dark eyes of a mob-movie hit man.

"Sawyerville," Harris croaked. "His father's sick and he took leave."

"When?"

"Friday."

And he'd grabbed Eve on Saturday, twenty-four hours ago. It was inconceivable that she was still alive and Latovsky felt the hope and energy drain out of him. He couldn't let them—he'd wind up in a helpless, fetal-shaped heap on the floor, and he made himself remember Rud Tyler, his best teacher at the academy. *Vote your hopes*, Rud used to say. *You can always give up; it's what people do best. Eighty out of a hundred mutts walk because someone gives up. Vote your hopes.*

He tried. It was *not* inconceivable that she was alive. She had a weapon no one else had, and Fuller might want to cut himself a piece of it, the way Latovsky had. If she played it smart, she could be alive and stay alive, and might even figure a way to get him before he got her.

"I need to use your phone," he said.

"Of course."

Harris led him into a pickled-pine-paneled room with white carpet and furniture, and a mantel faced in stainless steel that smearily reflected the room. Mrs. Harris had a sweet face, was probably a sweet woman, but her taste was abysmal.

"There." Harris nodded at a small white phone that looked impossibly flimsy. The newest thing in minitech, Latovsky thought. As he headed for it, Harris called softly after him, "Lieutenant." Latovsky paused.

Harris said, "I have to say this. I don't know what you think Adam's done but he's a fine and caring doctor. The best on our staff."

He meant it, and Latovsky allowed himself a second to stare at

Harris. Adam Fuller was a "caring" doctor; which must mean he tried with all his might to save his patients, then gentled them into death when he couldn't. And in between, he killed people. It was too stupendously weird to begin to contemplate and Latovsky didn't try.

He picked up the phone; his hand swallowed the tiny receiver with a mouthpiece that was small and flat and stuck out oddly from the handle. He looked at Harris. "Excuse me?"

"Of course." Harris edged out of the room and shut the door.

Latovsky got an information operator with a heavy West Indian accent who had trouble with *Sawyerville*. He finally got through the language barrier and a toneless computer voice gave Latovsky the number of the house he'd gone to last Sunday to ask about Raven Lake.

Raven Lake.

Adam Fuller had gone there on Thursday, maybe out of curiosity or to recapture a childhood summer . . . or to look for Eve. Didn't matter why; he'd gone and found an empty, isolated house on a lake the color of a raven's wing.

Raven Lake.

But Harris said *Sawyerville* and the phone started to ring in the house on Barracks Lane. Latovsky would try Sawyerville because he was not going to jump the gun this time; no shortcuts, everything by the book. He even let the phone ring the requisite five times; it was a small house but he wasn't going to screw up because Donald Fuller was on the can or drunk or hobbled by the spring-damp mizries and couldn't get to the phone on three rings. He let the fifth ring die away, then he depressed the key, popped it, and started to dial the general code to get Jed Brannigan's troop at Echo Lake ten minutes from Raven Lake.

Brannigan was no genius, but he was careful and restrained enough not to call out a SWAT team and act like the commander of a tank corps at the Battle of the Bulge when he heard *kidnap*. Brannigan was capable of finesse and would not get Eve killed if she were still alive.

Then Latovsky stabbed the key before it started to ring. He didn't have a scrap of evidence that Fuller even had her, much less had taken her to Raven Lake. Brannigan was too careful to break into a house without a warrant or a better reason than Latovsky could give him . . . *or permission.*

Latovsky ripped his notebook out of his pocket, tore through it to Mrs. Rodney's number, and dialed again.

"Of course, Lieutenant," she said, when he told her what he wanted. "If you think it's necessary."

"I do, ma'am. They may have to break in but we'll cover any damage."

"Can't say fairer than that," she said.

They hung up and he called Echo Lake.

● ●

It was Brannigan's show; if the house on Raven Lake was empty, Latovsky was heading for Sawyerville and Raven Lake was an hour in the wrong direction.

They went back to the station to wait, leaving Harris watching from his open front door, looking oddly abashed.

They drank coffee and tried not to stare at the phone; when the coffee was gone, Latovsky broke chunks off the rim of the Styrofoam cup.

It was after four, ten hours since he and Pete had beached the rubber dinghy on the shore of Chalice Lake and lifted the kids out to shore so they wouldn't get any wetter than they already were.

Brannigan and his men were in place by now; Brannigan would have at least five cruisers and maybe another couple from Echo Lake if the town was big enough to have its own force. They'd park down on the road and block the drive so Fuller couldn't get out.

Latovsky snapped a big piece out of the Styrofoam, ground it into squeaky rubble between his fingers, and let it fall on his desk.

One unmarked car would pull up the drive with a lone man wearing a sport jacket, baggy trousers, a light-blue Oxford-cloth button-down shirt, mostly polyester, and a polyester tie that the cop's kid had given him for Christmas. Must be some kind of given that all cops' kids bought atrocious ties. Last Christmas Jo gave him one that had what looked like blue and purple maggots rampant on a field of a color he thought was called teal.

The lone cop parks and goes up the steps of the porch. The house is silent, looks secret and hooded, a pretty cabin on the lake turned into the Wolfman's lair, with windows like blind glass eyes, a door that you know will creak like the lid of a coffin that's been in the ground a hundred years. He rings the bell, clears his throat, and stares expectantly ahead, trying to look like an encyclopedia salesman.

Latovsky's imagination failed him about what happened next. He threw the crushed cup into the wastecan, then swept the bits of it into his palm and threw them after it.

He rested his head on his hands and Lucci said, "Want a Milky Way?"

He nodded, Lucci stood up to go to the vending machine, and the phone rang on Latovsky's desk. Latovsky grabbed it and Brannigan said, "No dice."

"She's dead!"

"She's not there. No one's there, but they were. We found paper cups with dried coffee in the bottom and damp towels in the can. It's a damp day so the towels would take a while to dry. I'd say we missed 'em by an hour, maybe two. No more."

"Them?"

"*Them:* two cups, two balls of cellophane that they wrap doughnuts or sweet rolls in, two packets of instant coffee used . . . definitely *them.*"

"Body," Latovsky choked.

"No. Looked in the basement—floor's packed dirt, undisturbed for years. Grass out back's still wet from the rain so it would hold footprints, or tracks of dragging a body. No one's walked on that grass to the lake since before the rain started."

Brannigan *was* good and careful and smarter than Latovsky had thought.

"We started combing the woods," Brannigan went on. "Nothing right around the house, but there's lots of woods and we might find her yet, only I don't think so. Just a hunch, mind you. But I think he took her with him, wherever he went."

Sawyerville.

They hung up. Latovsky put out an all-points on Fuller's car, then went across the bullpen to Meers's office. The door was closed but a light showed under it. He took Bunner's tape out of his pocket and opened the door without knocking.

● ●

THE HOUSE WAS DREARY, LIKE THE OTHER HOUSES ON THE STREET, and Eve got a sense of deep-down decay as she went up the stairs to the scrap of a front porch. She imagined dry rot in the sill and post beetles chewing at beams and joists. The front steps were cracked and crooked. She stumbled and he grabbed her arm reflexively. It was the first time he'd touched her since he'd given her the shot last night.

He yanked his hand away as if he'd touched burning metal, but not before she got something from him; not a picture—she didn't see any more of what that bitch had done to him—or anything else about him. But she got a sense of spiraling darkness that was like looking down the throat of a roaring animal into a gullet that burned with rage.

Not at her, or she'd be dead. He had no more feeling about her than he would for a hammer or saw, or anything he *used. See Meg, I'm being useful,* she thought.

He opened the door with a key on a loaded ring: keys to here and wherever else he lived, keys to doors where he worked.

He held the door open with the gun on her. It was still light but it was Sunday afternoon and people must be having after-church dinners or watching TV, because the street was empty.

They went inside, he shut the door, and smells of old carpeting, dust too deep to be vacuumed up, and musty upholstery surrounded her. "Down the hall," he said. At the end was a shut door she knew was the kitchen.

"Open it." He prodded her with the gun. His voice sounded harsher than before and she tried to see his face, but it was too dark in the hall.

"Go on, open it."

She pushed it open and entered a kitchen with tarnished-looking light coming through a smeared window, giving everything a hazy gray aura.

He turned on the light and she saw the second kitchen.

In her vision it had been spotless, with shining windows, polished cabinets and appliances, and blinding white starched curtains. It wasn't dirty or clean now, just faded. The cabinets were dull, the refrigerator door had turned dull yellow and was covered with broken, fruit-shaped magnets holding money-off coupons and dry-cleaning tickets. She didn't know how she knew what they were, since she'd never used a coupon or taken or picked up dry cleaning in her life, but she did.

The curtains were yellowed and limp and milky water in the sink hid dirty dishes. It smelled of neglect, with the sour mustiness of that rot eating away at underpinnings. The bitch would be sorry to see her sparkling torture chamber come to this, and Eve wished she *could* see it because she hated her. It was the first time in her life she'd ever hated anyone.

"Same room?" he asked.

"Yes."

"It happened here too?"

"Yes."

"Same woman, same kid. You couldn't be wrong."

She didn't bother to answer and he sank down at the table and put the gun down with a clunk, but kept his hand on it. "So that's the big secret," he said quietly. "The deep, dark secret of my life." He looked up at her. "Lots of people cut up their kids, you know. It's become the national sport. Cut 'em up, smash their heads in, set 'em on fire . . . 'All he got for all his trouble was a hatful of rain.'"

"What?"

"Nothing." He looked away. "I feel like a kid on his birthday. Remember how you used to jump out of bed and run to look at the full-length mirror behind the bathroom door to see how you'd changed . . . and you hadn't?"

"I remember." Full-length mirrors on bathroom doors must transcend class and bank balances because every other bathroom door at home had one.

"I thought I'd *change* and I haven't."

But he had. He looked older and tired for the first time. His face was no longer blandly handsome like one of those TV-commercial models you got sick of watching in half a second. And there was something in his eyes that reminded her of the light on a fishing boat that had foundered on the rocks off Winter Harbor one night. It had left all its lights on for the Coast Guard and they had shifted and rocked, winked on and off in the dark as the little boat heaved in the swell.

"I guess I thought I'd be cured, like Ken Nevins," he said.

"Is he cured?"

"He's alive. Saw him at Rose's Coffee Shop on Main the other day and he smiled a lot and said hello to people. He ate an enormous breakfast, talked sports with the counterman, and after he left everyone said he'd never acted like that before."

So *the thing* had saved Meg's marriage and maybe cured Ken Nevins. It had also gotten Bunner killed, would probably kill Eve and die with her—*only it wasn't like that,* she thought suddenly. It wasn't a parasite or opportunistic infection that swarmed over her when her mother died. It was part of her, like the timbre of her voice, the Tilden-Dodd green undercast in her eyes, and *it always had been,* whether she'd known it or not. Power, Meg called it. "You were a woman with a power," she'd said when Eve thought it was gone. "Now you're just a helpless asshole, like the rest of us." But it wasn't gone and she wasn't helpless. He'd snatched her to use her; she'd told him what he wanted to know but that led to more: Who was his real mother? Where was she? Who was the bitch in the flowered dress? Was his father his father? Hours of tales to spin to buy time for Dave to find her.

"The old man could be a while yet. Why don't you sit down?" he said kindly.

She pulled out a chair and sat across from him at the table on which the woman in the flowered dress had cut him up and almost sliced his "dingus" off.

"I should warn you, he'll probably be drunk."

"I can handle it," she said drily. He laughed, and she let herself believe she saw the laughter in his eyes.

Then footsteps shuffled up the back stairs and he picked up the gun. The door opened and a man about seventy stood on the threshold holding a bulging paper bag.

"Adam," he cried, "Adam boy."

His name was Adam. Adam and Eve—primary characters, like primary colors. She wanted to laugh but was afraid she'd end up crying.

"Well, ain't you a sight for sore—" The old man stopped when he saw her. "What the hell . . . who's this, Adam?"

Adam stood up, holding the gun on the old man, but he didn't seem to notice. He gave a deep beery belch and said gaily, "No, don't tell me, son. Let me guess."

● ●

"Okay, we get there," Lucci yelled over the beat of the rotors. "Then what?"

Latovsky shrugged and Lucci yelled, "Great!" He was getting airsick. "At least get backup, Dave."

"No. Meers said Soames is a hotdog who'll hear kidnap, heiress, feds, and go ape. He'll get her killed if she's still alive."

Not a hope in hell she is, Lucci started to say, then thought better of it.

A gust hit the chopper and flung him against Latovsky. It was like lurching into the trunk of one of those thousand-year-old trees they were trying to save in Oregon, along with the cute little owl that'd die with the trees.

Not a hope in hell of saving them either, he thought.

"Big wind," he yelled, trying to get his mind off the hot uneasiness in his gut.

"Wing wind," Latovsky yelled back.

"What?"

"My mother would say it's the beat of the wings of chickens coming home to roost."

"Cute. You think that's what's going to happen in Sawyerville?"

"Could be."

Then Latovsky grabbed Lucci's arm and yelled in his ear, "Mike, Adam Fuller's the Wolfman."

"What?" Lucci forgot about being sick.

"You heard me. He did the women . . . we know he did Bunner. I got shit to prove it, but I know he did the Rileys too. That's eight. Nine if he's killed *her*."

Nine . . .

Then Latovsky screeched, "We don't have to be too picky about bringing him in."

Trying to cover his shock, Lucci yelled, "You mean what I think you mean?"

Latovsky nodded and let Lucci go. Lucci sank back in the seat, suddenly bereft and alone with his airsickness, the beat of the rotors, and the miles of plowed-mud fields sliding by under them. It must be warmer here than in Glenvale because some of the fields were misted with green.

Dave meant to kill Adam Fuller.

No arrest, arraignment, testimony, or trial. Just *You have the right to remain silent . . . blam blam.*

Lucci didn't know if he could do it or keep his mouth shut if Dave did. If he couldn't, he had to at least warn Dave. Then he could leave Lucci behind with the chopper on the clear assumption you can't bear witness to what you weren't there to see.

He had to decide and it had to be now, because the beat of the rotors changed as they sank toward the chopped-up, squared-off fields of mud stretching to nothing as the horizon darkened.

Nine people.

It was a wrap on Bunner; Fuller had taken the tape from his office and hidden it in a Bach slipcase. End of discussion about Bunner. But how did Dave know about the women?

From *her*.

Dill said Dave went to Connecticut on Monday; the cars in the drive of that house the night Reese got herself sliced had Connecticut plates. He could see the white on blue with *Connecticut, The Constitution State.*

That night, she'd put her hand against Latovsky's chest, told him about his oil bill, his ex, his kid, the kind of bread his mother baked, for fuck's sake . . . and Latovsky fell for it as Lucci had because you'd have to have rice pudding between your ears *not* to fall for it. Lucci was part Abnaki Indian on his mother's side. She'd told him a hundred tales of men and women witches of bygone days who'd had the gift.

So Dave went to Connecticut to see the seer and he'd taken Bunner's recorder or portable phone . . . or his jock strap for all Lucci knew. And she'd laid her thin, childlike, sallow hand with too-short nails on it and told him about Bunner and, as an extra added bonus (two for the price of one), about the women in the woods. And Latovsky went for it, as Lucci would have.

Soooo . . . Adam Fuller had killed six people (if you left out the Rileys), seven counting the seer, who was certainly dead by now.

For one murder they'd jug him; for two they'd jug him for good and he'd never eat another Big Mac. For seven they'd decide he was nuts and send him to the funny farm—Duyvilskill. At Duyvilskill they'd drug and shock him, sit him down with a shrink, then drug and shock him some more. In between, he'd eat chopped meat with a plastic spoon, watch TV, and get it in the ass from the guards and/or other inmates. In a few years—seven, maybe eight—they'd pronounce him "safe on medication" and let him go. It had happened before, more often than not. That meant one year per stiff and it wasn't enough for Bunner or the others. It wasn't enough for that poor babe Lucci had found in the woods with her guts steaming in the night air, and Lucci made his decision.

He hadn't fired his piece in the line of duty for so long he wasn't even sure it was loaded. He rarely went to the firing range because he was a crack shot and had been since his dad put his first piece in his hand at age ten; he was one of those naturals who could hit anything they could see.

He pulled the .38 (never cared for the 9mm. some of the others went for) and checked the chamber. It was full.

• •

THE OLD MAN WAS TALL AND SCRAWNY, WITH LOOSE POUCHES under his eyes and skin that looked untouched by the sun for a decade.

He grinned drunkenly at them, lurched to the refrigerator, and started loading it with beer bottles from the bag.

He moved aside a brown head of lettuce and a loaf of bread that looked petrified, then turned, holding one of the bottles. "Now where's me manners? Anyone want a beer?"

Adam said, "No," and Eve shook her head.

The old man took the bottle to an opener screwed into the Formica of one of the counters that had been as shiny as a mirror in the vision, and popped the top. Then he turned and raised the bottle. "To the day . . . and your news," he said, and took a deep swig.

Adam started to say something, but the old man held up his hand. "No, boy, you're supposed to let me guess."

He took another swig, then laid his forefinger along his nose and crowed, "I got it."

"You do?" Eve was having real trouble not laughing.

"Sure do," he cried. "My boy here, smartest kid ever went to Sawyerville High, has finally popped the question, ain't he, little lady? And you said yes, bless you. And you're here to break the news and give the old man a gander at the bride to be."

Wild laughter burst out of Eve, tears squirted out of her eyes, and it took every ounce of control to stop before she started to sob. She ran to the sink and tore a paper towel off the coat hanger holder tacked to the wall and wiped her eyes. She calmed down, turned to face them, and noticed that the sad-faced cookie jar on the counter in the vision was not there anymore.

The old man smiled uncertainly and Adam said, "That's not why we're here. Sit down, Father, I have to talk to you."

"Father! Shit, boy—'scuse my language, little lady. You ain't called me Father since your ma died." He grinned at Eve. "She said Pop and Pa was for hillbillies and insisted the boys call me Father. When she insisted, you went along, she was that kind."

"Indeed," Eve said weakly.

"Sit down." Adam gestured with the gun and the old man seemed to notice it for the first time. He peered nearsightedly at it. "So you took it. Knew it had to be one of you when I saw the box was gone and I figured even Mike wasn't dumb enough to keep a gun around with two kids."

He turned to Eve. "My oldest ain't smart like this one, but he makes up for it in sweetness." Then back to Adam. "You should'a asked me, son, I'd'a given it to you. Hell, I ain't even looked at it—"

"Sit down." Adam cocked the gun.

The old man looked at the gun, then at his son; his Adam's apple bobbed in his chicken neck swimming in the collar of his shirt, and he sank down in a chair clutching the beer bottle.

"Adam? Adam, boy—what's going on here?"

"Who was she?" Adam held the gun about a foot from the old man's face.

"Who was who?" The old man stared at the light gleaming on the barrel.

"The woman who insisted I call you Father."

"What kind'a nuts question's that? She was your mother."

"No, she wasn't," Eve said.

The old man tried to look nonplussed. "What is this? Who is this woman? What's she been filling your head full of—and put that fuckin' gun down. I'm your father."

"Are you?" Adam asked.

"Yes," Eve answered. You didn't have to be a psychic to see the resemblance.

"Damn tootin', and Barbara Healy Fuller was your mother!"

"No, she wasn't," Eve said again.

The old man shot her a look of shriveling hatred, then turned to his son. "Who're you gonna believe, boy? This female outta nowhere or your own pa?"

Adam's finger tightened on the trigger and the old man looked at the gun, then at his son. He closed his eyes slowly as if his lids were too heavy and kept them closed for a moment. When he opened them he was sober, and Eve felt the center of power in the room shift from son to father and she knew the old man was ready to die to protect his secret. Didn't care much about living anyway, and in a flash she saw his life of empty days with game shows in the morning, the trip to the local bar to watch soap operas in the afternoon. She imagined the hours of insipid, intermittent conversation with men just like him until it got dark; then he bought beer or whiskey, depending on how much he had left from his Social Security check. Then he made his careful way home, zapped something in the microwave, and drank and watched more TV until he passed out.

That terrible secret was all he had left.

"Who was she?" Adam asked again, and the old man answered, quietly, "Your mother."

Adam looked at Eve.

It was time to tell the truth, spin the final tale—*time to make the doughnuts*, she thought. She was sorry, because the old man had found a kind of dignity in his dogged protection of that lie and she was going to take it away from him. She could refuse, but Adam would kill her, and probably the old man and himself, and the kitchen that had been a gleaming testament to a houseproud monster would be awash in blood.

She didn't know how long this was going to take or if Dave had any idea yet where she was, but there was no way to put it off.

She glanced at the empty spot on the counter where the cookie jar had been and wondered where it was now. Then, moving as slowly as she dared, she went to the table. The old man was riveted on the gun aimed at his nose and didn't pay any attention to her.

She sat down next to him, slid her hand across the scarred Formica table, and grabbed his arm. He looked down as if he expected to see a hairy spider on his sleeve and she thought, *C'mon, it can't be that bad.*

He jerked his arm away, beer spewed out of the bottle, and his sad, sagging face with its slick of liquor sweat became a young woman's . . .

Who gazed lovingly at Eve. Then the camera in Eve's mind panned back and Eve saw it was a young version of the old man she was looking at. His dark brown hair was thick and wavy, his skin was ruddy from working outdoors, his body hadn't collapsed in on itself yet and was way too bulky for the kid's lap desk he'd crammed himself into.

The woman's hair was brown, her light brown eyes tilted a little, and she had wide Slavic cheekbones. She was small, fair, delicate, the absolute antithesis of the hefty bitch in the flowered dress.

They were in an old-time classroom with a blackboard and a big, scarred teacher's desk. The room smelled of chalk dust and dry heat from nickel-plated radiators under long windows that looked out on brown grass. Snow drifted past the window and he said, "It's snowing, Ed."

For Edna.

Eve had finally gotten a name and no sinking sensation or stuffed ears this time . . . or in the kitchen on Raven Lake, either. The trappings were gone and there was just her and *it* and whatever she'd gone back thirty some years to see.

"It's snowing, Ed." He made the mundane little observation

sound like a love poem and Edna laughed. "And it's too cold for the truck. We'll have to get a room."

She meant to make love in.

She had on a bulky orange sweater that made her eyes look tawny and picked out gold highlights in her hair, which was the exact color and texture of her son's.

● ●

IT WAS AN OLD STORY, THE KIND YOU COULD SEE ON PRIME-TIME TV any night of the week, but when it was over, and Eve took her hands away from her eyes, which she'd covered without realizing it, there were tears on them.

● ●

"HER NAME WAS EDNA," EVE SAID. THE OLD MAN SHRIEKED AS IF he'd been stung, then leaped up from the table and mashed himself against the refrigerator as if he wanted to melt into it.

"She taught at the high school," Eve went on quietly, "same school you went to. Adam is the name she gave you."

"Who is this woman?" the old man screeched. "*What* is she?"

She looked at him; he looked back in sick horror. "I'm sorry," she said, "I really am, because I know how much you loved her. You should've listened to her . . . you all should have."

She turned back to Adam. His eyes were riveted on her, the little light in them looked stronger, steadier, and his face seemed to be changing before her eyes, but that could be wishful thinking.

She went on. "He'd gotten a contract to build the addition on the high school, that's how they met. She was smart, like you. She liked to see how things worked, how they went together, and she'd watch the construction in her spare time . . . and they fell in love. Wildly, totally, madly in love. I doubt I'll ever love anyone that much." She shot the old man an admiring look, then looked back at Adam, whose face was losing more of that smooth, slack blandness every minute.

Eve said, "They made love in his truck, on the floor of the library one night, in her classroom, and when they couldn't find a place inside and it was too cold for the truck, they went to a little tourist court outside town. I didn't get the name of it, but it had a little pine tree on the sign, didn't it, sir?"

He answered with a low, sick moan and Eve said, "He'd been

married eight years when he met Edna. Gotten to where he thought work and misery and the sly drinking he did to numb himself out were all there were to life, and he accepted it, was faithful . . . until Edna. Then he wanted to play it straight, and when Edna told him she was pregnant, he went to the other one and asked for a divorce. Dumb, but that's what he did. She said no, of course. Didn't just say it, she raged and screamed and tried to kill him. Went for him with one of the knives I imagine she used on you later. He'd never seen such hate and rage, never imagined anything like it, did you, sir?"

He didn't answer, and Eve said, "She tried for his face but he feinted and she got him in the arm. You've still got the scar, don't you, sir."

No answer.

"I guess she liked knives. Anyway, that hour in this room when he told her about Edna was like a year in hell. Like an endless supper with the devil . . . and he had a short spoon." She smiled at the old man, trying to get a reaction from him. He didn't look at her and she went back to the story. "He knew it was no good after that. Worse, he knew the woman he'd married and had a child with was dangerous and he had to get Edna away. He played it smart; for once in his life, he came out of his daze and played it smart. He pretended he was cowed and would stay and make it up to Barbara, and she bought it. She was mean, not smart, right, sir?"

No answer.

"I guess it is easy to confuse them," Eve mused, "but lots of mean people are dumb. She was. Stupid as a sheet of plywood, he'd said about her. So he made his false peace and he and Edna made their plans on the sly. They waited until they couldn't any longer, because Edna was starting to show and there would be talk at the school.

"He waited for a Sunday when his wife was at church. She went every Sunday, used to cook and bake for the teas afterward and church suppers. It sounds like kindness, but it wasn't. She did it to show the other women up, because she hated them. Hate, conceit, possessiveness were all she could feel, weren't they, sir?"

The old man pretended to study the bottle in his hand.

Eve said, "He was making good money in those days. Might've gotten rich if things had worked out differently. He had enough to take care of both families, and he left his wife a whopping check and a note telling her he'd send more every month, then went to get his Edna.

"They'd rented a house in a town about thirty miles from here. Pretty place surrounded by hills, but a little isolated, and he was terrified *she'd* find them and show up with one of those knives when he was at work. He warned Edna, but he needn't have because Barbara Fuller was a coward—five-year-olds were her speed. She'd never face a grown woman, not even one she hated as much as she did Edna and, oh, how she hated her. Hate burned her up, kept her awake at night. But she kept her mouth shut because she couldn't bear people pitying her, talking behind their hands about how she lost her husband to another woman, a godless bitch who taught biology.

"People must've wondered, but she kept quiet and he kept quiet, and no one knew for sure where he went after work. Besides, Barbara Fuller was imperious, not the kind you'd question.

"So everyone kept the secret, and for five months he was happy. The only good time he ever had in his life, I think." She looked at the old man and said gently, "Some people never even get that much, you know."

Nothing from him.

"Then Edna had the baby—you. It was hard labor, even for a first baby, and, when it was over, Edna kept saying something wasn't right. But it was thirty-some years ago; doctors were *male* and males know as much about having babies as I know about pissing my name in the snow." She smiled; neither of them smiled back, but she didn't expect them to. "Anyway, Edna knew something was wrong, but they said she was hypochondriacal and hysterical like most women postpartum and they gave her tranquilizers." Her forehead creased as she fought for the name, then got it. "Milltown."

"Meprobamate," Adam said, as if the drug's generic name mattered.

"And they sent her home." She looked at the old man. "You didn't believe her either, did you?"

No answer.

"He didn't," Eve said. "He fed her the pills and looked after her and the baby and was wild with joy at his little family, sure that the postpartum whatevers would pass the way the doctor said and she'd be fine. Sad thing was, she believed it too. She'd been to college, had an M.A. in biology, understood the workings of her own body, but she believed them anyway, even though she *knew* they were wrong. She took the tranks and was calm, a little floaty, a little out of it. Then two days later, she got a feeling that no man can understand and probably no woman can describe adequately—the feeling that something's about to bubble out of you. She thought that was normal and got her sanitary supplies and went into the bathroom. She had on a white terry cloth robe, didn't she?"

Tears glittered in the old man's eyes.

"Then she looked down," Eve said, "and saw the toilet had filled to the rim with blood. But the tranks worked and she didn't panic, didn't even worry. She just flushed the toilet, and flushed it again when it filled back up, and flushed it again—"

"Stop it!" the old man shrieked.

"—and again," Eve shot at him, almost hating him, "and again—"

"Stooooopp," he screamed, and she wanted to, but she'd been gone twenty-six hours; every cop in the Northeast must be looking for her by now. Someone would find her—Dave would find her—if she gave him enough time, and she gathered herself and launched into the tale of the two kitchens. She drew it out, lingered on the descriptions of what Barbara had done to Edna's boy. It was 8:00 by the time she finished and getting dark out. The old man looked like a scarecrow with all the stuffing pulled out of him and she thought it was over; the old man and his lie were done for and she was out of tales and time.

Then slowly, slowly, as if he were a rubber doll on an air pump, the old man stiffened, raised his head, and straightened; he looked at Eve and raged, "Lying bitch. You lyin', fuckin' bitch."

He was still fighting for that rotten lie that had ruined his life and his son's. A macho point of honor, maybe, *A man's gotta lie like a man's gotta lie.*

"Stone fuckin' liar." The old man spat, then looked at his son. "She's spinnin' you a tale, you moron, and you're eatin' it up. Jesus Christ, what'd you think would happen, you poor booby?"

The attack took Adam by surprise. He backed up and the gun wavered in midair.

"You dumb shit," the old man yelled. "You get hold of her, whatever she is, stick a Colt Python in her face and say, 'Tell me the tale of the scars.' "

"You knew—" Adam cried.

"I knew shit. But you asked about scars every fuckin' month for twenty-five years, so I knew they were there, didn't I?"

"How?"

"How the fuck should I know how you got 'em? Maybe from some

game the other kids played with you because you were such a scrawny
little wimp and little boys love to see blood, so they tied you down and
cut you up a little. So what?"

"Want to see how they 'cut me up a little'?" Adam said softly.

"No! So they cut you up a little more than a little, and you made
the biggest deal out of it since the Mansons. And found this bitch."
He glared at Eve. "Stuck a gun in her face and told her to spin you a
tale and she spinned you a good one so you wouldn't blow her head off.
Spinned you a tale of passion and lies, torture and death, where your
ma ain't your ma and your past is a cross between *Days of Our Lives* and
Night of the Living Dead and you fell for it, you sucker."

Adam looked at Eve.

"It's a thought, isn't it?" he said softly.

"No, it's not, and you know it," she said.

"You *don't* know it!" the old man yelled. "Think, asshole! Just
think. Think people in this town'd keep quiet about a story like
that? Think they wouldn't tell their kids that Adam Fuller's a bastard?
Think the kids'd torment you more than she says your poor ma
did? Think Ida Van Damm wouldn't ferret out such a story and spread
it all over God's creation?"

"He's got a point," Adam said. The gun stopped wavering and
fixed on Eve. But it didn't faze her because she had an ace in the hole.

"That's it!" the old man screeched. "She's the one you should be
pointing that pistol at, not your ol' dad. Ask her, boy. Ask her how
a thing like that could happen in a town like this where everyone
knows every time you take a shit. Ask her!"

"I'm asking," Adam said.

"I don't know," she said. "I didn't see any more after Edna died,
except for something that happened later." (Years later, when the
bitch got her comeuppance, but there was no point in bringing it up
now.) "Maybe they said they adopted you. That wouldn't cause much
stir, even back then. But I don't know."

It sounded lame and the old man cackled, "See there . . . she
ain't got no answer."

Adam took a step toward her, the old man shivered with excitement, and Eve played her ace in the hole. She looked around the
kitchen, then back at Adam. "Where's the cookie jar?" she asked.
"There was a cookie jar with a sad face next to the sink. It looked like
it felt sorry for you . . . as if it could see what she was doing to you.
Where is it?"

There wasn't a sound in the kitchen except for the solid click of the railroad clock pendulum, then the old man blubbered, "She seen it at your house! She seen it—"

Adam leaped across the kitchen, grabbed the front of his father's plaid flannel shirt, and slammed him against the refrigerator. The beer bottle flew out of his hand and clinked across the floor, leaking foam, and the old man's eyes rolled back in his head. Adam dragged him to the table and shoved him in the chair. His head fell forward and Adam grabbed the back of his collar and yanked him upright, then jammed the gun into the soft meat under his chin and dug it in. "She didn't see it at my house, you old shit. She's never *been* to my house. She saw it when she saw the rest of it." He dug the gun deeper; the old man's face turned cheesy.

"Who was my mother?" Adam screamed in his father's ear. "What happened to her?"

The old man compressed his dry, cracked lips and Eve thought he would let his head get blown off before he'd give up the lie. She braced herself for the shot, then the old man sagged and moaned, "I killed her."

Adam eased up on the gun and stepped back, and the old man whispered, "Me'n the doctors killed her. Barbara the bitch killed her, 'cause if I didn't have to be scared of what she'd do, we could've stayed here, with a decent hospital, decent doctors. *You* killed her. Something previous, they called it."

"Placenta previa," Adam said.

"Yeah. We were out in Road Dust USA and it took the ambulance half an hour to get to us. Didn't matter, the doctors said, she'd'a died anyway, unless she was right there in the hospital, like she'd begged them to let her be *because she knew something was wrong.* So she bled to death."

"And the other one?"

"Barbara?" The old man grinned a little. "Barbara Healy Fuller was ready and waiting at poor Edna's funeral like the ol' spider in the parlor. Some other teachers came and the principal—can't remember his name now—and a few of the kids, but Edna'd been gone five months, kids forget fast. And Barbara. She took me off into this little room with lots of boxes of Kleenex and packs of smelling salts and made me this proposition.

"She had it all figured out, must've been studying on it from the second she heard Edna was dead. I'd left you back in Stanton with another new mother, a woman Edna'd made friends with. She made friends easy, people liked her. Anyways, Barb figured we'd take you to her mother's in Utica, and she'd stay there with you and Mike for a few months, then come home with *our* new baby. Maybe people would be suspicious, might whisper behind their hands, but everyone who knew Barb was a little scared of her, and she knew they wouldn't say a word. Not much they *could* say because she was a big woman, more'n possible she was a few months gone when we went to her mother's.

"So that's how we did it, son; that was her proposition and I accepted it. Made a pact with a flowered-dressed devil who made flaky piecrust that she'd raise you as her own and I'd pay the freight. Sold my soul to a demon Betty Crocker for your sake, boy. She said she didn't see as I had any choice, with those black eyes of hers snapping like there was a thousand lit candles in her head, and I wanted to kill her. But she was right, so I made m'pact, and I kept it. And thought she did too.

"Oh, Adam," he cried, "Adam, I knew she hit you more than she should 'cause you started getting real quiet and kind of strange. But I figured you'd get over it. Figured it was the hand life dealt you, and for a few extra licks you were kept clean and fed and as well turned out as Mike, and Christ knows what would'a happened to you with just me to look after you. So I let it go. I never, never"—he raised his right hand—"never knew about cutting you up or any of what she"—pointing at Eve—"says. Never would've imagined such things until you started asking me where the scars came from. Then I knew what Barbara'd done to you—to Edna's baby—but Barb was dead by then, too, and I didn't see any point telling you.

"I should've known right off," he went on miserably. "Would've if I paid attention, because there were signs. You used to adore me'n Mike, used to be all over me when I came in the door at night, used to follow Mikey around like a Chow dog with one master. That stopped and I should'a wondered why. Should'a wondered why she gave you your own room after a while instead of just taking it for granted it was so Mike could have *his* space, because he was a teenager by then. Now I know it was so Mike wouldn't see what she done to you, because he would'a stopped her. He'd never let anyone hurt you." He looked at Eve. "Heredity's funny, girl. That unwholesome bitch gave birth to the sweetest boy, who grew into the sweetest man you ever want to meet. Go figure, like Ben Levy at the dry cleaners says. Go figure."

"And my mother?"

"What about her?"

"Her name, Pop," Adam asked almost gently.

"Edna, like *she* said. How did she know—"

"Her whole name."

"Edna Janecki. Her pa died when she was little, her ma a few years before she met me. She had a brother, but I never met him. Don't know to this day if he knows his sister's dead. He never cared enough to come asking."

"Where is she?"

"Dead, boy," the old man snapped. "What've we been pissin' and moanin' about the last half hour—your mother's dead."

"Dead where?"

"Oh, I get you. Pine Ridge. Just up the hill from your—from Barbara."

"WELCOME TO SAWYERVILLE, GENTLEMEN,"
Captain Burt Soames yelled over the rotors.
They shut down, and the men introduced them-
selves and shook hands.

"Nice rig," Soames said, looking hungrily at
the chopper.

"Lem called . . ." Latovsky said.

"Oh, yes. Said to give you a car and anything
else you need and I'm ready to do just that."

Two cars were pulled up on the field, a spank-
ing new Olds Eighty-eight and a Caprice with
dented fenders.

"We're in kind of a hurry," Latovsky said,
edging toward the cars. Soames didn't move.

"Was wondering what all this was about," he
said. "Wondering if maybe it had something to do
with the Wolfman."

The Wolfman. If Riley's moniker had made it
to Sawyerville, it must be on wires all over the
country by now. *Riley'd've liked that,* Latovsky
thought.

"Wish it did," he said easily. "Fact is, it's
kind of a shit case. Rich woman supposed to be
kidnapped, but we don't think so. Seems she had
a boyfriend from around here."

"Runaway heiress." Soames sounded disappointed.

"So it seems. We take the Caprice?"

"What do you think?" Soames sounded a little nasty.

"Keys in it?"

"Look, I have to know where you're going, Lieutenant, this is my jurisdiction." Soames's chin jutted.

Latovsky smiled and pretended to misunderstand. "No sweat, Cap'n, we know the way. But thanks anyway, thanks a million."

He wheeled around and headed for the Caprice with his jacket flapping in the wind blowing across the field.

Soames started after him but Lucci grabbed his arm. "I wouldn't, Captain. He's had a lousy day, and I honest to God wouldn't." Soames wrenched his arm away from Lucci, but he looked at Latovsky's enormous back rushing to the car and didn't pursue him.

"Thanks again," Lucci said. "We'll make a full report . . . if there's anything to report."

"You better."

Lucci went after Latovsky and climbed into the passenger seat.

"Bet he follows," Latovsky said.

"Bet he doesn't, since I obliquely called attention to your size and disposition."

Sure enough, the Eighty-eight stayed put, with Burt Soames standing next to it and his minion silhouetted in the driver's seat as the Caprice pulled away.

The car was clean inside, with a cardboard pine-tree air freshener hanging from the mirror, and it started smoothly with the deep even rumble of an engine fed super gas. This was some lower-echelon detective's baby in spite of the dented fenders, and Lucci hoped they didn't wreck it for him.

They got to the end of the cyclone fencing where the road into town started and Latovsky said, "Fuller's car's a ninety-three light blue LTD, New York tag H278MD. There's no garage or driveway so it'll be parked on the street."

●　●

No light blue LTD, new or otherwise, was parked on Barracks Lane or the surrounding streets. The Fuller house porch light was on, but the front windows were dark.

"Now what?" Lucci asked.

"I don't know." Latovsky's face looked ghastly in the street light coming through the windshield, and the muscles of his jaw kept bunching and unbunching. He climbed out, and Lucci saw him un-snap the holster strap over his gun. Lucci did the same, and they went up the steps with their hands on the gun butts under their jackets.

"Badges?" Lucci whispered.

"Uh-huh."

Latovsky rang the bell, nothing happened, he rang again, and a voice behind them called, "Lieutenant?"

In the fading light, Lucci saw an old lady with hair like a rag mop and eyes the color of iridescent moth wings.

"Yes, ma'am," Latovsky whispered. "It's me."

"You still lookin' for Don?" she whispered back, coming up the steps.

"Yes, ma'am, seems like I missed him again."

"Nope, he's in there. Saw him go in, didn't see him come out. Bet he's in the kitchen, passed out on the table. C'mon, I'll take you 'round back." She turned and Latovsky took her arm. "Ma'am . . ."

"Mrs. Van Damm," she said. "You kin call me Ida."

"Ida, did you see his son?"

"Now how'd you know that? It's not his week, but he was here okay—and don't grab me like that, Mister, my bones're brittle as cooked chicken's."

He let her go. "You saw him?"

"Sure did. Saw him come, saw him go. Had a woman with him."

Latovsky took in a harsh gasp of air and closed his eyes. He cares too much, Lucci thought, cares in a way that wouldn't do him or Lucci—or the woman—any good.

"She was okay?" Latovsky asked hoarsely.

"I don't know about okay. She was walking on her own two legs."

"Mrs. Van Damm . . . Ida . . . ma'am," Latovsky pleaded. "You got any idea where they went?"

"Nope, 'cept back toward town, not out to the highway. Thought she might be a girlfriend finally and he was taking her out, maybe to the Elms. His sister-in-law works there."

Latovsky gave a strangled laugh and said, "I don't think so."

"Then to a bar or somep'n. All the churches are closed at this hour," she said drily. "Movie theater shut up five years ago. Don't know where else they'd be goin'."

"Maybe Mr. Fuller'll know," Latovsky said.

"Then let's ask him," she said excitedly.

"Mrs. Van Damm . . ."

"Don't be telling me I can't come along."

"You can't."

She glared at him with those incredible eyes and said, "Don't be an asshole, Lieutenant." She pronounced it *ace-hole.* "Somep'n's up for you to come sneaking around here late on a Sunday whispering on Don's porch, half breaking my poor arm when I tell you Adam's been here. Somep'n's up and it's lousy and ol' Don ain't gonna tell you what time it is, much less where his boy's gone. But he might tell me."

Lucci looked from one to the other, then Latovsky nodded and the old woman said, "Okay, follow me."

She led them around the house along an uneven cement walk. It was dim away from the porch light; the two men stepped carefully, but those iridescent eyes of hers seemed to see without light and she didn't falter.

They got around to the back, a scrap of a yard half cemented over and a patch of lawn that already needed mowing. Three wooden steps led up to a tiny back porch.

She went up and they followed, but there wasn't room for all of them on the porch and Lucci stopped one step down. The window in the back door and the windows along the back of the house were lit.

She looked through the glass, then hissed to them. "What'd I tell you, passed out on the table. Now tell me what you want to know, Lieutenant. And tell it straight or we're gonna waste a lot of time."

"Where Adam Fuller went," Latovsky said.

"Want to know what he was doing here at the wrong time of month in the first place and who that woman is?"

"We know who she is and I don't care why he came here. I just want to know where he is now. And fast, Ida. As fast as you can."

She opened the door, which was not locked, and went into the kitchen. Latovsky watched through the window; Lucci edged up into the small space and watched with him as the old woman tried to rouse the old man, whose upper body was sprawled across the table. The man's head lolled and a faint gleam of eyeball showed between the lids. He looked dead and Latovsky and Lucci looked at each other, then Latovsky put his hand on the doorknob and the old man's eyes flickered. The old woman disappeared, water ran and stopped, then she came back with a wad of wet paper towel and laid it gently across the back of his neck. He shivered and tried to raise his head, but couldn't. She kept the pad pressed to his neck and he tried again and made it this time. Bleary eyes looked at her, he tried to smile; at least that was how it looked from where they were. Then his face seemed to come apart and he started to cry. Thin, harsh sobs came faintly through the door and the old man's face looked like a sheet of paper being crushed by an invisible hand.

His sobs faded and Latovsky reached for the knob again because this was taking too long. Lucci put his hand on his wrist.

"No, Dave," he whispered, "you'll just screw it up. Let her do it."

He was right. Latovsky dropped his hand and waited. His mouth was dry; he raised some spit to swallow, afraid he'd cough and the old man would hear him and know someone was out there.

The old man finally stopped crying and he and the old lady murmured together a while. She got more wet towels and he took them from her, wiped his face, and she got a beer from the refrigerator. She opened it, gave it to him, and he swigged and talked some more. His eyes looked as brimming with blood as poor Pete Bunner's had the night his father died.

It felt as if they'd been out on the porch in the cool, damp evening air for hours, but it had only been a few minutes, not much more than five, Latovsky thought. He didn't want to look at his watch, afraid the old man would see movement through the window.

Finally the old man slumped forward again. Ida Van Damm waited a second, then came to the door. Lucci slithered down the stairs and Latovsky followed to give her room to get out. She stepped out on the porch and waved them farther away, then came down to them and whispered, "Pine Ridge. It's the Protestant cemetery north of town—the only cemetery. We don't hold with papists and I don't know what the three or four Jews in town do with their dead. He'll be on the North Ridge, up the hill from Barb Fuller's grave. God knows why."

"Thank you." Latovsky whirled away, but her skinny gnarled fingers caught his sleeve. "Don says Adam's got a gun, so don't come on like gangbusters. I've known Adam all his life. He was a sweet little boy to start with, then he turned into the kind'a kid that pours gas on cats and sets 'em on fire to see 'em run. You must'a come across the type."

He nodded.

"Point is, he ain't any nicer now," she said, "even if he is a doctor. If you rush him, he'll do what I figure you're scared he will to that woman and not turn a hair."

● ●

THE INSCRIPTION WAS WORN BUT STILL LEGIBLE: EDNA JANECKI, November 2, 1932—May 16, 1956. And an epitaph the old man must have composed, *Too good for this world.*

The plot was derelict, choked with weeds, and long grasses grew around the base of the stone. The stone had been badly set and had settled so the top sloped and it looked like it had been there for centuries.

"Cheap piece of shit he put up for her," Adam said. He stood on one side of the stone, Eve on the other. The gun was in his hand, hanging at his side, but he'd raise it any minute now.

" 'All he got for all his trouble,' " he murmured.

"What does that mean?"

"It's something I heard once, can't remember where."

As he talked, Eve looked around. It was almost dark; but the moon was up and his face and hands were dark gray blobs, the gun almost invisible. Flat black patches spread across the grounds with one at the foot of the rise that looked as thick as velvet. If she could get to it, lie flat in it, she might disappear. Her clothes were dark, he wouldn't be able to see her, and she could crawl away to the next patch and the next, then run through the gates to the road they'd come on. It had looked well traveled; she would flag a car.

"It goes, 'All he got for all his trouble was a hatful of rain.' " He said, "I feel like that a lot. All I got for all my trouble . . ."

She edged toward the impenetrable-looking shadow a few yards away.

"You got a lot for your trouble." She raised her voice slightly to hide the distance growing between them. "You got what you said you wanted."

"What I needed, or thought I did"—he stared at his mother's tombstone—"but it didn't change anything. Bunner said it would. Said the truth's down there, like a secret door only you could find. Pretty trite even for a shrink."

She edged away a little more; the black patch was close, but not close enough to make it in a single leap.

"I asked what I'd find behind the door," Adam said, "expecting some bullshit about the inherent satisfaction of self-awareness and knowledge being its own reward. But Bunner was honest, he said he didn't know."

"Bunner . . ."

"You met him, you were in his office. He was the one who told me about you."

"At the party?"

"Party? You mean the dance." He looked up, saw how far she'd gotten, and raised the gun. It was now or never. She tensed to leap the last couple of yards, and the grounds' lights came on in response to some signal that it was dark enough. The dense black patch turned into a softly rolling expanse of gray green that wouldn't hide a squirrel.

"I'm sorry," he said. His thumb slid up the gun butt to the lever at the top. "I really am because you tried to help and it's not your fault you couldn't. Maybe knowing isn't enough, maybe you have to be ready for what you know. I thought that meant taking the trouble to find out whatever it is, and Lord knows I've taken trouble, haven't I?"

He cocked the gun. "I'd've had to kill you no matter what, Eve, because you're the only one who knows for sure and there's still a chance I'll get away with it. Wouldn't bet the farm on it, but there's a chance. I've been careful, I don't think they've got anything that'll stand up in court, and you'll be the last, if it's any consolation. I never killed for fun, I did it to transform myself. But I can't and I'll have to live with it, if they let me. I'll still be a good doctor."

He came around his mother's headstone and took a couple of steps toward Eve. In the light from the grounds' lamps, he looked old, exhausted, handsome, and in pain. He didn't know how much he'd changed since yesterday, wouldn't believe her if she told him.

His finger wrapped around the trigger; she prayed he'd trip over the short lamppost and go sprawling, but he stepped smartly around it. She fought panic, made her mind take off to try to find words to fight with. Bunner would know what to say, but Eve had never taken psychology. It had been considered a nonsubject (like sociology) for people who liked multiple-choice tests. So she didn't have knowledge but she did have sense. She was the end product of generations of a family who'd had the sense to turn sugar bootlegged in 1680 into a vast fortune, and she tried to use it.

In the vision of the first kitchen, he'd been a sweet, pretty, frightened little boy, who'd loved the older brother who'd gone off and left him, and probably wanted to love the woman even though she terrified him; but by the second kitchen, here in Sawyerville, he'd turned into what he still thought he was, and couldn't feel anything even when he thought she was going to castrate him, because . . . because . . . Eve pushed her mind so hard she got dizzy.

Because if he felt, what he felt would be rage, hate, and the will to murder. But he couldn't let himself because she was his mother, and killing your mother was unthinkable, the worst crime. Worse than killing your kids. Medea killed her kids and the gods sent a chariot to take her away. Orestes killed his mother and the Furies pursued him for eternity.

But Barbara Fuller was not his mother.

She said it out loud. "She wasn't your mother."

"I know that. It doesn't matter."

"It does," Eve cried. "You can hate her."

"But I don't hate her. I don't feel anything about her. You haven't been listening. It didn't work."

Eve tilted her head back the way her aunt would and said in her coolest, most arrogant Tilden voice, "That's just silly. Of course you hate her, *I* hate her and she didn't do anything to me, she did it to you. *But she wasn't your mother.*"

He faltered and the gun moved off center.

"She was not your mother," she kept on in that tone that sometimes made her want to slap her aunt's face. "She was *not* your mother and of course you hate her. Of course you want to kill her, but it's okay, because she's already dead and *she was not your mother.*"

"I see what you're trying to do," he said, and moved the gun back to where it had been. "It won't work."

She'd give anything for a mirror to hold up to him so he could see how he looked.

"One thing is a shame," he said. The gun was back on target, his finger wrapped around the trigger.

"What?" Eve was sure her voice would quaver, but it didn't.

"She never got what was coming to her."

"Yes, she did."

"No. She was killed in an accident; the troopers said she never knew what hit her."

"They lied. Remember I said I saw something that happened years after your real mother died?"

He stared at her.

"Do you remember?" she asked haughtily.

"I remember."

"I saw Barbara Fuller alive, awake, and aware for an hour while they tried to cut her out of that car. She had so much glass stuck in her she looked like crystal, and the door had smashed into one side of her and drove the jagged ends of her bones out the other. She screamed and screamed. It sounded like a slaughterhouse and one of the troopers

went for his gun. The others wanted him to do it, because it was
unbearable and they'd shoot an animal in that kind of pain. But the
trooper couldn't; the others couldn't either because she wasn't an
animal and they didn't have the nerve. They could see in the light of
the flares around the car and the spotlights on their cruisers that she
was as good as dead because her brain was exposed and pulsing through
a crack in her skull, but they still couldn't do it. She was awake when
the ambulance got there, but the paramedic couldn't get close enough
to give her a shot. She was awake when they finally cut her free and
awake when they got her on the stretcher—*then* she died.

"Oh, she got her comeuppance, Adam." It was the first time
she'd used his name. "It didn't go on long enough, but it was horrible
while it lasted, if that's any consolation to you. And it can be, because
she was not your mother."

●   ●

THE TOWN ENDED ABRUPTLY AFTER A SHORT STRIP OF GAS STA-
tions, fast food joints, and car dealerships, and the muddy fields surrounded them. They thought they'd missed the turn and Latovsky got
ready to make a screeching U-turn, then saw a buckshot-pocked sign:
PINE RIDGE, with an arrow and a cross. He hit the brake and screeched
into the turn. There was a faint glow from the lights behind them,
nothing ahead but darkness, and one lone light that must be a farmhouse in the middle of a field. They topped a rise and saw more lights
low to the ground. Spots lit pillars and an open iron gate with a sign
over it that reminded Latovsky of iron letters on an iron strip:
AUSCHWITZ, ARBEIT MACHT FREI. This said PINE RIDGE PERFECT REST. He
didn't slow up going through the gates and missed a sharp curve at
sixty. The Caprice climbed a rise, plowing ruts in the lawn, and
headed for a large pale-gray monument with BIGGS on it.

He fought the wheel; the tires gouged more grass as the car swung
around and slammed onto the road, throwing Lucci against the door.
Pavement scraped the bumper, Latovsky fed gas, and they screamed
around the curve and missed the turn-off marked North Ridge. He
stood on the brake, the Caprice screeched to a stop, and the motor
died. "Shit!" He smashed his fist against the wheel and restarted the
motor. He raced it, then jammed the car into reverse. It screamed
backward and Lucci yelled, "Just like gangbusters, Dave. Just like the
old babe said not to—you're gonna get her killed."

He was right. Latovsky let the car lose momentum and took a
second to collect himself. Then he made the turn quietly and eased up

the North Ridge road for a quarter of a mile until the headlights hit the back of a light blue LTD, number H278MD. Latovsky killed the lights and motor and they coasted to a slow, silent stop behind Adam Fuller's empty car. Latovsky turned out the ceiling light so it wouldn't come on when they opened the doors, and they drew their guns and slipped out of the car.

● ●

ADAM SAID, "GOD, YOU'RE GOOD, YOU REALLY ARE. ALMOST HAD me going a little there, but not quite. I am *not* glad she suffered, Eve, I simply don't care."

"You do!" she said desperately. But he didn't believe her and she had told her last tale and had nothing left to fight with. He knew it and she saw pity in his eyes. But the emotion must be so new, so alien, he didn't even know he felt it.

He said, "It'll be awful for you to just stand there while I pull the trigger. Much easier for you to run, I think."

"Easier for you," she cried with all the defiance she could muster.

"No. I don't care either way. I'm not playing possum, Eve. *I don't care.* But you do—you want to live. And maybe I'll miss and keep missing until you're safely out on the road, or the gun'll misfire. It's an old gun, you might get lucky."

She saw his finger tense on the trigger. She couldn't get more than a couple of feet before he pulled it, if that, but she had to try and she whirled around and ran for her life.

The grass was dewy. Her shoes slid on it and she couldn't get up enough speed at first, then the soles gripped and she ran flat out, waiting to feel the bullet drill into her back like a dart and come out like a frisbee, taking her breastbone and most of her chest with it.

Nothing happened.

A tombstone loomed a few yards away. It would shield her if she could reach it, but she was too far away, she'd never get there . . . shouldn't have gotten this far. *He should have shot her by now.*

She reached the stone and threw herself behind it, then pulled her legs in. The stone was slate; when the bullet hit it, the slate would shatter in her face. She slid back in the grass and waited. She was covered with sweat, her knee stockings (favored by Bridgeton women, who uniformly avoided panty hose and short skirts) felt like hot rubber clinging to her legs, her hair was plastered to her forehead. Nothing happened.

She inched her head around the edge of the stone, looked out from behind it, and saw him at the bottom of the slope from his mother's grave, exactly where he'd been when she started running. The gun sagged in his hand; he didn't raise it when he saw her.

"I can't," he called calmly. "Just can't. Isn't that amazing?"

She came out a little farther. The gun drooped and pointed at the ground.

"Amazing," he called conversationally. "I can't. I guess something happened and I didn't even know it." His voice faded until he seemed to be talking to himself. "I just can't seem to do it."

Slowly, ready to duck again, she stood up and they faced each other. He looked helplessly at her; the gun hung uselessly at the end of his arm.

Buy him a forged passport, she thought crazily. *Get him to Switzerland or the Dominican Republic, where a man with twenty million was welcome, no questions asked. With her kind of money, she could send him to Paris, Monte Carlo . . . pay off cops, customs, immigration officials . . .*

Two figures topped the rise and paused beside Edna Janecki's tombstone. She knew one was Dave from his size, and that the dark lumps rising at the ends of their arms were guns.

"Nooooo . . ." she shrieked, and ran for Adam. "Noooooo!" She heard a muffled pop, saw a flame puff weakly at the end of one of the guns, and Adam jerked around like a doll on a pulled string. The gun flew out of his hand, did a loop-de-loop, and hit the ground.

"The gun's gone," she screamed, "the gun's gone."

The second shot smashed him forward. His hands flew up to his throat like pale moths in the ground light and he fell to his knees, then on his face.

Eve ran. The back of her skirt flew out behind her, the front plastered against her knees. She skidded on the wet grass, almost did a split, then caught herself and was up and running again. He'd flopped over on his back by the time she reached him and was quivering all over. Blood poured out of his neck, made a pool under his head, and started to soak slowly into the wet grass. She fell to her knees and tried to stanch it with her hands, but the blood poured through her fingers. His lips moved. She bent down until her cheek almost touched his. "What?" she whispered. "What, Adam?"

He made a low, slow, snorting noise she recognized instinctively even though she'd never heard it before; it was the sound her mother must have made when she'd died in the gray-walled room with gay chintz curtains they put up to make the rich feel at home in the private wing of Oban General.

His light brown eyes looked at her, saw her for an instant, then closed. They opened again halfway as his muscles lost the control to keep them shut and gazed past her at nothing at all.

Latovsky pounded down the rise from Edna Janecki's grave to Eve. He grabbed her shoulders, hauled her to her feet and ran his hands down her arms, then up to her neck, cupping her face. He looked her up and down to be sure she wasn't shot, cried her name, then pulled her to him and put his arms around her. He was too strong to fight; she let him hug her with her head mashed against his chest, turned so she could see the dark, elongated shadow of Adam's mother's tombstone.

The dark skinny one, who'd been at the house on Raven Lake the night Abigail Reese died, slid down the slope and approached the body, holding his gun straight out in both hands the way they did in the movies. He touched the body with the toe of his shoe, then bent and pressed his fingertips to Adam's neck.

"Nice shooting, Dave," he called. "He's dogmeat."

Latovsky ignored him and hugged Eve, murmuring her name; then he let her go, held her at arm's length, and ran his eyes down her body again as if he couldn't believe she was all there. That gave her room, and she pulled her arm back until her shoulder wrenched and slapped his face as hard as she could.

● ●

"You looking for Larry Simms?" asked the waitress.

She was neat and young, with short, dark blond hair and a bright, competent look. She had on pressed slacks and a plaid blouse that would stay crisp in spite of the heat because she looked like the kind who didn't sweat much, Latovsky thought.

She must be Mary Owens, whose big mouth had killed Riley and almost killed Eve. He had an impulse to tell her and watch her wilt before his eyes. But that would be mean and pointless and he kept quiet.

"He told me to look out for you," she said doubtfully, "if you're the lieutenant?"

"Yes," he said.

Her face cleared. "He's in back."

He forced himself to thank her and went down the bar to a back section with padded booths and lacquered pine tables. Simms was in the back booth, watching for him. He waved and half stood as they shook hands, then he maneuvered the table a little so they'd both fit in the booth.

"Want a beer?" Simms asked.

"Sure."

He signaled, and Mary Owens brought a frosted mug and set it on a cardboard coaster with BURT's printed on it. She smiled sunnily and left them alone.

"I wasn't exactly surprised to get your call, Lieutenant," Simms said after Latovsky had taken a drink. "But I don't know what we're doing here. I mean . . . I sort of do, but I don't know that it'll help."

"I had to try," Latovsky said. "She won't talk to me."

"Nope. She hates you."

"I still don't know what I did wrong." Latovsky was ashamed of the crack in his voice.

"You didn't do anything wrong—you saved her life. She doesn't believe that yet, but I do. See, he didn't shoot her when she thought he would, and she's made a whole frog-into-prince fairy story about what kind of man he would have been. Maybe some of it's true. Maybe he never would'a shot her and he'd'a wound up a trusty in whatever institution you stuck him away in, and maybe when he was sixty he'd've gotten out and atoned for eight murders. Maybe. But no matter what would've happened, he was no St. Francis."

"Is that what she thinks?"

"She's miserable and doesn't know what to think. She's eight months pregnant and she and Sam went to lawyers last June. The divorce will be final about the time the baby's born, and she's just purely miserable. It's sad, because Sam loves her, poor bastard, but he can't live with it . . . and I don't blame him."

"He's a fool," Latovsky said softly.

"Could you live with it?" Simms challenged gently.

Latovsky didn't answer, and Simms sat back in the booth and said, "I was afraid that's how things were. And I'm sorry . . . but I'm not sorry, because maybe you're the one who could hack it. Maybe. Thing is, Lieutenant, she's like our own; Franny and I love her and she's miserable and scared."

"Of what?"

"Of locking herself in a suite off the grand gallery of Tilden House while other people raise the child she's afraid to go near because of what she'll see. Like her mother . . ." Simms was quiet a moment, then he said slowly, "You could help her if she'll let you."

"How?" Latovsky leaned on the table and rocked the whole booth.

Simms smiled. "We don't want to wreck the joint."

Latovsky forced himself to sit back. "How?" he asked again.

"Give her something to do, to let her see that the thing *can* help, even if it didn't help Adam Fuller."

"It helped all the women he'd've taken into the woods between June and October."

"I know that—so will Eve eventually. She's stubborn, not dumb. Think of something for her to do, Lieutenant, and Franny and I'll do our best to see she does it."

"Like what?"

"Don't be dense," Simms said almost angrily. "You're a cop. You must have lots of things a woman who can go anywhere without a warrant could do."

Latovsky thought a second, then said excitedly, "An eight-year-old girl's been missing from Ticonderoga since Monday." It was Wednesday. "Maybe Eve could go up there, see the girl's room, talk to her folks." Touch her clothes, Latovsky thought, letting the idea race away with him, pick up her teddy bear. "And if they found the kid alive, because of her . . ."

"Or found her at all," Simms said.

"Yeah." Sweat dribbled down Latovsky's face and he wiped it away and drank more beer. "Lots of missing kids, lots of . . . other things. You think . . . ?"

"Yeah, I do," Simms said.

He'd given Latovsky the first hope he'd had in months, and he felt pitifully grateful.

"Look, I don't suppose—I mean, if you talked to her today . . . then I could talk to her since I'm here."

"You're that crazy to see her?" Simms asked gently.

That crazy, Latovsky thought, but he just shrugged.

"No soap," Simms said. "She's in Sawyerville."

"For what?" Latovsky cried.

"She went to his funeral in May, went back in June and ordered monuments for him and his mother. Went back today to see them put up. Stupid, pointless, self-destructive maybe. Me'n Frances tried to talk her out of it, but like I said, she's stubborn."

● ●

"Looks real nice, said Don Fuller. He was being kind. They looked huge and garish in the little cemetery with the simple, humble stones around them, and Eve was sorry she hadn't listened to the stone cutter. But she'd wanted the best.

"I'm sorry," she said softly. "I'll get them changed."

The two stone setters sighed and looked at each other and the old man cried, "You'll do no such thing, little lady. Those stones're terrific; *F— you,* they say, *F— the whole world.* I love 'em."

She looked at him. He was sober and beaming; he meant it, and maybe he had a point. Here lies Adam Fuller, the Wolfman: monster, fiend, murderer of eight . . . and a good doctor. And fuck you all. She and the old man smiled at each other suddenly, like conspirators.

"So they stayin' or goin'?" asked one of the stone setters.

"Staying," Eve said in her best Tilden voice.

The man pulled the brim of his cap, would have pulled his forelock if he'd had one, she thought, and the men went down the hill to the flatbed; the little back hoe trundled after them and they started loading it.

It was September, the sun beat down on her head, and she felt enormous, pushing that huge belly in front of her. She seemed to sweat more than the men and she took a handkerchief out of her purse and mopped her face. The sun shimmered on the fields, and smells of growing onions and cut alfalfa filled the air. Better than when the mills were going, she thought, and you smelled burning oil and tasted grit.

"You should get out of the sun," the old man said. "The way you are, I mean." He looked at her belly, blushed, and looked away.

"Car air-conditioned?" he asked.

She nodded.

"Well, get on in it. No use being any more uncomfortable than you need to be. You won't be back, I guess."

"I guess not," she said.

He held out his hand to her. She smiled, wiped her palm on her handkerchief, and shook with him, then didn't let him go. "Mr. Fuller, what kind of man would he have been?"

He pulled his hand away from hers, looked at the big hunks of the best marble money could buy, and shook his head. "You asked me that last time, too. And time before. I got no answer, little lady. No one does. So it's kind'a a stupid question, ain't it? No offense meant," he said quickly.

"None taken."

"Well, then, 'bye now. I do thank you for the nice monument for him and his ma. I do indeed."

He nodded at her and went down the rise to his pickup.

He stopped once and turned back. "You should get under cover, little lady. Sun's fierce."

"I will," she called back.

She waited until he'd pulled away, then she went down the rise to the small shallow valley at the base of it. She passed the slate stone with the willow on it that she'd taken shelter behind that night and kept going. The old man had said Edna Janecki was buried right up the rise from Barbara Fuller, so the stone must be right around there somewhere. She found a clutch of Fullers going back to the 1830s. One, another Donald, had a small bronze plaque for the Grand Army of the Republic on a metal stick in front of his grave, along with some long-dead flowers they must have put on the Civil War graves on Memorial Day. Then, at the end, with an empty plot next to it waiting for Adam's father, she found Barbara Healy Fuller: born June 9th, 1929, died May 20th, 1965. *Beloved Wife and Mother* said the epitaph, and Eve whispered to the stone, "My ass, you bitch."

She touched the top of the stone, then pushed a little, experimentally. The earth was dry and crumbly from the dry heat and the stone moved very slightly. Eve set her purse down, wiped her hands on her skirt, and set to work. She was covered with sweat and exhausted, all her muscles were jumping with strain, and she knew this was not work for a pregnant woman, but she felt a wild burst of triumph when she finally worked the stone loose and pushed it over, leaving a deep ridge in the dry dirt.